I0585187

John Brougham, William Winter, Noah Brooks

Life, Stories, and Poems of John Brougham

John Brougham, William Winter, Noah Brooks

Life, Stories, and Poems of John Brougham

ISBN/EAN: 9783743369108

Manufactured in Europe, USA, Canada, Australia, Japa

Cover: Foto ©Andreas Hilbeck / pixelio.de

Manufactured and distributed by brebook publishing software (www.brebook.com)

John Brougham, William Winter, Noah Brooks

Life, Stories, and Poems of John Brougham

LIFE, STORIES, AND POEMS

OF

JOHN BROUGHAM.

COMPRISING:

I. His Autobiography — a Fragment.
II. A Supplementary Memoir.
III. Sketch of his Club Life.
IV. Selections from his Miscellaneous Writings.

EDITED BY

WILLIAM WINTER.

BOSTON:
JAMES R. OSGOOD AND COMPANY.
1881.

Copyright, 1880,
By James R. Osgood and Company.

———

All rights reserved.

University Press:
John Wilson and Son, Cambridge.

✠

THIS MEMORIAL OF JOHN BROUGHAM

IS DEDICATED,

WITH CORDIAL SYMPATHY AND FRIENDSHIP,

TO

𝕳𝖎𝖘 𝕺𝖑𝖉 𝕮𝖔𝖒𝖗𝖆𝖉𝖊𝖘 𝖔𝖋 𝖙𝖍𝖊 𝕷𝖔𝖙𝖔𝖘 𝕮𝖑𝖚𝖇:

IN WHOSE SOCIETY

THE CHEERIEST MOMENTS OF HIS LATTER YEARS WERE PASSED,

AND TO WHOM HIS MEMORY,

ENDEARED BY ASSOCIATIONS OF KINDNESS,

WILL ALWAYS BE PRECIOUS.

✠

✠

"*To all my friends I leave kind thoughts.*"

JOHN BROUGHAM'S WILL.

"*The dearest friend to me, the kindest man,*
 The best conditioned and unwearied spirit
 In doing courtesies."

SHAKESPEARE.

"*For thou wert still the poor man's stay,*
  The poor man's heart, the poor man's hand;
And all the oppressed, who wanted strength,
  Had thine at their command."

WORDSWORTH.

"*First our pleasures die, and then*
  Our hopes, and then our fears, and when
  These are dead, the debt is due,
  Dust claims dust — and we die too !"

SHELLEY.

✠

PREFACE.

—◆—

THE suggestion that Mr. Brougham should write his Autobiography was made to him, more than ten years ago, by the editor of this volume, and it was received with favor. It was not, however, till within a short time of his death that he actually began the work. He had talked of it, often; he liked the idea of it, — although unaffectedly amused at the thought of talking so much about himself; and the fragment of it that he left, and that is here presented, affords ample evidence that he would have told the story of his life in an interesting manner. It was a life of much and varied activity, and its pathway — though not always smooth nor altogether unclouded — ran mostly through scenes of pleasure and of fame. Many of the famous men and women who have lived within the last forty years were personally known to him, and he had observed with a lively interest the great social experiences of his time. The mine of his recollections, accordingly, would have proved rich in portraitures of character, biographical facts, striking and humorous anecdotes, and philosophical reflection. To that treasure-house of the past he alone possessed the key. There is no one who can say for him what he would have said for himself; and no endeavor has here been made to finish the work that he began. This volume is a memorial — and nothing more; and perhaps its chief value will be found to consist less in what it contains than in what it suggests. Its contents,

*though, are representative of the man whom it commemo-
rates. Its outline of his life is complete and distinct, —
the narrative being mostly in his own language; and its
exhibition of his mind, imagination, tenderness of feeling,
mental activity, versatile talents, and command of the
resources of literary art — being made through the medium
of his best stories and poems — is obviously direct and
truthful. His best faculty as an author was that of
dramatic expression: his finest personal quality was his
humanity. The latter is felt in all that he wrote: the
former, of course, must be sought in his plays. These are
numerous, and there is not room even for specimens of
them in this volume. His stories and poems have been
selected from two volumes of miscellaneous writings that he
published a long time ago; from his comic paper, the
Lantern; and from various other sources. They are old-
fashioned, but they have the chimney-corner qualities of
comfort and kindness. He had himself begun the revision
of his works, with a view to their republication in a complete form. Had he lived a few years longer, he might
have made, in his completed Autobiography, a valuable
addition to the history of the stage of his time: he certainly
would have made his own choice of the writings that he
wished to preserve. To some slight extent this book is the
fulfilment of his wish. For his friends it is a relic; and
they, at least, will rejoice that the memory of a man so gentle and so much beloved is neither tossed away upon the
cold winds of time, nor left to moulder among the dead
leaves of the past.*

W. W.

*Fort Hill, New Brighton, Staten Island,
October 8th, 1880.*

CONTENTS.

✠

✠

LIST OF ILLUSTRATIONS.

✠

I.

AUTOBIOGRAPHY OF JOHN BROUGHAM.

A FRAGMENT.

AUTOBIOGRAPHY

OF

JOHN BROUGHAM.

———•———

CHAPTER FIRST.

EARLIEST. RECOLLECTIONS.

I make my "First Appearance upon any Stage," — What I remember of my Relatives. — My two Grandfathers, and their Characteristics. — My Father's Artistic Tastes and early Death. — A Recollection of my Mother. — Uncle William and his Companions. — His Religious Opinions, Public and Private. — The Stuttering Major. — Precocious Imitations. — A Monkey Rival, and how I got even with the Brute.

A LTHOUGH I have not the slightest personal recollection of the occurrence, yet, according to the register in our family Bible, backed up by credible concurrent testimony, in which I have always had implicit confidence, my very first appearance on the stage of life took place on the 9th of May, 1810.

What the individual characteristics were of those who immediately preceded me would scarcely interest any one to know; but, believing as I do in the hereditary transmission of certain innate qualities, I may be permitted to indulge the vanity of saying, that, through the accident of birth, I happened to spring from a tolerably well-blooded stock, especially upon the female side.

The paternal branch of our family tree was respectable enough, as far as the bearing of golden fruit could make it so ; but, indeed, I knew very little about it, as the then representative was furiously enraged with my father for marrying against his inclination ; having, moreover, aggravated the crime by choosing a wife whose dower consisted in the wealth of womanly virtue only, — one of the gentlest, kindest, and most lovable souls that Heaven ever lent to earth for a while, — my mother.

The consequence of that profitless act was, that our poor bough was lopped off from the ancestral trunk and flourished in its pride of place no more.   It must be admitted, however, at many critical periods of my life, when the hand of death had shaken its branches, a vague hope would cross my mind that some slight portion of the auriferous fruit might drop on my pathway ; — but it never did.

I saw the amiable old sinner but once, — an awe-inspiring, pompous individual, fat, florid, and gouty.   Very little cause have I to honor his memory ; for gout was the only legacy he left to me.   He did n't leave his son even that. He would, I have no doubt, had it been a physical possibility ; but podagra is one of " the ills that flesh is heir to " which does not follow in the direct line.   Let me here remark, parenthetically, that it seems somewhat unreasonable for a man's dietetic sins to be visited upon the grandchildren of the original transgressor, skipping, as this particular and painful malady does, the intermediary link ; but as there is no mention made of a *second* generation in the decalogue, I suppose it is all right.

My maternal grandfather was a fugitive from one of the periodical French revolutions, — which of them I cannot pretend to say.   Perhaps it will be as well for me to avow at once that I am no respecter of dates, neither am I me-

thodical enough to be consecutive in my story. Circumstances as they present themselves to my memory shall
be placed faithfully upon record, without regard to the
almanac.

My grandfather, with his wife and two daughters, rendered nearly destitute by the condition of things in his
own country, only too glad to escape with life, sought
refuge in England, where he fortunately had sufficient
interest to obtain a position in the Dublin custom-house.
It was not a very lucrative one, I fancy, but, as his was
a singularly philosophic nature, he was entirely content;
and he held this office during the remainder of his long
existence. That brave old gentleman is among the very
earliest of my recollections. Even now, while I pause for
a moment, he rises before my mental vision as distinctly
as when I last saw him, — a tall, dignified, and command-
ing figure, healthy, vigorous, and upright as a lance, notwithstanding that he carried on his broad shoulders the
weight of ninety-one years. I can see him in the dress he
usually wore, — a blue, square-cut coat with gilt buttons,
buff waistcoat with large lapels, immense white cravat,
black knee-breeches fastened by small silver buckles, his
scant hair powdered, and a carefully cherished "pigtail"
hidden beneath the coat-collar. In disposition he was
amiable, patient, and unambitious, floating quietly along
the current of circumstance, thoroughly satisfied with his
position, and never — for he was a man of curious passivity
— making the remotest effort to improve it.

Of my father I have no recollection whatever, as, unhappily for me, he died before I was old enough to retain
the impression of passing events; but of his ability as an
amateur artist, both in modelling and painting, I had abundant evidence in after years, as there were many creditable

2

specimens of his work in the house, consisting of clay statuettes and water-color landscapes, giving, perhaps, more promise of future excellence than evidence of present force; nevertheless most affectionately cared for, — it being a tradition amongst us that they were altogether incomparable. There was, also, a portrait of himself, done in oil, — one of his first efforts, — which was highly prized by my mother, though I always thought there was something strange about the eyes; and upon one occasion, having incautiously asked her if my father had a squint, I got such a whack on the ear as made me see domestic fireworks for an instant: it was the only time the dear soul ever laid her hand on me in anger, and the tears that followed the cuff assured me she felt it more than I did myself; so we kissed and made it up. I was as obstinate as Galileo, however, for I insisted that, if my father did not squint, the picture did; and with that compromise my offence was condoned, and the matter amicably disposed of.

If my father had lived, it is more than probable my pursuits in life would have been of a different character; yet I very much doubt if any other avocation than that into which I ultimately drifted could be so nicely adapted to my tastes and inclinations, or enable me to enjoy a pleasanter experience, made sunny by congenial association, and those valued friendships, few but heart-welcome, which have endured through all its vicissitudes. Fortunate, also, have I been in having my status confined to the safe plane of mediocrity, — not high enough to provoke envy or jealousy, and sufficiently low to prevent me from entertaining too exalted an idea of my own importance in the world.

The remembrance of my maternal grandmother when close upon her eightieth year, recalls a quiet, easy-tempered old lady, clad in some dark-colored dress, a black lace cap on her head, with her white hair in stiff curls, and her pale, much-wrinkled face lighted up by a pair of brilliant eyes. She was a Rousselle, pure blood, wonderfully proud of her Huguenot descent, — a voracious reader, strongly suspected, moreover, of writing anonymous stanzas for the "poet's corner" in the modish Della Cruscan vein. And yet, in spite of that malicious imputation, a worthy, reputable, inoffensive, darling old lady, whose uneventful life dawdled onward to the end, sustained by cheerfulness of spirit and a prodigious quantity of snuff.

I come now to what is indeed a labor of love, as I endeavor to describe one more figure in the family group, — the relative who, of all the others save one, clings closest to my memory ; for, supplying a father's place, he was the trainer, guide, and companion of my juvenile days, and, when heavy misfortune fell upon us, my mother's mainstay, counsellor, and steadfast friend, — my quick-tempered but warm-hearted Uncle William. Although possibly somewhat stand-offish and independent among his equals, — superiors he had none, — he was always considerately kind to all who were not as well positioned as himself ; and yet, when a fault was committed by any of the domestics, he would stun the ears of the offender with a tornado of strange oriental epithets, appalling enough to new-comers, but the older ones knew from experience that those storms of simulated anger were as harmless as stage thunder. The fact of his having passed the greater part of his early life at Calcutta, in the civil department of the East India Company's service, where he learned the British method of conciliating the natives, together with the irritating effect of a torrid climate upon his liver, fully account for those temporary gurgitations of bile.

It was at his hospitable home I spent the most of my

time, for he and his second wife, my mother's sister, —
(never, until memory lapses into the final sleep, can I forget
thee, dear, generous, indulgent, beautiful Aunt Mary!) —
had recently lost their first-born boy in childhood; and
as I, his namesake, was on the spot, they naturally trans-
ferred as much of their affection to me as served to fill, in
some measure, the void within their hearts. I am very
much afraid I did not then appreciate the advantages by
which I was surrounded, and must have given the worthy,
well-meaning couple a mighty heap of trouble; for that I
was a mischievous and intractable imp there is not a doubt
upon my mind. Suffered to do whatever I liked, without
reproof, as a matter of course I very soon arrived at the
thorough consciousness of my immunity, and played the
deuce, in a small way, with the greatest perseverance. I
ought to have known better, too, for I had emerged from
the spoilt-child era, and was gradually approaching toward
what are supposed to be " years of discretion," — an epoch,
I regret to say, never reached by me. I had been long
enough at a boys' school to have the inevitable fight with
the reigning bully; in which encounter being ingloriously
" knocked out of time," and ultimately carried home, not
on a shield, but on a shutter, Uncle William resented this
introduction of the " manly art " as an extra in my studies,
by exercising his oriental vocabulary upon all the parties
concerned, and swearing by some Brahminical deity that I
should never return to such a murderous place; whereat
his nephew, though sorely hurt, was not unhappy.

It is at the period of existence to which I had then
arrived that the human animal generally exhibits decided
traces of his simian predecessors in the Darwinian chain, by
a natural proneness for imitation; and this monkey-like
faculty began to develop itself in me at an early date,

chiefly for the reason that I had few companions of my own age, but especially because Uncle William and his immediate friends were persons of strongly marked peculiarities, — one of them remarkably so, a certain Major Stackpole, also a retired officer of the E. I. C. S. He was a gaunt, saffron-faced veteran, short-sighted in one eye, the other being glass, so that whenever he turned his head the stationary optic would glare rigidly in a fixed direction, while the other circulated in the liveliest manner. He was afflicted, too, with a curious kind of impediment or gasp in his speech, — a vocal obstacle in his conversation that he was compelled to jump over before he could get on. This he managed to do by introducing the words "you know" when he came to the difficulty. I very soon made him my victim, and got many a laugh by mimicking his obliquity of vision, which he did not see, and his halting phraseology, which he did not recognize. I was a little startled, however, upon one occasion, when the formidable Major twisted me suddenly round before the company, and, staring at me with his glittering eye, said, in a savage tone, "See here, young fif-fif-fellow, what the did — you know — devil do you mean by making gig — you know — game of me ? If I kick — you know — catch you at it, I'll bib — you know — box your ears." A sudden impulse seized me, and, putting on an amazed expression, I replied, "Why, my did — you know — dear Major, you don't sup — you know — pose that I would be gig — you know — guilty of such conduct!" and the hilarity was great when, relaxing his iron grip, he turned away, saying mildly, "Well, my bib-bib — you know — boy, I did not think it was pip — you know — possible."

It is a remarkable fact, that few persons can recognize an imitation of themselves, in voice and manner of enunciation, however evident it may be to all others. Charles Young, the tragedian, who had a pronounced lisp, went to hear Frederick Yates deliver his wonderful imitations of the celebrated actors of the day, in which he spoke Hamlet's advice to the players, giving passages applicable to each, in his peculiar style, and thereby convincing everybody but themselves that they had, severally, gone directly opposite to the rules laid down by Shakespeare. For instance, he gave the first lines precisely in the manner of Young: " Thpeak the thpeech, I pray you, ath I pronounth it to you, thrippingly on the tongue; but if you mouth it, ath many of our playerth do, I had ath lief the town-crier thpoke my lineth." Meeting Yates a few days afterwards, Young said to him, with the greatest seriousness, " Yateth, my boy, your imitathions are ecthellent, but you make one thingular mithtake : I don't lithp."

No one enjoyed the scene with the Major more than Uncle William, though he only understood the pantomimic part, as he was uncommonly deaf, and had to be spoken to very loudly before he could hear at all. Ah! poor, dear old boy! he little knew what a shameful advantage I took of his infirmity, incorrigible scamp that I was! Let me here premise, in mitigation of my offence, that it did not take away from his gratification, but on the contrary enhanced it, inasmuch as considerable amusement was created thereby ; and to see everybody happy about him was the delight of his benevolent heart.

Now Uncle William's topics of discourse, after the feminine part of the company had retired, were limited, and consisted invariably, either in very free expressions of his religious notions, which were heterodox, or in recitals of sundry highly colored personal adventures, which were mythical ; and both were repeated so often, and in the

same language, that it was not long before I knew every
word and sentence, even to the strong epithets and rather
questionable episodes. Upon religious matters he was
aggressive and promiscuous, thoroughly imbued with the
Asiatic and Grecian philosophies,— a result consequent up-
on- his Indian experience, — and yet a firm stickler for the
conservation of present ordinances. Ostensibly a member
of the English Church, he fulfilled all its public obligations,
had his own pew, attended divine worship with regularity,
and contributed liberally to its pecuniary requirements ;
" for," he was wont to say, "by Jove, sir, we must have
some moral law to keep the rascals of the human family
in order ; aside from that, it is incumbent upon every
gentleman to keep his word, particularly when he has no
discretion in the matter, but is simply bound in honor to
redeem the promise made for him at his baptism ; and, by
George, sir, the individual who does not is a disturber, a
social disturber, sir, and nothing else." But after the
decanter had circulated a few times, he would open his
batteries and discharge the real sentiments of his mind
with the confidence and volubility resulting from a frequent repetition of them.

As may be imagined, the frank expression of these pan-
theistic opinions gave rise to numerous discussions of a
more or less acrimonious nature, the details of which were
beyond my comprehension ; neither could I account for
the violent language the disputants used while arguing
about universal charity and brotherly love. During these
my first lessons in polemics, I remained judiciously silent ;
but when my uncle began to tell his regular series of after-
dinner anecdotes, from that instant he was at my mercy,
and I would anticipate, in an undertone, every sentence,
using his exact words without at all understanding their

sense, to the intense amusement of the listeners, who *could* hear me, and quite as much so to the dear old fellow who *could not;* for, attributing the uproarious mirth to his extraordinary success as a story-teller, he would laugh and splutter until the tears rolled down over his wine-colored nose.

The house we lived in was a perfect museum of hideousness in the way of Indian so-called curiosities, in the shape of josses, quaint and indescribable carvings, pot-pourri jars, perspectiveless paintings, and the usual agglomeration of rubbish collectors. Among other monstrosities, there was a mangy-looking old monkey, of the ringtail persuasion, a pet of uncle's, and an incurable demon of mischief; indeed, it was a toss-up which of us was the more successful disturber of domestic peace. He did much vicarious service, though, in the mean time; for whenever dishes were broken, cupboards rifled, or glass demolished, one of us had to bear the blame. The full name of this villanous brute was The Right Hon. William Pitt, bestowed from some unfriendly feeling, personal or political; but his familiar appellation was "Billy." I rather liked Billy at first, and he, on his part, condescended to be on friendly terms with me; but as we were both favorites with the reigning powers it naturally followed that a fierce and courtier-like jealousy sprang up between us. So, not being compelled to raise men or war material, hostilities began without diplomatic delay, and, like most family contentions, lasted long, carried on with as much cunning as persistence on both sides. To be sure, I had an unfair advantage in one particular; for, during the early part of the day, my antagonist was confined to his residence in the garden, secured by a long chain, — an opportunity for strategic operation I availed myself of by luring Billy to the end of his tether with an apple, holding a pitcher of water, an element he detested, behind my back, and, when he got within biting distance, dashing the water into his face, which caused the enemy to fly, screaming, back to his citadel. I must confess, however, as a candid military historian, that the victory did not always rest upon my side; for the beast was cat-like in watchfulness and fertile in resource. Viciously savage, too, when provoked, he would hurl all sorts of available missiles with the skill of a practised marksman, — a dangerous faculty, that induced Dan, the gardener, to say, after I had just dodged a first-rate shot : " Faix, and it's a crack in the gob you'll be gettin' one of these fine days, Masther John ; for that murtherin' baste is mighty handy with his fut."

But the most sanguinary of civil wars must come to an end in time, and ours ended with a veritable catastrophe. Thus it happened. There was a large dinner-party one winter evening, and as, after the manner of most boys, my leisure time was mainly devoted to experimenting in fireworks, fabricating small volcanoes and other amateur pyrotechnics, I on this occasion conceived a brilliant idea, and forthwith prepared to put it into execution, its sole purpose being the discomfiture of Master Billy, no further damaging consequence having entered my mind. I took the precaution to secure a confederate in the person of a neighbor's son, a youth of corresponding tastes, who entered into the new gunpowder plot with emphatic delight. While the substantial part of the meal was in progress, we obtained a large-sized squib, a kind of fire-cracker that burns noiselessly until the detonating point is reached, when it explodes with considerable energy. To this was attached a long fuse, to be ignited by my accomplice at the proper moment. When the dessert was served, I sauntered in with it, as usual, leaving the folding-doors that separated the two apartments slightly open, and while Billy, occupying his accustomed place on the back of Uncle's chair, had his whole attention directed to the cracking of filberts, and a lively conversation was going on, I managed to tie the squib to his tail, giving the pre-concerted signal to my fellow-conspirator. Immediately a faint spark crept slowly through the door and along the carpet, fading nearly out every now and then, so that I was apprehensive of total failure, and by and by crawling on again, occasionally emitting faint sputters that threatened discovery and made me perspire with fright. After a few moments of intolerable suspense it reached the chair, and, mounting rapidly, at last ignited the infernal machine, when — phit ! — phizz ! — bang ! — pshee-shee ! shee'! — off it went, amid showers of sparks and screams of consternation, for the inconsiderate brute had jumped into the very centre of the table, knocking down candelabra, upsetting flower-vases, and dancing a wild four-handed jig among plates, dishes, decanters, and wine-glasses. The panic was total. Women fainted, men were bewildered, and Uncle William thundered out the fiercest of his oriental expletives. As for me, utterly confounded at the unexpected result, and trembling at the consequences to myself that must ensue, I fled from the scene of terror and took refuge in my aunt's room, — the safe sanctuary on perilous occasions. My fears, however, were not realized ; for, as an instance of the untrustworthy nature of circumstantial evidence, it was the innocent small boy I had persuaded into complicity, who, captured in the act of running away with the compromising match in his possession, received punishment, and not the real culprit. How I obtained immunity I cannot call to mind.

At all events, the further consideration of the subject as concerned me was prevented by an opportune but exceedingly severe attack of quinsy, to which, and the savagery of the then medical system, as one physician after another experimented on my unhappy larynx, I had nearly fallen a sacrifice; but, contrary to all expectation, nature finally triumphed over both doctors and disease.

By the way, that disease is now called diphtheria; Greek being the prevalent language of the pharmacopœia, out of compliment, I presume, to the great masters of the healing art, to whom Greece paid divine honors. Rome, whose altars were principally raised to life-takers, never deified a doctor.

CHAPTER SECOND.

BOYHOOD AND SCHOOL.

Fondness for the Fine Arts. — First Attempt in Drawing. — Personal Characteristics. — My First School. — Trim, in the County of Meath. — Picturesque Ruins. — Interesting Associations. — Wellington. — Swift. — A Bad System of Training the Young. — An Adventure with Robbers. — My Brother George. — A Ruffian Schoolmaster. — Revolt.

AT the commencement of my sickness I was removed to our own house, where, at a very early age, I exhibited destructive proofs of a tendency toward the fine arts, as the disfigured pages of many a book could testify. But my over-partial mother forgave the vandalism, seeing only in the impossible horses, dogs, and houses I had scribbled on every blank space what to her were unmistakable evidence of latent genius. Therefore, a drawing-master was provided, with a view to the induction of myself, my brother George, and sister Essie — both of whom died young, of consumption — into the rudiments of the beautiful art by means of which, as my mother supposed, we were each and all destined to equal, if not surpass, the whole Royal Academy. For about two months I labored assiduously, copying geometrical figures, squares, circles, and triangles, — occasionally, by way of encouragement, indulged in the more advanced studies of a barn-door or a rustic bridge. It was in vain that I implored our instructor to let me have a dash at water-color: he was inexorable. At length I became impatient, and determined to make the effort without his permission ; so, taking into my room a sheet of drawing-paper and a box of Newman's colors, I went to work at once, and without allowing any one to see or know what I was employed at, meaning to produce a startling effect when my picture was completed.

I chose for the study a landscape of my father's, a composition of strong contrasts in light and shade, feeling satisfied that I should find it easy enough to reproduce. For several days, I devoted nearly all the time to this fascinating employment, scarcely caring to stop for food, while the hope of success stimulated exertion. At length, after sundry alterations and repeated efforts, the great work was accomplished, and my heart bounded with joy as I gazed upon the result of my intuitive genius. While I was thus wrapped in pleasurable thought, who should walk into the room but Uncle William ; and never had exalted anticipations such a sudden collapse ! The moment his eyes rested on it, "Why, John," said he, "where on earth did that miserable daub come from ?" The joy died out of my heart upon the instant. Divining the truth from my changed expression, and seeing a paint-box on the table, he continued, "Surely, you did n't do this yourself?" Upon my faltering out a timid "Yes," — "Oho !" he said, "that 's a different affair altogether. For the short time you have been learning, it is not so bad an effort." This good-natured but qualified praise humiliated me still more. "And pray what are you going to do with it?" he inquired. "To show it to mamma," I whispered. "I would advise you not to do anything of the kind," he said, in a gentle tone, laying his hand upon my shoulder ; "wait until you can let her see something worth looking at. You will be able to do

so in time: if you show her this, she will only do violence to her judgment, for, of course, she'll praise it at
the expense of the truth."

The result of this snub was salutary, for I never could
have attained satisfactory proficiency in that direction, and
mediocrity in the artist line is insufferable. Although I
have since, from time to time, when the fancy carried me
away from my legitimate avocation into the seductive but
unprofitable amusement of palette and pencil, wasted valuable hours coquetting with both, I have never pretended
to be an artist.

I may as well make the confession at once, that I very
soon became conscious of the organic defects in my individuality which have seriously damaged my interests, on
many occasions. The governing principles that dominated
my life and directed all its actions were not of my own
choosing: had they been so, I should, most assuredly,
have selected stronger types of character. In the first
place, I never could get over a lack of confidence in myself, or in any effort I should make. However hopeful I
might be about the work I was engaged at, a slighting
word would put me out of conceit with it altogether;
neither did I possess the useful bump of concentrativeness
sufficiently developed to make me stick to one road long
enough to be successful, without switching off to some side
speculation, or being persuaded into hazardous theatrical
ventures by unprincipled rascals.

"Everything by turns, and nothing long," I have been,
— a little of a painter, a little of a doctor, a little of a playwright, a little of a rhymester, a little of a musician, and
indulged for a brief period in the insane dash at comic
journalism, — and all without a scintillation of business
capacity, but with unbounded confidence in everybody

who made pleasant promises. A somewhat antagonistic
and wholly unproductive combination !

In process of time, it was determined that my brother
and I should endeavor to digest the amount of "*cram*"
needed to carry us through a college examination, and for
this purpose we were consigned to the care of Dr. Hamilton, who was the head of a preparatory academy at the
flourishing town of Trim, in the county Meath, about
twenty miles from Dublin ; said town consisting of a long,
improvised street, the houses mostly fashioned out of the
primitive mud, save here and there an ambitious brick
edifice, inhabited either by a lawyer or a doctor. It possessed a small, modest-looking court of justice, town-hall,
and market combined ; also an enormous jail, well popu-
lated generally, for it was the hanging era in Ireland, when
capital punishment ran through the whole gamut of crime,
from murder down to mutton-stealing.

Dr. Hamilton's establishment was delightfully situated,
close to the river Boyne, a most noble and picturesque ruin,
— the royal stronghold of the De Lacys, to whom Henry II.,
with kingly generosity, presented an entire province, after
having rendered its ruler incapable of continuing in possession, being in the vicinity, — together with another fragment of antiquity, known as the Yellow Tower. The former
is admitted to be the finest specimen of early Gothic in the
three kingdoms, — occupying an area of some ten or twelve
acres, in the centre of which stood the keep or citadel, an
immense square building, its external double walls nearly
intact. Open spaces, time-worn and irregular, showed where
doors and windows once had been, while the interior, a
desolate void, was roofed only by the sky. At the top, four
double walls were arched over, forming originally a castellated walk all around, where, centuries ago, the armed sen-

tinel kept watch and ward. Now, partly destroyed, the
protecting parapet gone and the narrow surface ruggedly
uneven from accumulation of rubbish, — considering, also,
the tendency to vertigo that so great a height induces, —
an attempt to scale it would be very hazardous. The winding stone stairway that led to this dangerous eminence,
dilapidated throughout, was, of course, the favorite scene
of emulation among the scholars, — in spite of the Doctor's
positive interdiction, many accidents having occurred there,
— and he who mounted highest was victor for the day ;
but the daring youngster who succeeded in reaching the
summit became the hero of a term. The inner castle was
surrounded by a wall of still more solid construction, with
a number of flanking towers of Cyclopean strength, and the
whole was clad in an evergreen mantle of ivy. Indeed, the
entire county of Meath abounded in places of interest. The
Castle of Daugan was but a few miles distant, — famous as
being, in popular belief, the birthplace of the "Iron Duke."
That, however, is doubtful ; but there is no doubt about
his having spent the best part of his youth there, when
the estate belonged to his father, the music-loving Earl of
Mornington, composer of "Foresters sound the cheerful
horn," "Here in cool grot," and many other pieces which
have become classic. His fighting son did not inherit
that placable disposition. Not far from Daugan lay the
rustic village of Laracor, the spire of its Liliputian church
half hidden in a mass of greenery. It was there Jonathan
Swift fretted many years of his "wild, tearing" life away,
between ministering sulkily to the sparsest and most uncongenial of congregations, and debating in his volcanic
mind which of his two erratic loves he would take to wife,
solving the question ultimately by living with both and
marrying neither. It was at this diminutive place of wor-

ship, the story is told, that he, as it was compulsory, had frequently to go through the prescribed service without a single listener except the parish clerk ; when he would vary the rubric thus : " Dearly beloved Dennis, the Scripture moveth you and me, in sundry places, to acknowledge," and so forth, reducing the ritual to a very personal affair. It was a daring innovation upon reverent custom, but exactly what such an impulsive, reckless, miserably disappointed man of genius, smarting from neglect and isolated from literary companionship, would do. There were many ancient and romantic memorials of former violence scattered through the county ; but as this is not intended for a guide-book I can only recommend those who are curious about such matters just to run over, and read, in the vast number of desolated castles, religious foundations, and lowly homesteads, one of the saddest national histories that ever were recorded in the unmistakable characters of ruin.

As our preceptor's scholastic family was limited to twelve, the institution was always full, with generally several applications to fill vacancies on its books. A most unruly dozen it was, of which I made a component cipher, — the only exception being my brother George. He had been in very delicate health from infancy. He was amiable in disposition and of almost feminine gentleness, and I loved him dearly, as he did me, so that we were nearly always inseparable ; for though after a short time the twelve segregated into congenial groups, we never were identified with any particular one. Our educational routine did not call for an overpowering amount of mental exertion, but it exacted much from the body. The principal, having been a noted gymnast in his early prime, looked upon calisthenics as of the first importance in the curriculum ; and,

3

judiciously directed, it unquestionably is, — health being as necessary to the growth of the perceptive faculties as to the development of muscle; but he fell into the error of most theorists, who, when they are mounted on their especial hobbies, care not whom or what they ride over. He left discretion and common sense far behind him. We had all to go through the same order and amount of exercise, without the slightest consideration for differences in health or constitution, — a strange inconsistency that, in time, led to a serious result. The same penitentiary system was the rule with regard to our dietary, no allowances being made for personal likes or dislikes. It did not matter whether the food was wholesome or injurious, consumed with a relish or wholly repugnant to the palate; day by day followed with the same gastronomic impartiality. Neither was it of any avail to declare one's inability to breakfast or dine upon such or such viands. The answer was, "Go without it until you can." This exasperating state of things resulted from the absence of a feminine housekeeper, the internal economy of the house being under the supervision of the head usher, Macadam, a Scotch-Irishman from Londonderry, who had the faculty of extracting profit from very strange elements.

George and I, however, plodded on uncomplainingly in the monotonous mill-horse round for several months. The only welcome sunshine in our clouded existence was when we got letters from home, inasmuch as they always brought us pocket-money, half a guinea each, hidden under the seals; and while that lasted, Macadam added considerably to his store of broken victual. He gave out that it was distributed in charity, but my impression now is that he must furtively have kept a small eating-house. With respect to the educational process, it differed very little, I

suppose, from all similar brain-mills, where every variety
of grain is flung into the hopper, the value of the result
depending altogether upon the capacity to sift the material.
The twelve neophytes were divided into three classes : the
first, consisting of the most advanced, had the place of
honor, at the head ; the second, next to them ; and the
third, new-comers and incapables, bringing up the rear, —
the ambition of each pupil being to displace the one above
him, until he reached the top. An excellent way it was to
stimulate exertion and incite to study ; moreover, it varied
the formality of examination, and occasionally led, in exercise hours, to personal encounters arising from real or imaginary favoritism on the part of the catechist. The Dean
himself, placid in temper, gracious of speech, and dignified
in demeanor, never entered the school-room without his
academicals, — proud as a medalled warrior of his well-worn
trencher cap and tattered gown. He was above suspicion ;
but of the huckstering usher's partiality I was entirely convinced. It might have been wrongfully, for I hated the
fellow from the bottom of my heart, — mainly, I presume,
because on him devolved the duty of punishing all infractions of school discipline ; and as that discipline was strict,
and those infractions many, such occasions were frequent.
The brutal, indecent, and humiliating indignity of flogging
being at this time prevalent, of course we came in for
our share. The instrument of castigation was a number of thin willow saplings, tough and pliable, tied together at one end for the convenience of handling, and the
other spread out for the purpose of covering the widest
possible space, — an invention, no doubt, of Macadam's.
The number of strokes varied, according to the degrees
of transgression. The ill-concealed satisfaction that ruffian
felt in his hangman's task caused me to regard him with

abhorrence, and it was not very long before I took an opportunity to demonstrate my disgust in a remarkably striking manner.

I had now just passed my fourteenth year, my brother being thirteen months younger. It was intended that we should remain at school for three years, and we had luckily worried through the first without being Macadamized to any abject degree, when we stumbled into an adventure that brought us an infinite deal of tribulation.

One morning, as he and I had gone out of the house together, according to custom, for the purpose of obtaining a supply of fresh air, we had not proceeded many yards from the entrance gate when we saw, lying in the middle of the road, — one very little frequented, — a good-sized leathern bag. I lifted it : it was heavy. "Open it," said George, "and let us see what's in it." I did so, and found that it contained a quantity of gold and silver. "What had we better do with it ?" said I. "Give it to the Dean," replied sensible George. There happened to be a sort of private jaunting-car some distance ahead, in which two men were riding. Some demon suggested to me that they must have dropped the bag. On the impulse of the moment I hurried after the car, and, when within hailing distance, cried out to them to stop. They did so. When I got there, I gasped out, with all the breath I had left, "Did you drop this ?" "What is it ?" inquired one. Even that did n't open my eyes. "Money," said I. "Why, of course we did," said the scoundrel. "How did it come open ? I hope you have n't been making free with any of our cash !" This combination of indignity and ingratitude made me so angry, that, without another word, I walked away in one direction while they drove off in another. Continuing our walk, we thought no more of the circumstance, until, about a fortnight after, while at dinner, a casual remark plunged us both into a perfect fever of apprehension. It was simply an inquiry, addressed to one of the party, if he had seen the reward offered for the recovery of a large amount of money, — notice of which was wafered on the court-house door. This startling intelligence so paralyzed our stomachs that eating was out of the question, and, as soon as it was possible to leave the table, we hurried off, anxious to know the worst. When we reached the place, sure enough there was the precious document, printed in frightfully conspicuous type : —

" FIFTY GUINEAS REWARD will be paid for the recovery of a LEATHER BAG, containing money in gold, silver, and bank-notes, *supposed to have dropped from a dog-cart on the road between Trim and Navan. All information upon the subject may be addressed to* SIR MARCUS SOMERVILLE, *High Sheriff of the County.*"

This was sufficiently appalling; but as the high sheriff was in some collateral way related to our family, there was just a possible hope that, by telling him the whole story, he might get us out of the scrape. Accordingly, we started off at once for his residence, a few miles distant, only to find, when we arrived there hot and fatigued, that he was in London, attending to his Parliamentary duties. Crestfallen and altogether miserable, we had no alternative but to return, frankly avow our predicament, and make a confidant of the good Dean. On reaching the academy, we found everybody in a state of evident excitement. In a place so barren of events, the least disturbance of its stagnant surface is sufficient to make a nine days' wonder, and the recent loss was now the town talk. They must have heard something, thought I, as my heart seemed to drop like a lump of lead, and poor George's pale, frightened

face told me too truly that he shared the impression, —
it was all discovered, beyond a doubt. When, like a
couple of convicted malefactors, we sneaked into the
school-room, half a dozen voices cried out at the same
instant, "Have you heard the news?" "Have you seen
the paper?" "It's all found out," — and such like ex-
clamations. This confirmation of our fears was the crown-
ing blow, a never to be forgotten moment of terror; but,
luckily, only momentary, for the daily newspaper from
Dublin, received during our absence, announced the to
us blissful intelligence that nearly all the missing funds
were restored to their owner, and the swindlers in the
hands of justice. Race-course gamblers of the lowest
grade, they had quarrelled over the distribution of the
spoil; and one of them, discovering that he had been
cheated out of his fair share, informed against the others,
whereupon the two were arrested and held for trial at the
autumn assizes, while the third was detained as king's evidence. The sudden revulsion of feeling had a severe effect
upon my brother, who, weaker in constitution and more
impressible than I, gave way under the strain, and kept
his bed for several weeks.

Shortly after he had sufficiently recovered to resume his
studies, an incident took place that put a sudden termi-
nation to our novitiate. It occurred on one of the examination days, conducted, in consequence of the Dean's
temporary illness, by Macadam. Well knowing the contempt in which I held him, — for I never took the trouble
to conceal it, — he was insolently aggressive in manner;
but, as I was well up in my task, he had no excuse for the
gratification of his savage nature. The villain knew, however, that he possessed the power to wound me very keenly
by harsh treatment of my brother. Many a time before

had he exercised that pitiful means of inflicting pain upon both of us, when it was as much as I could do to control my temper; but on this occasion he pushed his vindictiveness beyond all endurance. The poor boy, slow to learn and deficient in memory at all times, now rendered additionally nervous from recent illness, irritated also by the fellow's sneering tone and reiterated questioning, quitted his class, which was the second, and, bursting into tears, threw himself almost fainting into my arms. Trying to comfort him as well as I could, we were slowly leaving the room, when I was startled at hearing the usher yell out, "Stop! such negligence and insubordination cannot be too severely punished. You shall be flogged, sir, before the whole school."

I could hardly believe my senses. "What," I cried, while the hot blood was surging in my veins, "flog him, — flog any one in his condition of health! You dare not do it!" It was an impulse, — an unwise one, — but I could not help it.

The white rage froze in his face as he hissed through his clenched teeth, "You'll soon see whether I dare or not!" Then sending for "Collins," name of dread, — he was a huge, brawny porter, whose duty it was to officiate as assistant executioner, by holding the victim on his back during flagellation, — "Get to your work, sir!" shouted the dastardly tyrant.

The man, with evident reluctance, endeavored to separate us, but the terribly frightened boy only clung closer to me. At length, a sudden jerk unloosed his arms, and with a piteously appealing look, but never a word, he turned aside as passively as a lamb beneath the butcher's knife.

His very quietness, and the slow, deliberate way in

which that heartless ruffian made his preparations, so
fired my brain, that, with the brief madness of ungov-
ernable anger, regardless of all consequence, I exclaimed
wildly, "You shall not do this atrocious thing!" — "Indeed, and, pray, who is to prevent me?" he replied,
with a malicious grin, proceeding to strip the poor boy
down to his loins. But when I saw him about to strike
the first blow, I clutched a heavy slate from the desk
alongside, and, with a fierce cry, hurled it at his head.
My aim was a good one, for he dropped as though he
had been shot; and, taking advantage of the confusion,
we escaped to the dormitory, silent and awe-stricken, for
we knew not what mischief had been done. After a few
moments of dreadful suspense, we were told that Macadam
was in a fearful rage and very sick at his stomach, swearing that he would visit us with terrible retribution in
the morning. When we were left alone, after looking
regretfully at each other for a little while, I could see
that we both were thinking of the same thing. "How
much cash have you in your pocket?" I asked. — "Not a
half-penny," said he. — "And I have very little. Do you
think you are strong enough to take a long walk?" —
"Home?" whispered George, with a glad look. — I nodded. — "O yes," he replied; "once away from that cruel
man I should gain strength, I know." — "Very good;
say nothing to any one, and to-night, as soon as they are
all asleep, we will creep down stairs, undo the chain on
the door, and we will get home again, — home, George,
boy!"

It was now near dinner-time. We had determined not
to go down to table; but having heard that the disordered
state of the usher's internal economy would compel his
absence, we changed our plan, and prepared for the com-

ing risk by putting away a substantial meal. After collecting all that was portable of our *impedimenta*, it may be imagined that the intervening time was nervously exciting. We made a feint of undressing, but lay down in our clothes, and, when all was quiet, made our way out and started. The details of that momentous exodus I cannot recall without a shudder.

*   *   *   *   *

There is a break in the narrative here. — ED.

CHAPTER THIRD.

YOUTHFUL DAYS.

Entered at Trinity College, Dublin. — Thoughtless Choice of Companions. — Practical Jokes. — The Discomfited Tutor. — Sketch of Lord Norbury, "the Hanging Judge." — Caught napping on the Bench.

IN the mean time, it was necessary that I should undergo the usual amount of "cram," to enable me to pass an examination for college; and most dyspeptic provender it was.   But, bearing in mind the sage philosopher's axiom, that "of mental food as well as material it is not healthy to swallow more than you can digest," I lunched very lightly upon Homer and Horace, while Scott and Byron, then in the zenith of their popularity, I devoured with prodigious appetite, especially the former, frequently sitting up all night long rather than relinquish the fascinating volume.

At length, after two or three humiliating failures, I managed by some strange accident to scramble through the preliminaries, and entered the "College of the Holy and Undivided Trinity," — so denominated by Queen Elizabeth, its founder, — assumed the trencher cap and academic toga, took possession of a gloomy den in the Botany Bay quarter, bought a few prescribed books and a prodigious quantity of foolscap, with the stern determination to make up for wasted time by devoting myself to the most unremitting description of "grind."   That I was in dead earnest then I have no doubt; but many a strong resolution formed in the course of my experience has been rendered nugatory by my unfortunate tendency to let circumstances control the action of the moment. If, by chance, accident, or destiny, I had become associated, in the first instance, with reading men, perhaps the after results would have been different. But it is useless to speculate upon what might have been ; the truest philosophy consists in making the best of what *is*, — and, as my disposition is optimistic, it has enabled me to look on the bright side of things very often when there was but little brightness visible.

I very soon found out that my impulses were the reverse of studious ; and being naturally indolent, except in the pursuit of amusement, as a matter of course I segregated with " birds of a feather," — individuals as wild, reckless, and unreflecting as myself, — from whom I learned how absurd it was to pore over themes and exercises which would be forgotten long before examination day, when, by judicious " coaching" immediately preceding it, one's memory would be. fresh and serviceable. Unfortunately those arguments were so much in harmony with my own inclinations that my little stock of stationery remained intact, while, through the magnetism of congenial association rather than from premeditated effort upon my part, I was attracted to a companionship more delightful than disciplinary. This state of things, however, suited me exactly ; for, possessing, as I then supposed, an assured provision for the future, I had not the slightest ambition to go for honors, and consequently ran no risk of being in the unfeathered condition of " Plato's man."

The members of our set with whom I was most intimate were Hercules St. George, who ultimately gave his undivided attention to the race-course, and was a high authority on the horse question; Cornelius O'Callaghan, who, together with Dillon Brown and Richard Martin, son of the humane and eccentric Dick Martin of Galway, author of the first "Cruelty to Animals Act," developed into Parliament men; Collier and Poe, of whose after record I know nothing; Luke Dillon, nephew to the Earl of Roscommon; and two or three others whose names I have forgotten. Some of those fellows, notwithstanding their scholastic remissness, became persons of note; and one — the last named — of disgraceful notoriety, from what cause it would do no good now to revive the recollection. Suffice it to say, we were all sworn friends, pledged to take each other's part through thick and thin, whether in humbugging college dons inside the walls, or pitching into combative coal-heavers without.

That most reprehensible of all juvenile propensities, practical joking, was carried to a merciless extent about this time, and we exercised all our ingenuity in playing tricks, more or less mischievous, upon obnoxious dignitaries. It would be impossible to give an idea of their number or variety, but one instance may serve to indicate their nature.

There was a certain cross-eyed, red-nosed class tutor named Haggerty, who provoked our extreme displeasure by being so ridiculously particular as to insist upon the cessation of convivialities in our chambers after the closing hour. His predecessors having been humanely lax about enforcing the rule made old Haggerty's conduct the more unpardonable; therefore we resolved that he should be victimized, which he accordingly was, in the following manner. It is pretty generally known that for a female, whether a relative or not, to be discovered in any of the college rooms after "gating" is a crime of the most hei-

nous character, entailing expulsion, not only on the principal offender, but on all concerned in the enormity. Well!
The scene is Collier's quarters; in the centre a round table,
plentifully supplied with "Sneyd, French, and Barton's"
claret; surrounding it a group of festive youngsters and a
lady, apparently, who did not let the bottle pass without
replenishing. This was Collier himself, in one of his sister's
dresses; and, being a handsome, smooth-faced youth, with
the embellishment of some borrowed ringlets and an amaz-
ing head-gear of the period, which looked like an inverted
coal-scuttle, he might pass easily enough, in the dim candle-
light, for a favorable specimen of the incomparable sex.

When all was prepared, a suborned scout was despatched
to notify Haggerty of the irregular symposium, — a most
welcome message for the deliverer, inasmuch as domestic
treason was always liberally rewarded. Meanwhile, the
oak was sported, that is to say, both outer and inner doors
were locked, and we patiently awaited the coming of our
victim. It was not long before we heard him puffing and
wheezing up the stairs, for they were long and steep, and
he was short and asthmatic. A thundering rap was the
signal for us to get up a confused movement, one or two
wine-glasses were broken to give local color, and Collier
was hustled rather noisily into a closet, while Haggerty
shouted outside, as well as he could between snorts and
fatty suspirations, "It's no use, gentlemen. I know —
all about your — nice goings on, — so you may as well —
admit me at once." The doors were opened, and in he
waddled, a ludicrous expression of importance on his lying
face. I say a *lying* face, for if ever a speaking countenance
bore false witness against its owner his did; those dull,
watery eyes, with their heavy swollen lids, and those
tallowy cheeks, to which that mulberry-colored nose was

in vivid contrast, would have proclaimed him, before any bacchanalian jury at least, a "three-bottle man," whereas in reality it was nothing but a cutaneous libel, a scorbutic accusation, altogether false, as he happened to be one of the most abstemious of men.   "Well, young sirs," said he, after he had gained sufficient breath to articulate without much difficulty, "Will you be kind enough to introduce your fair companion? It is useless for you to deny that you have one here. I have been informed of your outrageous conduct."

"Devil take the informer!" cried O'Callaghan, angrily.

"Where is she?" inquired Haggerty.

Still no one spoke, but all bowed their heads as if in mortal shame.

"Ah! I see I must be my own master of ceremonies," said the old intruder, with grim facetiousness; "therefore, miss, or madam, or whatever you are, be pleased to honor me with your society only for an instant," — opening the closet-door and revealing Collier, who, with a handkerchief to his face, got up a respectable faint, and fell into a chair. "Very fine, sirs, ve-ry fine," grunted Haggerty, his scurvy nose glowing with a lovelier purple. "Of course you all know the penalty you will have to pay for this scandalous orgie. Such disreputable affairs have been too frequent, and examples must be made. Do not imagine that you can get rid of your delectable visitor, for I shall take the liberty of locking you all in until I return." Having given utterance to these portentous words as impressively as his apoplectic breathing apparatus would allow, he was about to quit the room, when he was astounded at hearing one of the roisterers yell out, "Hurrah for ould Hag in three times three!" which were given with a will. Gasping out some incoherent words, he shook his fist at the crowd, and made his exit, accompanied by a roar of laughter and the chorus of "He's a jolly good fellow."

The moment we heard the key turn in the lock, Collier rapidly divested himself of his borrowed plumage, which was carefully concealed, all bibitory appurtenances were cleared away, and in their place the table strewn with classic text-books; each man seized a volume, so that, when the two inquisitors entered, the indignation in their faces changed to blank surprise as they beheld, instead of a scene of dissipation, a group of students so intent upon their work that they were unconscious of the interruption.

"Why, Haggerty," said the proctor, "what does all this mean?"

"Mean!" replied the other, almost inarticulate from rage; "it means that they have hidden the woman somewhere; but I'll ferret her out."

"A woman in my chambers?" said Collier, in a tone of consternation.

Meanwhile, Haggerty had entered the closet. As he did so, the graceless delinquents looked compassionately after him, intimating, by suggestive pantomime, that the poor fellow was weak in the upper story; and, indeed, when he emerged from his unsuccessful search, "Well, sir," inquired the proctor, "what have you found?"

"Nothing," replied the puzzled tutor, "I do not know how they could have spirited her away, but that there was a woman here a quarter of an hour ago I'll take my oath."

"Mr. Collier, what answer do you make to this serious charge?" asked the proctor.

"A very simple one, sir," responded Collier, casting a pitying glance upon this accuser. "We all know our unfortunate friend's weakness : it was only an after-dinner hallucination."

Perfectly furious at the insinuation, Haggerty screamed out, "What, sir, have you the daring effrontery to tell me to my face that I did not find a woman here ? "

Instead of answering him, Collier simply shook his head mournfully, and addressed the proctor. "Sir," said he, "the thing is not only preposterous, but impossible. Mr. Haggerty certainly did break in upon our studies some-what unexpectedly, a short time ago, astonishing us very much both in speech and action ; when, after some inco-herent remarks, which we could not understand, he went away as abruptly as he came. If there had been a female in the room, how could she have vanished ? The windows are fifty feet from the ground, and he took the key of the door away with him."

The proctor was perplexed. He looked steadily for a moment or two at the accused and the accuser. The former returned his gaze with the calm, resolute expression of conscious innocence, while the latter, indignant at hav-ing his veracity doubted even by a look, utterly bewil-dered also by the audacious denial, glared open-mouthed into vacancy.

It was very evident that his embarrassed manner made an unfavorable impression upon the proctor, for it was in a sterner accent that he next addressed him, saying, "Are you quite sure, Mr. Haggerty, of what you assert? No possibility that you could be mistaken?"

"Mistaken ! " cried the exasperated man. "How could I be mistaken?"

"You saw a woman in this room?"

"If I can believe the evidence of my own senses."

"It is to be regretted, Mr. Haggerty, that in your case

such testimony is occasionally undependable," said Collier, in the most aggravating manner.

"Do you mean to insinuate that I am lying?" spluttered out the other, nearly choking with anger.

"By no means. I only assert very plainly that you have been laboring under some extraordinary optical illusion," responded Collier. "Mr. Proctor," he continued, in an earnest voice, "I solemnly assure you, sir, upon my honor, there has been no one here the whole evening except the persons you now see. I call upon them to substantiate my words," — which of course they did, most emphatically.

This settled the case as far as Haggerty was concerned, whose mortification was completed when the proctor observed, with a reproving head-shake, "Ah, Haggerty! Haggerty! I would advise you in the future to limit your potations."

Dublin at that period contained a number of eccentric individuals. First on the list was the notorious Lord Norbury, who achieved the peerage through his alacrity in thinning out the superabundant Irish population, but who was more generally known by his popular title of "the hanging judge." Many a time have I seen the sanguinary old ruffian jogging along through the streets astride of a fat cob, his eyes bleared and crimson-veined, as though he had been literally swimming in "the reservoir of innocent blood" alluded to in Robert Emmet's terrible denunciation; his great flabby cheeks distended to their utmost at every expiration, whence the nickname of "Bladderchaps," shouted at him by the juveniles, from all corners; his arms wagging by his sides; and an umbrella in his whip-hand, with which he whacked the flanks of his lazy steed with evident relish.

It was not a very difficult matter to diminish the numbers of the proletariat.   In those times capital punishment
quickly followed the commission of the pettiest offence,
from sheep-stealing up to the gravest and most unpardonable of all in Norbury's eyes, suspicion of complicity in the
" rising of '98."   When trying such cases, he set both law
and justice at defiance.   Instances are on record where
some unhappy, foredoomed victims were condemned to
death upon the testimony of a single witness, whereas the
English code required its confirmation by at least one more.
There could be no question of his having carried out the
depopulating programme with untiring perseverance.   It
was his wont, moreover, to vary the judicial atrocities
with a ghastly kind of humor, which, however amusing
to the briefless barristers, always ready to laugh at a judge's
witicisms, were but little appreciated by the poor wretches
waiting the inevitable result.   He also had a habit of drop-
ping his head upon the cushion before him in apparent
sleep, but was instantly alert when a legal point was in
dispute or the chance of making a jocular remark presented
itself.   Once, while he seemed to be in that somnolent
state, and the gifted advocate Curran was pleading, a don-
key happened to bray loudly in the street.   Up started
Norbury.   "One at a time, gentlemen," said he, to the
intense hilarity of his learned brethren.   But the great
pleader, who seldom failed at a rejoinder, turned the laugh
against the judge by quietly replying, "Your lordship is
laboring under a misapprehension; it was only the echo
of the court."

Upon another occasion he really was caught napping,
and with a singular consequence.   The accused being only
a rebel, he naturally anticipated the usual routine, and
therefore settled himself to enjoy an interval of repose,

waking up only when everything was over and the verdict rendered. Rising slowly and placing the fatal black cap on his head, to the astonishment and alarm of the prisoner, who too well knew what that signified, he began the formula he had so often repeated before. Referring to his notes, "Michael Fogarty," said he, in solemn tones, "you have been fairly tried by an intelligent jury of your countrymen, and convicted upon the clearest evidence —"

"But, my lord —" cried the trembling man.

"Silence in the court!" shouted his counsel. "Don't interrupt his lordship," — who continued : —

"Notwithstanding the praiseworthy efforts of the eloquent gentleman who defended you, your case is too flagrant, — examples are imperative, — the sentence of the court is — "

"Hem! May I be allowed to interpose a few remarks?" inquired the counsellor, amidst the suppressed merriment of the crowd.

"They will be entirely superfluous, sir," responded the judge, severely.

"I am thoroughly aware that the course I am pursuing is contrary to all precedent," said the other, blandly, "but I really think I have a plea in mitigation to offer."

"What possible plea can you have?" demanded the judge ; to which the lawyer quietly replied : —

"I acknowledge that it is very seldom, if ever, that your lordship commits a legal irregularity ; but it certainly appears to me a strange solecism in jurisprudence, the sentencing a man to death who has been acquitted."

"What! Acquitted!" thundered Norbury, looking savagely at the jury. "Then they are a pack of rebellious vagabonds themselves, and I hope I shall yet have the satisfaction of hanging the whole rascally lot."

CHAPTER FOURTH.

FIRST THEATRICAL EXPERIENCES.

The Theatre Royal, Dublin. — Habits of the Gallery Gods. — A
Convivial Musician. — Mr. Calcraft, the Manager. — John Balls,
the Comedian. — Liston. — Garrick. — Kean. — Booth. — Burton. — Mistaken Estimates of their Powers. — Amateur Theatricals. — Counsellor Plunkett. — Early Efforts in Acting. — A
Local Celebrity. — Monkey Tuthill. — Suppers after the Play.
— Introduced to Madam Vestris.

THE Theatre Royal in Hawkins Street was, at that
time, the almost constant resort of our set; scarcely
an evening passed that some of us could not be found
patronizing the shilling gallery, as much from the certainty
of enjoying some adventitious fun as for prudential reasons.
On certain special nights, when vice-royalty attended in
state, it was necessary to exhibit our loyalty in the dress
circle, — dull but decorous.   High times we used to have,
too, among the "Gods" of that unsavory Olympus, as we
listened to, and occasionally joined in, the fire of jokes,
sometimes rather sharp, which were directed against any
well-known or peculiar-looking individual.   The perspir-
ing deities — for it was as hot as Lucifer's kitchen in those
upper regions — conducted themselves with reasonable
propriety until the lights were raised through the house, a
proceeding usually hailed with applause, shouts, and clapping of hands.   Some fellow would cry out, "Hurrah,
boys! now we can see who's who."   And woe betide
the luckless persons who were unpopular with the crowd,

or whose appearance gave the slightest chance for ridicule !

With this agreeable kind of enjoyment, — agreeable to all but its victims, — the high-toned upper class would amuse itself, until the members of the band entered and took their seats. Then came a thundering cheer as Jemmy Barton, the leader, appeared, his face one genial smile as he acknowledged the compliment paid him, which would change to a supplicating expression as he glanced at his tormentors above, for he well knew what he was to expect. Jemmy was a prime favorite with the audiences, but he had his failings, and they were unfortunately exhibited so openly that there was no concealing the facts. Nobody presumed to dispute his standing as a musician, but whiskey-punch interfered with his standing as a man upon numerous occasions. Moreover, it was currently reported that his violin, a very costly one, was frequently instrumental in procuring from his "uncle" the means wherewith to gratify his rather Hibernian propensity, a pledge of affection accepted right willingly by his interesting relative.

Then some such colloquy would ensue as this : "Say, Jimmy, have ye got the ould cremorne out once more ?" And Barton, who thought it best to conciliate the ruffians, would hold up the violin, upon which another gallery boy would cry out, " None of your thricks, you thief of the world ! Look at his nose ! how it 's blushing for the lies he 's tellin' ! Tune up, you spalpeen, an' let 's see if it 's the real article, or one you borra'd from Andy Magra ! " If it so happened that the veritable instrument was not in temporary duress, Jemmy would play a few bars with such brilliancy as to elicit the hearty applause of the whole house. I once heard an enthusiastic neighbor exclaim, after a similar demonstration, "A' thin, more power to yer elbow, Jemmy avic ; but drunk or sober it's yerself can make good use of that convaynient jint in all sorts of wonderful ways, from rattlin' off a jig to emptyin' a jug."

The company performing in the theatre, although in my maturer years I might possibly consider it mediocre, was to me, as well as to my companions, a combination of histrionic perfection.   As a matter of course, there were some among the actors who were more highly favored by the audiences than the rest, upon whom they would lavish their plaudits with Celtic effusion, while the less fortunate ones were either listened to with indifference, or pelted with ironical compliments, likings and dislikings being expressed with equal frankness.

The lessee and manager, Mr. Calcraft, was first favorite by virtue of his position, together with the typographic opportunities it afforded to imprint his talent upon the public mind in big letters, and therefore was very naturally looked upon as a capital actor ; for persistency in self-assertion goes a great way toward manufacturing celebrities of every profession.   He, the manager, as a matter of precedent, monopolized all the heroic characters ; and although physically scarcely suited to represent them, being short and corpulent, he amply made up for these slight defects, and established the fact of his marvellous ability, by his voice, which was sonorous, and his deportment, which was majestic, his costumes, which were indescribable, and the opinion of the press, which was unanimous.

A few among the company, however, justified our early predilections, maintaining their reputations in other countries and before less impulsive critics.   Notably, the light comedian, John Balls, who afterwards achieved reputation both in England and America.* How well I remember him! — young, well-featured, and prepossessing; a form of perfect symmetry; eyes beaming with intelligence; a clear, ringing voice, infectious with merriment; and an inexhaustible wealth of animal spirits. He was vivacity personified, lacking, to be sure, the refinement that made his predecessor, Richard Jones, so pre-eminent in the higher walks of comedy; but in personations of a more farcical nature, requiring dash, sprightliness, and audacity, he was inimitable. It is not astonishing that the possessor of so congenial a temperament captured the heart with Cæsarian rapidity; and yet in private I have heard that man, so exactly fitted in every respect for the line of business in which he could have no competitor, so fêted and followed by high and low, deplore the blind obstinacy of the managers, who would not give him an opportunity to electrify the town with his tragic powers. On his benefit nights, when he had the privilege of choosing the entertainment, he invariably gratified his ambition by appearing as the hero of some lugubrious play or tearing melodrama, to the serious detriment of his reputation; for, while easy and

* Oct. 15, 1835. — Mr. J. S. Balls made his first appearance in America [at the old Park Theatre], as *Vapid*, in "The Dramatist," and *Singles*, in "Three and the Deuce." He will be remembered as a very excellent light comedian, of good personal appearance and mercurial temperament, — giving great effect to saucy footmen, eccentric fops, and shuffling spendthrifts. Like his forerunner, Abbott, he would have proved a desirable acquisition to the stock company, although not of sufficient weight to prove an attractive star. Mr. Balls was a native of England, born in 1799, appeared in London in 1829, last appeared in New York in 1840, returned to his native country, and died at Dublin in 1844. — J. N. IRELAND's *Records of the New York Stage*, Vol. II. p. 130.

graceful in characters adapted to his own individuality, in the others he was awkward, vociferous, and stagy. This was no temporary impulse, or the experiment of a beginner anxious to find out the true direction of his power, but a fixed belief, to which he was faithful during the whole of his theatrical life.

In the pursuit of every avocation, a certain probationary time has to pass before the beginner can find out whether or not his natural abilities are consistent with his inclining, and the chances of success are greatly dependent upon their assimilation. In many instances they are directly opposed, when the task is hard to reconcile the antagonism. At the commencement of a theatrical career the same contrariety frequently exists. John Liston, whose countenance was studded all over with dimples of fun, to which his deep voice and solemnity of manner formed a whimsical contrast, was so thoroughly satisfied of his capability to represent high tragedy that, ignoring the evidence of his looking-glass, and despising the laughter of the unappreciative crowd, he persisted in obtruding his comical-tragical efforts upon the provincial public, until that convincing argument, empty benches, compelled him to sacrifice predilection to prudence, and the disappointed tragedian became the greatest comedian of his time. That Garrick displayed a similar feeling is exemplified in the fact that he preferred *Abel Drugger* to *King Lear*.

Edmund Kean and the elder Booth were in the habit of playing farces at their benefits. Burton never was so happy as when indulging in some sentimental episode, and J. B. himself does not mind confessing to having had a decided preference for the buskin in his early days.

> "What they are not is what men fain would be :
> Few men are that, but what they are you see."

Private theatricals were much in vogue, and with one group of amateurs a few of our set became affiliated. The performances, ostensibly for a charitable purpose, but actually to show how easy the whole thing is, and how superior we were to the regulars, took place at a shabby old temple of the promiscuous drama, in Tattersall Street, mercifully dark, but unmercifully dirty. As is usually the case, we flew at the highest kind of game. No mousing owls were we! the eagle's flight or nothing!

Inasmuch as we had a superfluity of *Hamlets*, and no *Laertes*, to prevent jealousy or invidious distinction, the names of the characters were written on pieces of paper which were folded and thrown into a hat, and, when well shaken up, each of the aspirants drew out a slip, and whatever part fell to him he had to accept without a word. It was as good a way as any; for it would have been difficult to decide who was the worst of the lot. At all events, it had this advantage over the professional method, that, no matter how the subordinates might rail at the injustice of the fate that compelled them to appear in parts so far beneath their ability, the management escaped vituperation.

There was an individual then living whom all who can recall that period cannot but remember, Counsellor Plunkett, a man of excellent family, eminent in his profession, possessing ample means, and as rational as the majority of human beings upon all other subjects, but a monomaniac upon that of acting. Although beyond middle age, he had an enormous chest, ruddy face, bull neck, and Herculean limbs, — contrasting ridiculously with a thin, squeaky voice and strong Hibernian accent. He was under the hallucination that he possessed the united powers of Kean and Kemble. "What is there, I'd like to know, in this Masther Kane, that everybody's makin' such a fuss about, — a poor, wizen-faced, bandy-legged pygmy of a creature! Now, sir, I am two inches and a half taller than that solemn jackass, Kemble, and have some brains in my head, while he's nothing but an idjit. I'll take my oath that he doesn't know the meaning of half the words that's crammed into him. Now I do, — the sense as well as the sound, — which is more than any of the consated parrots can brag of." I have no doubt there was not an aspiring youth among us who did not entertain an exalted opinion of his own theatrical talents; but we had sufficient prudence to keep it to ourselves. Matters went on peaceably enough until the time arrived to prepare our next representation, the play chosen being "Richard III.," — rather a modest selection for youngsters utterly ignorant of stage tradition. As we were proceeding, in our usual way, to allot the several parts, Plunkett, who had just stalked in, inquired what hocus-pocus we were up to. "Finding out who is to play *Richard*," said one. "Who?" squealed the Counsellor, drawing himself up and pounding his brawny chest. "Why, who but the only man in the three kingdoms at this moment who has the requisite qualifications, both physically and intellectually, — and here he stands. Settle the rest of them among yourselves, but *I* shall enact *Richard!* Yes, and by the Lord, sir, I'll show them the true *Gloster*, the last and greatest of the Plantagenets, symmetrical in figure," (casting a complacent glance at his goodly proportions,) "not the wretched Lancastrian libel Shakespeare, degrading his genius and perverting history, drew from his imagination simply to curry favor with the vixenish, red-headed granddaughter of *Richmond*, the son of a poor Welsh farmer, and one of the meanest and most treacherous of kings." Upon somebody venturing to suggest that it was one of our rules, he became furious. "Rules!" he screamed out; "what are your confounded rules to me? Can you determine the degrees of mental capacity by throwing dice, or point out the brightest star in the firmament with your eyes shut; and am I, Counsellor Plunkett, to be dictated to by a litter of pup monkeys? To the devil with you and your rules! Genius breaks the fetters and emancipates itself. I am free. Go your own way and I'll go mine. Stick to your dirty Tattersall Street nursery. Wait till you see me coming out at the Royal, and cramming it too from the cellar to the cock-loft; then, maybe, you'll treat me with respect. But it serves me right for wasting my time with such a beggarly crew of Thrinity sizars." And so, with a petrifying look and contemptuous snap of his fingers, the learned Counsellor dismissed the society. And, strange to say, that daring prediction was, to a certain extent, verified; for many a time I have seen the mad lawyer, as he was called, upon charitable benefit nights fill the theatre to its utmost capacity, — appearing always in his favorite part, and although peal upon peal of laughter accompanied every word and gesture, culminating in a perfect tornado of ironical applause at one of the most astonishing single combats ever witnessed, and an indescribable death which was many times recalled. Yet such was his egregious vanity that he accepted the demonstration as a tribute to his superior talent, and, gracefully rising from the field of the dead, would acknowledge the compliment and the renewed acclamations, and go through his moribund contortions once more. In order to give the people an idea of his versatility he would sing, between the play and farce, "Scots wha hae" in character, — which consisted in going on in his shirt-sleeves with his pantaloons tucked up to the knees, a Scotch scarf twisted round his waist, and a tremendous bludgeon in his hands. The fun of this part of the entertainment lay between him and the band, as, not understanding a note of music and totally independent of time or tune, with his violent gesticulation, and thin, but high and penetrating voice, the singer was in constant discord with the musicians. You may be sure Jemmy Barton improved the opportunity; and the further the Counsellor strayed from the proper key, the more lustily Jemmy rattled away against him, making altogether a combination of ear-distracting sounds to which saw-filing would be seraphic; and yet this chaos of discord had to be repeated over and over again, until some merciful hand would send down the green curtain.

With regard to my own share in these performances, I must acknowledge that I felt no particular desire to incur much responsibility in the way of study; therefore, the smallest parts suited me best, and whenever chance assigned me a prominent character, I found it an easy matter to exchange it with some more ambitious tyro, thereby securing safety in my insignificance, and escaping the penalty consequent upon the treachery of an untrained memory, which, undisciplined by time and experience, is very apt to fly at the most critical moment. It was so, at all events, in my case, as the endeavor to give utterance, before an audience, to the few lines I had learned, invariably filled me with such trepidation and positive misery that I very soon concluded the greatest amount of success could not compensate for the indescribable horror of what is called " stage fright."

We had a frequent visitor, one Henry Tuthill by name. This singular person was then a noted celebrity in Dublin, being generally known as Monkey Tuthill, in allusion to

the extravagant nature of his street garments, of which he
had a wonderful variety, of every imaginable shade and
color.   A proud, generous, kind-hearted fellow he was,
beyond question, the only weak spot in his composition
being that of semi-insanity.   He did not belong to our
society, — indeed, rather looked upon its humble efforts
with the smiling complacency of a proficient in art ; for
had he not also seen his name in big type on the bills of
the Royal at sundry benefits? — with a different result,
truly, from that experienced by the Counsellor, — the
laughter in his case being real, as he represented certain
characters with much cleverness.   Harry was always welcome to us, for the reason that he usually was accompanied
by some notable member of the theatre stock, or, more
gratifying still, some London exotic, upon whom we looked
with the reverential awe such superior creatures seemed to
expect from commonplace humanity.   But those meteoric
visitors, however brilliant, never could outshine the fixed
stars of our dramatic firmament in the estimation of the
Dublin people, proverbially loyal to their favorites.   Henry
Tuthill, moreover, was a man to be cultivated, for the
reason that he gave the pleasantest kind of suppers three
or four evenings in the week, after the performances, and
which invariably consisted of a prodigious quantity of red-
bank oysters, — an incomparable bivalve, plump, firm, and
rich in flavor, a convenient mouthful in size, too, midway
between the London native and the American saddle-
rock.   These were washed down with draughts of Dublin
stout, from the pewter, and, after the repast, for the gentlemen unlimited tumblers of whiskey-punch, unacquainted
with lemon except the thinnest possible peeling of the
outer rind, containing sufficient of the citric oil to give
it the epicurean flavor, and, for the ladies, a bowl of hot

spiced claret, on which floated a roasted lemon stuck full of cloves.

At these suppers we were certain to meet the professional celebrities of the moment, both local and foreign. These agreeable symposia were presided over by Mr. Tuthill's mother, a delightful old lady, and as fond of theatricals as her son.

It was at one of her entertainments that I was favored with an introduction to a couple of individuals who afterwards, at an important turning-point in my life, were the means of determining its onward course. One was Madam Vestris, then in the zenith of her fame ; the other, a charming young fellow and an excellent singer, named Melrose.

*   *   *   *   *

[The fragment of Brougham's Autobiography ends here ; but the following synopsis of his career — written by himself, at my request, and given to me by him in 1868 — serves to piece out still further the authentic record of his life. It will be observed that he states his claim to a joint authorship with Dion Boucicault of " London Assurance "; and the reader will also find, in this off-hand summary, several characteristic touches of his ingenuous simplicity and kindly humor. — ED.]

SYNOPSIS OF BROUGHAM'S CAREER.

WRITTEN BY HIMSELF.

J. B., born in Dublin, 1810. Had decent opportunity for a liberal education. Obtained a tolerable amount of knowledge. Does n't himself know how. More probably by absorption than by application. Intended for the surgical persuasion — very much against his organization and impulses. "Walked" the Peter Street hospital for about eight months. Would very likely have been a lazy, worthless, and unendurable nuisance, if a severe family and pecuniary misfortune had not electrified him into personal exertion. Drifted accidentally into the histrionic. Made his *début* at the Tottenham Theatre, London, in 1830, — his first effort being the representation of some twelve or fourteen parts in "Tom and Jerry," then the sensation of the day.

Went with Madam Vestris to the Olympic, forming in process of time one of her famous stock company. Took vacation trips to the provinces, for practice, — playing everything, from "grave to gay." His first attempt at composition a burlesque for W. E. Burton, then an actor at the Pavilion Theatre, London; crude, undigested, in fact very bad, but by consequence curiously successful. Wrote numberless forgotten nothings. Migrated with Madam V. to Covent Garden, remaining there all the time she and C. Mathews had the direction. Wrote "London Assurance," in conjunction with Boucicault, who claimed the entire authorship, according to his usual ungenerous-

ness.   Had to bring an action against D. B., whose legal
adviser suggested payment of half the purchase money
rather than conduct so damaging a case.

Managed the Lyceum.   Wrote "Life in the Clouds,"
"Love's Livery," "Enthusiasm," "Tom Thumb the Sec-
ond," and, in connection with Mark Lemon, "The Demon
Gift."

Came to America, October, 1842.   Opened at Park Theatre, in the palmy days of light houses and heavy gas-
bills.   Took a starring trip through the country.   Made
considerable money.   Expended it, on a Mississippi steamboat, in the endeavor to master the intricacies of "draw
poker."   Arrived at New York a "wiser" and a poorer
man.   Attached himself to the Burton dynasty.   Wrote
for his place "Dombey and Son," "Bunsby's Wedding,"
"The Confidence Man," "Don Cæsar de Bassoon," "Vanity Fair," "The Irish Yankee," "Benjamin Franklin,"
"All's Fair in Love," "Irish Emigrant," "Haunted Man,"
and other "unconsidered trifles."

Managed Niblo's Garden.   Wrote "Home," a domestic
fairy tale, and "Ambrose Germaine," for Mlle. Blangy.
Opened Brougham's Lyceum, Dec. 23, 1850.   After a
brilliant commencement, the demolition of the building
next to the theatre gave it an unsafe appearance, which
frightened away the audiences; and finally a very dear
friend, by an adroit but perfectly legal proceeding, got
possession of his lease, leaving him with a load of indebt-
edness which mortgaged many years of his life-work.   He
had the satisfaction, however, of paying every dollar, and,
as soon as that task was accomplished, thought he was entitled to take a holiday : so visited Europe, intending only
to be absent a few months ; but, the war occurring in the
mean time, he determined to remain away as long as it

UNIV. OF
CALIFORNIA

lasted, not wishing to be a witness to the fratricidal strife. Advocated the integrity of the Union throughout, and opposed strenuously the madness of the projected dismemberment.

While at his Lyceum wrote "David Copperfield," "The World's Fair," "Faustus," "Spirit of Air," "Row at the Lyceum," "Actress of Padua," for Miss Cushman. When he was ejected from Broadway, tried the Bowery, but was a little too refined for that lax latitude. Presented the peanutters with a magnificent Shakespearian revival, — mounting "King John" as it has scarcely ever been given, — Mr. and Mrs. Davenport, Wm. Wheatley, J. B. Howe, and Miss Reignolds being in the cast, together with one hundred and fifty auxiliaries; scenery by Hilliard, in his best style. No go. Descended to the sensational, with better results. Wrote "The Pirates of the Mississippi," which knocked "the divine Williams" silly. Followed, in quick succession, by "The Gun-maker of Moscow," "The Red Mask," "Orion the Gold-beater," "Tom and Jerry in America," "The Miller of New Jersey," and such like sops to Cerberus. Singular results of a season of unexampled prosperity! — to the manager, *nil;* to a neighboring locality, an accession of brown-stone houses.

Accepted the position, and philosophically enlisted under the Wallack banner. Wrote, during his servitude, "The Game of Love," "Bleak House," "My Cousin German," "A Decided Case," "The Game of Life," "Pocahontas," "Neptune's Defeat," "Love and Murder," "Romance and Reality," "The Ruling Passion," "Playing With Fire," etc.

Again joined Burton, at the Metropolitan (Tripler Hall). Wrote for this establishment, "Columbus," "The Musard Ball," "Great Tragic Revival," "This House to be Sold." Burton parted with him rather than advance his salary to

5

$75 a week. Wrote, while in England, "The Duke's Motto," and "Bel Demonio," for Fechter; "The Mystery of Audley Court," and "Only a Clod," for Miss Herbert; "While there's Life there's Hope," played at the Strand Theatre; "The Might of Right," at Astley's; "The Golden Dream," at Manchester: also, the words of three operas, — "Blanche de Nevers," "The Demon Lovers," and "The Brides of Venice"; bushels of songs and miscellaneous rhymes, together with ambitious endeavors at polkas, waltzes, galops, — notably "The Bobolink," the especial favorite of its season in London. Inflicted society with a couple of volumes, — "A Basket of Chips" and "The Bunsby Papers."

Is of an indolent nature, and would like to be lazy, if he only had the time and patience to do nothing; yielding as water under small provocation, but somewhat granity if collided with roughly. Would rather be everybody's friend than anybody's enemy, from sheer selfishness, inasmuch as bearing malice weighs down the spirits and disturbs digestion. Stands five feet eight in his moccasins, and depresses the scale at one hundred and eighty.

A TALK ABOUT THE PAST.

An account of an interview with Brougham, written in the *New York Herald* by his friend Mr. Felix G. DeFontaine, gives additional particulars of his life, as taken from the lips of the veteran himself, and an extract from that bright and truthful narrative may, accordingly, be here incorporated into Brougham's Autobiography. The actor spoke as follows : —

MY American career, dramatically, commenced in 1842, on the stage of the old Park Theatre, opposite the Astor House, a site now occupied by stores. The American stage, at that early day, was in a lamentable condition. I had remained at Covent Garden during the career of Mme. Vestris. She played some of my early productions. When she relinquished the place, I happened to meet Mr. Stephen Price, the manager of the Park, and under an arrangement with him came to America. We started from Southampton in September. The voyage was pleasant enough, until, one evening, my attention was attracted to the peculiar condition of the sea. You could see the wake of the vessel almost to the edge of the horizon. The weather was calm, the clouds beautiful. It grew darker and darker, however, until there was a fearful hush on the water. I did n't understand it at all, and said, in my innocent way, to the second officer, " What a magnificent evening ! " His answer, accompanied by a shrug which I afterward recalled, was, " Don't put too much dependence on the night." Sure enough, in a few hours the ship was knocked about like a chip. We had steamed into a hurricane. For ten hours the tossing of the sea was terrific, and when the moon occasionally rushed across the clouds and disappeared, it seemed as if their great, black mouths had opened to swallow her. I recall the fact that, during all the commotion which occurred, I had no fear. Among the passengers was one who stuttered. In the midst of the turmoil nobody seemed to see him, but he turned up afterward, when people were congratulating themselves, with tears in their eyes, on their fortunate escape. On being questioned as to his whereabouts during the hurricane, he said he was " M-m-m-mostly asleep." — "Did n't you hear the storm?"—"W-w-was there a storm?"— "Of course there was." — "Th-th-that 's very st-t-t-trange." When the others went away, he turned to me and said : " The f-f-fact of it was, J-J-Jack, I heard it all and got sc-c-cared, b-b-but I was in my b-b-b-berth hedging like the d-d-d-devil. I wanted to win on the right s-s-s-side, you see."

On arriving in this country, I lived at the Astor House, which was then kept by the elder Stetson, and he and his sons ever after were among my dearest friends. The city was, of course, entirely new to me, in climate, people, and surroundings. I particularly remember the fire-flies, which I thought were the result of an atmosphere surcharged with electricity. Somebody told me that they were charged with flashes of lightning. At that time, too, the barbarous custom was prevalent of beating a gong to tell the animals that the feed was ready.

One of our earliest visits was to the Park Theatre, the company of which was one of the best ever gathered in America, consisting of the two Placides ; Peter Richings ; young Wheatleigh, then in the vigor of his youth, — an excellent light comedian ; John Fisher, the brother of Clara Fisher; James Brown, one of the most versatile

actors the stage has ever known; and John Povey, a useful man and everybody's friend. With the exception of
Brown, I think they were all Americans. Among the
ladies were Mrs. Wheatleigh, an admirable "old woman";
Miss Buloid, afterward Mrs. Abbott; and Mrs. Knight.
The play was "The School for Scandal," and when we
entered we found an audience of but six people besides
ourselves. The arrangements were similar to those which
exist now, only that, instead of a parquette, there was a
"pit." All told, there might have been a dozen or fifteen
present; but, to make up for the scarcity of spectators,
there was an inordinate number of rats, so admirably
domesticated that they sat on the ledge of the boxes and
looked you squarely in the face without moving a muscle.

This was a bad prospect for one who had come to
America, and expected an engagement in the following
week. Meanwhile, however, I had made the acquaintance
of N. P. Willis and General Morris, of the New York
Mirror, and through their efforts succeeded in stirring up
a little curiosity concerning our presence, so that we opened
to a large and friendly house. I remember the play was
"Love's Sacrifice," in which my wife played *Margaret
Elmore*, and I played the light comedy part. I did n't
make much of an impression at first, but my turn came
afterward, in the farce "His Last Legs." In those days
the interlude consisted of songs, dancing, &c. The success
of the farce seemed to have the effect of making the performance at least not a failure, and our first engagement was
renewed. It was a moment of supreme delight, I assure
you, when, at the end, the treasurer handed me a parcel
of bank-bills about the size of a brick. I congratulated
myself on the possession of so much filthy lucre, though
filthy enough it looked; but when I went to have it ex-

changed, it melted away, like my expectations, in the most marvellous manner. It was at that time called "wild-cat" money, and I had more of the feline commodity than was conducive to my convenience. Some of us had to pay seventy-five per cent discount; but enough was left to carry us on, and so we had to be satisfied.

New York at this time contained only the Bowery Theatre, then under Hamblin, and the Chatham. Niblo's Garden was supposed to be out of town; in fact, Mr. Niblo employed a private omnibus to convey people from the Astor House. Think of the distance now! I remember Mrs. Niblo well. Both husband and wife were models of host and hostess.

As viewed from the Astor House, New York was bounded on the north by Union Square. The latter was simply a great pile of dirt, with one or two dwellings in the vicinity, and a few farms near by. Greenwich village was in the neighborhood of Eighth Avenue. I used to shoot birds where the Fifth Avenue Hotel now stands. Our cricket ground was in a field somewhere near Thirty-fifth Street, and our suburban drive around the reservoir at Forty-second Street. Third Avenue was then a trotting ground, and a favorite place of resort was "Cato's," who kept, among other things, a popular "shuffle-board." The great peculiarity of the time was the versatility of the drinking. It was my first experience, but, as I have generally managed to economize my tastes and enjoyments through life, I never had a craving for the festive glass, and used it chiefly for the sake of association. With regard to this matter of appetite, you might as well find fault with the color of a man's hair as with this disease, — for it is nothing more, — and the well or virtuous man who is not afflicted deserves no credit.

From New York my wife and I went to Albany. It was in December, and we had no premonition of a sudden change until some time during the night, when the boat, with a sudden shock, ran into a field of ice, and stuck fast. The passengers walked ashore at Verplanck's ferry, where I secured a sleigh, and with the thermometer twenty degrees below zero started for Albany.

We managed to reach the city just half an hour before we went on the stage, and we played "London Assurance" that night. The manager was then John B. Rice, after-ward the Mayor of Chicago, an honest, independent gen-tleman. At this time the interval from engagement to engagement was like a long jump, and our next experience was in Chicago, and then in St. Louis, where the eccentric Sol Smith was managing. The Western stage was very rough. Everything, in fact, was in its infancy. As I recall the Chicago of those days, it was a dirty place, and consisted principally of Lake Street. Indians were sun-ning themselves on the corners, with here and there a soldier belonging to Fort Dearborn among the loungers.

The city is familiar to me in all of its phases; — the muddy stage, when mule teams were fished out of the depths with long poles; the hybrid stage, when the town and many of its edifices were raised six or eight feet with-out displacing a brick; and finally that which exists at present. While there, it was a question whether I should insure my life or buy some property. After consultation with my wife, — who was always a trustworthy adviser, — I determined to do the latter, and accordingly bought twenty acres of land from a certain Dr. Eagan at the rate of $600 an acre. Pretty hard scratching I had to meet my notes, but eventually they were all paid. Then it was dis-covered that this man had forged his wife's name to the

warranty deed, so that my purchase was absolutely void.
Here was trouble, but fortunately the matter was subsequently adjusted, and I came into the possession of the
property.   Then followed the inevitable taxes, assessments,
et cetera, and I became "kind of disgusted." Awhile
afterward — it was during the war — I went to England,
leaving a friend of mine in Chicago, in whom I had every
confidence, to represent my interests. He wrote that the
country was in a desperate condition, real estate not improving, and advised the acceptance of $20,000 for the
property.   I agreed to the sale, and it took place.   On my
return to America in 1868, *en route* to San Francisco, I
stopped at the Sherman House in Chicago, then kept by
the Gage Brothers, one of whom asked me incidentally
about the property.

   " Why, I sold it eight years ago, Sir." — "The devil ! "
said he, looking astonished ; " for how much ?" — " Twenty
thousand dollars." — "Why, man, it's worth two hundred
thousand to-day, and in five years it will be worth half a
million."   Sure enough, when I drove out with him in the
afternoon I found the property laid out in squares, and
people buying villa lots at so much a foot where I had
purchased by the acre.   And so you see how near I came
to being a millionnaire.   Ah me! if I had quarrelled with
misfortune, I should have been dead long ago.

   Becoming tired of travel, and being of a domestic nature, I came to New York to stay, and here produced at
the Broadway Theatre, then under Colonel Mann, (on the
corner of Leonard Street,) a five-act comedy, entitled,
" Romance and Reality," which had been offered in London and refused.   It had a very gratifying success, and
you may imagine how much more gratified I was when I
subsequently played it in London, at the theatre where it

had been refused by the manager, Mr. Buckstone, and heard him express astonishment at his oversight. On another occasion I offered an extravaganza called " Life in the Clouds" to Mme. Vestris, whose specialty was such pieces. Later she sat in the private box of a theatre the night it was played, and sent for me, for I was always a favorite with her. She said, " Why did n't you let me have that piece for my theatre, Mr. Brougham?" I replied, " My dear madam, you had it in your possession for three months." Sometimes, therefore, you see that an error of judgment on the part of a manager is costly. I have no doubt that many a golden opportunity is lost. After all, play-writing is like a lottery, — there are more blanks than prizes. Managers are not inclined to permit those who have not won their spurs to come to the front.

I then joined Burton's Theatre in Chambers Street as stage manager, at $50 per week, where I produced "Dombey and Son," in which Burton made such a great success as *Captain Cuttle.* He paid me for it a small sum, — I think about $10 a night, — and after three or four weeks said he thought he had done about enough. I answered, "Very well, if you are satisfied, I don't want any more." The play was taken from the stage for a week, but at the end of that time it was reproduced, and held the boards for two seasons, and laid the foundation of Mr. Burton's fortune. Then came " The Serious Family." In this was developed that quality which I seemed to possess of extemporaneous talking to an audience. It occurred in this manner. At the end of the piece the audience invariably called me out for a speech. Sometimes it was one thing, sometimes another, but always a lot of nonsense, born of the moment, until I came to regard it as an intolerable nuisance. I don't know whether Burton liked it or not, but, at any rate, on one occasion he rushed on the stage while I was speaking, and, assuming to be very much annoyed, exclaimed, " Don't believe a word that comes out of his Irish mouth ; he's so, and so, and so." I don't remember what he did say, but I answered him on the spot, and a war of words followed. The audience fairly yelled with delight, and after that they looked for and demanded that quarrel as a part of the business of the evening.

I remained at Burton's two seasons, and at the end of that time friends aided me in securing a theatre of my own, in Broadway near Broome, which became known as Brougham's Lyceum. I put all the money I could raise into the enterprise, and borrowed some from E. P. Christy, the old minstrel, for which he required a heavy interest. During the first season it was a brilliant success, but subsequently, owing to architectural changes in the neighborhood, it became necessary for me to assume new obligations. In making a certain loan I signed a paper which I supposed gave me the sole lease of the premises for a series of years. Instead of that, one of the parties took advantage of his legal rights, and, because on the instant I did not furnish $15,000, the amount of his demand, — although a few hours later, my friend, Col. H. J. Stebbins, offered to supply double the sum, — the sheriff entered and took possession of the theatre. I was dumfounded, knocked off my perch ; but it was of no use to cry. I had the satisfaction, however, of knowing that the property passed into the hands of the elder Wallack, who was an experienced manager. I became one of his company, and remained with him as long as I stayed in New York. He gave me a good salary, and in time I was enabled to pay all the indebtedness that had accrued. It mortgaged my exertions for nine years ; but when I finished,

I felt like a liberated slave, — threw up my hat, and went abroad. There I played at the Haymarket and through the provinces, in my own and other pieces.

While at Wallack's I had a severe surgical operation performed, which for some time kept me on my back. It was in this interval, with nothing to do but think, that I conceived and wrote "Pocahontas." It did n't make much of a sensation at first, for it was one of those things which had, as it were, to grow upon an audience. Still, it was nicely played, Charles Walcot being *Captain John Smith*, Peters the *Dutchman*, Miss Hodson *Pocahontas*, and so on. The piece was gradually rising in the public estimation, until one evening Mr. Lester Wallack came into the dressing-room, where Walcot and myself were preparing for the performance, with the announcement that *Pocahontas* was missing, and could not be found anywhere in the city.

What was to be done under the circumstances we could n't conceive. All sorts of plans were projected, but none would work. At last, in desperation, I said to Walcot, "Suppose we do it without Pocahontas." "Agreed!" said Charley, who was always bright, quick, and witty; "we'll do it anyhow!" Mr. Wallack went on the stage and made the announcement that, "owing to the absence of Miss Hodson," (the truth is she had eloped with somebody,) "the play would be produced without her, Messrs. Walcot and Brougham having kindly consented to fill her part," &c. For a moment a dead silence reigned; but, directly, the fun of the thing was taken in, and the people fairly screamed. We went on. First, Charley would say, "This is what Miss Pocahontas would remark if she were present," and then he would talk to himself. "Where is Pokey?" he would exclaim, to which I would reply, " Lost among the icebergs on Broadway. — [Broad-way was then a mass of refrigeration.] — Ah ! but if she were here I know she would answer you in this way," — and then I gave her speech. At the end, when it became necessary to join their hands in matrimony, we did n't know exactly what to do, but, looking around the stage, I saw a broom, and seizing it I boldly advanced to the front, saying as I handed it to Charley, " Take her, my boy, and be happy." It brought the house down, but it was a frightfully dangerous experiment.

The public, however, wanted it repeated, and it shows what a good-natured body a New York audience is when its sympathetic humor is fairly touched. It is one of the pleasant recollections of that piece that there was scarcely a camp in the army during the war, as I have been told, in which officers and men did not rehearse and enjoy " Pocahontas."

" Columbus " was produced by Burton, and drew tre-mendous houses. When we shook hands together as John Bull and Brother Jonathan, the applause was won-derful. He was a clever actor, but a close manager. Yet, after all, what good did it do him? He made $200,000, and not a twentieth part of it reached his children, — all devoured by lawyers and litigation. I remained at Wal-lack's until I left for Europe, producing a new piece almost every season.

In fact, I 'm never idle, and always want to be at work. I think my greatest infirmity is that I never have taken sufficient pains with my literary work. I know my short-comings as well as anybody, and there is no use in conceal-ing them. They are due in a measure to a great facility in composition. I don't have to consult books in order to obtain the groundwork or to fill in the patchwork of a play, or to spur myself up to it.

The brightest part of my artist life was passed in Wallack's Theatre. The management was generous, and the companionship congenial. The pleasantest of my recollections are associated with the "Old Shop."

On my return to America, in 1865, I played a star engagement which proved very remunerative, and would have continued but for the fact that inducements were presented to remain in New York and take control of a theatre which I was assured Mr. Fisk would build for me. When the building was completed, however, I found that I was not my own master; that capital, not art — that a taste with which I did not sympathize, proposed to take possession. The attempt was made to force certain people on me, and make me bear the brunt of a French company, then under the patronage of Mr. Fisk, all of which I believed would be detrimental in a business and moral point of view. I accordingly wished the principal good night, and went away, sustaining a loss of upward of $20,000. But I have n't regretted that. I returned to Wallack's and wrote "John Garth," so admirably played by Mr. Lester Wallack, because adapted to his lights and shades of character. Mr. Charles Fisher also made a point in it. After this I drifted into the hands of Mr. Daly, who wanted me to disport myself in the character of *King Carrot ;* but the Grand Opera House, after a costly and disastrous season, closed. Then I went to the Fifth Avenue, where I expected to produce some new plays; but inasmuch as Mr. Daly is a clever dramatist I missed an opportunity there.

Finally, I came to the conclusion that I was lingering rather long around the footlights, and that it was better for me, while I was yet in health and had not altogether lost my ability to afford gratification to an audience, to

take leave of the stage, in a series of plays of my own. I
have just finished the first act of an original and allegoric
fairy tale, in the Pocahontas vein, for which Mr. E. E. Rice,
the composer of "Evangeline," has written the music.

I have passed through the worst and the best portions
of the history of the American drama. When I began, I
found the stage in a bad condition, not from the lack of
good actors and actresses, for there was plenty of them,
but from a want of public attendance and popular appre-
ciation. The appetite had not been stimulated by adventitious means. Formerly a mere advertisement was the
only notification of a theatrical performance. Now we
are in the era of posters, — of Brobdingnagian type, pictures and pictorial effects, — fences covered with acres of
ink, — and they seem to have become a necessity of the
profession. No matter who the celebrity may be, amateur
or veteran, it 's a part of the abominable outlay. It 's an
ill wind, however, that blows nobody good. The wood-
engravers have made a fortune, and the printers have come
in for a share that would make their brethren of the last
generation envious. Artists of real ability have striven
against this influence, but at last they have had to swim
with the current.

· Circuses taught us that lesson first. In the time of
Richardson's show in England, everything was outside —
on canvas; nothing within. It was simply a swindling
superficiality, on paper, of fat women, monsters, snakes,
and abnormal beasts. But it drew the crowd. The crowd
saw a cheap collection of curiosities, and in half an hour
gave place to another. So our theatre bill boards have
become almost like a show at a fair.

Many other influences have affected the stage. The
war, for instance, let loose all sorts of people who never

thought of being actors before. Some of them acquired their first dramatic experience through recitations around the camp-fire. Others, half starved, drifted into local theatres, and there caught a smattering of the confidence and art that belong to the boards. Then again the variety business has had its effect. Men and women have double-shuffled into places on the stage, where twenty years ago they never would have been heard of. Making a little pecuniary headway, some ingenious body may have written a play for them that has hit the popular fancy, and it is ' astonishing to observe the success with which they have been received. Of course there are exceptions to the rule. But where there is one who wins, hundreds fail. In part, the public is to blame for this condition of affairs. It has been so highly stimulated by cheap champagne, that it fails to recognize the real article. It has almost lost the patience to sit and see performed throughout a first-class artistic drama. When Mrs. Siddons and John Kemble were at the zenith of their fame, they were obliged to produce " Blue Beard," and bring an elephant on the stage. That's the trouble with us now. We have too much elephant, and, intelligent as this generation has become, it seems to me that it should give its best praise to higher things. We pay high prices for small matters.

It is a custom to decry the theatrical profession ; but, if you will take the pains to investigate, you will find fewer crimes rightfully laid at its door than elsewhere. People behind the footlights have little time to be vicious. It is a strong light which blazes on the throne ; it is a stronger light which blazes upon actors ; but taking the thousands of instances of iniquity which may be drawn from social life, where diabolism reigns so boldly, I think that our profession will stand the test of the comparison. As a

class, we are laborious.   Our mornings are devoted to study
and rehearsals, our evenings to acting, and we have n't the
time to be very wicked.   In fact, speaking generally, the
vices of the theatrical profession end where the crimes of
some of the ministers begin.

EXTRACTS FROM BROUGHAM'S DIARIES.

[DURING many years of his active professional career,
as author and actor, Brougham kept a memorandum diary.
The greater part of it, however, would seem to have been
destroyed by him, — as the record covering the period
from January 1, 1855, to December 31, 1877, although
known to have existed, has not been found.   From the
fragment that remains a few extracts have been selected,
for use in this place.   The entries are disjointed, sketchy,
and barren of thought; but they have a flavor of the
writer's character, and perhaps they help to suggest the
picture of what manner of man he was, and what sort of
life he lived. — ED.]

1853.

Five-act Comedy: "Game of Life" (successful).
Farce: "Love and Murder."
Irish stories: "Ned Geraghty"; "The Fairy Circle";
"The Warning"; "Temptation"; "Elopement"; "Le-
gend of St. Patrick."
Host of small articles.
Four-act piece: "Bleak House" (successful).
Five-act play: "All's Fair in Love,"—altered from
"The Page."

*   *   *   *   *

Wrote, during the Dianian interregnum :— Not much, theatrically, being mainly busy at the devilish *Lantern*, — a mistake into which I entered *con amore.*

The *Lantern*, after being kept alive for eighteen months, exploded, June, 1853, costing the unfortunate subscriber about $4,000 !

*   *   *   *   *

Kept no diary since 1852, when, after a disastrous season, had to surrender the Lyceum to my friend Major Rodgers, who will, probably, be induced to do me justice at the arrival of the Greek Kalends.   Mr. Wallack took the theatre, and opened it in October, 1852, since when I have lived a quiet, laborious life, up to my under lip in debt, but getting out by degrees, — "Bent, but not broken," — waiting, like Micawber, for "something to turn up."

*   *   *   *   *

1854. — JANUARY.

January 1st, Sunday. — Saw old year out, as usual, with Annette and sundry friends.   Hope for better luck this year, with the blessing and help of Heaven.

2d. — Sent five act play, "All's Fair in Love," to New Orleans.   To receive third of benefit.

Note : Never heard a word about it.

FEBRUARY.

6th, Monday. — Stevens killed, — *skylarking.*

9th, Thursday. — Began new comedietta for Blake and Lester.   German subject.

11th. — Mr. Hunt died.

12th. — Stevens and Hunt buried at Greenwood.

APRIL.

5th, Wednesday. — Barry left for Europe to obtain novelty to open the new Boston theatre.

C

6th. — Mrs. Blake's benefit. Busy about Fund dinner.

8th. — Took a drive with Annette to Crystal Palace. Wrote article for Fund.

9th. — Wrote part of "Cousin German."

10th. — Sixth anniversary dinner of the American Dramatic Fund, at Astor House. Can't go; have to act. "Penelope's Web," first time. Not very bright.

11th. — Finished "Cousin German."

14th. — Mrs. Conway's benefit. A severe snow-storm. Settled to take house in Broome Street, — three years' lease.

16th, Sunday. — At home, writing "Red Mask." Great snow-storm. . Dr. Mackenzie spent the evening; did n't get off his pins till two o'clock.

17th. — Snowing still. Rehearsed "No. 1. Round the Corner."

18th. — "No. 1. Round the Corner," first night; successful. Fine weather.

21st. — Annette's benefit. "Game of Life," 22d time. "Immediate Satisfaction": successful, but not liked by the manager. Fine house; $700 (nearly).

22d. — Wrote Ode for Crystal Palace opening, by Barnum.

23d. — Wrote second Ode for opening of Crystal Palace.

26th. — Great fire in Broadway; many firemen killed, by falling of wall.

27th. — "Hearts at Fault," first time; pretty good. Very bad storm.

MAY.

1st, Monday. — Moved to 502 Broome Street.

10th. — Arranged to go to Philadelphia, with Blake; share after $125 and half benefit.

18th. — "A Nice Firm," — failure.

24th. — Charles Wallack's benefit. "The Scholar," "Rent-Day."

30th. — Blake's benefit. "Old Heads and Young Hearts," "Last Man." Bad rain-storm, — spoiled the house.

JUNE.

19th, Monday. — Last night of season.

20th. — Retrospect : —

Received	$5,934.39
Expended	5,582.00
	$ 352.39

Paying off debts on old Lyceum, and doing up new house, &c., gives me a poor show at the end of the season. Travelled to Philadelphia. Terribly hot.

21st, Wednesday. — At Philadelphia. "Rivals." Bad house ; weather fearfully hot. Shared nix.

22d. — "Poor Gentleman." Still excruciatingly hot. Small share.

25th. — Dined with John Drew.

26th. — "Game of Life." Fair.

28th. — Benefit. "Game of Life," "Sketches in India." $188, — *great for here !*

JULY.

4th, Tuesday. — Independence day. About twenty people in all !

18th. — Settled with Wallack for next season : $100 a week ; one half benefit and one third ; pieces as before.

23d, Sunday. — Lysander Thompson died.

27th. — Finished "Black Mask."

30th. — Sam Nichols, Burdick, and Burton to dinner.

AUGUST.

9th. — Began version of "Actress of Padua," for Matilda Heron.

12th. — Sold copy of "Romance and Reality" to Drew for $50.

15th. — "A Bachelor of Arts ": a hit.

23d, Wednesday. — Sent second act of "Mother's Gift" to New York.

26th. — Last night of engagement.

31st. — At home. Received at Philadelphia, $1,359.

SEPTEMBER.

5th. — Very hot. Went to the Broadway Theatre with Annette. Saw *Camille*, by Miss Davenport : well acted.

14th. — "She Stoops to Conquer": *Tony Lumpkin*, first time ; did n't please myself.

26th. — Played at Castle Garden, for Irish orphans. About 9,000 people, — 3,000 turned away.

OCTOBER.

11th. — Heard of total loss of *Arctic*, with several hundred souls. City wrapped in gloom.

13th. — Finished "Tisbe."

19th. — "London Assurance." *Début* of Miss Rosa Bennett. Rosa made a hit. *Sir Harcourt*, first time ; did well.

20th. — Began "Bride of Lammermoor," for Mrs. Alexina Baker.

NOVEMBER.

3d, Friday. — Finished version of "Bride of Lammermoor."

5th. — Home, working on "Jane Eyre."

8th. — Dined at Astor House; settled the business of Mrs. Thompson's benefit.

16th. — Received $300 from Baker for "Bride of Lammermoor."

21st. — First night of "Weeds among the Flowers": not very successful.

27th. — Made a sensation in *Andrew Wiley.*

DECEMBER.

2d, Saturday. — First meeting of the Garrick Club : Col. Joe Alston in chair.

4th. — *Goldfinch,* first time ; fair.

9th. — Meeting of Shakespeare Club.

11th. — "Gentleman from Ireland." *A hit.*

13th. — Began "Night and Morning." Extremely difficult to dramatize.

27th. — Finished "Night and Morning." Written in about eight days.

31st. — Last day of the year. In good health, tolerable spirits, sincerely grateful for all the comforts and blessings we have both received ; patient under the privations, and hopeful for the future.

Wrote this year : "Old Time and New"; "Love and Murder"; "Cousin German"; "Ode for Opening of C. P."; "Red Mask"; "Mother's Gift"; Weeds and Flowers" (altered); "Bride of Lammermoor"; "Night and Morning"; "Jane Eyre" (altered).

*   *   *   *   *

1878. — JANUARY.

1st, Tuesday. — 1877 is dead and buried, thank God ! It stole away my money, my watch, my health, and very nearly my life. I begin the new year more hopefully through the very generous assistance of my good friends, with improving health and a brighter prospect.

17th. — The "Grand Testimonial Benefit" for J. B. Afternoon and evening: Academy of Music. A brilliant occasion; all the theatrical celebrities volunteered.

FEBRUARY.

4th, Monday. — Rehearsed "Money" at Wallack's. Heartily glad to be at the old shop once more.

9th. — Was to have dined at the McCullough dinner, at the Lotos, but too ill to go.

14th. — Matinee benefit at Wallack's; $1,000 return.

18th. — Made my re-entrance as *Mr. Stout*, and had an overwhelming welcome from a large audience. Got through much better than I expected.

19th. — Second night of "Money." Another fine welcome.

21st. — Heard about the distribution of the benefit money. I am to have an annuity of $1,400 a year, which gives me $28 a week.

MARCH.

2d, Saturday. — G. F. Rowe's version, "The Exiles," makes a success. Bravo, George!

3d. — Feeling better. Letter from me in *Herald* explaining things: hope my duns will take the hint.

8th. — Drove in Central Park with Boucicault.

18th. — "London Assurance." Hit, as *Max Harkaway.* Dion called; told me he would have a part for me in the play for next season. Contracted with E. E. Rice to have "Lotos" ready by 1st of May. Terms, $150 a week, of eight performances.

30th. — "London Assurance." Concluded my engagement, which I thought was for the season, and I am disappointed.

APRIL.

1st. — " Diplomacy " produced at Wallack's ; a brilliant success.   Annual meeting of the Lotos Club ; I am elected a life-member.

2d. — Received my annuity papers, $340 a quarter, from 1st of July, proximo.   No fear of the almshouse, when I get to be ninety or a hundred !

3d. — Saw " Diplomacy " at Wallack's.   A very interesting play.

6th. — Dinner to Bayard Taylor.   Did not go ; too miserable.

8th. — Very down in the mouth ; in bad form to write comic songs.   Lord forgive me, I went in the evening to see " Uncle Tom's Cabin," a religious black burlesque.

13th. — Went out to get some air ; got too much ; caught cold from change of temperature.

15th. — Visited the armory of the 22d Regiment, with Cols. Porter and Lomas ; saw a very efficient drill ; was cordially received by the boys, and made a speech.

MAY.

9th, Thursday. — My birthday !   Sick and sicksty-eight. Finished " The Princess of Cashmere."   Bad title.   Not mine, however.

*   *   *   *   *   *

1879. — JANUARY.

1st. — Saw beastly old 1878 out, at the Westmoreland, with Mac, Col. Porter, and Hill.   God grant we may have better luck this one !

2d. — Saw Miss Claxton in Reade's "Double Marriage." A very interesting play.

15th. — Health better. Never give up the ship while there's a shot in the locker !

19th. — Spent the evening at Wallack's : George Freeman, Dr. Renny, Old Tom and cigars.

22d. — Very much better, which is fortunate, as I have to enact *Sir Lucius*, at Niblo's, to-morrow afternoon, for the benefit of the murdered policeman's family.

23d. — Benefit for family of the murdered policeman, at Niblo's. One act of " Rivals," by our company. An enormous house.

30th. — Getting better. Went to see George Edgar in *Lear.* A wonderful performance for an amateur, or, indeed, for anybody !

FEBRUARY.

2d. — Note from Dion, asking me to play the *O'Grady* in " Arrah-na-Pogue," at the Boucicault reunion.

4th. — Restudying *O'Grady :* rather a pill, but must be swallowed.

11th. — Played the *O'Grady* in " Arrah-na-Pogue," with Mr. and Mrs. Boucicault, and had a brilliant reception, — which the next day's *Sun* gave to John Gilbert.

24th. — Saw " Spellbound," with Col. Lomas. An unmistakable failure, I regret to say.

MARCH.

1st, Saturday. — Travelled to Boston. Left 11 A. M., arrived at 6.15, at Adams House.

2d. — Dined (with Dion), in company with Mr. Whittier and friends, — a glorious gathering of clever cusses.

3d. — "Arrah-na-Pogue," at the Boston.   Rather tired, but did well for a veteran of the Old Guard.

4th. — A fine house at the Boston ; had another fine reception.   Invited to supper at the Somerset Club, with Dion ; he went, but discretion kept me away.   Could not get a single morning paper, — all bought up by the "Pinafore" people.

8th. — Started for New York.

13th. — Saw "Through the Dark," at the Fifth Avenue, — an attack of dramatic lunacy in five fits, utterly beyond my poor comprehension.

APRIL.

5th. — Settled to migrate, this day week.

8th, Tuesday. — Sick, dull, and stupid.   Made up the little mind I have to retire quietly from the stage.   Have had many humiliating indications that I have become a *superfluous lagger.*

12th. — Told Wallack it was my intention to stop acting, and devote my time to writing.   He kindly said that, if he should want me in any play, he would give me an opportunity to revisit the glimpses of the foot-lights.

20th. — Reading French plays, — "Le Parvenu," "Les Pays des Amour," and "Les Sceptiques" : no good, any of them.

MAY.

7th, Wednesday. — Moved to 17 East 15th Street.

AUGUST.

6th. — Must be ready for the meeting of Boucicault's company at Booth's, on the 14th inst.

11th, Monday. — Wrote to Mr. ———, who is in mortal fear of losing the royalty on my plays.   He deserves but little consideration from me; nevertheless, I shall not interfere, though I am as badly off as he is.

14th. — Reading and rehearsal of Boucicault's new play, — one act of it. I fear it is of too quiet an order to satisfy the New York audience.

17th. — Studying *Felix*, after a fashion; cannot concentrate my mind on the work.

21st. — More rehearsal. My capacity for study is very much deteriorated, — the consequence of a year of sickness and ill-luck. Took a long ride, in three horse-cars.

30th. — Night rehearsal. Play very loose and disjointed; a very doubtful venture.

SEPTEMBER.

4th. — First night of Boucicault's play, "Rescued." The audience did not forget the old man; had a most cordial welcome.

12th. — "Rescued," ninth time. The sensation scene went properly, for the first time.

14th. — Dion dined his entire company; had a delight. ful time. The company to give him a return dinner next Sunday.

20th. — "Rescued" twice, 17th and 18th times. The best audience yet, and best performance.

21st. — Dion told me he intended to revive "The Duke's Motto."

24th. — "Rescued," 21st time. Had what might have been a serious accident, by stepping into a plug-hole for watering the horse of a 23d Street car, it being very dark, and no light to give warning of danger. It was merciful that I did not break my leg. — John Gilbert sick with typhoid fever.

28th. — Studying *Coitier* in "Louis XI."

OCTOBER.

1st, Wednesday. — Studying *Coitier*, — he's a pill of the blank verse order.

2d. — Rehearsed 1st and 2d acts of "Louis XI."

5th. — Hammering away at *Coitier*; think I have coiled round, but not quite swallowed, the cuss.

11th. — Production of "Louis XI." Brilliant reception of "Dot" Boucicault. Irish intonation — in fact, brogue — very prominent.

15th. — Dion sick of the part, and of the public's non-appreciation of the theatre. Play changed to "Rescued," 38th time. •

16th, Thursday. — Received the pleasant intimation that the season will be terminated the 22d of next month.

21st, Tuesday. — "Rescued," 44th time. Rose Coghlan left.

22d, Wednesday. — "Rescued," 45th. Wretched house; Dion very ill.

25th, Saturday. — "Rescued," 48th. Matinee. Ghastliest ! ! ! — Evening. Finished the brief and most disastrous season, with a house about half-full, — manifestly dead-heads. Seven weeks and two days. The whole company left to shift for themselves at the beginning of winter, with all opportunities for employment filled. What I shall do, God knows.

26th, Sunday. — Suffering from great mental depression.

NOVEMBER.

3d, Monday. — Moved to 81 West 12th. Thanks to Dion's houses, have come down to hard-pan, but am higher up in the world than ever.

1880. — JANUARY.

1st, Thursday. — Had very jolly New Year's dinner, — with Nan and Laura, — hoping we shall have better luck this year.

5th, Monday. — Finished the renovation of four plays : "The Witch of Domremi," "A Wilful Woman," "The Iron Cross," "The Irish Brigade."

8th, Thursday. — Had talk with French, about my farewell of the stage ; heartily tired, as I am, of the surroundings.

9th, Friday. — Sent the four plays to French, to be type-written. I wonder if I shall have a slice of luck out of any of them. I sincerely hope so, for I need it wofully.

19th, Monday. — Began writing "Home Rule." A great deal depends upon its success. That's so !

APRIL.

29th, Thursday. — Took lodging at 60 East 9th Street.

BROUGHAM'S WILL.

I JOHN BROUGHAM, of the city, county, and State of New York, actor and playwright, do make, publish, and declare this to be my last will and testament. I give, devise, and bequeath to my faithful friend, James A. Ship, all my wardrobe, private and theatrical. I give, devise, and bequeath all the rest and residue of my property, both real and personal, together with all my right, title, and interest in and to my plays, and the copyrights pertaining thereto, to Annie Deland Finegan (whose maiden name was Annie Deland), and I declare that said property shall be for her sole and separate use and benefit, and that her receipt, notwithstanding her present or any future marriage, shall be a valid and effectual discharge of the same. To all my friends I leave kind thoughts. I appoint Annie Deland Finegan and Laura Phillips the executrixes of this will.

In witness whereof, I, John Brougham, have, to this, my last will and testament, subscribed my hand, this 28th day of May, 1880.

JOHN BROUGHAM.

Witness :

II.

SUPPLEMENTARY MEMOIR.

[THE SKETCHES HERE REPRINTED, WITH A FEW EMENDATIONS,
FROM THE *NEW YORK TRIBUNE* AND *HARPER'S WEEKLY*, AND
THE TWO POEMS, ENTITLED "HONOR TO BROUGHAM" AND
"FAREWELL TO BROUGHAM," WERE WRITTEN BY THE EDITOR
OF THIS VOLUME, WHO ALSO CONTRIBUTES THE CHAPTER OF
"RECOLLECTIONS AND RELICS."]

SUPPLEMENTARY MEMOIR.

SKETCH OF BROUGHAM'S CAREER.

[*From the New York Tribune, June* 8, 1880.]

THOSE who have known and loved John Brougham — and of him truly it may be said " none knew him but to love him " — should be grateful that his earthly pilgrimage is over. For a long time he had been in sickness and sorrow. The malady from which he suffered was very painful, and it was incurable. He was more than seventy years of age; he had seen many of his friends drop away; he had outlived his once brilliant popularity with the public; he was, without being aware of it, losing his intellectual vigor; and the circumstances of his fortune were such as constantly preyed upon his mind. He still labored with his pen, and he still cherished plans for the future; but these labors were mostly frustrated by the weakness of age, and these plans were mostly of an impracticable character, and destined to disappointment. There seemed to be nothing left for him but trouble; and therefore the hearts to whom he was endeared should find their comfort in the thought that his toil-worn, sensitive, suffering spirit is now beyond the reach of earthly care and pain.

> " Alive, we would have changed his lot, —
> We would not change it now."

7

The life of John Brougham, notable for many things, has been especially remarkable for two qualities, — its brilliancy and its goodness. Fifty years of it he passed upon the stage; and, both as actor and author, his influence always tended to gladden and sweeten the human experience of which he was a part. The reason of this was, that back of the actor and author there was a true man. His heart was large, warm, and charitable; his mind was eager, hopeful, cheerful, and actively creative; his instincts were virtuous and kindly; his temperament was gentle; and his consideration for others, — which extended to the humblest of living creatures, was thoughtful of the most minute point of delicacy, found excuse for every fault, and gave forgiveness for almost every wrong, — sprang from the spontaneous desire that everybody should be happy. His thoughts, and very often his talk, dwelt upon the great disparity of conditions in society, the struggles and sufferings of the poor, and the relation of evil to the infirmities of human nature. He did not live for himself alone, but he was profoundly and practically interested in others; and this feeling, as potent as it was genuine, animated all his life, colored all his work, and so commended him to the responsive sympathy and good-will of his generation that his name, on every lip, was the name of a friend.

In his writings as in his acting the characteristic quality was a sort of off-hand dash and glittering merriment, a commingling of bluff, breezy humor with winning manliness. The atmosphere of his works was always that of sincerity, but it never had the insipidity of strenuous goodness. He was highly intellectual, and at times poetic and romantic; but he was human, and he was gay, and he loved to saturate life with the Celtic sparkle. His rich,

rolling voice, with a touch of the brogue in it, sounds in
all he wrote, and his happy, infectious laughter, for all
who recall his acting, will ring on in memory as long as
they shall live.   The scope and variety of his labors was
great.   He threw himself with the keenest zest into the
passing moment ; he dreaded no task ; he shunned no
emergency ; he attempted all sorts of composition to
which either his agile fancy impelled him, or which the
need of the hour exacted ; and, while he was not equally
successful in every line of literature or every walk of the
stage, he produced a surprising quantity of sterling dramatic work, and he acted many and diversified parts in
an admirable manner.   During the first twenty years of
his life, — which were passed in and around the city of
Dublin, where he was born, May 9, 1810, — he was provided with opportunities of liberal education ; and these
he improved, acquiring knowledge, however, as he has said
of himself, rather by absorption than application ; and all
his life he was a reader and a student ; so that his labors
were based on a solid foundation of good mental discipline.
In other words, he was a scholar ; and the operations of
his mind, however impulsive and erratic they sometimes
may have been, were usually guided and restrained by that
knowledge of the intellectual field, and that sense of pro-
portion and harmony, of fitness and of taste, which only
scholarship can give.

He began life as a student of surgery, and for several
months walked the Peter Street Hospital, Dublin ; but a
sudden stroke of adversity deprived him of the prospect of
fortune, and threw him upon his own resources, and he
thereupon went up to London, and by chance became an
actor.   This was an accident ; for, when quite destitute
of money, he had offered himself as a cadet in the East

India Company's service, and had only been restrained from enlisting by the recruiting officer, — a stranger, but a kind old man, — who gave him a guinea, and urged him to seek some other and fitter employment. A chance encounter with an old acquaintance, within an hour or two after this incident occurred, led to his engagement at what was then the Tottenham Street Theatre, afterward the Prince of Wales's; and there, in July, 1830, acting six characters in the old play of " Tom and Jerry," he began that sparkling professional career which death has closed, and which now is only a memory. In 1831, he was a member of the company organized by Madam Vestris for the London Olympic, and his name appears in the cast of " Olympic Revels," ("*Mars*, Mr. Brougham,") in the first full bill issued by that once famous manager. From the Olympic he made professional trips into the provinces, and played all sorts of parts. His first play was written at this time, and was a burlesque, prepared for William E. Burton, who then was acting in London, at the Pavilion Theatre. When Vestris removed from the Olympic to Covent Garden, Brougham followed her thither, and there he remained as long as Vestris and Charles Mathews were at the head of the theatre ; and it was while there that he coöperated with Dion Boucicault in writing the comedy of " London Assurance." In 1840, he became manager of the London Lyceum, which he conducted during summer seasons, and he wrote for production at this time, " Life in the Clouds," " Love's Livery," " Enthusiasm," " Tom Thumb the Second," and, in conjunction with Mark Lemon, " The Demon Gift."

His American career began in 1842, when, as *O'Callaghan*, in " His Last Legs," he came forward at the old Park Theatre in New York. Those days, he said, were " the

palmy days of light houses and heavy gas-bills." A starring tour of the country followed, and, incidentally, the
comedian lost all his earnings while endeavoring aboard
a Mississippi River steamboat, to learn our national game
of "draw-poker." A little later he was employed in Burton's company, in New York, and for Burton he wrote
"Bunsby's Wedding," "The Confidence Man," "Don
Cæsar de Bassoon," "Vanity Fair," "The Irish Yankee,"
"Benjamin Franklin," "All's Fair in Love," "The Irish
Emigrant," and a play on "Dombey and Son." Still later
he managed Niblo's Garden, producing there his fairy tale
called "Home," and the play of "Ambrose Germain,"
written for Mlle. Blangy. On December 23, 1850, he
opened Brougham's Lyceum, in Broadway, near the south-
west corner of Broome Street ; and while there he wrote
"The World's Fair," "Faustus," "The Spirit of Air,"
"Row at the Lyceum," a dramatization of "David Copperfield," and a new version of "The Actress of Padua," —
the latter for Charlotte Cushman. The demolition of the
building next to his theatre, however, made it appear to
be unsafe, and so his business, which had begun well, was
seriously injured ; and he always said that the misdealing
of a false friend took that property out of his hands and
left him burdened with debt, — all of which, however, he
subsequently paid. In theatrical management he was always unfortunate ; partly because he always acted from
principle and never from expediency, partly because he
would not consider the caprices of public taste, and partly
because he was gentle and yielding in nature.

From the Lyceum — which afterwards became Wallack's
Theatre, and so remained till 1860 — he went to the Bowery (July 7, 1856), where he revived "King John," with
superb scenery by Hilliard, and with a cast that included

Edwin L. Davenport, Mrs. Davenport, William Wheatley,
J. B. Howe, and Kate Reignolds; but this did not suc-
ceed; and he then wrote and produced a large number of
Bowery dramas, among which were "The Pirates of the
Mississippi," "The Red Mask" (based on a current tale
called "The Gun-maker of Moscow"), "Orion, the Gold-
beater," "Tom and Jerry in America," and "The Miller
of New Jersey." He then accepted employment in
Wallack's company, and for "the veteran's" theatre
wrote "The Game of Love," a version of "Bleak House,"
"My Cousin German," "A Decided Case," "The Game
of Life," the famous burlesque of "Pocahontas," "Neptune's Defeat," "Love and Murder," "Romance and Reality," "The Ruling Passion," and "Playing with Fire."
After several seasons at Wallack's, he rejoined Burton, —
then at the Metropolitan Theatre, formerly Tripler Hall,
and latterly the Winter Garden, in Broadway, nearly opposite to Bond Street, — and there he produced his burlesque
of "Columbus," "This House to be Sold," and several other
plays. In September, 1860, he went to England, where
he remained five years. While there, he adapted from
the French, for Mr. Fechter, "The Duke's Motto" and
"Bel Demonio," and wrote, for Miss Herbert, dramatic
versions of "Lady Audley's Secret" and "Only a Clod."
He also wrote "While there's Life there's Hope," acted
at the Strand; "The Might of Right," acted at Astley's;
"The Golden Dream," produced at Manchester; the words
of three operas, — "Blanche de Nevers," "The Demon
Lovers," and "The Bride of Venice," — several songs and
poems, and several pieces of music, one of which, "The
Bobolink Polka," subsequently became popular. His
comedy of "Playing with Fire" was produced at the
Princess's Theatre, and he himself acted there, and also

at the Lyceum. His reappearance in America was effected on October 30, 1865, at the Winter Garden Theatre, and he never afterwards left this land. He acted in a round of parts at that time, beginning with *Dr. Savage*, and continuing with *Foxglove* in his own "Flies in the Web," *Powhatan, Columbus*, and *McShane* in "The Nervous Man and the Man of Nerve"; and he wound up the engagement, which lasted three months, with his drama of "O'Donnell's Mission," in which he acted *Roderick O'Donnell*.

In February, 1867, a new piece by Brougham, entitled "The Christian Martyrs," was produced at Barnum's Museum, and in May of the same year he filled a brief engagement at the Olympic, appearing as *O'Donnell, Captain Cuttle, Micawber*, and *Powhatan*. In the following August he again played there, and at the same time his drama of "Little Nell and the Marchioness," written for Lotta (Miss Charlotte Crabtree) was brought out at Wallack's Theatre (August 14, 1867). In the summer of 1868 he produced, at the Walnut, in Philadelphia, "Hearts, or the Serpents of Society," and on June 8 in that year he brought forward, at Wallack's Theatre, his melodrama of "The Lottery of Life," and himself acted the chief part. This had a run of nine weeks. In December, that year, his play of "The Emerald Ring," written for Barney Williams, was produced at the Broadway Theatre, —Wallack's old house, — which Williams then managed. On January 25, 1869, he opened Brougham's Theatre, on the site of what is now the Madison Square Theatre, with a comedy by himself, called "Better Late than Never," — in which he acted *Major Fergus O'Shaughnessy*, — and the "Dramatic Review for 1868." He subsequently produced an adaptation called "Irish Stew," and his capital burlesque,

in which he enacted *Shylock*, entitled "Much Ado about
a Merchant of Venice." This theatre was taken out of
his hands by the owner, the notorious James Fisk, Jr.,
who behaved in a dishonest, tyrannical, and brutal manner,
and, on April 3d, Brougham closed his season, with a performance of "His Last Legs." On the 4th, a banquet in
his honor was given at the Astor House, and on May 18th
he received a farewell benefit, — performances being given
at the theatre which is now Haverly's, in Fourteenth
Street, and at Niblo's Garden. The attempt to establish
Brougham's Theatre was his final effort in management.
Since that time he has been connected with various stock
companies, but chiefly with Daly's Theatre and with Wallack's. Among his later works may be mentioned "The
Red Light," in which he acted at Wallack's Theatre, June
6th, 1870; "Minnie's Luck," produced at the same house;
"John Garth," given at Wallack's, December 12th, 1871;
"The Lily of France," brought out, December 16th, 1872,
at Booth's Theatre, by Miss Helen Temple, who enacted
Joan of Arc; and "Slander," and "Good Bye," in which
he made his last professional tour of the country, in the fall
of 1877. In 1852 Brougham edited a bright comic paper
in New York, called *The Lantern,* and he published two
collections of his miscellaneous writings, entitled "A Basket of Chips," and "The Bunsby Papers." On January
17th, 1878, he received a testimonial benefit, at the Academy
of Music, at which the sum of $10,278.56 was received;
and this fund, after payment of the incidental expenses,
was settled on him in an annuity, which expired at his
death. It was thought that he would live for many years,
and the desire and design of his friends, in the arrangement
then made, was to insure his protection from want in his
old age. He began, years ago, the composition of an "Au-

tobiography," at the earnest solicitation of a friend, but this remains unfinished. His last work was a drama, entitled " Home Rule," in which he treated the aspects of political and social affairs in Ireland. His last appearance on the stage was made, as *Felix O'Reilley*, the detective, in Mr. Boucicault's play of " Rescued," at Booth's Theatre, New York, October 25th, 1879.

The recital of these facts is indicative of the current of his career, the great vitality and industry by which it was marked, and the variable success with which it was crowned. Actors, more than most of the persons who live by their labor in the realms of art, are necessarily affected by the immediate influences of their time. Their characters, in other words, are to a considerable extent bent and moulded by public opinion and caprice. They feel the necessity of the instant response ; and, accordingly, they are not slow to make that direct appeal in which very often there is more of impulse than of judgment, the tinsel of artifice rather than the pure gold of art. Brougham, like many of his contemporaries, recognized this necessity ; but his sincerity of feeling, his sturdiness of character, his scholar-like taste, and his intense loyalty to the higher principles and best ideals of art were all combined in antagonism to worldly prudence and expediency ; and all through the story of his life it is easy to trace, not merely a roving, drifting, careless disposition, — the light-hearted heedlessness and yielding amiability of Goldsmith, whom in some ways he resembled, — but the resolute bent of a mind that spontaneously insisted on going its own way and fulfilling its own laws. There was, indeed, in his intellectual existence, no continuity of movement toward a definite goal, clearly seen afar off. But he was born to be a man of letters, a poetic artist, and a wit, and he could not, except in a fitful manner, take his cue from his circumstances. His experience, therefore, was often that of conflict with prevailing notions, and, toward the last, of considerable spiritual discontent.

The fact that fortune always, sooner or later, slipped through his fingers, was doubtless chiefly ascribable to his buoyant Hibernian recklessness of the ordinary precautions of prudence, and to his heedless trust in everybody. He adapted "The Duke's Motto" for Fechter, for instance, and it had a prosperous career in London, but all that he ever received for his work upon it was a box of cigars; and with transactions of this kind his whole business career was spangled. But, even with a harder temperament, he would still have been at odds with the practical spirit of his time. He had originality as a man, even more than as a writer, and he was often a dreamer in the midst of the battle. Those of his dramatic works in which he himself took the most pleasure, and in which the student will hereafter discern the most of the man, are the burlesque of "Columbus," the blank-verse drama of "The Lily of France," and the comedy of "Playing with Fire." They contain delicate thought, poetic suggestion, sweet-tempered satire, contemplative philosophy, and pathos. He often chose to appear to be, in a mild and elegant way, "the rantin', roarin' Irishman"; he was in fact nothing of the kind, but a pensive moralist, a poetic dreamer, a delicate, sensitive gentleman, as frank and honest as a child, and as gentle as a woman.

His rank among actors it is difficult to assign. He excelled in humor rather than in pathos or sentiment, and was at his best in the expression of comically eccentric character. Among the parts that will live in memory, as associated with his name, are *Stout*, in "Money"; *Dennis*

My dear friend, it was only natural, humanly of acknowledge... or rather attempt to do so — the fact compliment with which you have honour me but excessive anxiety, acting improperly upon by but excessive reaction, present condition of present condition formerly that prototype of little ... to been lovely ... formerly that prototype of ... things ... philosophy enough to ... Yes. One explains ... however ... Philosophy except ... impression that ... God forbear with ... enclose any amount of ... fade into account what equanimity — but I object not fade into ... and what ... the frequency of such circulating would have upon soothing effect and a ... whenever this welcome ... my own ... no easy tense ... daily to my anvil — liability ... ... my system ... since the first which was nearly every moment ... it lent the ... intimation I ... this the effort; and at any week have anyhow; thank you ...

that I am. bankrupted even in the article of Thanks).

(To see who have assisted in its furtherance, the New York Herald—especially the Ledger, for whom

they wrote the initiative reviews is a certainty—

) to the gentlemen of the Press, who have given them

believe and writ is anywhere more enthusiastic—and

unsparingly sent to my ever generous & liberal

in the character itself, acknowledge its importance

ever been also & may its resultant hereafter

so when my stable of its attitude. I am only hope and

pray that the contributed Comfort with what

my name crowned my trophy, new Year & many

be returned to them a thousand fold. (H)

LIBRARY

Brulgruddery, in "John Bull"; *Sir Lucius O'Trigger*, in "The Rivals"; *Cuttle; Micawber; Bagstock; O'Grady,* in "Arrah-na-Pogue"; *Dazzle*, in "London Assurance"; *Captain Murphy Maguire*, in "The Serious Family"; and *O'Callaghan*, in "His Last Legs." His animal spirits, dash, vigor, and brilliancy, in these parts, were great; he entered deeply into their spirit; he could be consciously joyous or unconsciously droll; he was never for an instant out of the stage picture; and he spoke the language with delicious purity. He has given an immense amount of pleasure; he has done no harm; he has gone to his grave in the fulness of years and honors; his best works live after him, in the usage of the stage and the admiration of the public; he is honestly and deeply mourned; and it will be a long time before any one who ever knew him can speak, without a sigh, the name of John Brougham.

HONOR TO BROUGHAM.

[*The following tribute to* BROUGHAM *was read, by its author, at a banquet in his honor, given at the Astor House, New York, April 4, 1869, just after his Theatre in Twenty-fourth Street had been unjustly taken from his hands.*]

I.

ONCE, where the Alpine hills arise,
    In glad desire to meet the day,
There wandered, under summer skies,
    A youth as glad and free as they.

Serenely sweet, his gentle face
  Could charm, and comfort, and subdue ;
And friends he found in every place,
  And every friend he found was true.

At noonday, resting in the shade,
  At eve, beside the cottage door,
His songs he sang, his flute he played,
  And laughed, and talked his wanderings o'er.

The birds made music round his way,
  In music spake the answering streams,
And all the world was lapped in May,
  And peopled from a land of dreams.

He scattered pearls where'er he trod, —
  Sweet fancy to pure thought allied :
And they who sow these pearls of God —
  They are not gone, although they died !

He passed away, his work complete, —
  A book of gold, to keep his fame,
A stainless fame, forever sweet, —
  And GOLDSMITH 's an immortal name !

II.

The same green isle that gave him birth,
  In after-time, inspired anew,
Sends forth a soul of kindred worth,
  A mind as sweet, a heart as true.

He walks the world for threescore years,
  In trouble, as in triumph, gay ;

He wakes our laughter, wins our tears,
  And lightly charms our cares away.

In him conjoined, once more we view
  High powers to conquer and command, —
The heart to feel, the hánd to do, —
  The Irish heart, the Irish hand.

Too proud a man to cringe and fawn,
  Too plain a man for craft to claim ;
Too great to put his soul in pawn
  And thrive upon the fruits of shame ; —

Haply he misses golden gain,
  But wins a wealth that 's prized above, —
Precious forever, without stain, —
  Honor, and dear and faithful love !

Our manly love is not the least
  Of all the laurel that he wears :
To-night he sits with us, at feast, —
  JOHN BROUGHAM is the name he bears !

God bless that name, and keep it bright !
  A beacon-flame, in evil days,
Of one who kept his conscience white,
  Through troublous scenes and devious ways.

And when at last (far hence the day !)
  His work is done, his story told,
Be that dear name inscribed, for aye,
  In Fame's immortal book of gold !

CHARACTER AND WORKS OF BROUGHAM.

[From Harper's Weekly, June 26, 1880.]

THE bereavement which the stage has suffered in the death of John Brougham is also the bereavement of society; for Brougham was one of those exceptional men who, while leading an intellectual life, devoted to art and its ambitious and engrossing labors, are at the same time able to win the heart of their generation, and make themselves the chosen comrades and cherished friends of the public. He was widely known; he was much and sincerely beloved; and at many a hearthstone throughout the land the news of his death has been felt with a sense of personal loss.   There was great force of character, singular beauty of spirit, and versatile, engaging, sustained industry, to cause this feeling and to justify it. In life John Brougham deserved his fame; in death he merits every tear that has been shed for him, and every kind and honoring word that can be spoken for his memory.

In the life of a man of letters, who is also an actor and a theatrical manager, there is room for much vicissitude. Brougham was each of these; and as he possessed prodigious vigor, much eccentricity of character, and a sunshiny, yielding, drifting temperament, his life naturally exhibited a surprising plenitude of incident and change.   He was born May 9, 1810, at Dublin, Ireland, and he died June 7, 1880, in New York, in the seventy-first year of his age. His youth was passed at home, and he received a good education.   He was at Trinity College in his native city, and he walked St. Peter's Hospital there, and it was intended that he should be a surgeon; but the rich uncle whose favorite he was, and from whom he had been taught to expect an inheritance of wealth, fell into poverty, and so the youth was forced to change all his plans of life, and to seek his fortune in new channels. He went to London, and became an actor, appearing at a little theatre in Tottenham Street, in July, 1830, in the rough old play of "Tom and Jerry." From that time onward he never left the stage. For half a century he was an actor and a writer of plays. He came to America in 1842; remained here till the autumn of 1860, when he returned to London; came back to New York in the autumn of 1865, and never afterward quitted this country.

At intervals within the last two or three years, Brougham has been engaged in writing an autobiography. His talk of old times was deeply interesting, full of anecdote, and various with sketches of character, witty comment, and professional learning. His recollections extended back to the days of Vestris, at the London Olympic, and afterward at Covent Garden. He had seen Munden and Liston and many another worthy of the old school. He knew Charles Mathews in his youth, and could have traced the whole growth of that sparkling mind and vigorous career which in our day became so famous. The first play that he wrote — it was in 1831 — was a burlesque for Burton, then acting in London. He saw the incidents which attended Sir Walter Scott's last sad journey through London, when that intellectual giant was forced to pause there, as he was going home to die. He was familiar with the last days of Campbell and Rogers, and contemporary with the opening careers of both Dickens and Thackeray. He was the comrade of Dion Boucicault when that author was little more than a boy, and he aided him in the composition of the com-

edy of "London Assurance."   His memories of the Kem-
bles and the Keans were perfectly distinct, and his descriptions of Macready and of Charles Kean in particular —
with both of whom he had acted, and for both of whom he
had managed the stage — were remarkably vivid, richly
humorous, and not a little pungent with drollery.   To
hear his account of a performance by Charles Kean, with
all the people about the stage shod in list slippers, was to
realize a truthful and instructive picture, and to enjoy a
complete exhilaration.   He possessed an unerring faculty
of mimicry; and as he said, "You take my life when you
do take the *beans* whereby I live," the listener heard again
the living voice of Charles Kean.   In felicity of theatrical
anecdote there has been no one like him here since George
Jamieson and John Sefton; and in this matter of simu-
lation of unconsciously comic attributes he has scarcely
left an equal among actors, unless, perhaps, it be Chanfrau
or Jefferson.

On the American stage he has been an important and
prominent figure since 1842, when he came forth at the old
Park Theatre as *O'Callaghan*, in Bernard's farce of "His
Last Legs," one of the strong characters of the brilliant
Tyrone Power.   He was at different periods associated with
Burton, for whose stage he wrote many plays, and with
whom he acted in various versions of the works of Dickens.
He opened "Brougham's Lyceum" in 1850; managed the
Bowery Theatre in 1856; acted for many seasons at
Wallack's; made starring tours of the country; opened
"Brougham's Theatre," in Twenty-fourth Street, in 1869;
edited a bright paper called "The Lantern"; published
"A Basket of Chips" and "The Bunsby Papers"; wrote
plays for many of the popular stars of his profession;
associated himself with the stock companies managed by

Daly and by Boucicault; and to the last kept busily at work, dying, as he had lived, in harness. His last play, finished about last Easter, was called "Home Rule," and was designed to exhibit the present social and political condition of Ireland, and to suggest a remedy for some of the evils which afflict that country. Brougham was an Irishman, though of French descent, and he loved his native land, and always desired and strove to promote the welfare of its people.

Of the brilliant attributes of his mind, the charm of his character, the vital force that he brought to bear upon his work, and the wholesome influence that he exercised upon society, it would be difficult to speak with too much admiration. He was the author of over seventy-five dramatic pieces, of all kinds, and many of them, by their sterling qualities of invention, movement, character, poetry, style, humor, and pathos, will long endure in literature, to testify to the solidity and sparkle of his intellectual powers. His comedies of "Playing with Fire," "Romance and Reality," "The Ruling Passion," and "The Game of Life," are among the most ingenious and brightly written of modern works of their class. His melodramas of "O'Donnell's Mission" and "The Emerald Ring" are pieces of marked originality, exciting interest, and picturesque stage effect. His "Lily of France" — a dramatic exposition of the story of Joan of Arc — is fraught with the imaginative glow and the soft romantic glamour of a true poem. His burlesques of "Pocahontas" and "Columbus" are wildly droll, exuberant in animal spirits, and — especially the latter — notable for melodious eloquence. He touched many styles, but, as Johnson said of Goldsmith, he touched nothing that he did not adorn. Although he lived in the library, and maintained and

8

cherished a high ideal of what the literary artist should strive to accomplish, he had neither the crudite prosiness nor the exclusive isolation of the abstract scholar ; he lived also in the world and with the life of his time. He clasped the hands of men and women ; he spoke to their hearts ; he was interested in their fortunes ; "their welfare pleased him, and their cares distrest"; and wherever he went, he carried the benediction of good deeds, and left the sunshine of love and laughter. The multitudes who have heard his off-hand speeches before the curtain will often call to mind what a ring of genuine kindness there was in his voice, what a light of sweetness there was in his face, what a glow of animal spirits he diffused around him, what a winning ideal of manliness he suggested, — with his native elegance of bearing, and the breezy heartiness and joyous dash of his manners. The men who were brought near to him in the business of life will not forget his thoughtful consideration, his delicate courtesy, his simple goodness. The poor had cause to bless him, though himself was poor. As he lay in his coffin, his noble face, grand in the awful serenity of death, was like the face of Shakespeare. The light, the merriment, the trouble, the pain, were all gone, and nothing but the majesty remained ; and looking on him there I thought of Shakespeare's words : —

> "Our cause of sorrow
> Must not be measured by his worth, for then
> It hath no end."

FAREWELL TO BROUGHAM.

*[In the summer of 1874, Brougham projected, and made his prepara-
tions for, a visit to his native land ; and, as he was in feeble health,
it was the thought of more than one of his friends that he would not
return to America. The Lotos Club, of New York, to signalize
his departure, gave a banquet in his honor, at the old club house,
No. 2 Irving Place, on the evening of June 4, 1874. Mr. White-
law Reid presided, and upwards of 175 gentlemen were present,
the stage being worthily represented by Mr. Lester Wallack, Mr.
John Gilbert, Mr. John McCullough, Mr. W. R. Floyd, and Mr.
George Fawcett Rowe. Several excellent and merry speeches were
made, and BROUGHAM himself spoke, with much emotion. It was
then that the following tribute was delivered by its author.]*

I.

IF buds by hopes of spring are blessed,
    That sleep beneath the snow,
And hearts by coming joys caressed,
    Which yet they dimly know, —
On fields where England's daisies gleam,
    And Ireland's shamrocks bloom,
To-day shall summer, in her dream,
    Be glad with thoughts of Brougham.

II.

To-day, o'er miles and miles of sea,
    Beneath the jocund sun,
With merrier force and madder glee
    The bannered wind shall run.

To-day great waves shall ramp and reel,
   And clash their shields of foam,
With bliss to feel the coming keel
   That bears the wanderer home.

III.

For he that, loved and honored here, —
   God bless his silver head! —
O'er many a heart, for many a year,
   The dew of joy has shed,
Longs for the land that gave him birth,
   Turns back to boy again,
And, bright with all the flags of mirth,
   Sails homeward o'er the main.

IV.

Ah, well may winds and waves be gay,
   And flowers and streams rejoice,
And that sweet region, far away,
   Become one greeting voice!
For he draws backward to that place,
   Who ne'er, by deed or art,
Made darkness in one human face,
   Or sorrow in one heart.

V.

He comes, whom all the rosy sprites
   Round humor's throne that throng
Have tended close, through golden nights
   Of laughter, wit, and song:
Whom love's bright angels still have known, —
   He ne'er forgot to hear

The helpless widow's suppliant moan,
  Or dry the orphan's tear.

VI.

Where boughs of oak and willow toss,
  His life's white pathway flows, —
With many an odor blown across,
  Of lily and of rose;
His gentle life, that blessings crown,
  Is fame no chance can dim;
And we honor manhood's best renown,
  When now we honor him!

VII.

Ambition's idols, crowned to-day,
  To-morrow are uncrowned;
Their fragments are of common clay,
  Strewn on the common ground;
But unto monarchs of the heart
  Are crowns immortal given,
And they who choose this better part
  Are anchored fast on heaven.

VIII.

Grief may stand silent in the eye,
  And silent on the lip,
When, poised between the sea and sky,
  Dips down the fading ship:
But there's one charm his heart to keep,
  And hold his constant mind, —
He 'll find no love, beyond the deep,
  Like that he leaves behind!

IX.

So, to thy breast, old Ocean, take
    This brother of our soul !
Ye winds, be gentle for his sake ;
    Ye billows, smoothly roll ;
And thou, sad Ireland, green and fair,
    Across the waters wild,
Stretch forth strong arms of loving care,
    And guard thy favorite child !

X.

And whether back to us he drift,
    Or pass beyond our view,
Where life's celestial mountains lift
    Their peaks above the blue,
God's will be done ! whose gracious will,
    Through all our mortal fret,
The sacred blessing leaves us still,
    To love — and not forget.

RECOLLECTIONS AND RELICS

A S already declared, it is not my purpose to endeavor to continue and conclude Brougham's biography. That would be a work of years, and even then it could be but inadequately performed. My effort has been to select with discretion, out of a great mass of material, and within a very brief time, the things that are best calculated to make up a life-like memorial of the actor, the author, and the man. The greater part of his story has now been told in his own language, and that part which is not told is clearly suggested. My personal recollections of him extend over a period of about twenty-three years, and from the moment when first we met till his eyes closed in death we lived in uninterrupted friendship. He was acting *Captain Murphy Maguire* when first I saw him, and he at once fascinated my youthful fancy, with that sweet manliness which to the last was his native and inextinguishable charm. I had frequent opportunities of seeing him, just before he went away to England, at the outbreak of the civil war ; and I was deeply impressed by the liberality of his mind, the gentleness of his judgment, and his great and constant charity for human infirmity and error. He saw things as they are, and not as he wished them to be, and never through a mist of prejudice ; he did not condemn because his taste or principle had disapproved ; he could praise a foe ; and he could go on doing kind deeds for others, with neither the thought nor the

expectation of gratitude. He was always helping the
poor, and he was always making merry in the passing
hour. That was the impression he left on my memory
when he went away ; and when he returned to America
I was one of the first friends whom he took by the hand.
His life after that time was known to me, every step of
its way, and it was full of goodness, of honorable labor, of
patience, and of beauty.

He made his re-entrance on the American stage, October
10th, 1865, at the Winter Garden Theatre, New York, as
Dr. Savage, in "Playing with Fire." The other parts were
cast as follows : *Herbert Waverley*, Charles Walcot, Jr. ;
Mrs. Waverley, Miss Rose Eytinge ; *Mrs. Savage*, Mrs. C.
Walcot, Jr. (Miss Isabella Nickinson) ; *Uncle Timothy*, Mr.
John Dyott ; *Pinchbeck*, Mr. W. S. Andrews ; *The Widow
Crabstick*, Miss Mary Carr : and this record of the occasion was made, the next day, by the present writer : " Time
has not robbed this accomplished comedian of any of
his spirit, his bluff manliness (that affects one like the
sound of sweet laughter and the pressure of an honest
hand), his humor, his fine play of feature, his dexterity
in the management of dialogue, his rare correctness and
rich melody in the pronunciation of the English language. Repeated rounds of applause materially delayed
the progress of the play. At the end of the first act Mr.
Brougham was called before the curtain, and again, with
enthusiasm, at the end of the fourth." His engagement
lasted three months, and from that time onward he was
seldom long absent from the public gaze, and always a
welcome and an honored presence ; although, toward the
last, a new theatrical generation having sprung up, he
was viewed rather as a legacy from the past than with
a clear idea of what he had been or what he had done.

There were several occasions, though, of more than ordinary moment and interest, when the good-will of the community was tested in his behalf, and was found to be ardent. When he opened his theatre in Twenty-fourth Street, — January 25th, 1869, — New York gave him a whole-hearted welcome; and the enforced closing of that theatre, on April 3d following, caused a deep regret. Brougham signalized his brief season of ten weeks at that house by producing his brilliant burlesque of "Much Ado about a Merchant of Venice"; and I do not think a more sparkling effect of comic humor can have been produced upon the stage than that which ensued upon his tempestuous entrance as *Shylock*, when, wildly rushing toward his brother Hebrew, he broke into song, with

> "O, Tubal dear, did you not hear
> The news that's going round?
> My Jessicay has cut away
> And nowhere can be found."

The air of "Wearin' o' the Green" had been made widely popular through the medium of Boucicault's "Arrah-na-Pogue," and the use of it, in this situation, was inexpressibly droll. There is uncommon intellectual force in this burlesque, combined with a delicate, silvery wit, and deep feeling. Brougham acted *Shylock* in the highest spirit of burlesque, — that is to say, in dead earnest, — revealing keen sympathy with the magnificent Hebrew nature; and over this solemnity — as over a gray ruin gleam the bright green leaves of the ivy — glanced the nimble lightning of his humor.

On his last night at that theatre Brougham acted the burlesque *Shylock*, after "His Last Legs," in which he appeared as *Felix O'Callaghan*, — always a favorite part with him, and one that he acted perfectly well. His farewell speech on this occasion was no less touching than witty, and, considering the injustice with which he had been treated by the owner of the theatre, temperate and reticent.

There was a banquet in honor of Brougham at the Astor House, the next night, April 4th, at which Mr. Charles Stetson presided, and Lester Wallack, Barney Williams, Edwin Adams, and many other leading members of the dramatic profession spoke in his praise, and at which was laid the foundation of a benefit for him, that occurred on May 19th, and brought him more than $5,000. The performances occurred at Niblo's Theatre in the afternoon, and at the theatre in Fourteenth Street (now known as Haverly's) in the evening; and, although a violent rain-storm prevailed, both houses were crowded. At the day performance "The School for Scandal" was given, with a remarkable cast:—

Sir Peter Teazle	John Gilbert.
Sir Oliver Surface	John Brougham.
Joseph Surface	Neil Warner.
Charles Surface	Edwin Adams.
Crabtree	A. W. Young.
Sir Benjamin Backbite . .	Owen Marlowe.
Rowley	T. J. Hind.
Moses	Harry Beckett.
Trip	J. C. Williamson.
Snake	Frank Rae.
Careless	J. W. Collier.
Sir Harry Bumper	R. Green.
Lady Teazle	Mrs. D. P. Bowers.
Maria	Miss Pauline Markham.
Lady Sneerwell	Mrs. John Sefton.
Mrs. Candour	Miss Fanny Morant.

THESE lists of plays, in Brougham's handwriting, are copied from the inner side of the cover of one of his old record books, and are without date : —

WORK DONE : — "Romance and Reality"; "The Game of Life"; "The Game of Love"; "Night and Morning"; "Bleak House"; "Dombey and Son"; "Capture of Cuttle"; "The Confidence Man"; "Vanity Fair"; "Cousin German"; "The Red Mask"; "Jane Eyre"; "David Copperfield"; "Love and Murder"; "Our Tom Thumb"; "The World's Fair"; "Love in Livery"; "Pocahontas"; "Distinguished Foreigners"; "The Rifle Corps"; "Ambrose Germaine"; "Franklin"; "Tom and Jerry in America"; "The Rival Magicians"; "Row at the Theatre"; "The Actress of Padua"; "A Decided Novelty"; "The Revolt of the Sextons"; "Don Cæsar de Bassoon"; "The Haunted Man"; "O'Harrigan and Jones"; "The Irish Yankee"; "Temptation"; "Dr. Faustus"; "Counterfeit Presentments"; "Life in the Clouds"; "The Pirates of the Mississippi"; "All's Fair in Love"; "The New Camille"; "The Gunmaker of Moscow"; "Owen, the Gold-Beater"; "A Decided Case."

WORK TO DO : — "Metamora"; "Quentin Matsys"; "Anne of Austria"; "Indian Uncle" (Australia); "Fille Bien Gardée"; "Christine of Sweden"; "Four Funny Screen Stories"; "Mystery of a Hundred Years"; "Columbus."

_____

JANUARY 23d, 1876. At his home, No. 139 East 17th St., N. Y., J. B. read to me his comedy, in five acts, named "Love's Champion."

_____

HERE is one of his letters, in which there is a bit of theatrical history, and which has the charm of his characteristic manner : —

DETROIT, Sunday (but no *sun*), 1869.

MY DEAR WILLIE : — Our letters crossed, a plain *spiritual* proof that our intangibilities were in communication with each other before the tardier humanity of which we are cognizant. I thank you deep down for the poem, which I read with dewy eyes and an impediment in my throat. Very pleasant pain, however. It is a lonely, wet day, and, in a provincial tavern, solitary as Crusoe, without my man Friday, that is to say Ship, you may imagine that my hilarity is not excessive. Opposite to my window stands a dilapidated city hall; next to it a deserted market, with empty stalls and a generally forlorn aspect. Not a soul to be seen; the only evidences that the universe still contains some fragment of animal life are exhibited in a pair of hungry pigeons.

You ask me to tell you something about the Broadway. My personal experience of the place is simply a story of hopes destroyed and confidence abused. When I started to build it, — I forget the year, — 1850, I think, — depending upon profuse promises, I put all I had then saved into the *foundation*, plunging into the affair with my usual recklessness. My means and the few subscriptions I obtained soon became exhausted, and I was compelled to execute a mortgage to Edwin P. Christy, entailing a very exorbitant interest. One very particular friend advanced me a large sum, and without the slightest acknowledgment from me. Indeed, I am certain he *then* had my interest truly at heart; and had not business matters gone wrong with him, he never would have acted as he subsequently did. However, I struggled through the preliminary difficulties, and the opening was a brilliant one, though the public opinion was that the place was entirely too far *up town*. In the first season, Trimble, the architect, was paid his entire bill : by the way, he has often told me it was the only theatre he had ever built for which he was entirely paid. There was every indication that the adventure would be profitable and permanent; but, unluckily for us, the corner building was torn down, which compelled us at our own expense to shore up the theatre, and this had the effect of making it *look* dangerous, — a report very industriously spread by a few disinterested people. The consequence was an abrupt desertion of the place and a period of much tribulation to " yours truly." A little assistance then would have enabled me to tide over the shallows, but I did not know how to solicit it. My successor did, though, and with a subscription of $5,000 from my friends he walked quietly into a place my money and work had partially set afloat. It was during this period of difficulty that my friend before mentioned asked me to give him some kind of security for the return of his loan. Induced by his great confidence in me to place equal reliance upon him I told him to go to my lawyer and have such papers made out as he liked. Well, they managed between them to draw up an instrument either carelessly read to me, or its principle not explained at all, by which I forfeited all right and title to lease and building if the debt were not paid *eleven* days after application, — " only as a matter of form, you know, my dear boy." The application was made, I could n't pay, and, stricken in a double sense, I had to clear out. Mr. Stebbins offered double the amount of the debt, but it was refused, and that 's the whole of the story. If you choose to say anything concerning the early history of the place, these random sentences may assist you to the knowledge of the facts. The rest you know all about.

Business very good here. I stay next week with "The Lottery of Life"; then for Pittsburg, Philadelphia, and "home, sweet home." Shall I ever be permitted to settle down in it? With best remembrances to Mrs. Winter. and my sincerest affection,

Ever your friend,

JOHN BROUGHAM.

BROUGHAM'S burlesque of "Pocahontas, or the Gentle Savage," was first produced, December 24th, 1855, at Wallack's Theatre, and it was the most successful work of its class that had been offered upon the American stage up to that time. The cast of parts was as follows : —

Powhatan	Brougham.
John Smith	Charles Walcot.
Cologog	J. H. Stoddart.
Rolf	Charles Peters.
Pocahontas	Miss Hodson.
Pootepet	Mrs. Stephens.
Weechevendah	Mrs. Sylvester.
Krosaskanbee.	Mrs. L. Thompson.

IN some of the cities of the old world they mark with memorial tablets the houses in which distinguished persons of the past have lived. The future antiquarian, for whom this note is made, may be pleased to know the places at which John Brougham resided while in New York. In 1854, at No. 502 Broome Street; in 1866, at No. 325 West Twenty-third Street; in 1867, at No. 14 West

Twenty-fourth Street, where occurred the death of his second wife; later, for five years, at No. 139 East Seventeenth Street; then, at various times, at No. 50 Irving Place, No. 17 East Fifteenth Street, No. 81 West Twelfth Street, and, finally, at No. 60 East Ninth Street, where he died. During the last years of his life he was very restless, and he changed his quarters no less than five times.

THE following play-bill may be interesting as a relic of Brougham's theatrical days in Boston, in the earlier part of his career : —

BOSTON THEATRE.
FEDERAL STREET.

MANAGER AND PROPRIETOR - - - - C. R. THORNE.

COMPLIMENTARY BENEFIT TO

MR. BROUGHAM.

Thursday Eve. Feb. 3d, 1848,

The Entertainments will commence with Buckstone's popular and interesting melo-drama of

PRESUMPTIVE EVIDENCE

Or..THE SAILOR'S RETURN!

With the following Unparalleled Cast.

Marmaduke Dorgan	. Mr. W. G. JONES	Jailor	. . . .	. Mr. Smith
Pryce Kynchela	. . J. B. BOOTH	Mr. Hammond	.	. H. B. Phillips
Lewey Madigan	. . . BROUGHAM	Judith	. . .	. Mrs. MUZZY
Fred	. . . . . Byrnes	Penny McLoughlin	.	Mrs. BROUGHAM
Brian	. . . . Phillips	Nelly	. . . .	. Mrs. Hathaway
Jack	. . . . Nelson	Shela	. . .	. Mrs. Mueller
Tom	. . . . Munroe	Cauthleen	. . .	. Mrs. Reid
Phedrig	. . . . . Watkins			

To be followed by Mr. Brougham's new Experiment, called the

LIVING PICTURES

Frank Vision, an artist, more in imagination than reality,   .   .   . Mr. Perry
Bob Plastic, his pupil and servant, with face enough for anything, Mr. Brougham
An Old Gentleman, recently seen in public, ... Mr. Brougham
Uncle Gabriel, an individual from whom Frank has some expecta-
tions, which are more than realized, ... Mr. Byrnes
Angelica, an angel of a creature of course, ... Mrs. Hathaway

In the course of the piece, Living Representations will be given of the following
well known pictures.

CHARLES I, after Vandyke.   FRANKLIN, the Red Cap Portrait.
WELLINGTON, after Sir Thomas Lawrence. NAPOLEON, after David's Celebrated Picture. WASHINGTON, after Stuart.

FAVORITE DANCE - - - - - - - - Miss MOWBRAY

After which, Mr. Brougham's new and original, aboriginal Indian
Burlesque, founded upon, and called

METAMORA

— OR THE —

LAST OF THE POLLYWOGS!

ANGLO-SAXONS.

Pappy Vaughan, an influential early settler, early settled,   .   .   . Mr. Spear
Lord Fitzfaddle, a highly to be envied individual, who has the
honor to die by Metamora's knife, ... Phillips
Master Walter, not the hunchback, but over head and ears in love,   . Watkins
Badenough, a most unpleasant individual, ... Byrnes
Worser, much the same, only more so, ...
Occana, old Vaughan's daughter, a chip of the old block,   .   . Mrs. Muzzy

POLLYWOGS.

Metamora, the ultimate Pollywog, an aboriginal hero, and a fa-
vorite child of the FOREST, ... Mr. Brougham
Kantshine, a friend, who gives excellent advice, and is treated as
all are who do it, ... McFarland
Old Tar, Indian Interpreter, from the Junk, half savage — half
sailor, ... H. B. Phillips
Whiskee T. Oddi, skilled in talk, so we are informed,   .   .   . Nix
Anaconda, a recreant red man, rather serpentine,   .   .   . Nelson
Tapiokee, La Belle Sauvage, the squalling squaw of Metamora,
killed with kindness, ... Mrs. Brougham
Papoose, being the last of the last of the Pollywogs,.   .   . Miss H. Mace

Printer's Ink Sketch of portions of the plot — Just sufficient to stimulate curiosity. A PRIMITIVE WOOD! Introducing a pair of unhappy lovers — one of whom discovers an interesting fact, and with considerable tact, redolent of college, communicates the knowledge. Description of a caitiff, another of a native; a doubtful sort of rhyme, but sufficient for the time. In a minute now or more, expect to hear the FOREST ROAR!! A mystery, in natural history, a deep weazle fast asleep — whom the maiden tries to catch, but meeting with her match, in a most uncommon fright, cries out with all her might, METAMORA COMES IN SIGHT. Savage quite and shows fight, with delight, and, without a scratch or bite, seals up the weazle's optics, in everlasting night; served him right. Then comes a conversation, all about the Indian Nation, bringing some recrimination, for the white man's usurpation, of a station in creation, lately in the occupation of the Pollywog's relation. After some exciting talk, Metamora waxes wroth, but to the maiden gives, who dared his deadly purpose baulk, a pinion which will save her from the savage tomahawk. THE WOOD IS CLEARED ; And you perceive, Mrs. Metamora grieve, at the absence of her love, like to any turtle dove, but meets comfort from her wild, interesting child. THE POLLYWOG IS RILED. Two messengers appear, from the council sitting near, and so, whether he likes it or no, Metamora has to go, for which he's rather green, to the FAMOUS COUNCIL SCENE. Which opens with a song, but it is n't very long. The Pollywog comes in, and the way he uses up the crowd to Moses is a sin! He gives it to them some, and anathematizes rum, says "you 've sent for me and I am come, if you 've nothing to say I must go home." At first they 're stricken dumb, and at nothing will they stick, so they're down upon him quick, swore 't was he "Threw that last Brick." They bring in a lying witness, objecting to his fitness, METAMORA GIVES HIM FITS, and frightens the assembly nearly out of their wits, by a wild denunciation of the whole Teutonic nation. Flying from the lodge, in a most unworthy dodge, delighted you will see, THE POLLYWOG IS FREE. In another pleasant scene, you 'll perceive a rather green, but excessively serene, gentleman of slender shape, of the genus we call ape. The article makes love, but don't successful prove. Many other things ensue, until the piece is through, that you and me between, TO BE APPRECIATED, MUST BE SEEN.

To conclude with Buckstone's popular Farce, of the

IRISH LION

TIM MOORE, a travelling tailor . . . . . MR. BROUGHAM

Squabbs . . . . . Mr. Spear	Mr. Yawkins . . . Mr. Nelson
Ginger . . . . . H. B. Phillips	Mr. Mackenzie . . . . . Mills
John Long . : . . . Phillips	Mrs. Fitzgig . . Mrs. BROUGHAM
Mr. Puffy . . . . . Byrnes	Mrs. Crummery . . . . . Reid
Capt. Dixon . . . . . Perry	Miss Echo . . . . . Muzzy
Mr. Wadd . . . . . Munroe	Miss Titter . . . . . Hathaway
Mr. Shin . . . . . Evans	Miss Smiler . . Miss Mowbray

To-morrow (Friday) will be presented a bill of Extraordinary Attraction.

In rehearsal, a New National Drama.

EASTBURN'S PRESS — STATE STREET.

A MORE recent theatrical relic is an Opening Address, which Brougham wrote for the occasion of the reopening

9

of Daly's Theatre, January 21st, 1873, in the old stone church near Astor Place, in Broadway. The theatre in Twenty-fourth Street had been burned three weeks before that date, and Daly's expeditious energy, in getting his new house ready within so short a time, prompted these lines. Miss Clara Morris, on this night, gave her first performance of *Alixe*, and gained one of the brightest of her laurels.

WILLIAM DAVIDGE.

Thanks, generous patrons, for that welcome cheer!
It shows us we have little cause to fear.
As our suspended play we here renew,
Our change of base will bring no change in you.

G. H. GRIFFITHS.

Stooping to conquer is our motto now, —
A kind of paradox, I must allow;
For, though your high esteem was won up town,
Higher we'll rise by coming farther down.

MRS. GILBERT.

Ill fortune is the truest, best of friends;
For all our ill your goodness makes amends
Most ample; and that favor to return
As far as in our power lies we *burn*.

MISS MORTIMER.

Not literally, mind you, gracious knows
'T is quite enough, I think, to burn our clothes.

SARA JEWETT.

I think so, too! — that lovely polk de soie —
The sweetest thing in silk I ever saw!
That Paris bonnet and manteau de cour —

RECOLLECTIONS AND RELICS.

LINDA DIETZ.

My beautiful marquise — trimmed with guipure,
And robe imperial that was so chic —

MARY CARY.

And my incomparable moire-antique,
Fiches d'Antoinette and point-lace berthe,
A thing of joy —

KATE CLAXTON.

The masterpiece of Worth !
I cannot now, so much I feel bereft,
Remember half the articles I left.

B. T. RINGGOLD.

The public will remember one, don't fear !

CLARA MORRIS.

Which one ?

G. H. GRIFFITHS.

"Article 47," my dear.

C. H. ROCKWELL.

They won't forget that easily, I 'll bet !

OWEN FAWCETT.

No ! no ! no ! no ! I 'm not so mad as that !

FANNY MORANT.

Ah well ! 't is useless vain regrets to nurse !
If you reflect, it might have been much worse ;
And the burned sacrifice is not in vain
That such abundant sympathy can gain :
As for the rest, my dears, I rather guess
That sumptuary grievance you 'll *re-dress.*

JAMES LEWIS.

Gone is the little stage we loved so well,
And now I'd find it difficult to tell
" The spot where she originally fell."

G. H. WHITING.

Sulky no longer, I accept my lot, —
Although I found that "Road to Ruin" hot.

LEMOYNE.

The way I bolted from it was a sin :
It was n't business, but " I throws it in."

GEORGE CLARKE.

And now, determined from our minds to cast
All gloomy recollections of the past,
Here is our home : no fitter could be found
Than this, — for it was on this very ground
Our manager and author's work began,
And " Under the Gas-light " took the town and ran.
It was the Broadway then ; the alteration
I shall account for in a brief narration.
Once, when old Judkins, of the Cunard Line,
Felt premature necessity to dine
His craving appetite outran the hour.
At sea those captains have peculiar power :
Hailing the watch, with grim and burly glee, —
"Ho, there ! what lacks it of four bells ?" said he.
"Some twenty minutes by the sun, sir, sure,"
The man replied ; when said the Commodore,
" The sun ? Can't wait for him, sir ! make it four !"
" Ay, ay, sir, four it is ! " So Judkins dined, —
Forcing the mystic hour to suit his mind.

CHARLES FISHER.

Has not *our* captain shown the selfsame skill
To make the hours subservient to his will ?
The scene before us now that skill displays, —
The work of months performed in twenty days !
You must acknowledge reason in this rhyme, —
Whatever else he lost, he lost no time.

LOUIS JAMES.

To call things as he pleases, too, he claims ;
For though this house has gone by various names,
In spite of custom or locality,
" Ho ! make it the Fifth Avenue," said he.
" Ay, ay, sir," said the printer ; " lucky words ! —
Fifth Avenue it is, sir, on the boards."

FANNY DAVENPORT.

The change one problem proves beyond a doubt, —
That Broadway *can* be thoroughly cleaned out
Without rough brigand hands to make it clear,
Or milder suasion of the atmosphere.
Here may we hope to pleasantly renew
Our late acquaintance shrivelled off with you.
Our purpose is to win you, head and heart !
For this we 'll practice every kind of art ;
So that like Man and Wife we may remain,
And never come Divorce betwixt us twain !

———

Mr. James A. Ship was, for twenty-three years, his
faithful attendant, serving him, alike in sickness and
health, with affectionate zeal. To him he left, by will,
a share of his personal property, and to him, on one

occasion, he sent a valuable watch, with the following characteristic letter : —

Nov. 9, 1874.

MY DEAR SHIP : — I have long thought that you required looking after, so I this day place an additional *watch* upon your movements. Sincerely hoping that it may tick off nothing but happy hours for the rest of your life !

From your friend,

JOHN BROUGHAM.

HERE is a bit of Irish humor that would not have been unworthy of the hand that wrote " Sir Lucius O'Trigger." It is an Irish gentleman's letter to his son in college, and was written by Brougham, as a specimen of the " Irish bull " : —

" MY DEAR SON : — I write to send you two pair of my old breeches that you may have a new coat made out of them. Also, some new socks which your mother has just knit by cutting down some of mine. Your mother sends you ten dollars without my knowledge, and for fear you may not spend it wisely, I have kept back half, and only send you five. Your mother and I are well, except that your sister has got the measles, which we think would spread among the other girls if Tom had not had it before, and he is the only one left. I hope you will do honor to my teachings ; if not, you are an ass, and your mother and myself your affectionate parents."

BROUGHAM was always ready to help others, and he acted for many benefits. In the Holland benefit (January, 1871), — an enterprise originated and conducted by me, — I received judicious advice and valuable support from him ; and he it was who suggested the idea of simulta-neous matinees at all the theatres in New York.   The net proceeds of that benefit amounted to $13,608.41, which went to the family of the late George Holland.

WHEN Mr. H. J. Byron's comedy of "Our Boys" was first produced in New York, Brougham wrote a little tag for it, which was thought characteristic and apt, and which is here preserved : —

> MIDDLEWICK (*to* SIR GEOFFREY *confidentially*).
> Our children, sir, are ticklish things to handle ;
> They can't be moulded as you would a candle.
> We were both wrong ; with customers like these
> The bullyragging system aint the cheese.
> When we first twigged as they was going to slope,
> We should have tried the vally of soft soap.

> SIR GEOFFREY.
> Ah, well ! the past is gone, beyond excuse ;
> This lesson, though severe, will be of use.
> Privation only heightens future joys ;
> Let's hope 't will bring success to *both* Our Boys !

THE American Dramatic Fund Association was one of Brougham's pet institutions, and he never tired of work-ing for it.   He felt a deep interest also in the success of the Shakespeare Memorial at Stratford, and he warmly advocated an idea which perhaps will yet be carried out to a successful result in this country, — the union, that is, of all the theatres on this continent in a simultaneous benefit performance for the Memorial.   This project is suggested in the following letter, addressed to him by his

THEATRE ROYAL

DRURY   LANE.

Lessee · · · · · Mr. F. B. CHATTERTON.

SHAKESPEARIAN

AFTERNOON PERFORMANCE,

FRIDAY, APRIL 23rd, 1875,

AT TWO O'CLOCK,

The Anniversary of the Birthday of the Great Poet.

Miss HELEN FAUCIT

(Mrs. THEODORE MARTIN)

Has kindly consented to appear, as ROSALIND, on this occasion.

Messrs. F. B. CHATTERTON and J. H. MAPLESON having
kindly given the use of this Theatre, a Performance
of one of Shakespeare's Comedies will take
place, in aid of the Funds now
being raised to erect a

SHAKESPEARE MEMORIAL THEATRE

AT STRATFORD-ON-AVON.

At Two o'clock, SHAKESPEARE'S COMEDY, in Five Acts, of

AS YOU LIKE IT,

Will be played with the following Powerful Cast : —

Jaques . . . . Mr. CRESWICK.
Orlando . . . . Mr. CHARLES WARNER.
Oliver . . . . Mr. JAMES FERNANDEZ.
Le Beau . . . . Mr. H. R. TEESDALE.
Banished Duke . . . . . Mr. ROGERS.
Duke Frederick . . . . . Mr. HOWARD RUSSELL.
Jaques de Bois . . . . . Mr. WEATHERSBY.
Lords . . . . { Mr. W. McINTYRE.
                      { Mr. F. DEWAR.
Amiens . . . . Mr. GEORGE PERREN.
   (Who will sing, " Blow, blow, thou wintry wind," and " Under
      the Greenwood Tree.")
Touchstone . . . . Mr. E. RIGHTON.
Corin . . . . Mr. LIONEL BROUGH.
Sylvius . . . . Mr. A. C. LILLY.
William . . . . Mr. BUCKSTONE.
Charles . . . . Mr. HARRY PAYNE.
Adam . . . . Mr. CHIPPENDALE.
Rosalind . . . . Miss HELEN FAUCIT.
                      (Mrs. Theodore Martin.)
Celia . . . . Miss HENRIETTA HODSON.
Phebe . . . . Miss ANNIE LAFONTAINE.
Audrey . . . . Mrs. E. FITZWILLIAM.

The Glees, " What shall be have that killed the Deer," and " Forester, sound the
Cheerful Horn," will be sung by the Chorus of the Royal Italian Opera, by
kind permission, all of whom have proffered their valuable aid.

Stage Manager . . . Mr. EDWARD STIRLING.

The above eminent artists will appear by the kind permission of their respective
Managers: Mrs. H. L. Bateman, Miss Litton, Messrs. F. B. Chatterton, J. B. Buck-
stone, W. Holland, S. B. Bancroft, J. Hollingshead, James and Thorne, R. Douglas,
Alexander Henderson, &c.

Costumier, Mr. S. MAY; Perruquier, Mr. CLARKSON : who have kindly
given their assistance.

Prices of Admission :— Private Boxes (Grand Tier), £3 3s.; Pit Tier, £2 2s.; First
Tier, £1 1s.; Second Tier, 10s. 6d. ; Stalls, 10s. 6d.; Dress Circle, 7s. 6d.;
Amphitheatre Stalls, 5s.; Galleries, 1s.

No fee for Booking. Box Office open from Ten till Five daily.

Chairman . . . Mr. T. SWINBOURNE.
Honorary Treasurer, Mr. H. GRAVES.
Secretary . . . Mr. GASTON MURRAY.

Subscriptions to the " Shakespeare Memorial Fund " will be thankfully received
by C. E. FLOWER, Esq., Avon Bank, Stratford-on-Avon, or by H. GRAVES, Esq., the
Honorary Treasurer, 6 Pall Mall, London.

old friend, Henry Graves, of London, which incorporates
an interesting play-bill : —

LONDON, April 24, 1875.

MY DEAR BROUGHAM, — Yesterday was the birthday of
Shakespeare, and we had, at old Drury, "As You Like
It," and took £300.   I escorted the Princess Louise to
the royal box.   We have now got £4,000.   The theatre
will now be begun at a cost of £5,000, but if we have the
picture gallery, and school or university for acting, we shall
want £5,000 more.

I propose that on April 23d, 1876, every theatre in
America and Great Britain shall give a Shakespeare play,
free, and the £5,000 will be got.   Can you get a promise
from the New York managers ?   I feel assured I can get
the London ones.   I only begun on Easter Monday, and
"did the deed."   Let me hope America will hear a noise,
but will not say, they did *not* do the deed.

Miss Lafontaine plays *Phebe* admirably.   Miss Faucit was rather slow, but still good.   If we do it next year,
I will get a great cast; and Simms Reeves has promised,
with Sothern as *Orlando*, and Ada Cavendish as *Rosalind*.   Miss Faucit drew, on a Friday afternoon, £300.
Had it been Saturday or Monday we should have had
£50 more in the gallery.   I hope erelong to see you in
London.

Yours sincerely,

HENRY GRAVES.

BROUGHAM was twice married : first, to Emma Williams,
in 1838; subsequently, to Annette Nelson, in 1847.   By
his first wife he had one child, a boy, who died at the age
of seven months, — an afflicting loss, which the father never

forgot. His second wife was a widow (Mrs. Hodges) ; to her he was tenderly attached, and they are buried side by side in Greenwood. Amy Fawsitt is also buried beside him, — a young actress who died in New York, December 26th, 1876, in extreme destitution, and to whose remains, although she was comparatively a stranger to him, he tenderly gave a place of rest.

From my friend Mr. Ireland's trustworthy and excellent "Records of the New York Stage" are copied the following statements respecting Brougham's wives : —

"Mrs. Brougham — known in London as Miss Emma Williams — was a model of physical beauty, of the Juno style, and, although not brilliant in talent, had sufficient good taste to get through her representations to the satisfaction of the audience, and, if she rarely thrilled one with delight, never proved offensive or disagreeable. She first played at the St. James's Theatre (London), in 1836, and afterward at Covent Garden, where she was the original representative of the *Empress*, in 'Love.' . . . . In 1845 Mrs. Brougham returned to England, and remained away for seven years. On her return, she appeared at the Broadway Theatre, February 16th, 1852, and played a short engagement, and in 1859 again made us a visit, being then Mrs. Robertson. She died in New York, June 30th, 1865."

"Miss Nelson was on the London stage as early as 1830, and made her American *début* at New Orleans, as the *Fairy Queen*, in 1833. She was generally called a beauty, and her hands and feet were so delicate and so exquisitely proportioned as to excite general admiration. Her talents were not, however, of the highest grade, although she danced and sung to the great delight of many youthful admirers, and her *Mountain Sylph* was considered a very attractive performance. She at one time had the direction of the Richmond Hill, which then went by the name of Miss Nelson's Theatre, and she was afterwards at Wallack's National, where she appeared as *Telemachus.* In 1847, Miss Nelson was announced as Mrs. Brougham, she being the second wife of John Brougham, and afterward occupied a prominent position at Burton's Theatre and at Wallack's." She died in New York, May 4th, 1870.

In his latter days Brougham declined into poverty. His last professional tour, made in 1877, proved a bitter disappointment, and therefore his friends organized a benefit for him. Performances with this object occurred at the Academy of Music, New York, on January 17th, 1878, and at Wallack's Theatre in February. The net receipts amounted to $10,278.56. The sum of $875 was used to pay a debt of Brougham's, and the sum of $9,403.56 was invested in an annuity for him in the New York Insurance Company. By that arrangement Brougham was to receive $1,380 a year during the rest of his life, and at his death the annuity would expire. The members of the Brougham Benefit Committee present when this plan was adopted were Mr. John Lester Wallack, Mr. John Gilbert, Dr. Charles Phelps, Mr. Theodore Moss, Mr. William Winter, Mr. Arthur Wallack, and Mr. Lovecraft. The plan received Brougham's sanction at the time, although subsequently he regretted it. But his friends — hoping and believing that he would live many years — deemed this the wisest way to secure him from want. The benefit had been arranged for him, and not for his creditors; and it was thought that, if kept afloat and guarded against trouble, he could by his pen — which was active to the last — retrieve his fortunes and set his affairs straight with the world. This anticipation was not destined to be fulfilled. The veteran's health had been more seriously impaired than even those nearest to him could perceive. His spirit had begun to break. He no doubt saw that the end was near. Yet he continued steadily at work, and his intercourse with society was marked by unaffected grace and gentleness. As late as the 25th of February, 1880, he was present at a dinner-party at the house of his friend, Mr. William Bond, — in whose companionship he found, as every one does, happiness and comfort, — given in honor of Miss Kate Field, who had but lately arrived from England, and whose purposed Monologue Entertainment was then first submitted to a little circle of kindly critics ; and I remember with what gracious courtesy and sympathetic kindness he entered into her plans and discussed the dramatic art and the public taste. Later, on the 24th of April, we dined together — it was for the last time — at the Westmoreland Hotel. He had much to say then of his new play of " Home Rule " ; but to his personal circumstances he made no reference. He was guarding — as afterward I sadly learned — the secret of hardship that many an affectionate friend would have been glad to relieve. Five days later he went out for the last time. During the remaining weeks of his life it seemed to be his purpose to secrete himself, if possible, from the knowledge of his friends. About the end of May it was suddenly made known that he was dying. Many who loved and honored him sought his bedside then, and took his hand for the last time. Wallack, Gilbert, McCullough, Sothern, Florence, Jefferson, Raymond, and Bangs were among. the old professional comrades whom he recognized with a greeting of

kindness and farewell.   He was tended to the last with
zealous and loving devotion by his trusted Ship, and by
his attached friends, Annie Deland and Laura Phillips,
whom he made his heirs.   The final scenes were inexpressibly sad.   He lingered till the 7th of June, in great
misery.   For twenty-four hours immediately preceding
death he was unable to speak, though apparently conscious.   He then sank into a deep sleep, and died without
a murmur.   It was a merciful release.

> " The storm that wrecks the winter sky
> No more disturbs his deep repose
> Than summer evening's latest sigh
> That shuts the rose."

THIS record of the funeral of Brougham is transcribed
from the New York *Tribune*, of June 10, 1880 : —
" The funeral of John Brougham took place at 11 A. M.,
June 9th, at the Church of the Transfiguration, in East
Twenty-ninth Street, New York.   The church was crowded,
while many persons who were unable to obtain admittance
remained standing outside during the service.   Delega-
tions from the Lotos Club, the Dramatic Fund Association, and the Theta Delta Chi Fraternity were present.
Of the members of the Lotos Club in attendance were
Messrs. Thomas W. Knox, G. P. Hiltman, William Apple-
ton, Jr., Col. R. Lathers, Daniel Bixby, B. R. Palmer,
H. N. Alden, George W. Colby, P. R. Molleson, P. Brod-
hurst, H. A. Mariotte, A. Kling, George II. Story, Mon-
tague Marks, James Beard, Chandos Fulton, Dr. A. E.
MacDonald, Charles P. Shaw, J. A. Pickard, Dennis Don-
ahue, Justice F. G. Gedney, W. R. Floyd, Judge H. W.
Allen, Dr. James Furguson, and A. P. Burbank.   Among

the other persons present were Lester Wallack, James A.
Ship, B. T. Ringgold, J. H. McVicker, of Chicago ; Charles
Pope, of St. Louis ; Joseph Murphy, of Philadelphia ;
Charles Leslie Allen, of Boston ; James Dunn, F. S.
Chanfrau, Mr. and Mrs. W. J. Florence, Madam Ponisi,
Franklin Mordaunt, W. P. Harrison, Stella Boniface, Lot-
tie Church, John A. Stevens, George F. Browne, Alfred
Joel, Emily Delmar, Col. T. A. Brown, Charles Wheat-
leigh, Benjamin Baker, George Edgar, Hart Jackson, Herr
Kline, Thomas Chapman, I. Daveau, E. E. Kidder, Dr.
Gillette (who had attended Brougham in his last illness),
Thomas Goodwin, Henry Pearson, Thomas E. Morris, J.
C. McCloskey, A. M. Palmer, E. H. Gouge, Edward Lamb,
C. T. Nichols, Henry Watkins, Clifton W. Tayleure, Frank-
lin Aiken, ex-Judge G. S. Bedford, J. B. Phillips, Louisa
Eldridge, Mrs. Chanfrau, Mrs. Boucicault, John L. Vin-
cent, Steele Mackaye, William Davidge, Sr., Maze Ed-
wards, Annie Ward Tiffany, W. S. Quigley, and Arthur
Gilman.

"The services were conducted by the Rev. Dr. G. H.
Houghton, assisted by the Rev. Alexander McMillan, both
of whom met the remains at the gate of the church-
yard. There were eight pall-bearers, — John R. Brady,
S. L. M. Barlow, Edwin Booth, William Winter, F. C.
Bangs, Charles Phelps, Noah Brooks, and John W. Car-
roll. The services were simple. At the head of the
coffin was a shield of flowers, in the centre of which was
a cluster of violets, arranged in the form of a lotos-flower.
This was sent by the Lotos Club. A few white flowers,
given by William Winter, were in the hand of the dead
actor, and were buried with him. Upon the coffin was
the inscription : 'John Brougham, died June 7, 1880,
aged 70 years and 1 month.' The coffin was not opened,

either at the church or cemetery. The remains were only
seen by the few friends who, with the bearers, met at
Brougham's late home, No. 60 East Ninth Street, before
the funeral. The burial took place in Greenwood Cemetery."

"In what new region, to the just assigned,
What new employments please the unbodied mind ?
A winged virtue, through the ethereal sky,
From world to world, unwearied does he fly ? . . . .
Or dost thou warn poor mortals left behind ? —
A task well suited to thy gentle mind.
O, if sometimes thy spotless form descend,
To me, thy aid, thou guardian genius, lend!
When rage misguides me, or when fear alarms,
When pain distresses, or when pleasure charms,
In silent whisperings purer thoughts impart,
And turn from ill a frail and feeble heart ;
Lead through the paths thy virtue trod before,
Till bliss shall join, nor death can part us more."

III.

BROUGHAM IN HIS CLUB LIFE.

By NOAH BROOKS.

✠

10

BROUGHAM IN HIS CLUB LIFE.

Lotos Club, 147 Fifth Avenue, New York,
Sept. 9, 1880.

MY DEAR WINTER : — Your request for a copy of the resolutions adopted by the directory of this club on the death of Mr. Brougham, and also for a reminiscence by me of our departed friend, brings to my mind a host of pleasant, tender, and sad recollections of the dear old man, whose title among the older members was " Uncle John." As you know, he was one of the founders of our club. Here he was more at home, during the latter years of his life, than anywhere else, I think. His increasing infirmities made it difficult for him to come to the club during the months immediately preceding his death ; but when he did come, he was greeted with a certain affectionate reverence and respect which were touching to witness, and which I am sure were keenly appreciated by him.

" Uncle John " was early chosen Vice-President of the Lotos, and he subsequently served two terms as President. As presiding officer at a business meeting, I am constrained to say he did not shine. It was utterly impossible for him to expedite the business of the hour ; and he interlarded his rulings and statements of pending questions with jokes and humorous remarks, which were vastly entertaining but highly irregular. Indeed, the spectacle of the good old man sitting at the head of the council-board, and flinging his quips and cranks and smiles about with absolute *abandon*, was an extremely ludicrous one. Often, when he was in high good humor, he would tolerate the most diffuse debate, throwing in his own amusing remarks, from time to time, until some restive member would insist upon the board being recalled to its regular business.

But at the head of a dinner-table (and Uncle John presided at many such) he was in his element. He was quick to turn a point in a humorous direction, and his unfailing wit, geniality, and vivacity insured a jolly occasion whenever he took command of the feast, and the fun began. Much of the time, however, during his presidency of the club, his professional engagements kept him from convivial reunions. As I was then Vice-President, it became my duty to attempt to fill his chair; and he never failed, so far as I can now remember, to remind me that he should not be able to attend, and that I must take his place. I think he rather enjoyed the position which he filled in the club, and he gave it up with great reluctance when he found that his growing physical weakness forbade his frequent attendance at the meetings and festivals of the members. "What's the use?" he once said to me: "when I'm not playing I'm sick, and when I'm not sick I'm playing; and between the two, it's little use I am to the club, anyhow." This was almost literally true, and his retirement from the chair seemed necessary. But the members could not let him go without some new tribute of affection and respect; and, at the expiration of his last term of office, he was unanimously elected a life-member of the Lotos. Although he accepted this somewhat unusual honor with his habitual gayety, he was deeply touched by it, and he privately assured us of his sense of the great kindness shown to him, and of his own humble deserts.

He took great pride in the increasing prosperity of the club, and he never spared himself any exertion which he thought, or others thought, might enhance the comfort and enjoyment of the members.   He never failed, when called upon, to respond with a song, a speech, or a story, and sometimes he generously gave all three, with a spirit and unction that were peculiarly his own.   Among the festal occasions which called out some of his happiest efforts, I recall the dinner to Edmund Yates, when Uncle. John (then Vice-President) was at his best.   He proposed the health of Mr. Yates in a jolly, rollicking speech, into which he introduced the titles of the novelist's best-known works very happily and wittily.   Once, however, Uncle John was fairly "flabbergasted" — to quote his own phrase — by one of his happy-go-lucky blunders.   Introducing William Black, the novelist, in an after-dinner speech at the club, he referred to him as "the author of *Lorna Doone*."   Somebody corrected him on the spot in an undertone, and Uncle John recovered himself as best he could, and went on with his speech ; but he afterwards said that he would much rather have made the mistake in referring to some better-known writer, "because," said he, "that would show that I was a blockhead ; whereas, in this case, William Black is not so well known in this country that a better man than myself might not confuse him with Blackmore.   At any rate, he is more Black than Blackmore."

When Uncle John made his arrangements to go to England in 1874, it seemed to many of us that we should never see him again in this country, where he had lived so long, and had so endeared himself to all who knew him.   His health had become very infirm, and it did not seem possible that he could live long enough to accomplish his plans for a visit to "the old country," and return to us. There is no event in the history of the Lotos Club which is cherished in the memories of its members with so much tenderness as the farewell dinner given to our dear old friend when he was on the eve of sailing. For once, Uncle John failed to bubble with mirth and jollity. You will remember how he finally did break down when your poem, the perfect flower of the occasion, fell from your lips. In place of conviviality, we had a flood of tears; and where we had looked for a jovial cheer at parting, we were met with a strain of plaintive melody. Nevertheless, no Lotos-eater, I am sure, would willingly give up his share of the recollection of that remarkable night. It was like a delightful poem in all its changeful passages. But under everything that was said and done was the perpetually recurring thought, "The old man is going away from us, never to come back again." Brougham afterwards, when his departure was indefinitely postponed, made many a joke at his own expense, protesting that he had roused all this sorrow to no purpose; but unto the day of his death, that farewell dinner, with all its train of delightful sentiment, was counted among the sweetest of his memories. There was no time when the respect and affection of the members of the Lotos Club for Mr. Brougham flagged or languished; but, if I were to refer to any point in his association with us as most significant of the tenderness of the relation which he held to us, my mind would involuntarily go back to that farewell dinner in 1874.

In a club, you know, men are disposed to exercise the privilege of members of a family, and to criticise each other, especially in club affairs, with great freedom. But I do not remember that Uncle John ever spoke an ill word of a member. Certainly, he never said an ill word of a man behind his back. If he had any criticism to make, he addressed himself, with a certain serious humor, to the object of his censure. Once, when provoked by a talkative wrangler at the whist-table, he burst out with "All we want out of you is play, and mighty little of that!" On another occasion, when a querulous, captious member was making a half-hearted apology for his failings, saying that he "could not help it," Uncle John fairly exploded with "Well, you can help making yourself so infernally disagreeable." And again, of a somewhat tedious acquaintance, he meditatively remarked, "——— is an acquired taste."

There was no sourness in his disposition, no gall in his ink. Harsh criticism of an absent friend or acquaintance uttered in his presence would invariably draw from him a gentle reminder of the good qualities of the absent. Gentleness, indeed, became more and more a prominent trait in his character as his life wore on to its close. His was not an old age embittered by fruitless regrets and repinings. He bore his infirmities of body with uncomplaining patience. The old servants of the club were swift to wait upon him, his manner was so gentle and full of kindly consideration. Even in the midst of pain, and when racked by ills which had become chronic, his urbanity was unbroken. It was an urbanity which came from a kind heart, not that which is taught by the rules of politeness.

Neither could any amount of suffering extinguish Uncle John's humor. When we visited him in the sick-room, to which he was so often confined, he received us with a joke, a hearty greeting, and a breezy joviality which belied and perhaps cheated his pain. When he was brought home, apparently to die, from his last Western trip, several gentlemen of his own profession received him, after much running back and forth, at the railway station, and accompanied him to his rooms, where, more dead than alive, he was propped up in an easy chair, while one of the party, who had just left a convivial dinner-table, made to him a speech of welcome. " Mr. Brougham," said the orator, holding by the back of a chair, "we are prepared to minister to your slightest want. We will stay with you ; we will sit up with you, if you need watchers ; and if you die, we will act as pall-bearers at your funeral." This was too much for the poor old man, who lifted his head painfully, and murmured, " Hear ! hear !" Uncle John outlived the orator, and he used to tell of this melancholy reception with great glee.

John Brougham's death, I need hardly say to you, came to us who knew him in the club like a personal bereavement. It was the sundering of a tie whose tenderness we had not fully known until it was snapped. It was not only that a gentle life was ended, that we mourned his demise ; it was not that we had lost an old and valued member of our organization, that we lamented his final departure ; it was because each of us must hereafter miss a welcome presence, a winning smile, a sympathizing friend, a delightful companion. If his last days had been happier, — if the life which had been spent in making existence for others more endurable had been less dimmed by care and sorrow, — Uncle John's friends would have beheld the gradual sinking of his sun with less poignant regrets. But troubles, which he concealed as far as he could, clouded his later days ; and, mingled with the grief which his death caused to us who knew and loved him so well, comes ever the painful reflection that this bright career should not have so ended, — that something might have been done to illuminate his closing hours. But, proud and sensitive to

the last degree, he concealed his poverty from his associates, and it was not until he was actually on his death-bed
that we knew how great were his needs.   I am glad to say
that the members of the Lotos Club were swift to minister
to the last necessities of their well-beloved associate.   And
when all was over, and affection could do no more for him,
the club was requested by its government to attend his
funeral.   It was also ordered that suitable floral emblems
should be sent to be laid on his coffin, and that his bust in
the club-house should be draped in mourning.   The following resolutions were adopted, June 7, 1880, and were
written on the records of the club : —

"*Resolved*, That the Lotos Club joins with a bereaved
community in lamenting the death of its ex-president and
life-member, Mr. John Brougham.   The club shares its
grief with the host of the late Mr. Brougham's friends and
admirers in every sphere of society.   He was a many-sided
·man.   He touched life at numerous points, and whatever
he touched he adorned.   As playwright, actor, poet, jour-
nalist, scholar, he was highly distinguished.   He graced
every social circle of which he was a part.   His brilliant
imagination, his bustling humor, were constant allies of
purity and goodness.   He wrote no line which, dying, he
would wish to blot.   He was never so happy as when pro-
moting the happiness of others.   Large-hearted and open-
handed, his were the deserts which won universal affection
and respect.   Such in his broad relations to his fellow-
men was the rare man whose loss we deplore.

"*Resolved*, That no tribute of words which this club can
render will fully discharge its obligation to Mr. Brougham's
memory.   As an officer of the club in the earlier years of
its existence, he was a nucleus around which clustered the
elements of geniality and good-fellowship."

" More than any other place, the Lotos Club was his home.
His cheerful presence, his thoughtful kindness, his ever-
ready wit, that never wounded, contributed greatly to stamp
the club, in its formative era, with a character which is one
of its best claims to distinction.   As a club man — the
relation in which he was nearest to us — he was a beloved
personality, whose name will always be tenderly enshrined
in our recollection, and preserved on the roll of our honored dead."

It seems to me that I have very inadequately complied
with your request.   What I have written in this familiar
and desultory manner is at your service, to make of it whatever disposition you may choose.   I knew Uncle John in-
timately, and, if I had the time, it would give me great
pleasure to set down, with what skill I may have, a thoughtful and appreciative estimate of his personal character.   He
was, in many respects, a rare man.   I shall never see his
like again.   But other and abler hands must do him that.
justice which too partial friendship cannot render to the
dead.   We who lament his death must chiefly grieve that
in this work-a-day and selfish world we lost a great brightness when we lost John Brougham.

Faithfully yours,

Noah Brooks.

To William Winter, Esq.

IV.

BROUGHAM'S SELECTED WRITINGS.

✠

TERRY MAGRA

TERRY MAGRA'S LEPRECHAUN.

AMONGST a people so simple-hearted and enthusiastic as the Irish, it is not at all surprising that a firm and implicit belief in supernal agency should be almost universal. To vivid imaginations, ever on the stretch for the romantic, yearning always for something beyond the dull realities of commonplace existence, there is something extremely fascinating in the brain revellings of Fairy Land.

Now the Irish fairies are very numerous, and all as well classified, and their varied occupations defined and described by supernaturalists, as though they really were amongst the things that be. The "learned pundits" in such matters declare that the economy of human nature is entirely carried on through their agency. Philosophers have demonstrated the atomic vitality of the universe, and the believer in fairies simply allots them their respective places and duties in the general distribution. They tell you that every breath of air, every drop of water, every leaf and flower, teems with actual life. Myriads of tiny atomies, they say, are employed carrying on the business of existence, animal, vegetable, and atmospheric. Here are crowds of industrious little chemists, extracting dew from moonbeams, which they deliver over to relays of fairy laborers, by them to be applied to the languishing grass. The noxious exhalations of the earth are, by a similar process, gathered from decaying vegetation, and dispersed or condensed into refreshing rain. The warm sunbeams are by them brought down and scattered through the fields; it is the beautiful ministry of one class to breathe upon, and gently force open, the budding blossoms, while another sedulously warms and nurtures the ripening corn, and tends the luscious fruits. Mischievous fellows there also are, whose delight it is to try and frustrate the exertions of the workers. They travel from place to place, loaded with malign influences; blight and mildew, and all the destructive agents that blast the hopes of the agriculturist, are under their control; and, with an industry nearly equal to their opponents, they employ their time in training caterpillars and other devouring insects to assist them in the work of desolation.

Many are the battles, we are informed, that occur between the two opposing classes, and it depends upon which side has the best of the contest what the result may be to the defeated object; whether they contend for the life of some delicate flower, or whether the poor farmer's toils were to be rewarded or rendered hopeless by the safety or the destruction of his entire crops.

But to leave this fanciful, and, it must be admitted, poetical theory, our business now is with an individual of a highly responsible class in the world of Fairydom, — *the Leprechaun.* A most important personage he is; being the custodian of all hidden treasure, it is he who fabricates the gold within the rock-encircled laboratory. The precious gems, the diamond, sapphire, ruby, amethyst, emerald, and all the world-coveted jewels, are in the safe guardianship of the Leprechaun; and fatal it is to him when aught is discovered and torn from his grasp, — for his fairy existence, his immortal essence, is lost with it; he can no longer sport through the air, invisible to mortal ken, but is compelled to take a tangible form, and to work at a degrading. occupation, — that of making and mending the shoes of his former fairy companions.

In the little village of Templeneiry, situated at the base of one of the Galtee mountains, whose summit looks down upon the diminutive hamlet from the altitude of two thousand feet, there dwelt a very celebrated and greatly sought-after individual, one Terry Magra, the piper; there was n't a *pathern*, fair, wake, wedding, or merriment of any description, for miles round, in which he and his dhrones were not called into requisition.

Now, with grief it must be recorded, Terry was too much addicted to the almost national failing, that of intoxication. Whiskey was to him the universal panacea ; did his sweetheart, and he had plenty of them, frown upon his tender suit, whiskey banished the mortification ; was his rent in arrear, and no sign of anything turning up, whiskey wiped off the account instanter ; did all the ill-omened birds that flock around the head of poverty assail him, he fired a stiff tumbler of whiskey-punch at them, and they dispersed. On the whole, it was a jolly vagabond, reckless, and variegated life, that of Terry Magra.

It was one moonlight night that Terry, after having attended a grand festival in the neighborhood, brought up, as was his usual custom, at a Sheebieen house, where a few seasoned old casks like himself invariably "topped off" with a round of throat-raspers. Here he was the Sir Oracle. The lord of the soil himself (did they ever see him, which was not at all probable, for upon the means wrung by his agents from the poor wretches by Providence delegated to his care — those same agents, by the way, managing to squeeze out a comfortable percentage for themselves — he lives in London) could not be served with readier obedience, or listened to with more profound attention.

The roaring song, and joke, and fun, abounded upon this occasion, and Terry improvised so wild and inspiriting a strain upon his famous pipes that it was generally conceded, with enthusiasm tinctured with awe, that no mortal hand could have produced such astounding music.

At length the sleepy proprietor of the place put a sudden end to the jollification by stopping the supplies, the only way in which the Widow Brady — for I'm sorry to say it was a woman, and a decent-looking one too, who presided over this Pandora's box, where Hope forever lies imprisoned — could break up the party.

Terry, after vainly endeavoring to mollify the widow, gathered up his magic pipes, and sallied forth. Adieus were exchanged; friendly hugs and protestations of eternal friendship passed between the stammering, roaring crowd, to be ratified hereafter, it might be, by a crack on the skull from a tough *alpieen.* At last they separated, each to find, as he could, his way home by the devious light of a clouded moon.

Now Terry lived a smart way up the mountain, and so, with, as he said, "the sense fairly bilin' in him everywhere but his murdherin' legs," that persisted in carrying him in the opposite direction to that which his intention pointed, the contest between his will and his locomotive powers making his course somewhat irregular, our bold piper proceeded on his way, humming snatches of songs, and every now and then, by way of diversion, waking the echoes by a fierce blast from his "chanter."

Whether Terry resorted to these means for the purpose of keeping his courage from slumbering within his breast, I know not; but, inasmuch as the ground he was traversing had a general fairy repute, I think it more than likely that, notwithstanding the whiskey valor with which he had

armed himself, it was not without considerable trepidation
he endeavored to make his way through the enchanted
precincts.

There was one isolated mound, which tradition had positively marked as a favorite resort of the "good people,"
and, as Terry neared it, apprehension smote against his
heart lustily. For the first time, he faltered. The moon,
which had hitherto seemed to light him famously, shot
suddenly behind a dense, black cloud, and Terry thought
that blindness had fallen upon him, so black did everything
appear. At the same moment, a gust of wind shook the
crisp leaves of the aspen-trees, with a noise like the rat-
tling of dry bones, that sunk into his very soul. He was
frightened, — he could n't go a step further. Down on
his knees he fell, in the middle of the road, and, as a last
resource, tried to collect himself sufficiently to mutter
through the form of exorcisement used by the peasantry
in similar emergencies. To his horror he discovered that
he could n't remember a syllable of the matter. He resorted to his prayers, but his traitor memory deserted him
there also.

Now his perturbation and dismay increased, for he knew
by those signs that he was "fairy-struck." There was
nothing left him but to run for it ; but, to his yet greater
terror, on endeavoring to rise from his knees, he found
himself rooted to the ground like a tree ; not a muscle
could he move. Then — as he described it — "The fairy
bells rung like mad inside of me skull. The very brains
of me was twisted about, as a washerwoman twists a wet
rag ; somethin' hit me a bat on the head, an' down I
dropped, as dead as a herrin'."

When Terry came to himself again, the darkness had
vanished, and the whole scene was glowing with the mel-

11

low softness of an eastern morning. The atmosphere was imbued with a delicious warmth, while a subdued crimson haze hung between earth and sky. The common road-stones looked like lumps of heated amber. The very dew-drops on the grass glittered like rubies, while the noisy little mountain-fall, where it broke white against the rocks, flashed and sparkled in the rosy light, like jets of liquid gold, filling the air with living gems.

"Be jabers, an' this is Fairy-land, sure enough," said Terry; "an' if the little blaggards has got anything agin' me, it's in a murdherin' bad box I am, the divil a doubt of it. I've nothin' for it, anyway, but to take it aisy." So he sat upon a large stone on the wayside, and gazed with intense admiration on the lovely scene before him, wondering what kind of demonstration the inhabitants of this enchanted spot would make when they discerned his audacious intrusion.

Several minutes had elapsed, and Terry heard nothing but a small, musical hum, barely discernible by the sense, which every warm current of air caused to rise and fall upon his charmed ear, in undulations of dreamy melody. Suddenly, however, his attention was directed towards a fallen leaf, which some vagrant breeze appeared to toss to and fro in merry play. For a long time he watched its eccentric movements, until at last a gust of wind lifted it up, and, whirling it round and round in circling eddies, dropped it on the piece of rock where he was sitting.

Now Terry perceived a multitude of tiny creatures, ant-like, busied around the still fluttering leaf, and, on stooping to examine them closely, his heart leaped like a living thing within his bosom, his breath came short and gasping, and his tongue clove to his palate.

"There they are, an' no mistake," thought he ; "an' my time is come.   May the blessed saints stand betune me an' harm ! "

The crowds of atomies which he had supposed to be ants were beings of the most exquisite human form ; anon, the air grew thick with them.   Some, winged like butter-flies, disported around his head, and alighted upon his garments, pluming their bejewelled pinions and then dart ing off again.

"It's mighty quare that they don't give me a hint that I'm out of me element," thought Terry, as, emboldened by their passiveness, he gently took the leaf up in his hand, on which were dozens of them yet clustered ; he held the fairy-laden leaf up to his eyes ; still they kept gambolling about it ; they overran his fingers, and clam-bered up his sleeve, but no intimation did they give that Terry was of other material than one of the rocks by which they were surrounded ; they invaded his face, examined his mouth, and peered into his eyes, yet there was no indication that his presence was acknowledged.

Resolving to test the matter at once, with an effort of courage, he rose up gradually, and looked around him ; all was quiet.

"If anything will make them spake, the pipes will," said he, bravely, and so, filling his chanter, he gave one preliminary blast, and finding that it met with no response, save from the distant echoes, that sent it sweeping back in multiplied reverberations, he commenced to play one of his most lauded planxtys : never had he satisfied him-self better, but never had he exerted himself before a more unappreciative assembly ; the universal fun and frolic went on as before.

His artistic self-love was sadly wounded.   "The divil

such a lot of stupid fairies did I ever hear tell of," said he, throwing down his pipes in disgust. "An' bad luck attend the grunt more yez'll get out o' me; such ilegant music as I've been threatin' yez wid, an' the never an ear cocked among the lot of yez."

"Athin, Misther Terry Magra," said the smallest possible kind of a voice, but which thrilled through the piper as though it were thunder-loud. "Shure, an' you're not goin' to concate that it's music you've been tearin' out of them tree-stumps of yours; be the powers of war, it's a tom-cat I thought you wor squeezin' undher yer arms."

"Thank you, kindly, yer honor, for the compliment, whoever you are," replied Terry, when, on turning round to the quarter whence the voice proceeded, he saw, sitting on the branch of a tree beside him, a diminutive piper, in all respects a perfect resemblance to himself; dressed in similar garments, even to the dilapidated *caubieen*, with an atom of a *dhudieen* stuck in it; but what elicited his admiration most of all was the weeny set of pipes the swaggering little ruffian carried on his arm.

"Your soul to glory," cried Terry, his excitement completely mastering his apprehension. "An' if you can blow any music out of them, I'll give in soon an' suddent."

"Howld yer prate, you ugly man, an' bad Christian," cried the little fellow; "shure, an' it's plinty of help I'll have." With that, he put the bellows under his arm, and blew a blast that sounded like the whistle of a tom-tit in distress; a signal which was quickly answered by similar sounds, issuing from all directions; and very soon Terry saw groups of little pipers climbing up the tree until the branch was fairly alive with them, each one an exact counterpart of the first.

"May I never sin if the sowls of all the Terry Magras,
past, present, an' to come, ain't to the fore, it's my belief,
this minnit," said the piper, in an ecstasy of amazement.

"We must graize our elbows before we begin, boys,"
said Terry's friend, producing a fairy bottle.

"Here's your health, Misther Terry Magra," says the
little vagabond, with a ghost of a laugh ; and up went the
bottle to his head.

"Here's your health, Misther Terry Magra," they all
repeated, as the real mountain dew went merrily round.

"Faix, an' it's glad enough I'd be to return·thanks for
the favor," said Terry, "if it's a thing that I had a toothful
of sperrits to join yez in ;. more bo token, I'm as drouthy as
a sand-bag this blessed hour."

"Never be it said that a dhry Christian should keep
cotton in his mouth while we can give him a dhrop to
wash it out," said the little piper, throwing his bottle at
Terry.

"Bedad, it's a *dhrop*, sure enough, that I'll be suckin'
out of this," said Terry, as he regarded the tiny atom that
rested in the palm of his hand. "Bad 'cess to me, if a
scooped-out duck-shot would n't howld more nourishment.
I'm obleeged to you for your good intentions, anyway,
but I b'leeve I won't be robbin' you this time."

"Don't be refusin' your liquor, you fool," said the piping
little chap, with a wicked look out of his mites of eyes.
"I'll be bound that such liquor never tickled your throat
before."

"Well, rather than appear onfriendly, I'll just go
through the motions ; so here's jolly good luck to yez
all," said Terry, raising the pellet-like material to his lips,
when, to his intense satisfaction and wonder, his mouth
instantly filled up, and ran over, with a perfect flood of

such whiskey as he owned never yet had blessed his palate ;
again and again he repeated the experiment, and with the
like delicious result.

"Hollo there ! give me back my bottle, you thief of the
world; would you ruin us, intirely?" cried the little
piper. "If the blaggard would n't drink the say dhry,
I 'm not here."

"By the sowl of me mother," said Terry, with a loud
smack of enjoyment, "if the say was made of such stuff
as that, may I never if I would n't change places wid a
mermaid's husband, and flourish a fish's tale all the days
of me life."

"But this has nothin' to do concarnin' the music," says
the fairy, "so, here goes to show how much you know
about humorin' the pipes." So saying, the whole army
of pipers set up a chant, so small, and yet so exquisitely
sweet and harmonious, that Terry scarcely dared to breathe,
for fear of losing the slightest echo of such bewitching
strains.

"What do you say to that ?" inquired the little fellow,
when they had finished.

"Say to it," cried Terry, flinging his hat upon the ground
in an ecstasy of delight; "what the mischief can I say ?
Bedad, there never was a mortial had the concate so complately licked out o' him as it 's been deludhed out o' me at
this present writin', an' to make my words good, av there
was a bit of fire near, if I would n't make cindhers of that
murdherin' ould catherwauler of mine, I 'm a grasshopper."

"It does you credit to own up to it so readily, Terry
Magra," said the head fairy, pleased enough at the compliment. "An', by the way of rewardin' you for that same,
we 'll give you a blast of another sort." With that they
turned to and executed a jig-tune, so swiftly fingered, so

lively and irresistibly *sole*-inspiring, that, with a wild
scream of delight, Terry whipped off his great coat, and,
jumping on the level rock, went through the varied complications of the most intricate description of Irish dance.

"Murdher alive, av I only had a partner now," he cried.
"Such ilegant music, an' only one to be enjoyin' it!"
Faster and faster played the fairy pipers, and yet more
madly Terry beat time upon the stone, making the mountains resound to his vociferous shouts, until, exhausted at
last, he jumped off, and sunk panting on the ground.

"Oh! *tear an' aigers!*" he cried, "an' av yez have a
grain of compassion in thim insignificant tiniments of
yours, fairies darlin', won't yez lend us the loan of a pull
out of that same bit of a bottle, for it's the seven senses
that you've fairly batthered out o' me wid that rattlin' leg-
teaser of a chune.".

"Wid a heart an' a half, my hayro!" said the little
piper, flinging Terry the fairy-bottle; "it's you that has
the parliaminthary unction for the creather, if ever a sowl
had. Don't be afeard of it, it won't hurt a feather of you,
no more nor wather on a duck's back."

Thus encouraged, Terry lifted his elbow considerably,
before he thought it prudent to desist, the fairy liquor appearing more delicious with each gulp, when, all at once —
for Terry had a tolerable share of acuteness for a piper —
the thought struck him that the little schemers might have
a motive in thus plying him with such potential stuff.

"If you're at all inclined for a nap, Terry, my boy,"
said the fairy, blandly, "there's a lovely bank of moss for-
nent you, that'll beat the best feather-bed at the Globe Inn,
in the town of Clonmel. Stretch yourself on it, *aroon*, an'
we'll keep watch over you as tindherly as av your own
mother was hangin' over yer cradle."

"Ho! ho! is it there yez are, you sootherin' vagabonds," said Terry to himself. "It's off o' my guard you want to ketch me, eh?" He was determined, however, to diplomatize, so he replied, with equal politeness, "It's thankful that I am to yer honors for the invite, but I would n't be makin' such a hole in my manners as to let a wink come on me in such iligant company."

"O, well, just as you like, Terry Magra," observed the fairy, with just enough of lemon in his tone to convince Terry that his surmise was correct. "At all events, if you 're not sleepy now, you soon will be," the little fellow continued, "so, when you are, you will lie down without fear. In the mean time, we must go and inform our king how famously we 've amused you, and what a fine fellow you are." So saying, with a sharp little squeal of a laugh, that Terry thought carried with it a sufficiency of sarcasm, the little piper and his companions rapidly descended from their perch, and vanished from his sight.

No sooner had they departed when Terry's ears were saluted by a singularly delightful buzzing noise, that, in spite of his endeavor to resist it, caused a growing drowsiness to steal over him. The declining daylight deepened into a still more roseate hue. Once or twice his eyelids drooped, but he recovered himself with a vigorous effort.

"By the ghost of Moll Kelly," he cried, "I 'm a lost mutton, as sure as eggs is chickens, if the sleep masthers me; the pipes is my only chance." So saying, he shook off the slumberous sensation, and, seizing the instrument, blazed out into a stormy attack upon "Garryowen," and, sure enough, something like a distant groan, as of disappointment, reached him at the very first snore of the chanter.

"Ha! ha!" he exclaimed, "it is n't an omadhaun all

out yez has to dale wid this time, you little rascals, as cunnin'
as ye think yerselves. Bedad, it won't do me any harm to
make use of my eyes hereabouts ; who knows but I may
light atop of a fairy threasure, and drive the imptiness out
of my pocket for ever and ever."

With this determination, the bold piper proceeded to
investigate the character of the ground in his immediate
neighborhood. For a short time he saw nothing remarkable
except the circumstance of the whole surroundings being
alive with fairies, to whose presence he was becoming more
and more habituated ; occasionally he would pause in his
search to view with admiration the energetic way in which
a group of workers attended to their specific duties. Ob-
serving at one time a more than usual commotion, he was
led to give the affair particular scrutiny, when he discovered that it was the scene of a most animated contest between two distinct bodies of supernaturals.

An infant lily-of-the-valley was just raising its head
above the yielding earth, softened and broken to assist its
upward progress by scores of busy atomies. Numbers
showered its tender leaf with refreshing dew, procured, as
Terry observed, by plunging into the hollow cup of some
sturdy neighboring flower, then flying back to their charge,
and shaking the nutritious drops from their wings ; others,
with mechanical ingenuity, held glasses by which they
could concentrate the passing sunbeams upon the spot,
when necessary ; while others drove there with their united
pinions the stray breezes, whose invigorating breath was
needed.

While Terry was rapt in the delightful contemplation
of this curious scene, all at once he saw that there was
something of uncommon interest going on amongst the
crowd. He observed, in the first instance, that, although

the labor was not for a moment suspended, yet a solid phalanx of armed fairies had formed about the immediate workers. The reason was soon obvious ; for, careering round and round, or darting to and fro in zigzag courses almost as swiftly as the lightning itself, was an enormous dragonfly, carrying on its glistening back a diminutive form of a brilliant green color, that flashed in the glancing light like living emerald. Wherever there was a tender young plant there its fierce attack was directed, and in all cases repelled by the brave little guardians.

This terrible monster — as it appeared even in Terry's eyes, when compared with the tiny creatures that surrounded him — seemed to have singled out the fragile lily-of-the-valley for its especial ferocity, for again and again it darted furiously against the unyielding defenders, only, however, to be repulsed at each charge, writhing and twisting its snaky body, punctured by the thorn-bayonets of the fairy-guard.

The indomitable courage and resolution of the defence at length prevailed, and after a last ineffectual effort to break through the chevaux-de-frise that protected the beleaguered flower, the dreadful enemy wheeled angrily two or three times around the spot, and at length darted upward rapidly, and disappeared, to the manifest delight of the fairies. Soon, however, a yet more formidable danger threatened, for in the distance there approached a gigantic snail, dragging its noxious slime over everything in its destructive path. Terry now observed evidences of the most intense solicitude and perturbation. The guard around the flower was trebled ; scouts seemed to be called in from all quarters, hastening to a common rendezvous. Meantime, the snail moved on in a direct line with the object of their care and anxiety.

"Now, my fine fellows," said Terry, completely absorbed in the interesting scene, "how the mischief are yez goin' to manage that customer?"

Nearer and nearer crawled the snail, and at every onward movement the little crowd grew more agitated, scampering here and there, and overrunning each other in a perfect agony of apprehension and excitement, like a disturbed colony of ants. Multitudes of them cleared the small stumps of decayed grass, and rolled off the pebbles from a side path, in the hope of diverting Mr. Snail's course; but their engineering skill was fruitless, — still on he came, crushing every delicate germ in his progress. He was now only about six inches away from the lily, and the trepidation of the fairies became so excessive that it smote upon Terry's heart. He forgot for a moment or two that he himself was the arbiter of their fate.

"Mother o' Moses," said he; "it's afeared I am that yez goin' to get the worst of the fight this time; heigh! at him agin, yer sowls," he shouted, clapping his hands by way of encouragement, as a crowd would try to push the snail from the direct path.

"Where's yer sinse, you little blaggards? why don't yez all get together, and you'd soon tumble the murdherin' Turk over."

Despair seemed to be spreading through the fairy ranks, when it suddenly occurred to Terry that it was in his own power to put an end to their fears at once by removing the cause; another and more personal idea flashing across his mind at the same time.

"Why, then, bad cess to this thick skull o' mine," said he, as he picked up the snail and hurled it to a distance. "It well becomes me to be stickin' here, watchin' the antics of these little ragamuffins, instead of mindin' my own business of threasure-huntin'." So, without waiting to see what effect his timely interference had upon the supernals, he commenced vigorously to prosecute his search.

For some time he diligently explored the crevices and deep hollows on the mountain's side, without finding the slightest indication to stimulate his quest. One particular opening, however, he was loth to penetrate; the insects were so numerous therein, and flew so spitefully against his face, that, although it evidently extended to some distance into the heart of the mountain, again and again he was driven from his purpose of ascertaining that fact by the pertinacity of the annoying creatures. Now, a prodigious horned beetle would bang sharply against his cheek; anon, he would be entirely surrounded by a cloud of wasps, through which he had to fight his way lustily.

Thrice had he entered the cavity, and, having been ignominiously driven back each time, had determined to give up the effort to penetrate further. " Faix, an' it's mighty quare, intirely," said he, " that this is the only spot in the place that's so throubled with the varmint : it's my belief there's somethin' in that, too," he continued, a new light seeming to break upon him. " What should they be here for, more nor at any other openin', unless it was to keep strangers from inthrudin'? May I never, if I don't think that same hole in the rock is the turnpike-gate to somethin' surprisin' in the way of a fairy road; here goes to thry, anyway, in spite of the singin' and stingin'."

Once more, therefore, my bold Terry attempted to enter the cavern, and was attacked as before, but with tenfold fury ; legions of stinging flies, wasps, and hornets raised a horrible din about his ears ; but, setting his resolution up

to the fearless point, on he went, without regarding their
unpleasant music, expecting, of course, to be stung desperately.   What was his astonishment and relief to discover
that the noise was the only thing by which he was at all
distressed!   Not one of his myriad of assailants even as
much as touched him, and before he had proceeded many
steps further into the cavity every sound had ceased.

He now found his onward progress most uncomfortably
impeded by a stubborn species of wild hedge-brier, whose
sharp, thorny branches interlaced through each other, forming a barrier, whose dangerous appearance was sufficient to
deter the boldest from risking a laceration.   Not an opening large enough to admit his head could Terry see, and he
was about again to give the attempt up as unattainable,
when, by the merest accident, on turning round, his foot
slipped, and, with that inward shudder with which one
prepares for an inevitable hurt, he fell against the prickly
wall ; when, to his utter amazement, it divided on each
side as though it were fashioned of smoke, and he tumbled
through, somewhat roughly, to be sure, but altogether unharmed by the formidable-looking interposition.

"By the mortial of war," he cried, rubbing his dilapidated elbow, and looking round to examine his position,
"I'm on the right side of that hedge, anyway."

Now, Terry perceived that the barrier he had just so
successfully passed was slowly regaining its original appearance, and, to his mortification, as it gradually closed up the
aperture of the cavern, the light, hitherto quite sufficient
for him distinctly to see every object, faded away slowly,
and finally left him in utter darkness.

"Bedad, an' a tindher-box an' a sulphur match would
be about the greatest threasure I could light on at this
present," said Terry, as he groped about cautiously to find

some kind of an elevation whereupon he might sit and wait
for luck.

He had not been many minutes, however, in the blackness, when his quickened sense became aware of a light red-
dish spot, which faintly glowed at some distance. This
was the first sign of an encouraging nature he had experienced, and with a beating heart he proceeded to feel his
way toward the bright indication.

Getting gradually accustomed to the dimness that surrounded him, he suddenly discovered that he was opposed
by a solid wall of rock, in the very centre of which the
pale red glimmer still shone, like a star seen through a summer mist.

"The divil a use in my thravellin' any longer in that
direction," said Terry, turning sharply round to retrace his
steps, when, to his amazement and consternation, he encountered the same rocky barrier. Whichever way he
looked, all was alike stern and impassable. He was enclosed within a stony wall, whose circumference was but
little more than an arm's length, but whose height was lost
in the unsearchable darkness.

"Musha, then, how the divil did I stumble into this
man-thrap?" cried Terry, in consternation. "There's no
way out that I can see, an' where the mischief the top of
it is, is beyant my comprehendin'. Bedad, there's nothing for it but to thry an' climb up." So saying, Terry
placed his foot upon what he supposed, in the uncertain light, was a bold projection of the rock, when down
he stepped through it, and before he could recover his
perpendicular his body was half buried in the apparent
wall.

"Be jabers, if it ain't more of their thricks! — the never
a rock's there, no more nor the briers was; they may

make fools of my eyes, but they can't of my fingers, an' it's thim I'll thrust to in future," said he. And so, keeping the light in view, he boldly dashed through all the seeming obstacles, and soon found himself once more in an open space. It was a kind of vaulted tunnel that he was now traversing, his onward path still in profound darkness, with the sole exception of the red light, which Terry imagined grew larger and more distinct each step he took. A rush of warm air every now and then swept by him, and his tread echoed in the far distance, giving an idea of immense space.

Somewhat assured by the impunity with which he had already explored the enchanted districts, he was beginning to pick his way with freer breath, when his ears were smitten by a sound which filled him with dismay. It was the loud and furious barking of a pack of evidently most ferocious dogs, which approached rapidly, right in his path. On came the savage animals, louder and louder grew their terrible bark, and Terry gave himself up for lost in good earnest. It was no use to turn about and run, although that was his first impulse; so, flinging himself down on the ground, he awaited the attack of his unseen foes. He could now hear the clatter of their enormous paws, while their growlings echoed through the cavern like thunder.

"Murdher an' nouns, there's a half a hundred of them, —I know there is; an' it's mince-meat they'll make of me in less than no time," cried Terry, mumbling all the prayers he could remember; and in another instant, with a tremendous roar, they were upon him, and, with stunning yells, swept over him as he lay; but not an atom did he feel, no more than if a cloud had passed across.

"If they're not at it again, the blaggards," said he, get-

ting up, and shaking himself; "the divil a dog was there
in the place at all, — nothin' but mouth; but, bedad,
there's enough of that to frighten the sowl out of a nar-
vous Christian"; and once more the bold piper started in
pursuit of the coveted light. He had not proceeded very
far before he heard the distant bellowing of a bull; but,
warned by his past experience, he shut his ears against the
sound, and, although it increased fearfully, as though some
mad herd were tearing down upon him, he courageously
kept on. To be sure, his breath stopped for a moment,
and his pulse ceased to beat, when the thing seemed to approach his vicinity, but, as he anticipated, the terror fled
by him as he stood up erect, with the sensation only of a
passing breeze.

Terry received no further molestation, but plodded along
quietly, until he came to the place whence the light proceeded which had hitherto guided him, and here a most
gorgeous sight presented itself to his enraptured gaze.
Within a luminous opening of the cave he saw groups of
living atomies, all busied in the formation of the various
gems for which the rich ones of the world hunger. In one
compartment were the diamond-makers; in another, those
who, when finished, coated them over with the rough exterior which they hoped would prevent them from being
distinguished from common pebbles. Here was a tiny
multitude, fashioning emeralds of astonishing size; there
a crowd of industrious elves, putting the last sparkle into
some magnificent rubies.

With staring eyes, and mouth all agape with wonder
and delight, Terry watched the curious process for a few
moments, scarcely breathing audibly for fear of breaking
the brilliant spell. What to do he did not know. Heaps
of the coveted jewels lay around within his very grasp, yet

how to possess himself, without danger, of a few handfuls, he could n't imagine.

At last, resolving to make one final effort to enrich himself, he suddenly plunged his hand into the glittering mass of diamonds, presuming they were the most valuable, and, clutching a quantity, thrust them into his pocket, intending to repeat the operation until he had sufficient; but the instant that he did so, the entire cavern was rent asunder as with the force of an earthquake, the solid rock opened beneath him with a deafening explosion, and he was shot upwards as from the mouth of a cannon — up — up through the rifted cave, and miles high into the air. Not a whit injured did he feel from the concussion, saving a sense of lightness, as though he were as empty as a blown bladder. So high did he go in his aerial flight that he plainly saw to-morrow's sun lighting up the lakes and fields of other latitudes. As soon as he had reached an altitude commensurate with the power of the explosive agency, he turned over and commenced his downward progress, and, to his great relief, found that his fall was by no means as rapid as he had anticipated, — for his consciousness had not for a moment left him; on the contrary, the buoyant air supported him without difficulty, and each random gust of wind tossed him about like a feather. Well, day came, and shone, and vanished; so did the evening, and the starry night, and early morning, before Terry had completed his easy descent; when at length he touched the earth, gently as a falling leaf, and found himself lying beside the very stone whence he had departed on his late exploration. The marks of the recent terrible convulsion were visible, however, for the vast mountain was gone, ·and in its place a deep, round chasm, filled to overflowing with a dark yellow liquid, that hissed and bubbled into

12

flame like a Tartarean lake. The rocks around him, that before had shone so resplendently, were now blackened and calcined, — the lovely vegetation blasted, — the paradise a desert.

"Athin, maybe, I have n't been kickin' up the divil's delights hereabouts," said Terry, as he looked round at the desolation. "But never a hair I care; have n't I got a pocket full of big diminds, an' won't they set me up anyway?" he continued, drawing forth the precious contents of his pocket, and placing them on the rock by his side; when, to his infinite mortification, the entire collection turned out to be nothing but worthless pebbles.

"Musha! thin, may bad luck attend yez for a set of schemin' vagabones; an' afther all my throuble it's done again I am," he cried, in a rage, emptying his pocket, and flinging away its contents in thorough disgust. "Hollo! what's this?" he cried, with a start, as he drew forth the last handful; "may I never ate bread if I have n't tuk one of the chaps prisoner, an' if it is n't a Leprechaun I'm not alive." And sure enough there, lying in the palm of his hand, was as queer a looking specimen of fairyhood as ever the eye looked upon.

The little bit of a creature had the appearance of an old man, with wrinkled skin and withered features. It was dressed, too, in the costume of a bygone age. A mite of a velvet coat covered its morsel of a back; a pair of velvet breeches, together with white silk stockings, and little red-heeled shoes, adorned its diminutive legs, which looked as if they might have belonged to a rather fat spider, and a stiff white wig, duly pomatumed and powdered, surmounted by a three-cornered hat, bedecked its head.

The leprechaun seemed to be in a state of insensibility, as Terry examined minutely its old-fashioned appearance.

"It's just as I've heard tell of 'em," he cried, in glee; "cocked hat, an' breeches, an' buckles, an' all.   Hurroo! I'm a made man if he ever comes to."   With that, Terry breathed gently on the little fellow as he lay in his hand, as one would to resuscitate a drowned fly.

"I wondther if he'd have any relish for wather, — here goes to thry," said Terry, plucking a buttercup flower, in whose cavity a drop of dew had rested, and holding it to the lips of the leprechaun, "O, murdher! if I only had a taste of whiskey to qualify it; if that would n't bring the life into an Irish fairy, nothing would.   Ha! he's openin' his bit of an eye, by dad; here, suck this, yer sowl to glory," Terry continued, and was soon gratified by seeing the leprechaun begin to imbibe the contents of the buttercup with intense avidity.

"I hope you're betther, sir," said Terry, politely.

"Not the betther for you, Mr. Terry Magra," replied the fairy, "though I'm obleeged to you for the drop o' drink."

"Indeed, an' yer welcome, sir," Terry went on, " an' more betoken, it's mighty sorry I am to have gev you any oneasiness."

"That's the last lie you towld, Mr. Terry, and you know it," the leprechaun answered, tartly, "when your heart is fairly leapin' in your body because you've had the luck to lay a howld of me."

"Well, an' can't a fella be glad at his own luck, an' yet sorry if anybody else is hurted by it?" said Terry, apologetically.

"You can't humbug me, you covetious blaggard," the fairy went on.   "But I'll thry you, anyway.   Now listen to me.   The fairies that you have just been so wicked as to inthrude your unwelcome presence upon were all leprechauns like myself, — immortal essences, whose duty it was to make and guard the treasures that you saw in spite of all the terrors that we employed to frighten you away. So long as they were unobserved by mortal eyes, our existence was a bright and glorious one; but, once seen, we are obliged to abandon our fairy life and shape, take this degrading form, and work at a degrading occupation, subject to the ailments and mishaps of frail humanity, and forced to live in constant fear of your insatiate species. Now, the only chance I have to regain the blissful immortality I have lost, is for you to be magnanimous enough to relinquish the good fortune you anticipate from my capture. Set me unconditionally free, and I can revel once more in my forfeited fairy existence; persevere in your ungenerous advantage, and I am condemned to wander a wretched outcast through the world. Now, what is your determination ? " .

Terry's better feelings prompted him at first to let the little creature go; but love of lucre got the upper hand, and, after a slight pause of irresolution, he replied, " Indade, an it's heart-sick that I am to act so conthrary, but 'I'll leave it to yerself if it ain't agin nature for a man to fling away his luck. Shoemakin' is an iligant amusement, an' profitable; you'll soon get mighty fond of it; so I'm afeared I'll have to throuble you to do somethin' for me."

" I thought how it would be; you're all alike," said the fairy, sadly, — " selfish to the heart's core. Well, what do you want ? I'm in your power, and must fulfil your desire."

" Long life to you; now ye talk sense," cried Terry, elated. " Sure I won't be hard on you, — a thrifle of money is all I wish for in the world, for everything else will follow that."

"More, perhaps, than you imagine, — cares and anxieties," said the leprechaun.

"I 'll risk all them," replied Terry; "come, now, I 'll tell you what you may do for me. Let me find a shillin' in my pocket every time I put my fist into it, an' I 'll be satisfied."

"Enough! it 's a bargain; and now that you have made your wish, all your power over me is gone," said the leprechaun, springing out of his hand like a grasshopper, and lighting on the branch beside him. "It 's a purty sort of a fool you are," it continued, with a chuckle, "when the threasures of the universe were yours for the desire, to be contented with a pitiful pocketful of shillin's! Ho! ho!" and the little thing laughed like a cornkrake at the discomfited Terry.

"Musha, then, may bad cess to me if I don't crush the fun out of your cattherpillar of a carcass if I ketch a howlt of you!" said Terry, savagely griping at the fairy; but, with another spring, it jumped into the brushwood and disappeared.

Terry's first impulse was to dive his hand into his pocket to see if the leprechaun had kept his word, and to his great delight there he found, sure enough, a fine bright new shilling. At this discovery his joy knew no bounds. He jumped and hallooed aloud, amusing himself flinging away shilling after shilling, merely on purpose to test the continuance of the supply. He was satisfied. It was inexhaustible, and bright dreams of a splendid future flitted before his excited imagination.

With a heart full of happiness, Terry now wended his way homeward, busying himself as he went along in conveying shilling after shilling from one pocket into the other, until he filled it up to the button-hole. On arriving at the village, he met a few of his old companions, but so altered that he could scarcely recognize them, while they stared at him as though he were a spectre.

"Keep us from harm," said one, "if here ain't Terry Magra come back."

"Back," cried Terry with a merry laugh, "why, man alive, I've never been away."

"Never away, indeed, and the hair of you as white as the dhriven snow, that was as brown as a beetle's back whin you left," said the other.

It then struck Terry that his friends in their turn had aged considerably. The youngest that he remembered had become bent and wrinkled. "The saints be good to us," he cried, "but this is mighty quare intirely. How long is it sence I've seen yez, boys?" he inquired, eagerly.

"How long is it? why, a matther of twenty years or so," said one of the bystanders; "don't you know it is?"

"Faith, an' I didn't until this blessed minute," said Terry. "Have I grown ould onbeknownst to myself, I wondher?"

"Bedad, an' it's an easy time you must have had sence you've been away," said another.

"Well, won't you come an' taste a sup, for gra' we met?" said Terry, beginning to feel rather uneasy at the singular turn things had taken; but they shook their heads, and, without any other observation, passed on, leaving him standing alone.

"Stop!" he cried, "wait a bit; it's lashins of money that I have. Here, look!" and he drew forth a handful of the silver. It was no use, however. All their old cordiality and love of fun were gone; off they went, without even a glance behind them.

"Twenty years," said Terry to himself. "O, they're makin' fun of me. I don't feel a bit oulder nor I was yesterday. I'll soon be aisy on that point, anyway." So he proceeded toward the old drinking-place that he had so often spent the night in, but not an atom of it could he find. In the place where he expected to see it there was a brand-new house. He entered it, however, and, going straight up to a looking-glass which stood in the room, was amazed on seeing reflected therein an apparition he could not recognize. So withered and wrinkled did it appear, and so altogether unlike what he anticipated, that he turned sharply around in the hope of finding some aged individual looking over his shoulder; but he was entirely alone, — it was his own reflection, and no mistake at all about it.

"By the powers of war, but my journey into the mountains has n't improved my personal appearance," said he. "It's aisy to see that. But niver mind, I've got the money, an' that'll comfort me "; and he jingled the shillings in his pocket as if he could never weary of the sound.

In a short time the fame of Terry's wealth spread abroad, and, as it may readily be imagined, he did n't long want companions. The gay and the dissolute flocked round him, and as he had a welcome smile and a liberal hand for everybody, the hours flew by, carrying uproarious jollity on their wings, and, notwithstanding his infirmities of body, Terry was as happy as the days were long.

Now, while he had only to provide for his own immediate wants, and settle the whiskey scores of his riotous friends, he had easy work of it. It was only to keep putting his hand into his pocket two or three dozen times a day, and there was more than sufficient. But this kind

of existence soon began to grow monotonous, and Terry
sighed for the more enviable pleasures of a domestic life;
and inasmuch as it was now well understood that Terry
was an "eligible party," he had no great difficulty in making a selection. Many of the "down-hill" spinsters gave
evident indications that they would be nothing loth to
take him for better or for worse; and — I'm sorry to have
to record the fact — not a few even of the more youthful
maidens set their curls at the quondam piper. Neither
his age, nor the doubtful source of his revenue, render-
ing him an unmarketable commodity in the shambles of
Hymen.

In process of time, Terry wooed and won a demure-
looking little *collieen*, and, after having shut himself up for
two or three days, accumulating money enough for the interesting and expensive ceremony, was duly bound to her
for life. Now it was that his inexhaustible pocket began
to be overhauled continuously, and Terry cursed his imprudence in not asking for guineas instead of shillings.
Mrs. Terry Magra possessed a somewhat ambitious desire
to outvie her neighbors. Silk dresses were in demand,
and shawls and bonnets by the cart-load. The constant
employment gave Terry the rheumatism in his muscles,
until at last it was with the greatest difficulty he could
force his hand into his pocket.

Before many months had elapsed, Terry was prostrated
upon a sick-bed, his side — the pocket side — completely
paralyzed; and as he was not one of those who lay by for
a rainy day, his inability to apply to his fairy exchequer
caused him to suffer the greatest privation. And where
were the boon companions of his joyous hours now?
Vanished, — not one of them to be seen, — but haply fluttering around some new favorite of fortune, to be in his

turn fooled, flattered, and, when the dark day came, deserted.

When Terry grew better in health, which he did very slowly, there was a considerable back-way to make up, and the best part of his time was occupied in the mere mechanical labor of bringing out his shillings. Mrs. Magra also became more and more exacting, and the care-worn piper began to acknowledge to himself that his good fortune was not at all comparable with the anxiety and annoyance it had produced. Again and again he deplored the chance which had placed the temptation in his way, and most especially blamed his own selfish greed, which prevented him from behaving with proper generosity toward the captured leprechaun.

"He towld me plain enough what would come of it," cried he one day, as, utterly exhausted, he threw himself on the floor, after many hours' application to the indispensable pocket; "he towld me that it would bring care and misery, an' yet I was n't satisfied to profit by the warning. Here am I, without a single hour.of comfort, everybody dhraggin' at me for money, money! an' the very sinews of me fairly wore out wid divin' for it. This sort of life ain't worth livin' for."

Before long, Terry's necessities increased to such a degree that, out of the twenty-four hours of the day and night, more than two thirds were taken up with the now terrible drudgery by which they were to be supplied. No time had he left for relaxation, — hardly for sleep. The thought of to-morrow's toil weighed on his heart, and kept him from rest. He was thoroughly miserable. It was in vain that he called upon death to put an end to him and his wretchedness together. There was no escape for him, even by that dark road; the fear of a worse hereafter, made imminent by the consciousness of an ill-spent life, kept him from opening the eternal gate himself, to which he was often sorely tempted.

To this great despondency succeeded a course of reckless dissipation and drunkenness. Homeless at last, he wandered from one drinking-shop to another, caring nothing for the lamentable destitution in which his family was steeped; for, as is usually the case, the poorer he became, the more his family increased. His deserted wife and starving little ones were forced to obtain a scanty subsistence through the degrading means of beggary. He himself never applied to his fairy resource unless to furnish as much of the scorching liquor as would completely drown all sense of circumstance. The slightest approach to sobriety only brought with it reflection, and reflection was madness. So, the very worst amongst the worst, in rags and filth, he staggered about the village, a mark of scorn and contempt to every passer-by, or else, prone upon some congenial heap of garbage, slept off the fierceness of his intoxication, to be again renewed the instant consciousness returned.

With that extraordinary tenacity of life indicative of an originally fine constitution, which, added to a naturally powerful frame of body, might have prolonged his years even beyond the allotted space, Terry crept on in this worse than brutal state of existence for many months, until at last one morning, after a drinking bout of more than usual excess, he was found lying in a stable to which he had crawled for shelter, insensible, and seemingly dead. Perceiving, however, some slight signs of animation yet remaining, his discoverers carried him to the public hospital, for home he had none, and his own misdeeds had estranged the affections and closed the heart against him of her whose

inclination as well as duty would have brought her quickly
to his side, had he but regarded and cherished the great
God-gift to man, — a woman's love, — and not cast it aside
as a worthless thing.

Tended and cared for, however, although by stranger
hands, Terry hovered a long time betwixt life and death,
until at length skill and attention triumphed over the as-
sailant, and he was restored to comparative health.

It was then, during the long solitary hours of his con-
valescence, when the mind was restored to thorough consciousness, but the frame yet too weak for him to quit his
bed, that the recollection of his wasted existence stood
spectre-like before his mental vision. Home destroyed,
wife and children abandoned, friendships sundered, and
himself brought to the brink of a dreaded eternity, and all
through the means he had so eagerly coveted, and by which
he had expected to revel in all the world's joys.

He prayed, in the earnest sincerity of awakened repentance; he prayed for Heaven's assistance to enable him to
return to the straight path.

"O, if I once get out of this!" he cried, while drops
of agony bedewed his face, " I'll make amends during the
brief time yet left me, — I will, I will. Come what may,
never again will I be beholdin' to that fearful gift. I now
find to my great cost that wealth, not properly come by, is
a curse, and not a blessing. I'll work, with the help of the
good God and his bright angels, an' maybe peace will
once more visit my tortured heart."

It was some time before he was able to leave his bed,
but when at last he was pronounced convalescent, he
quitted the hospital, with the firm determination never
again, under any circumstance whatsoever, even to place
his hand within the pocket whence he had hitherto

drawn his resources. As a further security against the
probability of temptation, he took a strong needle and
thread, and sewed up the opening tightly.

"There," he cried, with an accent of relief, "bad luck
to the toe of me can get in there now. O, how I wish
to gracious it had always been so, and I would n't be the
miserable, homeless, houseless, wifeless, and childless vagabone that I am at this minute!"

As he was debating in his mind what he should turn
to in order to obtain a living, — for so great a disgust
had he taken to the pipes, to which he attributed all his
wretchedness, that he had determined to give up his pro-
ductive but precarious profession of piper, and, abandoning
the dissolute crowd who rejoiced in his performances, betake himself to some more useful and reputable employment, — it suddenly occurred to him to visit the scene of
his fairy adventure, in the hope that he might get rid of
the dangerous gift his cupidity had obtained for him.

No sooner had he conceived the idea than he instantly
set forward to put it in execution. The night was favorable for his purpose, and he arrived at the identical place in
the mountain, without the slightest interruption or accident.
He found it just as he had left it, a scene of the wildest
desolation. No sound fell on his ear save the mournful
shrieking of the wind as it tore itself against the harsh
branches of the dead pine-trees. He climbed the rugged
side of the hill, and looked into the black lake that filled
the dark chasm at its summit. It seemed to be as solid as
a sheet of lead. He flung a pebble into the gulf; it was
eagerly sucked in, and sunk without a ripple, as though
dropped into a mass of melted pitch. One heavy bubble
swelled to the surface, broke into a sullen flame that flashed
lazily for an instant, and then went out. A small, but in-

tensely black puff of smoke rose above the spot; so dense
was the diminutive cloud that it was rejected by the
shadowy atmosphere, which refused to receive it within its
bosom. Reluctantly it seemed to hang upon the surface
of the lake, then slowly mounted, careering backwards and
forwards with each passing breeze.

The singular phenomenon attracted Terry's attention,
and he watched, with increasing interest, the gyrations of
the cloud, until at length it took a steady direction toward
the spot where he stood. It was not long before it floated
up to him, and he stepped aside to let it pass ; but as he
moved, so did the ball of smoke. He stooped, and it followed his movement ; he turned and ran, — just as swiftly
it sped with him. He now saw there was something su-
pernatural in it, and his heart beat with apprehension.

"There's no use in kickin' agin fate," he said, " so, with
a blessin', I'll just stop where I am, an' see what will
come of it ; worse off I can't be, an' that's a comfort anyway."

So saying, Terry stood still, and patiently waited the result. To his great surprise the cloud of smoke, after making the circuit of his head two or three times, settled on
his right shoulder, and, on casting his eye round, he perceived that it had changed into a living form, but still as
black as a coal.

" Bedad I'm among them agin, sure enough," said Terry,
now much more easy in his mind ; " I wondher who this
little divil is that's roostin' so comfortably on my showldher."

" Wondher no longer, Misther Terry Magra," grunted a
frog-like voice into his ear ; " by what magic means, O
presumptuous mortal, did you discover the charmed stone
which compelled the spirit of yonder sulphurous lake to

quit his warm quarters, thus to shiver in the uncongenial air? Of all the myriad pebbles that are scattered around, that was the only one which possessed the power to call me forth."

"Faix, an' it was a lucky chance that made me stumble on it, sir," said Terry.

"That's as it may turn out," replied the spirit. "Do you know who and what I am? but why should you, ignorant creature as you are? Listen, and be enlightened. I am the chief guardian of yon bituminous prison, within whose murky depths lie groaning all of fairy kind who have by their imprudence forfeited their brilliant station."

"You don't tell me that, sir? By goxty, an' I wouldn't like to change places with them," said Terry, with a great effort at familiarity.

"There's no knowing when you may share their fate," replied the spirit. "The soul of many an unhappy mortal, who has abused a fairy gift, lies there as well."

Terry shivered to his very marrow as he heard those words, for full well he knew, that, amongst all such, none deserved punishment more than he; he was only wondering how his immortal part could be extracted from its living tenement, when, as though the spirit knew his very thoughts, it uttered, "I have but to breathe within your ear a word of power, and with that word the current of your life would cease."

Terry instinctively stretched his neck to its fullest extent, as he said to himself, "I'll keep my lug out of your reach if I can, my boy." But the spirit either knew his thought, or guessed it from the movement.

"Foolish piper," it said, "I could reach it, did I so incline, were it as high as Cashel Tower." And to prove that the assertion was not a mere boast, the little fellow

made a jump, and perched upon the bridge of Terry's
nose, and sat there astride ; and as it was of the *retroussé*
order, a very comfortable seat it had ; light as a feather, it
rested there, peering alternately into each of Terry's eyes,
who squinted at the intruder, brimful of awe and amazement.

" I give in," said he.   " It 's less nor nothin' that I am
in your hands ; but if it 's just as convainient for you, I 'd
be much obliged to you if you 'd lave that, for it 's fairly
tearin' the eyes out of me head that you are, while I 'm
thryin' to look straight at you."

" It 's all the same to me intirely," replied the spirit ;
" and now that you have come to a full sense of my power,
I 'll take up my position at a more agreeable distance."

So saying, the spirit bounded off of Terry's nose, and
alighted on a branch of the same tree on which the legion
of little pipers had before assembled, while Terry wiped
his relieved eyes with the sleeve of his coat, and sat upon
the piece of rock that stood beside.

" And now, Masther Magra," said the spirit, " we 'll proceed to business.   Had you picked up any other stone but
the one you did, or had you refrained from obstructing the
lake in any way, your soul would have been mine for ever.
You see what a small chance you had.   But inasmuch as
your good luck pointed out the talismanic pebble, you have
yet the privilege of making another wish which I must
gratify whatsoever it may be.   Think well, however, ere
you ask it ; let no scruples bound your desires.   The
wealth of the world is in my distribution."

Terry's nerves thrilled again, as his mind conjured up
images of purchased delights.   But for an instant only did
he hesitate what course he should pursue.

" The temptation is wonderful," said he.   " But no :

I've endured enough of misery from what I've had already."

"What can I do for you?" said the spirit, sharply. "Don't keep a poor divil all night in the cold."

"Well, then, sir, I'll tell you," replied the other. "I suppose you know already — for you seem to be mighty knowledgable — that some years back I kotch a leprechaun on this very spot; and though he towld me that it would be the desthroyin' of him out an' out, I meanly chose to make myself rich, as I thought, by taking a fairy gift from him, rather than lettin' him go free an' unharmed. It was a dirty an' selfish thransaction on my part, an' it's with salt tears that I've repinted of that same. Now, if that leprechaun is sufferin' on my account, and you can give the creather any comfort, it's my wish that you'll manage it for me, — ay, even though I was to bear his punishment myself."

"You have spoken well and wisely," said the spirit; "and your reward will be beyond your hope."

Simultaneously with those words, Terry was still more astonished at beholding a gradual but complete change taking place in the neighborhood: the blasted trees shot forth fresh branches; the branches, in their turn, pushed out new leaves; thick verdure overspread the rugged sides of the mountain; while, gushing joyously from an adjacent hollow, a little rill danced merrily through the shining pebbles, singing its song of gratitude, as though exulting in the new-found liberty; unnumbered birds began to fill the air with their delicious melody; the rifted and calcined rocks concealed their charred fronts beneath festoons of flowering parasites; the murky lake sank slowly into the abyss, while in its place a tufted, daisy-spangled field appeared, to which the meadow-lark descended lovingly,

and, fluttering a short space amidst the dewy grass, sprang
up again, with loud, reverberating note.

The primeval change, when the beautiful new world
emerged from chaos, was not more glorious than was the
scene now presented to the rapt beholder.   He felt within
himself the exhilarating effect of all this vast and unexpected wonder; the free, fresh blood cast off its sluggish-
ness, and once more bounded through his veins; the flush
of vigor and excitement bedewed his brow; the flaccid
muscles hardened into renewed strength; elasticity and
suppleness pervaded every limb, stiffened and racked erewhile with keen rheumatic pains.   It was not, however,
until, attracted by the pure limpid stream that filtered into
a sandy hollow near him, he stooped down to carry the
refreshing draught to his lips, that he was aware of the
greatest change of all; for, instead of the sunken cheeks
and wrinkled brow, the bloodshot eyes and thin, gray hairs
that he had brought with him, the ruddy, health-embrowned
and joy-lit features of years long gone laughed up at him
from the glassy surface.

And now a merry little chuckle tinkled in his ear, and,
on looking around, he discovered that the black spirit had
vanished, and in its place sat the identical leprechaun,
about whose melancholy fate he was so concerned.

"By the piper that played before Moses, but it's glad I
am to see you once more, my haro; have they let you
out?" inquired Terry, with considerable anxiety.

"I have never been imprisoned," replied the little fellow,
gayly.

"Why, then *tear an nounthers*," said Terry.   "You
have n't been gostherin' me all the time, an' the heart of me
fairly burstin' wid the thought of them weeshee gams of
yours strikin' out among the pitch that was beyant."

13

"It was that very feeling of humanity, which I knew yet lingered in your heart, that saved you," replied the leprechaun.

"As how, sir, might I ax?"

"How long is it since you saw me before?"

"Don't mention it," cried Terry, with an abashed look, "a weary life-time a'most has passed since then."

"And *what* a life-time!" observed the leprechaun, reproachfully.

"Indeed, an' you may say that," replied the other. "There's no one knows betther nor I do how sinfully that life was wasted, how useless it has been to me an' to every one else, how foolishly I flung away the means that might have comforted those who looked up to me, among heartless, conscienceless vagabones, who laughed at me while I fed their brutish appetites, and fled from me as though I were infectious when ill-health and poverty fell upon my head."

"Then the fairy gift did not bring you happiness?"

"Happiness!" replied Terry, with a groan, "it changed me from a man into a beast, it brought distress and misery upon those nearest and dearest to me, it made my whole worldly existence one continued reproach, and, God help me! I'm afeared it has shut the gates of heaven against my sowl hereafther."

"Then I suppose you have the grace to be sorry this time that you did n't behave more generously in my case," said the fairy.

"True, darlin'; if I was n't, I would n't be here now," replied Terry. "It was to thry and find you out that I took this journey, an' a sore one it is to a man wid the weight of years that 's on my back."

"O, I forgot that you were such an ould creather

intirely," said the little fellow, with a merry whistle, " but
what the mischief makes you bend your back into an
apperciand, and hide your ears on your showlders, as if
the cowld was bitin' them."

" Faix, an' it's just because I'm afeared to sthraighten
myself out, that murdherin' thief rheumatism has screwed
the muscles of my back so tight."

" You can't stand up then, eh, Terry ? "

"Not for this many a long day, sir, more is the pity,"
replied the other, with a heavy sigh.

" You don't tell me that," said the leprechaun, with a
queer expression of sympathy.   " There could be no harm
thryin', anyway."

" If I thought there would be any use in it, it's only
too glad that I'd be," said Terry.

" There's no knowin' what a man can do, until he makes
the effort."

Encouraged by these words, Terry began very gingerly
to lift his head from its long sunken position ; to his infinite delight he found the movement unaccompanied by
the slightest twinge, and so, with a heart brimful of joy,
he drew himself up to his full height without an ache
or a pain, — tall, muscular, and as straight as a tailor's
yard.

The hurroo ! that Terry sent forth from his invigorated
lungs, when he felt the entire consciousness of his return to
youth and its attendant freshness and strength, startled the
echoes of the mountain, like the scream of a gray eagle.

" And now, Misther Terry Magra," said the leprechaun,
" I may as well tell you the exact period of time that has
passed since I first had the pleasure of a conversation
with you ; it is now exactly, by my watch," and he pulled
out a mite of a time-keeper from his fob, — " there's noth-

ing like being particular in matters of chronology, — jist fourteen minutes and fifty-nine seconds, or, to be more explicit, in another second it will be precisely a quarter of an hour."

" O, murdher alive ! only to think ! " cried Terry, gasping for breath. " An' the wife an' childher, and the drunkenness and misery I scattered around me."

" Served but to show you, as in a vision, the sure consequences which would have resulted had you really been in possession of the coveted gift you merely dreamed that you had obtained ; the life of wretchedness which you passed through, in so short a time, is but one of many equally unfortunate, some leading even to a more terrible close. There are a few, however, I am bound to say, on whom earthly joys *appear* to shed a constant ray ; but we, to whom their inmost thoughts are open as the gates of morning to the sun, know that those very thoughts are black as everlasting night. What say you now, Terry? Will you generously give up your power over me, and, by leading a life of industry and temperance, insure for you and yours contentment, happiness, and comfort, or will you, to the quelling of my fairy existence and its boundless joys, risk the possession of so dangerous though dazzling a gift as I am compelled to bestow upon you, should you insist on my compliance with such a wish ? "

It must be confessed that Terry's heart swelled again at the renewed prospect of sudden wealth, and inasmuch as he exhibited, by the puzzled expression of his countenance, the hidden thoughts that swayed, alternately, his good and evil impulses, the leprechaun continued, " Take time to consider, — do nothing rashly ; but weigh well the consequences of each line of conduct, before you decide irrevocably and forever."

"More power to you for givin' me that chance, any-way," said Terry. "It would n't take me long to make my mind up, if it was n't for what I've gone through; but 'the burnt child,' you know, 'keeps away from the fire.' Might I ax, sir, how far you could go in the way of money? for, av I incline that way at all, bedad it won't be a peddlin' shillin' that I'll be satisfied with."

"Do you know Squire Moriarty?" said the fairy.

"Is it Black Pether? who does n't know the dirty thief of the world? Why, ould Bluebeard was a suckin' babby compared to him, in the regard of cruelty."

"How rich is he?"

"Be gorra, an' they say there's no countin' it, it's so thremendous. Is n't he the gripin'est an' most stony-hearted landlord in the barony, as many a poor farmer knows, when rint-day's to the fore?" said Terry.

"And how did he get his money?" inquired the leprechaun.

"Indeed, an' I b'lieve there's no tellin' exactly. Some says this way, an' others that. I've heard say that he was a slave marchint early in life, or a pirate, or something aiqually ginteel an' profitable," replied Terry.

"They lie, all of them," the little fellow went on. "He got it as you did yours, by a fairy gift, and see what it has made of him. In his early days, there was not a finer-hearted fellow to be found anywhere; everybody liked, courted, and loved him."

"That's thrue enough," said Terry, "and now there ain't a dog on his estates will wag a tail at him."

"Well, you may be as rich as he is, if you like, Terry," said the fairy.

"May I?" cried Terry, his eyes flashing fire at the idea.

" He turned his poor old mother out of doors, the other day," observed the leprechaun, quietly.

Terry's bright thoughts vanished in an instant, and indignation took their place; for filial reverence is the first of Irish virtues. "The murdherin' Turk!" he exclaimed, angrily, "if I had a howld of him now, I'd squeeze the sowl out of his vagabone carcass, for disgracin' the counthry that's cursed with such an unnatural reprobate."

"It was the money that made him do it," said the fairy.

"You don't tell me that, sir!"

"Indade but I do, Terry. When the love of *that* takes possession of a man's heart, there's no room there for any other thought. The nearest and dearest ties of blood, of friendship, and of kin, are loosed and cast away as worthless things. You have a mother, Terry?"

"I have, I have; may all good angels guard and keep her out of harm's way!" cried Terry, earnestly, while the large tears gushed forth from his eyes. "Don't say another word," he went on rapidly; "if it was goold mines that you could plant under every sthep I took, or that you could rain dimonds into my hat, an' there was the smallest chance of my heart's love sthrayin' from her, even the length of a fly's shadow, it's to the divil I'd pitch the whole bilin', soon an' suddent. So you can keep your grand gifts, an' yer fairy liberty, an' tak my blessin' into the bargain, for showin' me the right road."

"You're right, Terry," said the leprechaun, joyously, "an' I'd be proud to shake hands with you if my fist was big enough. You have withstood temptation manfully, and sufficiently proved the kindliness of your disposition. I know that this night's experience will not be lost on you,

but that you will henceforth abandon the wild companionship in the midst of which you have hitherto wasted time
and energy, forgetful of the great record yet to come, when
each misused moment will stand registered against you."

"And now, Terry," he continued, "I'll lave you to
take a little rest ; after all you have gone through you
must sorely need it." So saying, the leprechaun waved a
slip of osier across Terry's eyelids, when they instantly
closed with a snap ; down he dropped all of a heap upon
the springy moss, and slept as solid as a toad in a rock.

When Terry awoke, the morning was far advanced, and
the sun was shining full in his face, so that the first impression that filled his mind was that he was gazing upon a
world of fire. He soon mastered that thought, however,
and then, sitting down upon the famous stone, began to
collect his somewhat entangled faculties into an intelligible focus. Slowly the events of the night passed before
him ; the locality of each phase in his adventures was
plainly distinguishable from where he sat. There, close
to him, was the identical branch on which had perched
the legion of little pipers ; a short distance from him was
the mazy hollow through which he had so singularly
forced his way ; half hoping to find some evidence of the
apparently vivid facts that he had witnessed, he put his
hand into his breeches pocket, but only fished out a piece
of pig-tail tobacco.

As he ran over every well-remembered circumstance he
became still more puzzled. It was clear enough that he
had been asleep, as he had but just waked ; but then
he was equally certain that he was wide awake when the
leprechaun touched his eyelids with the osier. Indeed, he
looked round in the expectation of seeing it lying somewhere about ; but there was no trace of such a thing.

The conclusion he came to was a characteristic one. "By the mortial," said he, as, taking up his pipes, he saun- tered down the mountain road, "there's somethin' quare in it, sure enough ; but it's beyant my comprehendin'. The divil a use is there in botherin' my brains about it ; all I know is that there's a mighty extensive hive o' bees sing- in' songs inside of my hat this blessed mornin'. I must put some whiskey in, an' drownd out the noisy varmints."

The chronicler of this veracious history regrets exceed- ingly that he cannot, with any regard to the strict truth, bring it to a conclusion in the usual moral-pointing style, except in its general tendency, which he humbly considers to be wholesome and suggestive ; but the hero of the tale — the good-for-nothing, wild roysterer, Terry, who ought, of course, to have profited by the lesson he had received and to have become a sober, steady, useful, somewhat bil- ious, but in every way respectable member of society, dressed in solemn black, and petted religiously by ecstatical elderly ladies — did not assist the conventional *dénouement* in the remotest degree. With grief I am compelled to record the humiliating fact that Terry waxed wilder than ever, drank deeper, frolicked longer, and kicked up more promiscuous shindies than before, and invariably wound up the account of his fairy adventures, which in process of time he believed in most implicitly, by exclaiming, "What a murdherin' fool I was not to take the money !"

O'BRYAN'S LUCK.*

A TALE OF NEW YORK.

CHAPTER I.

THE MERCHANT-PRINCE.

IN the private office of a first-class store sat two individuals, each thoroughly absorbed in his present employment, but with very different feelings for the work.
One — it was the head of the establishment, the great Mr.
Granite, the millionnaire merchant — was simply amusing
himself, as was his usual custom at least once a day, figur-
ing up, by rough calculation, the probable amount of his
worldly possessions, they having arrived at that point when
the fructifying power of wealth made hourly addition to
the grand total ; while the other, his old and confidential
clerk, Sterling, bent assiduously over a great ledger, mechanically adding up its long columns, which constant use
had enabled him to do without the possibility of mistake.
With a profound sigh of relief, he laid down his pen, and,
rubbing his cramped fingers, quietly remarked, " Accounts
made up, sir."

" Ah ! very good, Sterling," replied the stately principal,
with a smile, for his arithmetical amusement was very
satisfactory ; " how do we stand ? "

* The author has treated the subject of this story in his touching
play called " The Irish Emigrant." — ED.

"Balance in our favor, two hundred and fifty-seven thousand eight hundred and forty-seven dollars, and twenty-three cents," slowly responded the old clerk, reading from his abstract.

"You're certain that is correct, Mr. Sterling?" inquired the merchant-prince, in a clear, loud voice, which indicated that the old, time-worn machine was wearing out. He was so deaf that it was only by using his hand as a conductor of the sound that he could hear sufficiently to carry on a conversation.

"Correct to a cipher, sir," he replied. "I have been up and down the columns a dozen times."

"Good."

"Did you speak, sir?"

"No."

"Ah! my poor old ears," the old clerk whispered, half aside. "Five and forty years in this quiet office has put them to sleep. They'll never wake up again, never, never."

"You have been a careful and useful assistant and friend, Sterling," said the merchant, in a kindly tone, touching him on the shoulder with unaccustomed familiarity, "and I thank you for the great good your services have done the house."

"Bless you, sir, bless you! — you are too good. I don't deserve it," replied Sterling, unable to restrain the tears which this unusual display of good feeling had forced up from the poor old man's heart.

"I shall have no further need of you to-day, Sterling, if you have any business of your own to transact."

"I have, I have, my good, kind friend, and thank you for granting me the opportunity," said Sterling, descending with difficulty from his place of torture. — Why will they not abolish those inflexible horrors, those relics of barbarism, those inquisitorial chattels, — office stools ? " I 'll go now, and mingle my happiness with the sweet breath of heaven.   And yet, if I dared to say what I want — I — "

" Well, speak out, old friend." The merchant went on, with an encouraging look: " If your salary be insufficient — "

" O, no, no ! " interposed the other suddenly. " I am profusely paid, — too much, indeed, — but — " and he cast down his eyes hesitatingly.

" This reserve with me is foolish, Sterling.   What have you to say ? "

" Nothing much, sir ; indeed, I hardly know how to bring it out, knowing, as I well do, your strange antipathy — " Granite turned abruptly away. He now knew what was coming, and it was with a dark frown upon his brow he paced the office, as Sterling continued, " I saw *him* to-day."

" Travers ? "

" Yes," replied the other, " Travers. But don't speak his name as though it stung you. I was his father's clerk before I was yours."

" You know what I have already done for him," moodily rejoined the merchant.

" Yes, yes, — I know it was kind, very kind of you, — you helped him once ; but he was unsuccessful. He is young, — pray, pray, spare him some assistance. You won't miss it, — indeed you won't," pleaded the clerk.

" Sterling, you are a fool," Granite replied, sternly. " Every dollar lent or lost is a backward step that must be crawled up to again by inches. But I am inclined to liberality to-day. What amount do you think will satisfy this spendthrift ? "

"Well, since your kindness emboldens me to speak —
it's no use patching up a worn coat, so even let him have
a new one — give him another chance — a few hundred
dollars, more or less, can't injure you, and may be his
salvation. About five thousand dollars will suffice."

"Five thousand dollars! are you mad, Sterling?" cried
the merchant, starting to his feet in a paroxysm of anger.

"Your son will have his half a million to begin with,"
quietly suggested Sterling.

"He will, he will!" cried the other, with a strange,
proud light in his eye, for upon that son all his earthly
hopes, and haply those beyond the earth, were centred.
"Wealth is power, and he will have sufficient; he can lift
his head amongst the best and proudest; he can wag his
tongue amongst the highest in the land, — eh, my old
friend?"

"That can he, indeed, sir, and be ashamed of neither
head nor tongue, for he's a noble youth," replied the clerk.

"Here, take this check, Sterling. I'll do as you wish
this time; but mind it is the last. I have no right to injure, even in the remotest degree, my son's interests, of
which I am simply the guardian. You can give it to —
to — *him*, and with this positive assurance."

"Bless you! this is like you, — this is noble, princely,"
murmured the old clerk, through his tears, which now
were flowing unrestrainedly; "when I tell — "

"Hold! repeat his name again, and I recall the loan.
I repent already of having been entrapped into this act of
folly."

"You wrong your own liberal nature," said Sterling,
mildly. "You are goodness itself, and fear not but you
will receive your reward fourfold for all you have done
for — "

"Away, you prating fool," cried Granite, in a tone that hurried the old clerk out of the office, full of gratitude for the service done, and of unaffected joy that Providence had selected him to be the bearer of such happy intelligence to the son of his old employer.

Meantime, the merchant-prince flung himself into his comfortable easy-chair, a spasm of agony passing across his harsh features. "O Travers, Travers!" he inly ejaculated, "must that black thought ever thrust itself like a grim shadow across the golden sun-ray of my prosperity?"

CHAPTER II.

THE MAN OF LABOR.

THE accommodating reader will now be kind enough to accompany me to a far different place from that in which the foregoing dialogue was held. With an effort of the will — rapid as a spiritual manifestation — we are there. You see, it is an exceedingly small habitation, built entirely of wood, and excepting that beautiful geranium-plant on one window, and a fine, sleek, contented-looking puss winking lazily on the other, — both, let me tell you, convincing evidence that the household deities are worshipped on the hearth within, for wheresoever you see flowers cultivated outside of an humble house look for cleanliness and domestic comfort on the inside, — little of ornament is visible. Kind people dwell within, you may know; for, see, the placid puss does n't condescend to change her position as we near her; her experience has n't taught her to dread an enemy in our species.

Lift the latch; 't is but a primitive fastening. Nay!

don't hesitate ; you know we are invisible. There! you are now in the principal apartment. See how neat and tidy everything is. The floor, to be sure, is uncarpeted, but then it is scrupulously clean. Look at those white window-curtains ; at that well-patched table-cloth, with every fold as crisp as though it had been just pressed ; the dresser over there, each article upon it bright as industry and the genius of happy home can make it. What an appetizing odor steams in from yonder kitchen! and listen to those dear little birds, one in each window, carrying on a quiet, demure conversation, in their own sweet way! Do they not say, and does not every quiet nook echo : "Though poor and lowly, there is all of heaven that heaven vouchsafes to man, beneath this humble roof; for it is the sphere of her who is God's choicest blessing — that world angel — a good, pure-hearted, loving WIFE."

But hark! who is that singing? You can hear him, although he is yet a block off; and so can she who is busy within there; you can tell by that little scream of joy.

That is Tom Bobolink, the honest truckman, and the owner of this little nest of contentment.

But, if you please, I will resume my narrative in my own way, for you are a very uncommunicative companion, reader, and it is impossible for me to discover whether you like the scene we have been looking at, or do not.

In a few moments, Tom rushed into the little room, his face all a-glow with healthy exercise, and a joyous song on his lips.

"Hello, pet! where are you?" he cried, putting down his hat and whip.

"Here am I, Tom!" answered as cheerful a voice as ever bubbled up from a heart full of innocence and love.

"*Din* in a *sec*," meaning dinner in a second; for "Tom and Pol," in their confidential chats, abbreviated long words occasionally; and I give this explanation as a sort of guide to their pet peculiarity.

"Hurry up, Polly!" cried Tom, with a good-humored laugh, "for I'm jolly hungry, I tell you. Good gracious! I've heard of people's taking all sorts of things to get up an appetite; if they'd only have the sense to take *nothing*, and keep on at it, it's wonderful what an effect it would have on a lazy digestion."

Polly now entered with two or three smoking dishes, which it did not take long to place in order. Now, I should dearly like to give you a description of my heroine, — ay, heroine, — for it is in her station that such are to be found, — noble spirits, who battle with privation and untoward fate, — smoothing the rugged pathway of life, and infusing fresh energy into the world-exhausted heart. O, what a crown of glory do they deserve, who wear a smile of content upon their lips, while the iron hand of adversity is pressing on their hearts, concealing a life of martyrdom beneath the heroism of courageous love!

I say I should like to give you some slight description of Polly's appearance, but I choose rather that my readers should take their own individual ideas of perfect loveliness, and clothe her therein; for, inasmuch as she is the type of universal excellence, in mind and character, I wish her to be so in form and beauty.

"What have you got for me, Polly?" says Tom.

"It ain't much," she replied; "cos you know we can't afford *lux'es;* but it's such a sweet little neck of *mut*, and lots of *wedges*."

"Gollopshus!" says Tom; "out with it! I'm as hungry as an unsuccessful office-seeker."

" Office-seekers ! what are they, Tom ? "

" Why, Polly, they are — faith, I don't know what to
compare them to ; you 've heard of those downy birds, that,
when some other has got hisself a comfortable nest, never
rests until he pops into it. But them's politics, Polly, and
ain't *prop* for *wom* to meddle with."

" I agree with you there, Tom, dear ; there 's enough
to occupy a woman's time and attention inside of her
house, without bothering her head with what 's going on
outside."

" Bless your little heart ! " cried Tom, heartily. " O
Polly, darling ! if there were a few more good wives,
there would be a great many less bad husbands. This is
glorious ! If we could only be sure that we had as good a
dinner as this all our lives, Pol, how happy I should be !
but I often think, my girl, if any accident should befall
me, what would become of you."

" Now, don't talk that way, Thomas ; nor don't repine
at your condition ; it might be much worse."

" I can't help it. I try not ; but it 's impossible, when
I see people dressed up and titevated out, as I go jogging
along with my poor old horse and truck — I envy them in
my heart, Pol — I know it 's wrong ; but it 's there, and it
would be worse to deny it."

" Could any of those fine folks enjoy their dinner better
than you did, Tom ? " said Polly, with a cheering smile.

" No, my girl ! But eating is n't all, Pol. This living
from hand to mouth — earning with hard labor every
crust we put into it — never seeing the blessed face of a
dollar that is n't wanted a hundred ways by our necessities — is rather hard."

" Ah, Tom ! and thankful ought we to be that we have
health to earn that dollar. Think of the thousands of

poor souls that are worse off than ourselves! Never look above your own station with envy, Thomas; but below it with gratitude."

This moment there appeared at the open door a poor, wretched-looking individual, evidently an Irishman, and, from the singularity of his dress, only just landed. He said not a word, but upon his pale cheek was visibly printed a very volume of misery.

"Hello, friend! what the devil do you want?" asked Tom.

"Don't speak so, Thomas. He's sick and in distress," said Polly, laying her finger on his mouth. "There! suppose you were like that!"

"What? a Paddy!" replied the other, with a jolly laugh; "don't mention it!" then calling to the poor stranger, who was resignedly walking away, "Come on, Irish!" he cried. "Do you want anything?"

"Av you plaze, sir," answered the Irishman, "I'd like to rest meself."

"Sit down, poor fellow!" said Polly, dusting a chair, and handing it towards him.

"I don't mane that, ma'am; a lean o' the wall, an' an air o' the fire 'll do. The blessin's on ye for lettin' me have it!" So saying, he placed himself near the cheerful fire-place, and warmed his chilled frame.

"A big lump of a fellow like you, would n't it be better for you to be at work than lounging about in idleness?" said Tom.

"Indeed, an' its thrue for ye, sir, it would so; but where is a poor boy to find it?"

"O, anywhere, — everywhere!"

"Bedad, sir, them 's exactly the places I 've been lookin' for it, for the last three weeks; but there was nobody at

14

home.   I hunted the work while I had the stringth to crawl afther it, an' now, av it was to come, I 'm afear'd that I have n't the stringth to lay howld ov it."

"Are you hungry ?" inquired Polly.

" I 'm a trifle that way inclined, ma'am," he replied, with a semi-comic expression.

"Poor fellow, here, sit down and eat," said Polly, hurriedly diving into the savory stew, and forking up a fine chop, which she handed to the hungry stranger.

" I'd relish it betther standin', if you plaze, ma'am," said he, pulling out a jack-knife and attacking the viands with vigorous appetite, exclaiming, " May the heavens bless you for this good act ! sure it 's the poor man that 's the poor man's friend, afther all.   You 've saved me, sowl and body, this blessed day.   I have n't begged yet, but it was comin' on me strong.   I looked into the eyes of the quality folks, but they carried their noses so high they could n't see the starvation that was in my face, and I would n't ax the poor people for fear they were worse off than meself."

" Ain't you sorry, Thomas, for what you said just now ?" inquired Polly of her husband.

" No," he replied, striking his fist on the table.   " I 'm more discontented than ever, to think that a few hundred scoundrel schemers, or fortunate fools, should monopolize the rights of millions ; is n't it devilish hard that I can't put my hand in my pocket and make this poor fellow's heart jump for joy."

"Point out to him where he can get some employment, Thomas, and his heart will be continually jumping," replied Polly.

By this time the poor stranger had finished his extempore meal, and shut up his pocket-knife, which he first carefully wiped on the tail of his coat.   " May God bless

you for this!" said he. "I'm stronger now. I'll go an'
hunt for a job; maybe luck won't be a stepfather to me
all my days."

"Stop," cried Tom, "suppose I were to give you something to do, what would you say?"

"Faix, I would n't say much, sir," said the Irishman,
"but I'd do it."

"Come along with me, then, and if I get any job, I'll
get you to help me."

"O, then, may long life attend you for puttin' fresh
blood in my veins!" responded the excited Milesian,
giving his already curiously bad hat a deliberate punch
in the crown, to show his gratitude and delight.

"Bless his noble, honest, loving heart!" cried Polly, as
Tom, having impressed his usual kiss upon her lips, started
to his labor again. "If it were not for those little fits of
discontent every now and then, what a man he'd be! but
we can't be all perfect; don't I catch myself thinking silks
and satins sometimes, instead of cottons and calicoes? and
I'll be bound, if the truth was known, the great folks that
wear nothing else but grand things don't behave a bit
better, but keep longing for something a little grander still,
so *he* must n't be blamed, nor he sha'n't, neither, in my
hearing."

CHAPTER III.

THE BOARDING-HOUSE.

TURN we now to the highly genteel establishment where
Henry Travers and his young wife are now resident,
presided over by a little more than middle-aged, severe-
looking personage, who rejoices in the euphonious name

of GRIMGRISKIN : her temper, phraseology, and general dis-position may be better illustrated by the conversation which is now going on between her and her two unfortunate in-mates. The midday accumulation of scraps, which was dignified by the name of dinner, but just over, Henry Tra-vers, in his small, uncomfortable bedroom, was ruminating upon the darkness of his present destiny, when a sharp knock at his door admonished him that he was about to receive his usual dunning visit from his amiable landlady.

"Come in," he gasped, with the articulation of a person about to undergo a mild species of torture.

"You'll excuse me, good people," said Grimgriskin, "for the intrusion ; but business is business, and if one don't attend *to* one's business, it's highly probable one's business will make unto itself wings, and, in a manner of speaking, fly away : not that I want to make you feel uncomfortable. I flatter myself, in this establishment, nobody need be under such a disagreeable apprehension ; but houses won't keep themselves, at least *I* never knew any so to do. Lodgings is lodgings, and board is board ; moreover, mar-kets — specially at this season of the year — may reasonably be said to be *markets ;* beef and mutton don't jump spon-taneously into one's hands, promiscuous-like ; neither do the hydrants run tea and coffee, — at least as far as my knowledge of hydrants goes."

"The plain sense of all this is — "

"Exactly what I am coming to," interrupted the voluble hostess. "I'm a woman of few words ; but those few, such as they are, I'm proud to say, are generally to the purpose. I make it a point to send in my bills regularly every month, and I presume that it's not an unreasonable stretch of imagination to expect them to be paid. Now, for the last three months they have come up to you receipted, and down to me with what one might call the auto-graphical corner torn off. Now, as it is not in my nature to make any one feel uncomfortable, and being a woman of very few words, I would merely intimate to you that rents is rents — and, moreover, must be paid — and mine, I am sorry to observe, is not a singular exception in such respect."

"My dear Mrs. Grim — "

"One moment!" interposed the woman of few words. "Perhaps you may not be aware of the circumstance, but I have my eyes open, — and, moreover, my ears. Whispers is whispers, and I *have* heard something that *might* make you uncomfortable; but as that is not my principle, I won't repeat it; but talkers, you know, will be talkers, and boarders can never be anything else in the world but boarders."

"What have they dared to say of us?" inquired Henry.

"Nothing — O, nothing to be repeated — dear, no! I'm proud to observe that my boarders pay regularly every month, and are therefore highly respectable; and respecta-ble boarders make a respectable house, and I would n't keep anything else. Thank heaven, I have that much consideration for my own respectability!"

"May I be permitted to ask what all this amounts to?" asked Henry, with commendable resignation.

"Just two hundred dollars," sharply replied Mrs. Grim-griskin; "being eighty for board, and one hundred and twenty for extras. I'm a woman of few words — "

"And I'm a man of less," said Henry, "I can't pay it."

"I had my misgivings," cried the landlady, tartly, "not-withstanding your boast of being connected with the rich Mr. Granite. Allow me to say, sir," she continued, seating herself upon a chair, "I've just sent for a hackman to take your trunks away, and I mean to retain the furniture until some arrangement is made."

"May I come in?" murmured a small, but apparently well-known voice at the door, from the alacrity with which Henry's poor young wife rushed to open it, admitting old Sterling, the clerk.

"Let me look in your eyes," cried she; "is there any hope?"

Sterling shook his head.

"No, — no more!"

"Heaven help us!" she exclaimed, as she tottered back to her seat.

"Heaven has helped you, my bright bird," said Sterling. "I only shook my head to make your joy the greater."

"What say you?" exclaimed Travers; "has that stony heart relented?"

"It is not a stony heart," replied Sterling; "I am ashamed of you for saying so. It's a good, generous heart. It has made mine glow with long-forgotten joy this day."

"Does he give us relief?" inquired Henry.

"He does," said the old man, the enthusiasm of generous happiness lighting up his features; "great, enduring relief. What do you think of five thousand dollars?"

"You dream, I dream!" cried Travers, starting up in astonishment; while Mrs. Grimgriskin, smoothing her unamiable wrinkles, and her apron at the same time, at the mention of so *respectable* a sum, came forward, saying, in her newest-lodger voice, "You'll excuse me; but I'm a woman of few words. I hope you won't take anything I've said as at all personal to you, but only an endeavor, as far as in me lies, to keep up the credit of my own establishment; as for that little trifle between us, of

course you can take your own time about that." So
saying, and with a profusion of unnoticed courtesies, she
quitted the room.

She had scarcely done so, when, with a deep groan of
agony, Sterling pressed his hand against his head, and
staggered to a chair. In an instant, Henry and his wife
were by his side.

" What is the matter, my dear Sterling ? " cried Henry.

" Don't come near me," replied the old clerk, the very
picture of despair and wretchedness ; " I am the destroyer
of your peace, and of my own, forever. O, why was I
allowed to see this dreadful day ? Curse me, Travers !
Bellow in my blunted ear, that my vile sense may drink it
in. I 've lost it, — lost it ! "

" Not the money ? " exclaimed Henry and his wife at a
breath.

" That 's right ! Kill me ! kill me ! I deserve it ! " continued Sterling, in an agony of grief. " O careless, guilty,
unhappy old man, that in your own fall must drag down
all you love, to share your ruin ! Lost — lost — lost,
forever ! "

" Forgive even the appearance of injustice, my good,
kind old friend," soothingly observed Travers. " It is I
who am the doomed one. There is no use in striving
against destiny."

" Don't, Henry, don't ! " gasped the old clerk, through
his fast-falling tears. " This kindness is worse than your
reproof. Let me die ! let me die ! I am not fit to live ! "
Suddenly starting to his feet, he cried, " I 'll run back, —
perhaps I may find it. O, no, no ! I cannot ; my old
limbs, braced up by the thought of bringing you happiness, are weakened by the effect of this terrible reaction ! "

"Come, come, old friend, take it not so much to heart!" said Travers, cheering him as well as he could. "There, lean upon me; we'll go and search for it together, and even if it be not found, the loss is not a fatal one, so long as life and health remain."

"You say this but to comfort me, and in your great kindness of heart, dear, dear boy!" cried Sterling, as he rose from the chair, and staggered out to retrace his steps, in the hope of regaining that which had been lost.

CHAPTER IV.

THE PIECE OF LUCK.

IT so happened that the very truckman who was sent to take Henry's trunks was our friend Bobolink, who was plying in the vicinity, and, as it was his first job, he was anxious enough to get it accomplished; therefore, a few minutes before Sterling came out, he and his *protégé*, Bryan, the Irishman, trotted up to the door.

"There! away with you up, and get the trunks," said Bobolink; "I'll wait for you here."

Bryan timidly rung at the bell, and entered. In the mean time, Tom stood at his horse's head, pulling his ears, and having a little confidential chat. Taking out his wallet, he investigated its contents.

"Only fifty cents," he exclaimed, shrugging his shoulders, "and this job will make a dollar, — that's all the money in the world."

In putting back his greasy, well-worn wallet, his eye happened to fall upon an object which made the blood rush with a tremendous bound through his frame. Lying close to the curb, just below his feet, was a large pocket-book.

"Good gracious!" he exclaimed, "what's that? It looks very like" — (picking it up hurriedly, and taking a hasty survey of its contents) — "it is — money — heaps of money — real, good money, and such a lot — all fifties and twenties!" First, he blessed his good luck; then, he cursed the heaviness of the temptation; at one moment he would whistle, and endeavor to look unconcerned; at another, he would tremble with apprehension. What to do with it, he did not know; but the tempter was too strong; he at last determined to retain it. "It's a wind-fall," said he to himself; "nobody has seen me take it. Such a large sum of money could not have been lost by a poor person, and nobody wants it more than I do myself. I'll be hanged if I don't keep it!"

Just then Bryan emerged from the door, with a most lachrymose expression of countenance, and was very much astonished to find that his stay did not produce an equally woe-begone effect upon Tom.

"There's no thrunks goin'," said Bryan. "The fellow as was leavin' ain't leavin' yet; because somebody's after leavin' him a lot o' money."

"Come, jump up, then," cried Bobolink, "and don't be wasting time there."

At that moment his eye caught that of Sterling, who, with Travers, had commenced a search for the lost pocket-book. Instinct told him in an instant what their occupation was, and yet he determined to keep the money.

"My man," said Travers to Bryan, "did you see any-thing of a pocket-book near this door?"

"Is it me?" replied Bryan. "Do I look as if I'd seen it? I wish I had!"

"What for? you'd keep it, I suppose?" observed Travers.

"Bad luck to the keep," replied Bryan, "and to you for thinkin' it! but it's the way of the world, — a ragged waistcoat's seldom suspected of hidin' an honest heart."

"Come, old friend," said Henry to Sterling, "these men have not seen it evidently"; and off they went on their fruitless errand, while a feeling of great relief spread itself over Bobolink's heart at their departure.

"How wild that ould fellow looked," said Bryan.

"Humbug!" replied Bobolink; "it was only put on to make us give up the pocket-book."

"Make us give it up?"

"Yes; that is to say, if we had it. There, don't talk. I'm sick. I've got an oppression on my chest, and if I don't get relief, I'll drop in the street."

"Indeed, an' somethin's come over ye since mornin', sure enough," said Bryan; "but you've been kind, an' good, an' generous to me, an' may I never taste glory, but if I could do you any good by takin' half yer complaint, I'd do it."

"I dare say you would," replied Tom; "but my constitution's strong enough to carry it all. There, you run home, and tell Polly I'll be back early. I don't want you any more."

As soon as Bryan was off, Bobolink sat down on his truck, and began to ruminate. His first thought was about his wife. "Shall I tell Polly?" thought he. "I've never kept a secret from her yet. But suppose she would n't let me keep it? I sha'n't say a word about it. I'll hide it for a short time, and then swear I got a prize in the lottery." It suddenly occurred to him that he was still on the spot where he had found the money. "Good heaven," said he, "why do I linger about here? I must be away, — away anywhere! and yet I feel as though I was leaving my life's happiness here. Pooh! lots of money will make any one happy." So saying, and singing — but with most constrained jollity — one of the songs which deep bitterness had called up spontaneously from his heart, he drove to the nearest groggery, feeling assured that he should require an unusual stimulant of liquor, to enable him to fitly bear this accumulation of good luck which did not justly belong to him.

CHAPTER V.

HOME.

"WHAT a dear, considerate, good-natured husband I have, to be sure! The proudest lady in the land can't be happier than I am in my humble house," said Polly, as she bustled about to prepare for Tom's coming home, having been informed by Bryan that she was to expect him. "Poor fellow! he may well be tired and weary. I must get his bit of supper ready. Hush! that's his footstep," she continued. But something smote her as she noticed the fact that he was silent. There was no cheering song bursting from his throat, — no glad word of greeting; but he entered the door, moody and noiseless. Another glance. Did not her eye deceive her? No! The fatal demon of Liquor had imprinted its awful mark upon his brow. She went up to him, and, in a voice of affection, asked what was the matter.

"Matter? What should be the matter?" he answered, peevishly.

"Don't speak so crossly, Thomas," said she, in a subdued voice; "you know I did not mean any harm."

"Bless your little soul! I know you did n't," he exclaimed, giving her a hearty embrace. "It 's me that 's the brute."

"Indeed, Thomas, you are nothing of the kind," she went on, the cheerful smile once more on her lip.

"I am, Polly; I insist upon being a brute. Ah! you don't know all."

"All what? you alarm me!"

"I wish I dared tell her," thought Bobolink; "I will! I 've found a jolly lot of money to-day, Polly."

"How much, Thomas?"

"Shall I tell her? I 've a great mind to astonish her weak nerves. — How much do you think?" cried he, with a singular expression, which Polly attributed but to one terrible cause, and she turned sadly away. That angered him, — for men in such moods are captious about trifles. "I won't tell her," said he; "she does n't deserve it. Well, then, I 've earned a *dollar*."

"Only a dollar?" replied Polly. "Well, never mind, dear Thomas, we must make it do; and better a dollar earned, as you have earned yours, by your own honest industry, than thousands got in any other way."

Somehow Tom fancied that every word she said was meant as a dig at him, forgetting, in his drunkenness, that she was ignorant of what had passed. The consequence was, that he became crosser than ever.

"Why do you keep saying savage things, that you know must aggravate me?" he cried. "I can't eat. Have you any brandy in the house? I have a pain here!" and he clasped his hands upon his breast, where the pocket-book lay concealed. "I think the brandy would relieve me."

"My poor Thomas," replied his wife, affectionately, "something must have happened to annoy you! I never saw you thus before; but you are so seldom the worse for drink that I will not upbraid you. The best of men are subject to temptation."

At that word Bobolink started from his seat, and, gazing intently in her face, exclaimed, "What do you mean by that?"

"Why, even you, Thomas, have been tempted to forget yourself," she replied.

"How do you know?" he thundered, his face now sickly pale.

"I can see it in every feature, my poor husband!" said she, sorrowfully, as she quitted the room to get the brandy he required.

"I suppose you can," muttered Bobolink to himself, as he fell into the chair, utterly distracted and unhappy; "everybody can. I'm a marked, miserable man! and for what? I'll take it back. No, no! I can't now, for I've denied it!"

"Something has happened to vex you terribly, my dear husband!" cried Polly, as she returned with a small bottle of brandy.

"Well, suppose there has," replied he, in a loud and angry tone, "is a man accountable to his wife for every moment of his life? You've had such a smooth road all your life that the first rut breaks your axle. Come, don't mind me, Polly! I don't mean to worry you, but — but you see that I'm a little sprung. Leave me to myself, there's a good girl! Come, kiss me before you go. Ha! ha! I'll make a lady of you yet, Pol! see if I don't. Did n't you hear me tell you to go to bed?"

"Yes, Thomas, but —"

"But what ? "

"Pray, drink no more."

"I 'll drink just as much as I please ; and, moreover, I won't be dictated to by you, when I can buy your whole stock out, root and branch. I 've stood your nonsense long enough, so take my advice and start."

"O Thomas! Thomas!" cried his weeping wife, as she hurried to her little bedroom; "never did I expect this, and you 'll be sorry for it in the morning."

"Damn it! I am an unfeeling savage. ·Don't cry, Pol!" he shouted after her, as she quitted the room; "I did n't intend to hurt your feelings, and I won't drink any more, there. Say God bless you, before you go in, won't you?"

"God bless you, dear husband!" said the loving wife.

"That's right, Pol!"

As soon as Tom found himself quite alone, he looked carefully at the fastenings of the doors and windows, and, having cleared the little table of its contents, proceeded to examine the interior of the pocket-book. With a tremulous hand and a quick-beating heart, he drew it forth, starting at the slightest sound; tearing it open, he spread the thick bundle of notes before him; the spectacle seemed to dazzle his eyes; his breath became heavy and suffocating; there was more, vastly more, than he had even dreamed of.

"What do I see?" he cried, while his eyes sparkled with the fire of suddenly awakened avarice, "tens — fifties — hundreds — I do believe — thousands! I never saw such a sight before. What sound was that? I could have sworn I heard a small voice call out my name. For the first time in my life, I feel like a coward. I never yet feared to stand before a giant! now, a boy might cow me down. Pshaw! it's because I 'm not used to handling money."

Again and again, he tried to count up how much the amount was, but grew confused, and had to give it up. " Never mind how much there is," he cried at last ; " it's mine, — all mine ! Nobody saw me ; nobody knows it : nobody — but One — but One ! " he continued, looking upward for an instant, and then, clasping his hands together, and leaning his head over the money, he wept bitter tears over his great *Piece of Luck.*

CHAPTER VI.

THE WILL.

AT a splendid escritoire Mr. Granite sat, in his own room, surrounded by the luxurious appliances which wait upon wealth, however acquired. The face of the sitter is deadly pale, for he is alone, and amongst his most private papers. He has missed one, upon which the permanence of his worldly happiness hung. Diligently has he been searching for that small scrap of paper, which contained the sentence of death to his repute. O the agony of that suspense ! It could not have been abstracted, for it was in a secret part of his writing-desk, although by the simplest accident in the world it had now got mislaid ; yet was he destined not to recover it. In hastily taking out some papers, it had dropped through the opening of the desk, which was a large one, upon the carpet, where it remained, unper- ceived. In the midst of his anxious and agonized search, there was a knock at the door, and, even paler and more heart-broken than the merchant himself, Sterling tottered into the room.

" Well, my good Sterling," said the merchant, with a

great effort stifling his own apprehension, "I am to be troubled no more by that fellow's pitiful whinings. I was a fool to be over-persuaded; but benevolence is my failing, — a commendable one, I own, — but still a failing."

"I am glad to hear you say that, sir, for you now have a great opportunity to exercise it."

"Ask me for nothing more, for I have done," — interrupted Granite; fancying for an instant that he might have placed the missing document in a secret place, where he was sometimes in the habit of depositing matters of the first importance, he quitted the room hurriedly.

"Lost! lost forever! I have killed the son of my old benefactor!" cried Sterling. "He can't recover from the shock — nor I — nor I! my heart is breaking. To fall from such a height of joy into such a gulf of despair! I, who could have sold my very life to bring him happiness." At that moment his eye caught a paper which lay on the carpet, and, with the instinct of a clerk's neatness solely, he picked it up and put it on the table before him. "The crime of self-destruction is great," he continued, "but I am sorely tempted. With chilling selfishness on one side, and dreadful misery on the other, life is but a weary burden." Carelessly glancing at the paper which he had taken from the floor, he read the name of Travers; he looked closely at it, and discovered that it was an abstract of a will. Curiosity prompted him to examine it, and his heart gave one tremendous throb, when he discovered it to bear date after the one by which Henry, in a fit of anger, was disinherited by his father.

The old man fell upon his knees, and if ever a fervent, heartfelt prayer issued from the lips of mortal, he then prayed that he might but live to see that great wrong righted.

He had just time to conceal the paper within his breast, when Granite returned.

"You here yet?" he cried. "Have I not done enough to-day? What other beggarly brat do you come suing for?"

"For none, dear sir," said Sterling. "I would simply test that benevolence of which you spoke but now. The money which you sent to Travers —"

"Well, what of it?"

"I have lost!"

"Pooh! old man," continued the other, contemptuously, "don't think to deceive me by such a stale device; that's a very old trick."

"You don't believe me?"

"No."

"After so many years!" cried the old man, with tear-choked utterance.

"The temptation was too much for you," bitterly replied the merchant. The old leaven exhibited itself once more. "You remember —"

"Silence, sir!" cried the old man, drawing up his aged form into sudden erectness, while the fire of indignation illumined his lustreless eye. "The majesty of my integrity emboldens me to say that, even to you, your cruel taunt has wiped out all of feeling that I had for you. Fellow-sinner, hast thou not committed an error also?"

"Insolent! how dare you insinuate?"

"I don't insinuate; I speak out; nay, not an error, but a *crime*. I *know* you have, and can prove it."

"Away, fool! you are in your dotage."

"A dotage that shall wither you in your strength, and strip you of your ill-bought possessions," exclaimed the old man, with nearly the vigor of youth; "since humanity

15

will not prompt you to yield up a portion of your *stolen* wealth, justice shall force you to deliver it all, — ay, all ! "

" Villain ! what riddle is this ? " cried Granite, with a vague presentiment that the missing paper was in some way connected with this arraignment.

" A riddle easily solved," answered Sterling. " Behold its solution, if your eyes dare look at it ! A will, devising all the property you hold to Henry Travers ! There are dozens who can swear to my old employer's signature. Stern, proper justice should prompt me to vindicate his son's cause ; yet, I know that he would not purchase wealth at the cost of your degradation. Divide equally with him, and let the past be forgotten."

There was but one way that Granite could regain his vantage-ground, and he was not the man to shrink from it. With a sudden bound, he threw himself upon the weak old clerk, and, snatching the paper from him, exclaimed, " You shallow-pated fool ! think you that you have a child to deal with ? The only evidence that could fling a shadow across my good name would be your fragment of miserable breath, which I could take, and would, as easily as brush away a noxious wasp, but that I despise you too entirely to feel your sting. Go, both of you, and babble forth your injuries to the world ! Go, and experience how poor a conflict starveling honesty in rags can wage against iniquity when clad in golden armor ! I defy ye all ! Behold how easily I can destroy all danger to myself, and hope to him, at once." So saying, he held the paper to the lamp, and, notwithstanding the ineffectual efforts of Sterling to restrain him, continued so to hold it until a few transitory sparks were all that remained of Henry Travers's inheritance.

Sterling said not a syllable, but with a glance at the other, which had in it somewhat of inspiration, pointed upward, and slowly staggered from the room.

CHAPTER VII.

MORNING THOUGHTS.

THE early gray of dawn peeped furtively through the shutters of Tom Bobolink's home, and, as they strengthened and strengthened, fell upon a figure which could scarcely be recognized as the same joyous-hearted individual of the day before. On the floor lay Tom; the candle, which had completely burned out in its socket, close to his head; one hand grasped the empty bottle, and the other was tightly clutched within his breast.

And now another scarcely less sorrowful-looking figure is added. Polly gazes, with tearful eyes, upon the prostrate form. He is evidently in the maze of some terrible dream, for his head rolls fearfully about, his limbs are convulsed, and his breathing is thick and heavy.

Polly stooped down to awake him gently, when, at the slightest touch, he started at one bound to his feet, muttering incoherent words of terror and apprehension; his eyes rolled about wildly. He seized Polly, and held her at arms' length for an instant, until he fairly realized his actual situation, when he burst into a loud laugh, that chilled his poor wife's blood.

"Ha! ha! Pol, is that you?" he cried, wildly. "I've been a bad boy, I know; but I'll make up for it gloriously, my girl. Ugh! what a dream I've had! Ah! the darkness is a terrible time to get over when one's conscience is filling the black night with fiery eyes." Then, turning to his wife, he said, loudly : " Polly, darling, I 'm ashamed of myself ; but it will be all right by and by. You were cut out for a rich woman, Pol."

" Dear Thomas, let me be rich in the happiness of our humble home ; 't is all I ask."

" O, nonsense ! Suppose now you got a heap of money, a prize in the lottery, would n't you like to elevate your little nose, and jostle against the big bugs in Broadway ?"

" Not at the price of our comfort, Thomas," she answered, solemnly.

" You 're a fool ! Money can buy all sorts of comfort."

" What do you mean, Thomas, by those hints about money ? has anything happened ?"

" O, no, no ! " he replied quickly, turning his eyes away ; " but there 's no knowing when something might. Now I 'll try her," thought he. " It 's my dream, Pol. Shall I tell it to you ?"

" Do, my dear Tom. O, I 'm so glad to see you yourself once more ! "

" Well, dear," he continued, sitting close to her, and placing his arm around her waist, " I dreamed that, as I was returning from a job, what should I see in the street, under my very nose, but a pocket-book, stuffed full of money. Presently the owner came along. He asked me if I had found it. I said no, and came home a rich man, — O, so rich ! "

" I know your heart too well, Tom, to believe that such a thing could happen except in a dream," said his wife, to his great annoyance. He started up, and after one or two turns about the little, now untidy room, exclaimed angrily : " Why not ? I should like to know if fortune did — I mean — was to fling luck in my way, do you think I'd be such a cursed fool as not to grab at it?"

"Thomas, you have been drinking too much," said she, sadly.

"No, no," he interrupted, "not enough; give me some more."

"Not a drop, husband," she replied, seriously, and with determination. "If you will poison yourself, it shall not be through my hand."

"Don't be a fool," he cried, savagely, "or it may be the worse for you. I'm master of my own home, I think."

"Home! ah, Thomas, some evil spirit has stolen away our once happy home forever," said Polly, as she slowly and sorrowfully returned to weep in the silence of her own room.

"There has, there has," cried Tom, as she quitted him. "And this is it," — pulling out the pocket-book, which he had not left hold of for an instant, and frowning desperately at it. "Confound your skin! it's you that has stolen away our comfort. I'll take the cursed thing back; I wouldn't have Polly's eyes wet with sorrow to be made of money. I'll take it back this very blessed morning; and somehow that thought brings a ray of sunlight back to my heart." So saying, he thrust the pocket-book, as he thought, safely within his vest, but in his eagerness to take extra care of it, it slipped through, and dropped upon the floor; his mind being taken off for a moment by the entrance of Bryan, to tell him that the horse and truck were ready.

"Very well, I'm glad of it," cried Tom. "Now I'll see what the fine, bracing morning air will do for this cracked head of mine; now, then, to take this back," — and he slapped his chest, under the full impression that the pocket-book was there. "Bryan, I don't want you for half an hour; just wait till I come back, will you?"

"That I will, sir, and welcome," said Bryan, and with a merry song once more at his lip, and a cheerful good-by to Polly, to whose heart both brought comfort in her great sadness, Bobolink mounted his truck, and trotted off.

Meantime Bryan, now left alone in the room, dived into the recesses of his capacious coat-pocket, and, producing a piece of bread and cheese, moralized the while upon the pleasant change in his prospects.

"Long life to this tindher-hearted couple," said he. "Shure an' I'm on the high road to good luck at last; plenty of the best in the way of atin', and an elegant stable to sleep in, with a Christian-like quadruped for company; av I had only now a thrifle o' money to get myself some clothes, — these things does n't look well in this part of the world," — casting his eyes down in not over-delighted contemplation of his nether integuments. "A little bit o' money now would make me so happy an' industrious, I could take the buzz out of a hive o' bees. The saints bechune us and all mischief, what's that?" he continued, starting to his feet, as his glance fell upon the pocket-book which Tom had dropped. "It serves me right," he went on, his face suddenly becoming pale as paper, "to wish for any such thing. I don't want it, — it was all a mistake," cried he apologetically. "This is the Devil's work; no sooner do I let a word out o' me mouth, that I did n't mane at all at all, but the evil blaggard sticks a swadge of temptation right before me. I won't have it, — take it away."

At that instant Polly returned into the room. "Take care how you come, — don't walk this way," said Bryan. "Look!"

" What is it ? " cried Polly, in alarm.

" Timptation ! " shouted Bryan. " I was foolish enough just now to wish for a thrifle of money, and may I niver see glory if that lump of a pocket-book did n't sprout up before me very eyes."

" Pocket-book, eh ? " cried Polly, seizing it in her hands, despite of the comic apprehension of Bryan, who insisted that it would burn her fingers. The whole truth flashed across her mind at once. Tom's dream was no dream, but a reality, and the struggle in his mind whether to keep or return it had caused that miserable night. " Bryan," said she, quickly, " did you hear any one say that he had lost any money yesterday ? "

" Let me see," replied the other. " Yes, to be sure, 44 came out of the hall-door, and axed me if I saw a pocket-book."

" It must be his. Thank God for this merciful dispensation ! " cried the agitated wife. " Quick, quick, my bonnet and shawl, and come you, Bryan, you know the place ; this money must be that which was lost."

" I 'm wid you, ma'am," answered Bryan. " Who knows but that may be the identical pocket-book ? At any rate it 'll do as well if there 's as much money in it, and if there is n't, there 'll be another crop before we come back."

CHAPTER VIII.

RETRIBUTION.

SNUGLY ensconced in his own apartment, Mr. Granite had flung himself in post-prandial *abandon* into his easiest of easy-chairs. Leisurely, and with the smack of a true connoisseur, he dallied with a glass of exquisite Madeira. The consciousness of the enviable nature of his worldly position never imbued him so thoroughly as at such a moment. Business was flourishing, his health was excellent, and his son, on whom he concentrated all the affection of which his heart was capable, had recently distinguished himself at a college examination. Everything, in fact, seemed to him *couleur de rose*.

It can readily be imagined that to be disturbed at such a period of enjoyment was positive high-treason against the home majesty of the mercantile monarch.

Fancy, therefore, what a rude shock it was to his quiet, when he was informed that Mr. Sterling wished to see him on a matter of the greatest importance. "I cannot, I will not see him, or anybody," said the enraged potentate; "you know, he knows, my invariable rule. It must not be infringed, for any one whatever, much less for such a person," — and, closing his eyes in a spasm of self-sufficiency, he again subsided into calmness, slightly ruffled, however, by the outrageous attack upon his privacy.

He had just succeeded in restoring his disturbed equanimity, when he was once more startled into ill-humor by the sound of voices as if in altercation, and a sharp knock at the chamber-door.

The next instant, to his still greater surprise and anger, the old clerk, Sterling, who had been ignominiously dismissed since the last interview between him and Granite, stood before him. Every particle of his hitherto meekness and humility had apparently vanished, as for a few moments he regarded the merchant with a fixed and penetrating look.

"What villanous intrusion is this? Where are my servants? How dare they permit my home to be thus invaded?" cried Granite, with flashing eyes and lowering brow.

"I am here, not for myself," replied Sterling, calmly, "but for the victim of your rapacity, — of your terrible guilt. I have intruded upon you at this unusual time to inform you of the extremity in which Travers is placed, and from my carelessness, — my criminal carelessness. Will you not at least remedy that?"

"No!" thundered the exasperated merchant. "Your indiscreet zeal has ruined both you and those for whom you plead. I'll have nothing to do with any of ye, — begone!"

"Not before I have cautioned you that my lips, hitherto sealed for fear of injury to him, shall henceforward be opened. Why should I hesitate to denounce one who is so devoid of common charity?"

"Because no one will believe you," responded the other, with a bitter sneer. "The denunciations of a discharged servant are seldom much heeded; empty sounds will be of no avail. Proof will be needed in confirmation, and where are you to find that?"

"Ah! where, indeed! you have taken care of that; but have you reflected that there *is* a power to whom your machinations, your schemes of aggrandizement, are as flimsy as the veriest gossamer web?" solemnly ejaculated Sterling.

"Canting sways me as little as your hurtless threats. What I have I shall keep in spite of —"

"Heaven's justice?" interposed the old clerk.

"In spite of anything or everything," savagely replied the irritated merchant. "You have your final answer, nor is it in the power of angel or devil to alter it; and so, the sooner you relieve me from your presence the better I shall like it, and the better it may be for your future prospects."

"Of *my* future, God knows, I take no care ; but for the sake of those poor young things, so cruelly left to struggle with a hard, hard world, I feel that I have strength even to oppose the stern rock of your obstinacy, almost hopeless though the effort may be. I am going," he went on, seeing the feverish impatience working in Granite's face, "but, as a parting word, remember that my dependence is not in my own ability to unmask your speciousness, or contend against the harshness of your determination. No, I surrender my case and that of my clients into His hands who never suffers the guilty to triumph to the end. The avalanche falls sometimes on the fruitfullest vineyards, as well as on the most sterile waste."

"By heaven! you exhaust my patience," roared the other, as he rung the servants' bell impetuously ; "since you will not go of your own accord, I must thrust you forth into the street like a cur."

"There shall be no need of that," meekly replied the clerk, turning to leave the apartment, just as the servant entered, bringing a letter for Mr. Granite.

The latter was about to address an angry sentence to the servant, when he perceived that the letter he carried was enclosed in an envelope deeply bordered with black.

His heart gave one mighty throb as he snatched it, — tearing it open, and gasping with some terrible presentiment of evil, he but glanced at the contents, and with a fearful shriek fell prostrate.

Sterling rushed to his side, and, with the aid of the servant, loosed his neckcloth, and placed him in a chair, using what immediate remedies he could command in the hope of restoring animation. It was some minutes before the

stricken man, clutched from his pride of place in the winking of an eyelid, gave signs of returning vitality. During
his unconsciousness, Sterling ascertained from the open
letter lying at his feet, that the merchant's son, the sole
hope of his existence, for whom he had slaved and toiled,
set at naught all principle, and violated even the ties of
kindred and of honesty, had died suddenly at college.
No previous illness had given the slightest shadow of an
apprehension. He had quietly retired to his bed at his
usual hour on the previous night, and in the morning was
found stark and cold. None knew the agony which might
have preceded dissolution. No friendly tongue was nigh
to speak of consolation, no hand to do the kindly offices
of nature.

Slowly and painfully the wretched parent returned to
consciousness, and, with it, the terrible reality of his
bereavement. Glaring around him fiercely, " Where am
I ? — what is this ? — why do you hold me ? " he cried,
madly. At this instant his glance fell upon the fatal
letter. " O God ! I know it all, — all ! My son ! my
son ! " Turning upon Sterling, fiercely, he grasped him
by the throat. " Old man," he cried, " you have murdered him ! you, and that villain Travers ! " Then he
relaxed his grip, and, in an agony of tears, fell to supplication. " It cannot be, — it shall not be ! Oh ! take me
to him. What am I to do ? Sterling, my old friend,
O, forgive me ! — pity me ! — let us away ! " He tried to
stand, but his limbs were paralyzed. " The judgment has
fallen —.I feared it — I expected it, but not so suddenly
— it may be that there is still hope — hope, though ever
so distant. Perhaps a quick atonement may avert the
final blow. Quick, Sterling — give me paper, and pen."
They were brought. " Now write," he continued, his

voice growing fainter and fainter : "I give Travers all, — all, — if this late repentance may be heard, and my son should live. I know I can rely on his benevolence. Quick, let me sign it, for my strength is failing fast."

With extreme difficulty, he appended his signature to the document Sterling had drawn up at his desire. When it was done, the pen dropped from his nerveless grasp, his lips moved for an instant as though in prayer, — the next, he was — nothing !

CHAPTER IX.

SUNLIGHT.

OUR scene shifts back to Mrs. Grimgriskin's elegant establishment, where poor Travers's affairs are once more in a very dilapidated state, as may be inferred from the conversation now progressing.

"People as can't pay," said the now curt landlady, smoothing down an already very smooth apron, "need n't to have no objections, I think, to turn out in favor of them as can. I 'm a woman of few words, — very few indeed. I don't want to make myself at all disagreeable; but impossibles *is* impossibles, and I can't provide without I have the means to do so with."

"My good lady," interposed Travers, "do pray give me a little time; my friend Sterling has again applied to Mr. Granite —"

"Pooh ! I 'm sick of all such excuses ; one word for all, — get your trunks ready. I 'd rather lose what you owe me than let it get any bigger, when there 's not the remotest chance, as I can see, for its payment; and, dear me, how lucky ! I declare there's the very truckman who came the other day. I'll tell him to stop, for I don't mind giving you all the assistance I can, conveniently with my own interest."

So saying, she hailed Tom Bobolink, who was indeed looking somewhat wistfully towards the house. He was just cogitating within his mind what excuse he could make to get into the place, and so rid himself of his unfortunate good fortune at once.

" Your trunks, I presume from appearance, won't take a long time to get ready," said the delicate Grimgriskin. " Here, my man; just come in here," she continued, as Tom, in a state of considerable trepidation, entered the room; "this young man will have a job for you."

The poor wife now joined Travers, and, on inquiring the cause of the slight tumult, was told by Henry that she must prepare to seek an asylum away from the hospitable mansion which had recently afforded them a shelter.

" Come, my love," said he, with a tolerable effort at cheerfulness, " let us at once leave this mercenary woman's roof."

" Mercenary, indeed !" the landlady shrieked after them, as they entered their own room. " Because a person won't suffer themselves to be robbed with their eyes open, they're mercenary. The sooner my house is cleared of such rubbish, the better. Mercenary indeed ! " — and with an indignant toss of her false curls, she flounced out of the room.

" Now for it !" cried Tom; "the coast is clear; what the deuce shall I do with it ? I dare not give it openly, suppose I say I found it under the sofa. Egad, that will do famously ; here goes." So saying, he plunged his hand into his bosom, and to his horror and consternation it was

not there. "O miserable, miserable wretch! I 've lost it,
I 've lost it! what is to become of me!" In vain he
searched and searched; it was gone. "O, how can I
face Polly again?" he groaned. "My life is made unhappy forever; cursed, cursed luck! That ever my eyes
fell upon the thing at all! — Ha!" a shadowy hope flitted
across him, that he might have left it at home. "Could I
have been so drunken a fool as to leave it behind me?
if so, where is it now? At all events, I must go back
as fast as I can, for if I cannot recover it, my God! I
shall go mad." With a few big jumps he reached the
street, and, hastily mounting his truck, drove rapidly
home, unmindful of the public observation his demented
look and unusual haste produced.

A short time after Tom's sudden departure, which was
a perfect mystery to Mrs. Grimgriskin, and also to Henry
and his wife, a timid ring was heard at the hall door, and
soon Travers, to whom every sound brought increase of
apprehension, trembled as he became aware of an altercation between his irate landlady and the new-comers,
whoever they were.

"I tell you I must see 44, the man that had the thrunks
goin' away a few days agone," said an unmistakably Irish
voice, rich and round.

"O, if you please, ma'am!" placidly continued a small,
silvery one.

The dispute, however, was very suddenly cut short by
the owner of the loud voice exclaiming, "Arrah, get out o'
the road, you cantankerus witch of Endher," and O'Bryan
and Polly rushed up the stairs without further ceremony.
The door of Travers's room was flung open. "Ha! ha!"
cried O'Bryan, "there he is, every inch of him; that 's
44; long life to you! and it 's glad I am I 've found you,

and glad you 'll be yourself, I 'm thinkin', if a trifle o' money will do yez any good."

" What 's the matter with you, my friend ? what do you seek from me ? " demanded Travers.

" O, sir, I beg your pardon for breaking in upon you so suddenly," said Polly, " but have you lost any money ? "

" I have, indeed," replied Henry, " a large sum. Do you know anything about it ? "

" Yes, sir," cried Polly, with a radiant flash of her eye. " Here it is " ; — handing over the wallet, with its contents, with a sigh of the greatest possible relief. " Tell me one thing, sir," she hesitatingly went on, " was it — was it — taken from you ? "

" No, my good woman, it was lost by an old friend of mine, — dropped, he believes, in the street."

" It was, sir, just as you say, thank heaven for it ! Yes, sir ; my husband found it. Is it all there, sir ? O, pray relieve me by saying it is ! "

" Yes, every penny."

" Then, sir, whatever joy you may feel at its restoration cannot equal what I feel at this moment," said Polly, while the tears gushed forth unrestrainedly from her eyes.

" Here, my good woman, you must take a portion and give it to your honest husband," said Henry, handing to her a liberal amount of the sum.

" Not a shilling, sir, not a shilling," Polly firmly repeated. " I hate to look at it."

" Then would you, my friend, take some reward," continued he, addressing O'Bryan.

" Is it me ? not av you were me father, I would n't," said the Irishman, with a look of horror. " I know where it came from ; bedad, I know the very soil it sprouted out of. I 'll tell you how it was, sir. You see I was sittin' by meself, and, like an ungrateful blaggard as I am, instead of thankin' the blessed heavens for the good luck that had fell a-top o' me, what should I do but wish I had a bit o' money, for to dress up my ugly anatomy, when all at once that swadge of temptation dropped on the floor before my very face."

"Don't heed him, sir, he knows not what he talks about," said Polly. "It is all as I told you, sir. My husband — "

She was interrupted by O'Bryan, who cried, "Here he comes. May I niver stir if he does n't, skelpin' along the street in a state of disthractitude ; by me sowl, it 's here he 's coming, too."

"Yes, I know," said Henry, "he is employed, I believe, by our worthy landlady, to remove our things."

At this moment Tom burst into the room, but on seeing Polly and O'Bryan he stopped short, as if arrested by a lightning stroke. "You here, Polly? have you heard of my crime?" he said, wildly : but she restrained him by gently laying her hand upon his arm.

"Yes, Tom," she said, quietly, "I know all about it, and so does this gentleman. I have restored the money."

"What?" exclaimed Bobolink, while a thrill of joy went through his frame ; "is this true?"

"Hush! husband, dear, hush !" she continued; "I did as you told me, you know. I have brought and given back the lost money to its owner. You know you left it at home for me to take."

"Ah, Polly, I wish I could tell this fellow that," said Tom, laying his hand upon his heart; "but I did intend to give it back. I did, by all my hopes of happiness."

"I know you did, my dear Tom," replied Polly, earnestly. " Your true heart could not harbor a bad thought long."

" My good friend," said Travers, approaching the truckman. " Your wife has refused any reward for this honest act."

" She's right, sir, she's right," interrupted the other.

" At least you'll let me shake you by the hand, and proffer you my friendship?"

" I can't, Pol, I can't," said Tom, aside, to his wife. "I'm afraid — I'm half a scoundrel yet — I know I am; but I've learned a wholesome lesson, and while I have life I'll strive to profit by it."

Urged to it by Polly, he did, however, shake hands with Travers and his wife, just as old Sterling, his face shrouded in gloom, and Mrs. Grimgriskin, stiff and tigerish, entered the room.

" Ah, Sterling, my good old friend, rejoice with us! This honest fellow has found, and restored the money lost," said Travers, gaily; " but how is this? you don't join in our gladness. Has that old rascal — "

" Hold!" interrupted the old clerk, in an earnest voice, and impressive manner; " Heaven has avenged your wrongs in a sudden and fearful manner. Mr. Granite is dead."

" Dead!" exclaimed Henry, in a subdued tone; " with him let his misdeeds be buried. His son will perhaps be more merciful; he will inherit — "

" He has inherited — his father's fate," solemnly replied the old clerk. " Justice may slumber for a while, but retribution must come at last. You are now, by the merchant's will, his sole heir."

" Ho, ho!" thought Mrs. Grimgriskin, who had been an attentive listener, "I'm a woman of few words, but if I had been a woman of less, perhaps it would be more to my

16

interest ; but sudden millionnaires are usually generous " ;
— and so, smoothing her feline demeanor into quietude,
she approached Travers. "Allow me most sincerely to
congratulate you upon your good fortune," she simpered.
"*Apropos*, the first floor is somewhat in arrear; lovely
apartments, new carpet, bath, hot water."

"Plenty of that, I'll be bail," remarked O'Bryan ;
"arrah, howld yer prate, Mrs. Woman-of-few-words, —
don't you see there's one too many here?"

"Then why don't you go, you ignorant animal," sharply
suggested the other.

"Because I'm not the *one*."

Suffice it to say, Henry, with his young wife, and dear
old Sterling, were soon installed in a house of their own,
and, to their credit, never lost sight of the interest of Tom
Bobolink and Polly, who from that day increased in content and prosperity.

As for O'Bryan, the last intimation we had of his well-
doing was the appearance of sundry gigantic street-bills
which contained the following announcement : —

VOTE FOR

THE PEOPLE'S FRIEND.

O'BRYAN,

FOR ALDERMAN.

ROMANCE AND REALITY.

CHAPTER I.

IT was morning in the neighborhood of Belgrave Square, that is to say, fashionable morning, very considerably past midday, when calls are orthodox, and belles and beaux emerge from their respective beautifying retreats. Untenanted carriages dash along in one general round of unsubstantial etiquette; visits are paid by proxy; an inch or two of enamelled pasteboard representing, frequently, dukes, earls, or marquises, perhaps fully as well as they represent their individual constituency. West End morning is a period of factitious politeness and unreal industry ; everybody is supposed to be out, but everybody is known to be at home.

Sir Henry Templeton, of Templeton, one of the wealthiest baronets of England, the deeds of whose ancestors, are they not registered in that sublimest of works, Burke's Peerage ? sat within his splendid library, so called from the fact of its containing an unlimited number of books. But what they themselves contained was matter of profoundest mystery, both to him and his household. A *moiety* of the diurnals, the Times, the Morning Post, and hebdomadally the Bull, comprised the staples of this " fine old English gentleman's" literary labors. Be it observed, that he was too good a Tory to cast a glance over the pages of any paper emanating from the opposition ; being one of those who like some one else to do their thinking, he confined his opinions to those of the leader of his own party.

He had just got to the " Hear ! hear ! " and " Great cheering ! " with which the imaginative reporter had introduced an unpretending speech of his own, which, until this moment, he has been under the disagreeable impression had been a lamentable failure.   Imagine his surprise when he finds his half-dozen scarcely intelligible phrases swollen into a goodly column of well-rounded, nicely-perioded, polysyllabic English, garnished with a Miltonic quotation, and classically tailed up with a line and a half of Homer.

" Well," said the Baronet, and not without a pardonable glow of vanity at the contemplation of his eloquence, " those reporters certainly have long ears.   I had no idea in the world that I made or could make so sensible a speech ; but I suppose I did.   In point of fact, I must have been rather luminous.   Latin, too, by Jove !   I did n't know that I could recollect so much."

In the full bloom of his *amour propre*, a footman entered and announced " Lord Sedleigh."

" At home."

In the interval between the announcement and the appearance of his lordship, as he is a stranger, perhaps I had better give you the benefit of a descriptive introduction.   The Lord Sedleigh, but newly arrived from All Souls' College, Oxford, is a tolerably fair specimen of the reputable portion of England's young nobility.   Rich without ostentation, generous without extravagance, prudent without parsimony, and learned without pedantry ; his title lent him no lustre that his virtues did not pay back with interest.

Hoping, dear reader, that you will not repent of the acquaintanceship, behold him ! he enters.   Do you not

agree with me in saying that he looks the very imperson-
ation of that oft-desecrated phrase, a *noble*-man ?

The greeting between Sedleigh and Sir Henry is hearty
and sincere. The last new singer having been discussed,
and the last *liaison* deplored, with some slight embarrassment Sedleigh broke the primary object of his call.

" Sir Harry," said he, with almost startling abruptness,
" you have a ward ? "

" Egad, Sedleigh, you 're right there," replied Sir Henry,
with a good-natured chuckle, " nor would you have erred
had you said two."

" Yes, yes, I know," rejoined the Viscount.   " But —
ah ! — I — the fact is, there 's no use in mincing the matter,
I have taken a most insurmountable interest in one."

" Lucy ? "

" No.   Arabella — pardon me — I mean Miss Myddleton."

" I 'm sorry for that, Sedleigh," replied the baronet, —
" very sorry, for I like you."

" Why ? why ? " eagerly interposed the other.   " Is she
engaged ? "

" No, not exactly that ; but — "

" But what ?   Do, for pity's sake, relieve my suspense."

" Upon my soul, Sedleigh, instead of being a neophyte
in love, one would suppose you an amorado of some years'
experience.   Ah ! in my day, people never married head
over heels.   But you don't want to hear anything about
that.   Seriously, I should like to give you encouragement
if I could, but you don't know the wild, wayward gypsy
Arabella.   Would you believe it, she 's a perfect little
Chartist, an absolute leveller, sneers at a title, and declares
that, if she ever does marry, it will be with some son of
toil, some honest yeoman.   By Jove, I don't know

whether it's that fellow Bulwer, with his cursed empty love-in-a-cottage balderdash, who has turned her little brain topsy-turvy or not, but she absolutely and positively restrains me from presenting anybody of the suitor order, who is tainted with, as she calls it, the adventitious possession of hereditary worthlessness. I'm very sorry, by George, I am! But now, there's Lucy, could n't you transfer your affection to her?"

Sedleigh, who fortunately had not heard the last morsel of mercantile philosophy, suddenly exclaimed, " She objects to a title?"

" In toto."

" Full of romance?"

" Brim."

" Do *you* object to my trying to influence her?"

"Not in the least. But, by Jove, I can't introduce you."

" I don't ask you, if I have your consent. I 'll manage the rest myself."

" That you have, Sed, my boy, and my best wishes for your success. But what do you mean to do? By Jupiter, I don't think you 'll ever get her consent."

" We shall see."

CHAPTER II.

Lucy and Arabella Myddleton were orphans, with good, though not great fortunes, — both left to the strict guardianship of their uncle, Sir Henry, the will expressly premising, that, in case either married without his consent, her fortune was to revert to the other.

There was but one year's difference in their age. Arabella
was the older, but being a blonde, with exceedingly beautiful, young-looking hair, — glossy hair, — looked many
years the junior. Lucy, on the contrary, was a beauty of a
severer nature; a magnificent brunette, with large, lustrous
eyes of the darkest hazel, and hair like a raven's wing.
Their dispositions were as opposite as were their complexions. Lucy was a proud, high-souled creature, with a step as
stately as a pet fawn, and a sort of regnant look, that plainly
kept familiarity aloof, while Arabella was all life, spirit,
elasticity, and wildness. The very soul of joy beamed from
her sparkling eyes, and mirth itself dwelt within the ringing echo of her laugh. So that, although Lucy attracted
every eye by the majesty of her appearance, and the fawn-
like gracefulness of her deportment, yet Arabella won
every heart by the yielding sweetness of her temper and
the gladsome smile that played on her lips.

Two or three mornings subsequent to that on which
the conversation mentioned in the last chapter took place,
as Arabella was leisurely strolling through the conservatory,
which opened with glass doors into the drawing-room, she
perceived a young man, plainly but elegantly dressed, with
his collar thrown back à la Byron, displaying a throat of
womanly whiteness, climb up the trellis-work, and jump at
once through the open window. Her first impulse was to
scream ; but, perceiving that the stranger was remarkably
handsome, and moreover, as she was in the act of reading
" Zanoni," her susceptible heart was predisposed for any
romantic incident. Seeing that his attention was directed
towards a bust of Byron, which ornamented the conservatory, and that she was as yet unperceived, she quietly
waited the result.

Sedleigh, for it was he, approached the bust with reverence. Giving his hair the conventional thrust back from his forehead, and flinging himself into a theatrical attitude, he exclaimed, "O thou undying one, upon whose ample brow high intellect doth sit enthroned, from whose expressive eye the lightning of the soul, the fire of genius, seems incessantly to flash, upon whose every lineament the mighty hand of nature hath irrevocably stamped the evidence of an immortal mind, — spirit of poesy, my soul doth kneel to thee!"

What an exceedingly nice young man! thought Arabella, as he, with increasing fervor, proceeded, —

"And thou wert of that tinsel throng men bow, and cringe, and fawn on, and call *lord*. *I* cannot call thee so; thy genius lifts thee higher than the highest pinnacle of rank could e'er attain. I'll call thee what thou wert, a *man*, spurning the gauds of title, — an inspired, an independent, but ah! most persecuted MAN!"

These sentiments so entirely coincided with those of the romantic Arabella, that, forgetting the time, place, her ignorance of the individual she addressed, everything except the glow of enthusiasm which his words had kindled, she flung "Zanoni" aside, and rushed forward, exclaiming, "He was! he was! You're right, sir, he was a persecuted man."

Sedleigh started with well-simulated astonishment, exclaiming, in a faltering tone, "Miss Myddleton, here — I — pray your pardon. I —"

"Don't apologize, I pray," said the rapt girl, "sweet poet — but —" Suddenly recollecting herself, and blushing deeply, she continued, "I beg your pardon. You are a stranger, — at least, I do not remember having had the pleasure of an introduction."

"Alas, never!" exclaimed Sedleigh, sighing profoundly.

"But that I *have* seen you before, I am certain."

"Many a time, and in many a guise hast thou observed me : nor didst thou know that all those varied forms contained but one devoted heart."

"Indeed ! what mean you ? "

"As at the balmy twilight hour the other eve you walked, a mendicant sailor you did encounter, with leg of wood, a pitiable patch across his face, — 't was I. I asked for charity. You gave me sixpence, but the coin was naught compared with the sweet sigh of sympathy which hallowed the donation. In menial garb for months I 've waited on thee, paid by a look, enchanted by a smile. At Beulah-Spa, a gypsy I did personate, and as I gazed upon thy beauteous palm, I promised thee what from my soul I wished, and still do wish, — a long, a joyous, cloudless, sunny life."

"I don't recollect the sailor or the gypsy," said Arabella, feeling, as he spoke, in a strange, incomprehensible flutter, for his voice was sweet, and his manner peculiarly impressive.

"Sweet lady," he continued, "will you deign to pardon the presumption of one, who, although a simple unit from the presumptuous herd, yet dares to utter his aspiring thoughts within thy hearing ? "

"How like Claude Melnotte he speaks," thought Arabella, rather flatteringly, it must be confessed ; it was sufficient to show that Bulwer was a piece of golden-colored glass within the windows of her soul. "Would it be too much, sir," said she, in that matter-of-fact way which romancers frequently fall into, as the exception, — "would it be too much to inquire who and what you are ? "

The question was almost too abrupt for Sedleigh, too earthly, now that his imagination was abroad upon the

wings of fancy.   However, with a still more extensive
respiration, he replied, —

"Madam, to be frank with you, I'm a gentleman; but
alas! the spirit and plaything of hard destiny, which, had
it emptied all its store of woes upon my head, makes
ample recompense by now permitting me to speak to thee.
O, let the soft music of thy voice, steeping my soul in
melody, bid me not despair.   'T is strength of love alone
that lends me boldness, for I feel, I know, that I am
unworthy of you.   The possessor only of a poor cottage-
home, where love might make its rosy dwelling, but where
worldly riches enter not."

Arabella felt strangely excited.   Here was the realiza-
tion of her every wish, untitled, wealthy only in abundant
love.   She hesitated, and in accordance with the veracious
proverb, in that moment's unguardedness, Cupid, the
vigilant, abstracted her heart forever.

Sedleigh was crafty enough not to prolong this introductory visit, which was meant but to show Arabella that she
had a devoted adorer.   Affecting to hear an approaching
footstep, he cried, in an agitated voice, "Some one comes!
O, do not send me away without a ray of hope to light
existence!"

"What can I say?" replied the really agitated Arabella.

"That you do not hate me?"

"No."

"You'll let me see you again?"

"No."

"I must, I must.   O, say but yes!   Remember the
happiness or misery of a life depends upon your answer."

Arabella was most imprudently silent; for Sedleigh,
construing it advantageously, exclaimed, "O, thanks, ten
thousand thanks, for that voiceless eloquence!   And now,

for a time, farewell, my first, my only, everlasting love, farewell." And hastily opening the window, he withdrew by the same uncomfortable way in which he had entered, leaving Arabella in a fearful maze, but whether of joy or apprehension she hardly knew. But the chord of sympathy had been touched, and still vibrated to her very heart; for she acknowledged that, of all men, he was the only one for whom she had ever felt the slightest approach to a sentiment of love.

Now would she laugh at the absurdity of being so taken with a mere stranger, and suddenly find her recollection dwelling on his features, — thus struggling like a bird in the net of the fowler. Slowly and silently she returned to the drawing-room, hearing, as she went, the loud, hearty laugh of her uncle in the library, little thinking that she had furnished him with matter for such uproarious mirth; for Sedleigh was at that moment relating to Sir Henry the success of his first interview, and the tears rolled down the old gentleman's crimsoned cheeks as he listened.

Next day Arabella was very busy at her toilette, and Lucy, curious to know what could so occupy her attention, crept stealthily across, and, peeping over her sister's shoulder, beheld the half-finished likeness of a remarkably nice-looking young man, with beautiful dark hair, and brilliant eyes. Pulling down the corners of her mouth with a good-gracious-me sort of an expression, she quietly returned to her chair and said nothing, — sensible girl!

CHAPTER III.

FOR several weeks had those secret interviews — so secret that they were known to the whole household — occurred, and Arabella, who tolerated them at first, from the mere caprice of a romantic disposition, soon began to look forward to their coming with what one might call a heart-hunger. The truth was, she loved Sedleigh, the — as she imagined — poor, unfriended youth, with an affection the most ardent and overwhelming, and now, for the first time, a shade of gloom dimmed the radiance of her brow as the thought incessantly arose before her that Sir Henry could never, by any possibility, be induced to countenance a match so unworthy. Many a time did she determine to throw herself on her knees before her uncle, and try the unequal contest of woman's tears against a man's will, but as often did her heart fail her, at the full certainty of refusal, and the consequent dismissal of Sedleigh.

Poor Arabella's perturbation of mind and uneasy demeanor, as one might suppose, were matter of pleasant observation to Sir Henry and Lucy, who, in full possession of everything that occurred, could construe every look and action of her who thought herself the very focus of mystery, the very incarnation of romance.

It was now near the time at which her lover usually made his stolen visits, and Arabella, making some trivial excuse, rose, and, with a beating heart, sought the conservatory, Sir Henry and Lucy stealing quietly after, and ensconcing themselves within a seeable, though not a hearable distance, — treasonable encroachment upon the precincts of Eros, King of Hearts.

Not long had Arabella to wait. With a mysterious glance around, and with a noiseless, stealthy step, Sedleigh approached.

"Dearest love," whispered he, most tenderly, "again am I in the presence of my soul's ray, again the cheering influence of those beaming eyes imbues my seared and withered heart," — for as he was making love medicinally, he was no homœopathist. "O," he continued, with a glance of unspeakable affection, "how have I languished for this blissful hour! a blank, a void, a dull, cheerless nullity has been the intervening time since last we parted, and were it not that thy bright image ever dwelling here within my heart of hearts shot through my breast a ray of joy, and kindled hope within my soul, despair and death had, ere now, claimed their victim."

Now Sedleigh thought, at first, that by enacting these scenes of high-wrought and overcharged romance, he would disabuse the mind of Arabella, and thereby induce her to listen to him in his real character; but he was much mistaken, and but little knew the page he had to study; for, as the purest, deepest love had taken possession of her enthusiastic young heart, she looked on all he said or did as the perfection of their kind. O bounteous dispensation of the heart's disposer, that so inclines and tempers each to each, that to its own choice the enraptured soul can find no parallel! What, a short time since, even in the midst of her romance, she would have deemed absurd, now, in the very soberness of her reflective moments, her partial heart found full excuse for — only because his was the expression of a true and sacred love, although in an exaggerated mask.

"The sun will warm, though it do not shine."

This interview, lengthened out to an unprecedented extent, — outstaying even curiosity, for Sir Henry and Lucy were tired in about half an hour, — brought a definite issue, which may be inferred from the following conversation that took place in the library a short time later.

"Well, Sed, my boy, my gay deceiver, how do you get on, eh?"

"Famously!"

"Does she surrender at discretion?"

"No. Most indiscreetly."

"How so?"

"Be in the drawing-room, but not in view, at twelve o'clock to-night, and you shall see."

"Why, zounds! You don't mean that you are going to —"

"Gretna Green, by the Lord Harry."

"Ha! ha! ha!" roared the Baronet. "Give me your hand; by Jove, that's capital. An ELOPEMENT EXTRAOR-DINARY, a young lady running off with a Viscount and ten thousand a year, and thinking that she's throwing away a good fifteen thousand to unite her fate with a cottage-keeper's grow-your-own-vegetable sort of a fel-low! Ha! ha! ha! try that port! It's too good, by George, it is." Whether the Baronet meant the wine or the joke was doubtful and immaterial.

The evening wore on, and all around bore an aspect of abstraction. A sort of mysterious atmosphere seemed to envelop the place; never were the girls so silent, and never did the Baronet go off into so many unaccountable explosions of laughter without condescending to explain the various witticisms. At last Arabella rose, and, as was her custom before retiring for the night, embraced her sister and her uncle. There were tears in her eyes as she gave Lucy a long, long kiss; but when she approached Sir Henry, something again appeared to tickle him amazingly, for it was full five minutes before he subsided sufficiently to receive his ward's affectionate salute.

"Good-night, you little — pooh! hoo! ha! ha!" and off he went again.

"What *can* be the matter, uncle?" gravely inquired Lucy, with the slightest possible smile resting on her proud lip.

"Nothing, child, nothing; a good joke I heard to-day, that's all; a capital joke. But come, 't is foolish to laugh so much," — and with an altered, and now serious countenance, the good, kind-hearted old gentleman kissed Arabella affectionately, saying, "God for ever bless you, my pet! good night," — and she retired.

Some two hours after, the lights being all out in the drawing-room save one small lamp, and Lucy and Sir Henry, with a cambric handkerchief stuffed into his mouth, snugly concealed behind the ample window-curtains, a soft step was heard gently approaching, and the little fluttering run-away crept into the apartment. It was as much as the Baronet and Lucy could do to restrain their emotion as they saw the seeming giddy child fling herself upon her knees, and, burying her face in her hands, burst into an agony of tears.

A few moments after, a signal was heard. Hastily wiping away the pearly drops from her eyes, Arabella started to her feet, threw a note on the table, and, snatching up thence two miniatures, one of her uncle and the other of her sister, kissed them fervently, and then placed them in her bosom.

Sedleigh joined her, and it was with much and earnest

persuasion that he at length induced her to accompany him. They went out, and, as they crossed the garden, Arabella thought she heard either a smothered laugh or a sob, or both.

Crack went the postilion's whip, and off they dashed, northward, at the rate of twelve miles an hour. They need not have been in so great a hurry, — nobody followed them.

CHAPTER IV.

GENTLE reader, oblige me by filling up the hiatus as your imagination may suggest, and skip with me three weeks. Having done so, now let me show you the interior of a small, but for the life of me I cannot say comfortable, cottage in Devonshire, the humble residence of Mr. and Mrs. Sedleigh. He is sitting on a chair, dressed in a gamekeeper's sort of fustian jacket, cord continuations, and high leather gaiters. A gun rests on his arm, and a magnificent pair of thorough-blooded pointers recline at his feet, with mouths all agape, and tongues quivering in proof of recent exercise. Seated opposite to him is his sister, the Lady Emma Sedleigh, her noble contour but ill-concealed beneath a maid-of-all-work's coarse habiliments. You may hear Arabella in the adjacent small garden, singing like a bird, and as happy as one. Now for our story.

"Well, brother," rather pettishly exclaims the Lady Emma, " this notable scheme of yours does n't promise much success. Just listen to that extraordinary wife of yours, warbling away as though this were a palace, and not an odious, unendurable hovel."

"Patience, Emma love," replies Sedleigh, "all will yet be as I wish. I have noticed already *moments* of discomfort; they 'll soon swell to *hours*, hours to *days*, and then for my lesson. Depend upon it, we shall soon contrive to make her feel uncomfortable."

"Do, do, for gracious sake," replied the petted child of fortune, who undertook this matter as much from the excitement of novelty as for sisterly love; and now the former had passed away, the latter scarcely sufficed to keep her to her promise.

"I have begun already," replied Sedleigh, "by placing a brick across the chimney, — and see the result," as a puff of smoke clouded into the room.

"O, delicious!" exclaimed his sister, clapping her hands, "she 'll never be able to endure that. Hark! she 's coming; I must return to my *place* in the hope of soon changing it"; and the Lady Emma, or rather *Mary*, as she is now called by that familiar term, vacated the parlor for the poor kitchen, heartily sick and tired of her *situation*.

In bounded Arabella, radiant with happiness, and all aglow with health. "My own, own husband," she exclaimed, "never did I in my wildest dreams anticipate the fulness of joy that now inhabits my soul."

"My beautiful, my wife," ardently responded Sedleigh, "happiness is but a fleeting shadow, and its opposite may obtrude itself even among these rosy bowers."

"How! you look sorrowful, my Sedleigh. Dear husband, has anything happened to vex? any light word of mine? O, I would not bring the slightest shadow of a cloud upon thy brow for millions of worlds," tenderly exclaimed Arabella, the mere alteration in his tone chasing her smile away upon the instant.

Sedleigh, with difficulty obliging himself to go through

17

with his design, said, "The fact is, dearest, I am rather close pressed, in the pecuniary way, just at present. I owe a trifle; my creditor has been here, and — "

"Pay him! pay him, certainly. I will myself," energetically cried Arabella, — but suddenly checked by the thought, for the first time in her life, of being without the means.

"But no matter," rejoined Sedleigh, "that I can put off, but present wants must be supplied; dinner is imperative. I must away and try and shoot some game if his lordship's well-stocked grounds be not too closely watched."

"Are you obliged to leave me, Sedleigh?" said she with a small pout.

"Else we have no dinner," he replied. Giving her an affectionate embrace, he left her to digest this, her first practical lesson, in the comforts of "Love in a Cottage," and, to say the truth, poor Arabella felt at this moment very far from happy; the leaves began to drop from the roses and the concealed thorns to make themselves seen and felt.

It was in this mood, that, on sitting down to reflect, a puff of smoke descended the chimney, covering her in a black cloud of soot. Putting her hands over her eyes, she screamed for Mary several times, stamping her pretty little foot in positive anger. At last, with the characteristic listlessness of her *rôle*, the Lady Emma crawled into the room. Wiping her hands on her apron, she drawled out, "Did you call, mum?"

"Call, mum," replied Arabella, with a rather dangerous expression of eye, — "I did *call* enough to waken the dead."

"If they were n't too far gone, I s'pose, mum," provokingly rejoined the maid-servant.

" No impertinence ! "

" What do you please to want, mum ? "

" Why, don't you see ? " said Arabella, pettishly.

" See what, mum ? "

" The chimney."   .

" Yes, mum."

" It smokes."

" Law, *do* it, mum ?   Well, so it *do*, a little, I declare,"
said she, as another volume of sooty vapor swept into the
place. " But don't take on, mum," she continued, " it
always do smoke when the wind is in one direction, and
it generally almost always is, so that you 'll soon get used
to it."

" Good heaven," said Arabella, " I cannot endure this ;
I must go out into the air.   Come here ! put my collar
straight."

" Can't, mum."

" Why not ? "

" Cos my hands is all black-leaded," said the lady-ser-
vant, going out of the room with an internal consciousness
that matters were progressing to a climax.

And now poor Arabella began seriously to deplore the
dark prospect which rose before her imagination.   Her
little feet went pat pat upon the uncarpeted floor, and, if
she had been asked at that moment how she felt, she
would have replied, decidedly miserable ; but her true
woman's heart soon conquered every discomfort, and she
said within herself, 't is my Sedleigh's fate ; if he can
endure it, so shall *I*, without a murmur.   So that, when he
returned, instead of finding her, as he supposed he should,
in sorrow, her beautiful face greeted him with smiles more
gladsome than ever.

It was some days before Sedleigh could make up his

mind to bring matters to a crisis. He was becoming him-self rather fatigued with his rustic life, and so, with a view to investigate the state of Arabella's feelings, he one morning seated her beside him, saying, " Now, dearest love, since you have had some experience in this our homely country life, tell me frankly how you like it. Does it come up to, or exceed, your expectation ? "

" Sedleigh," she replied in a tone of earnest seriousness, " I married *you*, and not your station, swearing at the holy altar to be yours, in health or in sickness, in joy or in sorrow. If I can shed one ray of happiness upon your onward path, though ne'er so humble, 't will be my glory and my pride."

" But now," continued he, " were I to find myself within a somewhat better sphere, were fortune to bless me with increase of means, — say, now that by some strange freak a title were to fall to me."

" Sedleigh, husband," replied Arabella, with enthusiasm, " I *would* not love you *less* were you a beggar, I *could* not love more were you a king."

" I 'd like the former chance before the latter," smil-ingly rejoined Sedleigh. " Heaven reward your sweet, disinterested love. I *have* a somewhat larger and more commodious house ; it has just been put in order at some little cost ; we shall remove there, dearest, after dinner. 'T is but a short walk from this. Now for our meal. Mary ! "

In vain they called ; Mary had incontinently vanished, and, with her, all hope of dinner.

" Never mind," said Sedleigh, " we *may* find something at the other house."

" I hope so," gayly responded Arabella, " for I am furi-ously hungry."

Delighted at the anticipation of being anywhere out of the atmosphere of smoky chimneys, Arabella put on her little plain straw bonnet, and, taking the arm of her husband, sallied forth. In a few minutes they came in view of a splendid castellated mansion, situated in the centre of a spacious park, with herds of deer browsing here and there, upon the velvety grass.

"Goodness me, what a lovely place!" said Arabella, as they entered; "may we go through here?"

"As often as you please, dearest," replied Sedleigh, "the owner, I think I may venture to say, will not interdict you."

"Indeed, then I shall take many a walk beneath the shade of those fine old elms," replied Arabella.

"I hope so, most sincerely," replied Sedleigh, "and I too: and then we *might* fancy this delightful place our own, and stroll about as though we had a right."

They now neared the entrance to the castle, and Arabella, perceiving that the marble steps were lined with servants in rich liveries, shrunk timidly back. But what was her surprise to find her husband walk directly towards the group!

"You are not going in there, Sedleigh!" she cried in a voice of alarm, a sensation akin to fear creeping over her.

"Yes, dearest," he replied, "I know some persons connected with the household. Indeed, I believe you have met them occasionally; so come, — fear nothing."

In a sort of wondering maze, Arabella entered, and, leaning heavily on the arm of her husband, traversed the statued hall and noble picture-gallery. As she neared an inner apartment, a sound proceeded from it that made her thrill with vague, indefinite anticipation. It was a peculiar

laugh.   She could have sworn that she knew it, and
she was right.   A pair of large folding-doors flew open,
and in a rich, elegantly appointed room, mellowed by the
soft light of a glorious tinted window, Arabella almost
fainted with overpowering excitement as she beheld, rushing forward to embrace her, Sir Henry Templeton and
her sister Lucy.   Scarcely had she recovered the shock
of pleasurable surprise, when the quondam Mary, splen-
didly attired, flung her arms around her neck, exclaiming,
"Dear sister, let me be the first to welcome the Vis-
countess Sedleigh to the domain of her husband.   His, by
right of heritage, hers by right of conquest."

Arabella gave one glance of unutterable love at her *lord*,
through eyes made brighter by tears

> "That came not from a soul-cloud charged with grief,
> But were from very over-brightness shed,
> Like heart-drops falling from a sun-lit sky."

KIT COBB, THE CABMAN.

A STORY OF LONDON LIFE.

INTRODUCTION.

In which the Author frankly acknowledges his Ignorance.

IT is not in my power to give you the slightest account of my hero's birth and early experience; indeed, it would be very hard if I were called upon to do anything of the kind, seeing that my worthy friend Kit himself was equally ignorant upon the subject. His recollection did not carry him back further than his tenth year; why it took so limited a retrospect it is impossible for me to determine; perhaps he was a *forward* boy, too strongly imbued with the go-a-headativeness of Yankeetude to waste time in Parthian glances, — perhaps, like Swift, and other great geniuses, whose juvenile dulness has become matter of history, he indulged in no precocious draughts upon memory. However the reader may exercise his ingenuity in establishing an hypothesis, I can't say more than I know, and, what's more, I won't; but should you speculate on the subject, you can bear in mind that the probability is he must have been tolerably easy in his circumstances, for early discomfort makes a notch in the memory not easy planed off. How far that may have been the result more of a contented disposition than of the velvet accessories of wealth can, I think, be safely de-

duced from the relation of a simple fact. He wore his first
pair of shoes, strong, double-soled, and hob-nailed, after
he had attained his fourteenth year, — that is to say, there
or thereabout, for poor Kit never had a birthday but once,
and he could n't even swear to that, for no man can give
evidence in a case which concerneth himself. That he
had a father we have only the same circumstantial proof,
utterly invalid in a legal point of view, and, inasmuch as
no clearer testimony could be adduced to establish the fact
of maternity, according to the unerring dictum of English jurisprudence, he was an absolute nullity ; to be sure
he lived, and breathed, and moved, but of what avail was
that, — *he could n't prove it.*

Poor Kit, he certainly was a waif upon the road of life,
a stray fly in the great sugar-hogshead of the world, a thing
of chance, an incomprehensible atom; for aught he, or
any, know to the contrary, he might have been "evolved
from contingent matter," hatched in the "Eccalobeion," or
won at a raffle ! No matter, there he was, an inexplicable
human riddle, a fine, fat, chubby, laughing, squalling,
hungry mystery !

CHAPTER I.

Which is to be hoped will give you a better Opinion of the Author, and of his Subject.

A COLD, gray, drizzly, uncomfortable November morning began reluctantly to tint the eastern sky with a dull
something which might be almost mistaken for light, holding a deadly-lively contest for precedence with sundry
pale, sleepy-looking gas-jets that reeled and flickered in
their lamps with a tipsy, up-all-night sort of undulation.

Silence brooded over the west end of the town, broken only by the echoing tread of the ever-watchful police-man, and now and then the sudden rattle of a furiously driven cab, containing some belated son of Nox, some titled ruffian, who, sheltered by a name and wealth, defies all law, owns no restraint, and breaks through every social tie, upheld by the mean-souled worshippers of Mammon. Save these, all was stillness; but in the abodes of wretchedness and continual labor, to which I am about to conduct the reader, all was astir.

Perhaps no other city on the face of the globe can par-allel the utter destitution and misery, both apparent and actual, which are to be found in the very core of London. Within this great metropolis, surrounded by evidences of superabundant wealth, with the palaces of the nobility bounding it on one side, and the scarcely less splendid mansions of the merchant kings on the other, stands, or rather rots, the parish of St. Giles, the very focus of squalid poverty, the nucleus of disease, the nurse of vice. Year after year has it been denounced as the hot-bed of conta-gion, the "normal" school of crime. Yet there it re-mains, and will remain unless the hand of Heaven, by the purification of fire, averts a second plague.

In a wretched stable, in the most wretched lane of this wretched neighborhood, the sound of a merry voice might be heard, in startling contrast to the surrounding scene. The singer is Kit Cobb, now about fifteen years old, and the happy owner of a hack cab and horse. Although the most of his life hitherto had been passed in lounging about, running of messages, pulling down shutters, with intervals of dangerous inactivity, yet he had curiously es-caped the vitiating influence of the society into which fate had cast him.

About a year previous to this time, a large cab-owner, struck by the boy's frank countenance, had engaged him as a driver, and, as a reward for his integrity and industry, sold him a vehicle, consenting to receive payment for it weekly, in small instalments.

Last night the purchase was made, and this morning behold him. Alexander the Great, when Darius owned him conqueror, Napoleon, when with his own hands he placed the crown of Charlemagne upon his head, were not a whit more happy than poor Kit Cobb, when, in the extravagance of his joy, with eyes streaming, and a choking voice, he cried, "Horse and cab, all mine, mine!" And then he would laugh, and dance, and sing, with all his might, now squaring up at the horse and punching him as though he had n't a greater enemy in the world, now hugging and kissing the brute's long face with most alarming emphasis.

He was fond of the animal; the truth is it was his first affection, and I'm happy to say the feeling was reciprocated; for, as Kit would rub his horse down, pluck his ears, and bestow such like evidences of partiality, the animal would neigh, and sniff, and wink knowingly at him, as much as to say, "You're my particular friend, Kit; stick to me, and I'll stick to you."

And Kit held an interesting conversation with his favorite, but, inasmuch as they were both rather excited, it's not worth while to relate the substance of it; indeed, it was very well for them that they were not observed by the keeper of a lunatic asylum, for no madman could possibly exceed the extravagance of Kit's demeanor, and if ever a horse deserved a strait waistcoat, it was Old Turk.

CHAPTER II.

Which is Short, but (or else the Author flatters himself) Pithy.

GENTLE reader, with your kind permission, we jump two years, and find, in addition to his horse and cab, Kit has persuaded an unfortunate little girl that he could n't live without her; she, with the innocent simplicity of her sex, believed him, and they were married. Our poor friend's worldly store was but little augmented by this procedure, for his bride brought him, by way of dower, one stuff gown, one doubtful colored silk ditto, one imitation French shawl, one Dunstable bonnet, with other smaller matters, not mentioned in the category, and all settled tightly on herself; but no matter, Kit loved her with an overweening love, and, when the heart is driver, prudence gets the whip. The result of Kit's domestic arrangement was, in due time, a duodecimo edition, so that there were soon three mouths to provide for, besides that of Old Turk, the most expensive of all; for though Kit might and did stint his own appetite, yet he held it part of his religion that the horse should have no cause to complain for lack of food.

Things began to look gloomy; the outgoings exceeded the incomings, notwithstanding their most stringent exertions; for the first time Kit had been unable to make up the instalment of purchase-money; he became despondent, and the old horse moped for sympathy.

One morning poor Kit took the last truss of hay and feed of oats, discoursing as was his custom with his early friend, and the person who had the temerity to say that the horse could n't understand every word would have been looked upon by him as an intensely ignorant individual.

"Come up, you old brute," said he. "I've had no breakfast myself yet, but here's yours. We've a precious long day's work before us, and if you don't earn more than you did yesterday, it ain't much you'll get to-morrow, that I can tell you."

Old Turk sniffed, and pushed his nose out in anticipation of the coming meal.

"What a hurry you're in, you precious old rascal," said Kit, rather offended at Turk's evident want of sentiment; "let me tell you a bit of my mind before you eat a morsel," and he snatched back the sieve of oats just as Turk had licked his teeth round for the second mouthful, a proceeding at which he made his displeasure tolerably evident.

"O, I don't care!" continued Kit, "you may blow up as much as you like, but it's my belief that you're a selfish old reprobate." The horse gave Kit one reproachful look that went directly to his heart. "There, take it," said he; "I beg your pardon. I didn't mean to insult you; pitch into it; it does my heart good to see you enjoy it," — and, flinging the feed into the manger, Kit folded his arms and watched his pet as he plunged into the welcome food. It was not long before he nuzzled up every grain.

"Now, then," said Kit, stroking down the old horse's mane as he spoke, "I'm going to tell you something that will break your heart, — leastways I think it will. I wouldn't say anything of it before, for fear of spoiling your breakfast; but things are getting worse and worse, Turk, and if something don't turn up in the course of this very day, we — we'll have to part. You — you and I'll have to part — to *part*, Turk," he repeated sternly, — one round, big tear settling in the corner of his eye, — and gently pulling the horse's ears as he spoke.

The old brute, for the purpose of enjoying the luxury to an extent, placed his head on Kit's shoulder. That was enough ; construing it into an appeal to his affection, he could stand it no longer, but burst into a flood of tears, exclaiming through his sobs, "Don't, don't, Turk ! you deceitful old beast, don't you go to take advantage of my weakness. I tell you my mind's made up. I — I have a w-hi-hife ! now — I have ! and a chi-hi-hild ! They've had plenty as yet, but they don't know how I have pinched myself to get it. I can't let *them* want. You would n't if you were me, bless your old bones ! I know you would n't ; so let us part friends. I can't pay for you, and I must give you up again. You must go, — indeed you must. Come, now bear it like a Christian. I 'll give your ears another pull, if you want me. There, there, come ! "

And poor Kit wept like a sick child, while he harnessed old Turk for, as he thought, the last time.

CHAPTER III.

Which is essential to the Story, and contains, moreover, a Moral Lesson, though inculcated in a curious Way.

"DEAR Kit, you don't eat."

" Never mind me, Betsey, love, go on. I — I 'm not hungry yet ; I shall be sure to get something by and by."

Now that was a lie, — a deliberate lie ; he *was* hungry, and would have thought no more of demolishing the entire of that meagre meal than if it were but a mouthful ; but he struggled manfully against his inclinations, and, having watched his darling wife and child make a sufficient breakfast, kissed them both with his heart upon his lips, and departed upon his almost hopeless toil.

"God bless and preserve *them*," said he, "whatever may become of me; I can battle with the world's strong arm; I *will*, Heaven help me in the effort! It is not for myself I ask it. No, no; were I alone, like a stray weed on the surface of the waters, I'd make no opposition to the whelming tide, but float along wherever fate impelled me; but while these two helpless and uncomplaining creatures look to me, I *will* work, I *will* strive, for I love them so that I could willingly give up my life to rescue them; nay, if it would insure their happiness, I do believe — God forgive me! — that I would *sell my very soul to the fiend.*"

Who can tell at what time an "idle word" may meet its recompense, or the mental invocation be answered, and the destroyer permitted to fling his specious lure upon the sea of circumstance?

Kit spoke from the very promptings of his heart, feeling sincerely what he said, but without the vaguest notion of supernal aid in this debtor and creditor age; it was merely a common saying uttered heedlessly, yet, even as he spoke the words, the soul-ensnarer had begun his work. He was hailed by a sedate-looking, middle-aged, but no further remarkable gentleman, who engaged him for several hours, giving promise of a good day's work, from so favorable a commencement, and poor Kit's heart bounded again with joy at the thought of home, and this cheering omen of better fortune. Great cause had he for joy!

At the self-same moment that the stranger entered Kit's cab, two suspicious-looking individuals might be observed creeping stealthily up the rickety stairs which led

to his miserable home; as they seem to move slowly
and with difficulty, I'll describe them as nearly as I can,
while in progression. The first was an apoplectic son of
Iscariot, short, squab, and intensely fat, his huge carcass
decorated in the very extremity of gaudy show, his capacious chest enveloped in a flaming plaid velvet waistcoat,
about which an endless convolution of snake-pattern,
imitation gold chain played at hide and seek, now fantasti-
cally twining round an exaggerated breastpin of some red
material, then flitting through sundry button-holes, and
finally plunging into his side pocket; his continuations, or
pants, to use the Yankee abbreviation, were composed of
light, very light blue material, and made so uncomfortably
tight as to give one a sensation of pain, while his feet were
squeezed into French gaiter boots, with patent-leather tips.
The coat was of that economically fashionable material,
generally worn at night, when rows are expected, mostly
patronized, though, by ambitious apprentices, in the last
year of their time, when they begin to be intrusted with
the door-key, and, from a laudable anxiety to go to bed
early, invariably defer it until next morning. His hands
— fins — flippers, or whatever they were *au naturel*, were
surrounded on all sides with kid gloves, but where he got
the gloves, how he got into them, or when he did, are
matters as mysterious to me as Mesmer, Hahnemann, or
Pusey.

His follower, literally, was in every way antithetic; long,
scraggy, and cadaverous, he looked like a slender, consump-
tive ninepin by the side of a plethoric ball.

"Phew!" ejaculated Solomon Duggs, our adipose friend,
following it up with a series of fatty suspirations. "*Dim*
these *dim* stairs. Phew!— stop, *le's* rest— *dim* the
dim thing— how *dim* fatigued I *em!* Why, Badger,

you *dim*, watery-blooded anatomy, how *dim* cool you look ! "

" I *am* cool," gruffly responded the thin-ribbed follower, " I have only myself to carry."

" *Dim* your impudence ! " puffed Duggs, " do you mean to insinuate that I am so *dim* fat ? "

" Not I ; I only thought it would be convenient to be a *shade* smaller," said Badger, the ghost of a smile shivering on his lips.

" You lie, *dim* you, it would n't : I like it — phew ! " — and Duggs fanned himself with his great fist.

" O, very well, I 've done. I 'm sorry I spoke. If you like it, may your shadow never be less, that 's all " ; and Badger fairly laughed, — a breach of discipline and of decorum which raised the ire of Duggs to such an extent that he punched him in the ribs, which was about as much use as flinging putty against iron bars.

" Come, come, no more of this *dim* nonsense, but *le's* to business ; phew ! " and he fanned faster than ever. " Are you sure this is the *dim* place ? "

Badger nodded, for he was an economist in words.

" Well, knock, *dim* you."

Badger knocked a small, crafty, neighbor-like knock — a miserable, mean, *dirty* " summons."

Poor Betsey flew to open the door, and started back again with astonishment and vague apprehension, as Duggs, followed by Badger, waddled in ; utterly unable to speak, and gasping from an indefinite sense of dread, she gazed on the intruders.

" Sarv'nt, *mim*, don't be so alarmed ; we aint agoing to hurt you," blandly simpered Duggs, flourishing his cane, while Badger, with the practised eye of an appraiser, in one glance round the room calculated to a sixpence the profits of his brokerage.

"Take a *cheer, mim,*" continued Duggs; "hem," — and he cleared his throat for his stereotyped introductory speech. "I 'm extremely sorry that so unpleasant a *dooty* should *revolve* upon me as a legal functionary, but laws *is* laws, and *dooties* is *dooties,* and if I *warn't* to do it, *p'r'aps* some one else as is not so tender *'ud* be *obligated.*"

"For heaven's sake," cried the agitated Betsey, "tell me what all this means." Duggs shrugged up his shoulders, and began fumbling in his pocket, pointing at the same time to Badger, who, seated cross-legged on the bed, was noting down with callous indifference every article of furniture. The extent of her misfortune struck her in an instant, her brain reeled, the blood rushed upward from her heart, and she fell.

"*Dim* the *dim* thing," gasped Duggs, "she 's fainted."

"So she has, I declare," said Badger, dryly, without moving.

"Then *dim* you, come and help." Badger got slowly up, and helped to raise the poor victim, giving her a shake, and saying, gruffly, "I hate your fainters; don't put her on the cheer; we 'll want that. Here, drop her on the mattress at once; there, she 'll come to time enough."

"Give her some water, *dim* you."

He did so; it seemed to revive her a little; she swallowed about half a glassful. Badger threw the remainder under the grate, and, pocketing the tumbler, proceeded with his inventory.

"Come, *mim,*" said Duggs, "don't take on so; 'taint for much, — only a paltry *fip-poun ten; dimme,* I 'd pay it myself, only that dooties is dooties. Can't you give it us, and we 'll be *hoff.*"

"God knows," said poor Betsey, her eyes streaming with tears, "I have n't five farthings in the world, but do

18

wait until my husband comes home : he'll give it you, I know ho will, for he's as honest as truth itself."

" Why, you see, *mim*, there aint no honosty in the case," replied the amiable Duggs, speaking the truth, by mistake ; " the long and the short of it is, if you have n't the *dim* money we must take the *dim* things."

But why linger over a scene, which, to the disgrace of British laws, is enacted daily in the British metropolis. Suffice it to say, Kit had neglected, from perfect ignorance, to answer a summons before the Court of Requests, summary execution was issued, and amidst the agony of grief and ineffectual remonstrances of that poor, lonely mother, the humble apartment was stripped of every article except the bed she lay on, even to the very cradle of her infant, to satisfy the greed of a stony-hearted creditor, and the rapacity of a shameful and cruel law.

CHAPTER IV.

In which Kit spurns at Fortune in a most unaccountable Manner.

" So ho ! old Turk, we've done well to-day, old boy, ha ! ha ! I've paid my instalment, and have ten good shillings in my pocket. So ho ! good old fellow, who's afraid ? There's life in a muscle yet. There, there, now don't be impatient, you shall have such a feed presently, you'll feel in your stall like a bishop, only you won't have no wine. So much the better. Water's the good, wholesome drink that nature provides for all sorts of animals, and how mankind got to like anything else puzzles me ; but the sense is leaving us and going into the brutes — there, you 're unharnessed, now give yourself a

shake — that's right — now just wait until I go cheer up
my darling Bessie, and kiss that varmint, young Kit."

So saying, with a light step and a joyous heart, Kit
bounded up stairs, singing as he went, —

"O, there's nothing like luck all the universe over,
Misfortunes don't always stay with us, 't is clear;
To-day we're in sorrow, to-morrow in clover,
The light follows darkness throughout the long year.
O, the light follows darkness — "

At that moment, with a gladsome smile on his lips,
he rushed into the room. Heavens! what a sight met his
view! the quick revulsion of feeling almost drove out
sense. It was as though one were suddenly to wake fresh
from the glories of a blissful dream, to find a devouring
flame enveloping his bed. In the confusion of his first
dismay he had a vague conception of some sweeping
destruction, and that wife, child, and all were lost; but
when he saw that they were safe, a deep feeling of relief
came over him, the blood flowed again, and full consciousness returned.

"Great heaven! Bessie!" he cried in dry, husky accents, "what's the meaning of this? who has been here?
what has happened?"

"O Kit," she replied, flinging her arms round his
neck, and breaking into a flood of tears, "dear Kit! why
did n't you come sooner? — they have been here — and —
everything is gone."

"Who — who has done this?" said Kit, with a savage
glance in his eye, seldom lighted there, but, once it was,
most fearful to encounter.

"That man, you know, — that grocer, dear Kit," said
Bessie.

"Higgins!" cried Kit. She nodded. "The grasping

cur, the sneaking, dastardly slave, to take advantage of my absence," said Kit, fiercely, clenching his hands and grinding his teeth. "May" — the large tears rolled in streams down his cheeks; burying his face in his hands, he continued, "May God pardon him for this day's inhuman work, forgive me for the harsh words I've used, and avert the strong hate that in my own despite springs up within me towards him. O, 't is hard! — hard to be thus dashed, dear Bessie, with a soul full of hope. But come, it's over now, and we must make the best of it."

"Bless you, bless you," replied the devoted wife, "we will, we will; for your sake, and for the sake of our child, I can endure anything."

"Heaven reward your true woman's love, Bessie, darling," fervently replied Kit. "I have enough for present want, here," — placing his hand in his pocket to take out the piece of gold which he had carefully deposited there, when, to his utter dismay, he could not find it. He hunted through every crevice, but to no purpose : it was gone. "Fool! fool that I am!" he exclaimed, bitterly. "I've lost it."

"Never mind, dear Kit," replied Bessie, tenderly, "there's enough for the boy's supper, and I do not want anything."

"What have I done?" pettishly exclaimed Kit. "Great heaven! what have I done, that everything should so conspire against me?" At that instant they both started, — hearing the peculiar chink of gold. "Ha!" shouted Kit, "there it is," and, rushing over to the place whence the sound proceeded, he saw a sight which made his brain reel. Seated on the cab cushions which he had brought in with him, his little boy was playing with a *bag of gold;* he had just managed to untie the string, and the precious metal poured out in a perfect shower.   Kit's first thought was one of unmitigated delight, but ere an instant had passed, he and his wife looked intently at each other, with faces painfully livid.

"Bessie," said he, grasping her hand tightly, and speaking through his teeth with compressed energy, "these walls are naked, you and your child are pinched by hard want, misfortune dogs our very footsteps, — let us pray that a merciful God may give us strength to battle with this strong temptation."   And with clasped hands they knelt in silent supplication.

The mingled aspirations of two hearts as pure as ever tenanted this mortal clay wended upward from those miserable walls to the throne of Him who hears, and who, in His own good time, will answer the prayer of the wretched.

CHAPTER V.

In which Kit does an extraordinary Thing, and is recompensed in an extraordinary Way.

NEITHER Kit nor Bessie slept a single wink all that night ; the consciousness of having so great a sum of money in their possession, which did not belong to them, effectually drove off slumber.   Kit had counted it, and found there were one thousand pounds in the bag.   How it could possibly have escaped his notice, as he removed the cushions from the cab, puzzled him exceedingly, but he conjectured the string had by some means got twisted round one of the buttons.   Having replaced the money, he put it carefully under his pillow, and if he felt once, he felt a hundred times to see if it were safe.   Bessie was equally fidgety, and at last, far from being inclined to retain any, they both heartily wished it anywhere but with them. Now would they fancy footsteps were approaching the bed; now Kit would jump up and put some additional fastening on the door and window, for the first time experiencing the truth of the old proverb, —

> "He who has naught to lose
> Need never his doors to close."

Poor Bessie, in the simplicity of her heart, exclaimed, " Dear Kit, if money makes people feel as I do, I would n't be rich for all the world."

Long before morning, they were both up, and when Kit cast his eyes first upon his scant breakfast and then upon the treasure within his grasp, his heart bounded up to his throat. Bessie, guessing his thoughts, with true woman's tact, diverted them into the one broad, over-whelming current of paternal love, presenting the laughing boy to receive his father's kiss. "See, see," she exclaimed, "how beautiful he looks this morning. Does it not seem as though heaven had sent one of its own angels to reward us for shunning this devil's lure? Is it not a great thing, dearest, to meet his smile without a blush of shame?"

"It is, it is," he exclaimed, regarding his child with the strong emotion of a father's love. "No, no; *you* shall never curse your father's memory. The anger of a just God, who visits the father's sins upon the children, shall never reach you from my misdeeds, if through His abundant mercy my soul be still strengthened in the right."

With placid minds, and even cheerfully, they sat down to their insufficient breakfast, Kit cheering his wife the while, by saying, "Take heart, love, take heart! I shall

take the money down to Somerset House. No doubt I shall
see the owner; he will be grateful for its return, and will
perhaps reward me with a trifle. At all events, the greatest
pleasures money could obtain would n't approach the thou-
sandth part of the joy I feel at the anticipation of returning to that old man his no doubt almost hopelessly lamented treasure."

When Kit arrived at Somerset House, he found the office
for the reception of valuables found in cabs was not open,
so he sat down on the curbstone to wait, amusing himself
by *hefting* the bag in his pocket, and wondering what its
owner would give him for the recovery. His cab was
standing in the entrance ; suddenly he was startled by an
authoritative voice, shouting to him to get out of the way.
With habitual deference, Kit flew to lead his vehicle into
the enclosure, when a splendid carriage, driven by a pair
of blood-horses, dashed up the avenue, stopping short with
a sudden pull.

In an instant after, one of the liveried servants touched
Kit on the shoulder, and, upon looking up, in the occupant
of the carriage he beheld the owner of the treasure.

" Come in, come in," said the old man, and poor Kit
was handed into the magnificent vehicle.

" Good fellow, good fellow, have you brought it ?" said
the stranger quickly, and with the slightest possible evidence of agitation.

" To the uttermost farthing, sir," replied Kit, as, un-
twisting the string from around his neck, he placed the
bag in the old man's hands.

" You're an honest fellow," said the latter, " what 's your
name ? and where do you live ?"

Kit told him.

" I won't forget ; I won't forget. Shake hands, I honor

you!" and, with a hearty grasp, wealth paid homage to honesty. "Now, good by," continued the old man; "I've business of great importance to attend to." And without any acknowledgment except that unsubstantial handshake, poor Kit was left standing on the curbstone, while the carriage of the ungrateful stranger whirled furiously away.

Stunned and mortified, Kit could hardly believe his senses. "What," cried he, "not a guinea, not a shilling, after restoring that vast sum! Mean, miserly! Well, I've done *my* duty, and, after all, I had no positive right to expect anything for it." Thus he argued, in the endeavor to shake off his annoyance, but vainly; he was bitterly disappointed.

After a few hours spent in his usual occupation, utterly despondent and almost hopeless, Kit sought his wretched home, scarcely knowing how to meet his wife, or break the mortification to her. He found her in tears, which, when she saw him, she strove to restrain, but could not; in her hand was a large, lawyer-like, suspicious-looking letter, with an enormous seal, — just such a document as brings a shudder through an individual in straitened circumstances.

"So, so," said Kit, "more wretchedness, more misfortune! Who is this from? Some other charitable soul, who fain would help to sink a drowning wretch still deeper."

Seizing the letter he tore it open, when, glancing at the contents, he gasped for breath, his eyes dilated, the big tears bursting from them in torrents; he jumped up, shouted, laughed, danced, kissed Bessie, and squeezed his child until he fairly hurt it, and behaved altogether in a most mysterious and alarming manner.

"Merciful heaven!" cried Bessie, a cold shiver running through her frame, "he's mad!"

"He's not, he's not," shouted Kit. "Look here, read, read," and, pushing the letter towards her, between laughing and crying they slowly deciphered the following :—

"I hereby grant to Christopher Cobb, for the term of his natural life, the sum of Two Hundred Pounds, lawful British money, annually, for which this shall be deemed sufficient instrument, in gratitude for an essential service, and as the inadequate reward of exemplary honesty.

"EGREMONT."

Reader, art thou in prosperity, be grateful to Him from whom all earthly good proceeds. Art thou in adversity, remember that He who rules the thunder is all-powerful to cast from thee the bitter cup.

THE MORNING DREAM.

"The dream of the night there's no reason to rue,
But the dream of the morning is sure to come true."
OLD SAYING.

PRETTY Peggy May; a bright-eyed, merry-hearted, little darling you are, Peggy! there's no gainsaying that fact; a cunning little gypsy, and most destructive too, as many an aching heart can testify. But who can blame you for that? as well might the summer's sun be blamed for warming the sweet flowers into life. It is a natural ordination that all who see you should love you.

Pretty Peg has just completed her eighteenth year; in the heedless gayety of youth, she has hitherto gambolled through the road of life, without a grief, almost without a thought. O for the sunny days of childhood, ere, wedded to experience, the soul brings forth its progeny of cares! Why can we not add the knowledge of our wiser years, and linger over that most blessed, least prized period of our existence, when every impulse is at once obeyed, and the ingenuous soul beams forth in smiles, its every working indexed in the face, ere prudence starts up like a spectre, and cries out, "Beware! there is a prying world that watches every turn, and does not always make a true report." Prudence! how I hate the cold, calculating, heartless term! Be loyal in word, be just in act, be honest in all; but prudence! 't is twin-brother to selfishness, spouse of mistrust, and parent of hypocrisy! But methinks I hear some one say, "This is a most cava-

Paddy. How do ye do, Misther Aicho?
Echo. Mighty well thank you, Paddy!

lier way of treating one of the cardinal virtues." To
which I reply, "It certainly has, by some means or other,
sneaked in amongst the virtues, and thereby established a
right to the position; but it is the companionship only
which makes it respectable, and it must be accompanied
by *all the rest* to neutralize its mischievous tendency."

If you have taken the slightest interest in little Peg,
prepare to sympathize in her first heart-deep sorrow. She
is in love! Now, if she herself were questioned about the
matter, I'm pretty sure she would say it's no such thing;
but I take upon myself to declare it to be true, and, for
fear you should think that I make an assertion which I
cannot prove, permit me to relate the substance of a
conversation which took place between Peg and her
scarcely less pretty, but infinitely more mischievous cousin,
Bridget O'Conner. They had just returned from one of
those gregarious merry-meetings where some spacious
granary, just emptied of its contents, gives glorious opportunity for the gladsome hearts of the village, and "all the
country round," to meet and astonish the rats — sleek,
well-fed rascals dozing in their holes — with uproarious
fun and revelry.

A sudden, and indeed, under the circumstances, extremely significant sigh from Peg, startled Bridget from
the little glass where she had been speculating as to how
she looked, for the last hour or two. I may as well say
the scrutiny was perfectly satisfactory; she had not danced
all her curls out.

"Gracious me!" she exclaimed, "Peg, how you *do*
sigh!"

"And no wonder," rejoined Peggy, with a slight squeeze
of acid, "after having danced down twenty couple twenty
times, I should like to know who wouldn't?"

"Ah! but that was n't a tired sigh, Peg. I know the difference; one need n't dive as low as the *heart* for them. A tired sigh comes flying out upon a breath of joy, and turns into a laugh before it leaves the lips; you are sad, Peg!"

"How you talk! why, what on earth should make me sad?"

"That's exactly what I want to know; now there's no use in your trying to laugh, for you can't do it. Do you think I don't know the *difference* between a laugh, and that nasty deceitful croak?"

"Bridget!" exclaimed Peg, with a look which she intended should be very severe and very reproachful, "I'm sleepy."

"Well, then, kiss me, and go to bed," replied Bridget. "Ho, ho!" thought she, "there's something curious about Peg to-night. I think what I think, and if I think right, I'm no woman if I don't find out before I sleep." Craftily she changed the conversation, abused the women's dresses, and criticised their complexions, especially the pretty ones. At last, when she had completely lulled the commotion of Peg's thoughts into a calm, she suddenly cried out, "O Peg! I forgot to tell you that one of the boys we danced with had his leg broke coming home to-night."

Peggy, surprised into an emotion she found it impossible to conceal, started up, pale as snow, and gasped out, "Who was it? — who?"

"Ha! ha!" thought the other, "the fox is somewhere about, — now to beat the cover."

"Did you hear me ask you who?" said Peg, anxiously.

"I did, dear," replied Bridget, "but I'm trying to recollect. I think," and she looked steadily into Peggy's eyes, "I think it was Ned Riley."

Peg did n't even wink.

"She does n't care about him, and I 'm not sorry for that," thought Bridget, thereby making an acknowledgment to herself which the sagacious reader will no doubt interpret truly. "No, it was n't Ned," she continued. "Now I think of it, it was — it was — a — "

"Who? who?" cried Peg, now sensibly agitated; "do tell me, there 's a dear."

Not she, not a bit of it, but lingered with feminine ingenuity, now making as though she recollected the name and then, with a shake of her head, pretending to dive back into memory, just as the inquisitors of old used to slacken the torture to enable the recipient to enjoy another dose.

"Now I have it," said she, — "no, I have n't; I do believe I 've forgotten who it was, but this I know, it was the pleasantest-mannered and nicest young fellow in the whole heap."

"Then it *must* have been Mark!" exclaimed Peg, throwing prudence overboard, and fixing her large, eloquent eyes full on Bridget's mouth, as if her everlasting fate depended upon the little monosyllable about to issue from it.

"It *was* Mark! that *was* the name!"

Peggy gave a gasp, while Bridget went on, with a triumphant twinkle in her wicked little eye which did not show over-favorably for her humanity.

"*Mark Brady!*" dwelling on the name with slow, distinct emphasis, which made Peggy's heart jump at each word as though she had received an electric shock.

She knew the tenderest part of the sentient anatomy, Bridget did, and took intense delight in stabbing exactly there; not mortal stabs, *that* would be mercy, but just a little too far for tickling. That sort of a woman was Bridget, who, if possessed of an incumbrance in husband shape, would take infinite pains to discover the weakest points in his temper, and industriously attack those quarters, piling up petty provocations, one upon another, none in itself of sufficient importance to induce a sally, but making altogether a breastwork of aggravation that must at last o'ertop the wall of temper. Phantoms of crutches and of wooden legs came crowding on Peg's imagination, contrasting themselves with the curious agility with which poor Mark had "beat the floor" in the merry jig, until he made it echo to every note of the pipes. Then rose up vague spectres of sanguinary-minded surgeons, with strange butcherly instruments; then she saw nothing but fragmentary Marks, unattached legs, a whole roomful dancing by themselves; there they were, twisting and twirling about, in the various difficult complications of the "toe and heel," "double shuffle," "ladies' delight," and "cover the buckle"; she shut her eyes in horror, and was sensible of nothing but a gloomy blood-red. There's no knowing to what lengths her terrible fancies might have gone, had they not been dispersed like wreaths of vapor by a hearty laugh from the mischievous Bridget. Peggy opened her eyes in astonishment. Was she awake? Yes, there was her cousin, enjoying one of the broadest, merriest, wickedest laughs that ever mantled over the face of an arch little female.

"Poor Mark!" she cried, and then burst forth again into ringing laughter, which dimpled her crimson cheeks like — what shall I say? — like a fine healthy-looking cork-red potato, an Irish simile, to be sure; but had we seen Bridget, and were we acquainted with the features of the aforesaid esculent, I'm pretty certain you would acknowledge its aptness.

"What in the name of gracious are you laughing at?" exclaimed Peggy, a gleam of hope breaking on the darkness of her thought.

"Why, that you should take on so, when I told you Mark had broken his leg," gayly replied Bridget.

"Has n't he?"

"Not half as much as your poor little heart would have been broken if he had," said the tormentor.

"Bridget! cousin!" said poor Peg, now enduring much more pain from the sudden revulsion of feeling, "you should not have done this; you have crowded a whole lifetime of agony into those few moments past."

"Well, forgive me, dear Peggy. I declare I did n't know that you had the affection so strong on you, or I would n't have joked for the world. But now, confess, does n't it serve you right for not confiding in me, your natural born cousin? Did I ever keep a secret from you? Did n't I tell you all about Pat Finch, and Johnny Magee, and Jack, the hurler, eh?"

"But not one word about Edward Riley, with whom you danced so often to-night," observed Peg, with a very pardonable dash of malice.

It was now Bridget's turn to change color, as she stammered out, "I — I was going to, — not that I care much about _him_; no, no, Mark is the flower of the flock, and I've a mighty great mind to set my cap at him myself."

Peggy smiled, a very small but a peculiar and it might have been perfectly self-satisfied smile, as she replied, "Try, Miss Bridget, and I wish you success."

"Truth is scarce when liars are near," said Bridget. "But I say, Peg, does Mark know you love him?"

"Don't be foolish; how should he?"

"Did you never tell him?"

" What do you take me for ?"

" Did he never tell *you* ? "

" What do you take *him* for ?"

" For a man, and moreover a conceited one ; don't you mean to let him know his good fortune ? "

" It is n't leap-year, and if it were, I 'd rather die than do such a thing," said Peggy.

" Come, I 'll bet you a new cap, that I mean to wear at your wedding, you *will* let him know the state of your feelings, and that before a week is over your head," provokingly replied Bridget.

Peggy said nothing.   Prudent Peg.

" Is it a bet ? "

" Yes, yes, anything ; but go to sleep, or we sha'n't get a wink to-night."

" True for you, cousin, for it 's *to-morrow* already ! Look at the daybreak, how it has frightened our candle, until it 's almost as pale as your cheek."

" Good night, Bridget."

" Good night, dear Peg, don't forget to remember your dreams.   Recollect it 's morning now, and whatever we dream *is sure to come true.*"

Before she slept, Bridget formed a project to insure the winning of her bet.

———

Very early in the day Mark Brady and Ned called to inquire after the health of their respective partners.   It so happened that Bridget received them ; and very quickly, for she was one of those tyrants in love who make their captives feel their chains, on one frivolous pretence or another dismissed her swain, and began to develop her plot with Mark.

Now Mark, I may as well tell you now as at another time, was a very favorable specimen of a class I regret to say not over numerous in Ireland ; a well-to-do farmer, his rent always ready, his crops carefully gathered, and a trifle put by yearly, so that he enjoyed that most enviable condition in life, "a modest competence." As to his personal appearance, there's scarcely any occasion to describe that. Suffice it to say, Mark was a man! A volume of eulogy could not say more.

Mark was apparently very busy, sketching imaginary somethings on the floor with his blackthorn stick, and seemingly unconscious of Bridget's presence, when she suddenly interrupted his revery by saying, " A penny for your thoughts, Mr. Brady!"

" Eh ! what !" he replied, blushing till the blood stung his cheek like a million of needles. " A penny is it, miss ? Faith, an' it's *dear* they 'd be at that same."

" And what might you be thinking of, may I ask, Mr. Mark?" said Bridget, accompanying the question with one of her very sweetest smiles.

" Just nothing at all, miss," replied Mark.

" ' Nothing !' then they *would* be '*dear*,' and that's true, Mark ; but supposing, now," she continued, archly, " I only say, supposing it happened to be your sweetheart you were thinking of, you might find another meaning for that same little word ! "

Mark felt as though he had been detected in a fault, as he replied, sketching away on the floor faster than ever, " But what if I had n't a sweetheart to think of, Miss O'Connor ? " It was a miserable attempt at prevarication, and he felt that it was.

" Why, then, I should say, as you 're not blind, it's mighty lucky that you don't carry such a thing as a heart

about you. I'd be ashamed if I were you, rising twenty
years old, and neither crooked nor ugly; it's disgraceful
to hear you say so, — a pretty example to set to the boys!"

"True for you, and so it is," said Mark, "and more
betoken, it's a much greater shame for me to tell any lies
about the matter. I *have* a sweetheart, though she does n't
know it; ay, and have had one for this nigh hand a twelve-
month."

"Only to think," replied Bridget, casting down her eyes,
and affecting to conceal some sudden emotion, "and for a
twelve-month nigh hand! O dear! I don't feel well!"

Mark was puzzled, in point of fact embarrassed. There
was something in Bridget's manner which he could n't
understand; he had a vague presentiment that there was a
mistake somewhere, but when she, pretending to be overcome, flung herself into his arms, the truth burst upon him
at once. He was in a precious dilemma; Bridget was in
love with him, and he felt downright ashamed of himself
for being so fascinating. What he was to do, or how to
extricate himself, he could n't tell, as she, casting a fascinating glance at him, said softly, "Dear Mark, those
good-looking eyes of yours told me of your love, long, long
before your lazy tongue."

"Love," interrupted Mark, endeavoring to put in a
demurrer.

"To be sure," said she; "I saw it, I knew it and well,"
she continued, seeing he was about to speak. "When do
you mean to talk to Aunty? You know my fifty pounds
are in her hands." She was an heiress, was Bridget.

"Pounds! Aunty! yes, to be sure," replied Mark, perfectly bewildered; "but I thought Ned Riley was —"

"Peggy's sweetheart, — well, we all know that," interrupted Bridget, inly enjoying the consternation that painted

Mark's cheek a livid white. "And you to be so jealous of Riley," she went on, "not to dance with me last night; I knew the reason, but the jealousy that springs from love is soon forgot, so I forgot yours."

"Peggy! *his* sweetheart? Riley's?"

"To be sure; don't you know they are going to be married?"

"No!" vacantly replied the sorely bewildered Mark.

"O, yes! and now I want to tell you a pet plan of mine, if you don't think me too bold, Mark, and that is, how nice and cosey it would be if we could only all be married on the same day."

This was too much for Mark; he could n't endure it any longer; he started up, pushed his hat very far on his head, saying, in what he intended to be a most severe tone, "Miss O'Connor, I don't know what could have put such an idea into your head. Marry indeed! I 've enough to do to take care of myself. No, I 'm sorry to wound *your* feelings, but I shall never marry!"

"O, yes, you will," said Bridget, placing her arm in his, which he disengaged, saying bitterly, "Never! never!"

"Nonsense; I 'll bet you will, and, if it was only to humor me, Mark, on the very same day that Peggy is!"

"Bridget, I did n't think I could hate a woman as I 'm beginning to hate you."

"Better before marriage than after, Mr. Mark. Come, I 'll bet you a new Sunday coat, against a calico gown, and that 's long odds in your favor, that what I 've said will come true."

"Nonsense!"

"Is it a bet?"

"Pooh! I 'll bet my life, against —"

"What it 's worth, Mr. Mark, — just nothing at all."

"True for you, now, Bridget; true for you," and Mark suddenly quitted the house, in such real sorrow that it touched for a moment even Bridget's heart; but only for a moment. "Pshaw!" thought she, "let him fret; it will do him good, and make the joy greater when he comes to know the truth. A hunt would be nothing without hedges and ditches." Proceeding to the window, she uttered an exclamation of surprise.

"Ha! as I live, here comes Peg herself. She must meet Mark; what fun! He sees her and stops short; what a quandary he's in! She sees *him!* How the little fool blushes! Now they meet. Mark does n't take her hand. I wonder what he's saying. 'It's a fine day,' I suppose, or something equally interesting. He passes on, and Peg looks as scared as if she had seen a ghost."

A sudden thought at this moment seemed to strike Bridget; she clapped her hands together, and laughed a little, sharp laugh, saying, "I'll do it, I will; I'll have a bit of fun with Peg, too." So she pretended to be very busy at her spinning-wheel as Peggy entered, and, hanging up her cloak and bonnet, sat down without saying a word.

"Ah, Peg!" Bridget began, "is that you? Mark has just been here."

"Indeed?" replied Peggy, twisting up one pretty curl so tightly as to hurt her head.

"The blessed truth," continued the wicked little tormentor. "Did you meet him?"

A very desponding "Yes" was the response.

"Well," demanded Bridget, anxiously, "did he say anything, — I mean, anything *particular?*"

"He only said the weather was pleasant, and then passed on, without ever even shaking hands with me," sadly replied Peggy.

"Mark need n't have done that; whatever happens, he ought to be civil to *you*," said Bridget, with a peculiar expression that made Peggy's heart flutter within her like a pigeon.

"Civil to me! what *do* you mean, Bridget?"

Bridget hummed an air, and, as if suddenly wishing to change the conversation, said, gayly, "O, I forgot! we were to tell each other's dreams this morning. Peg, you begin; what did *you* dream about?"

"Nothing, Bridget, I did n't sleep."

"Then you could n't have dreamed," sagely responded the other, "but I did."

"What?"

"I dreamed that I had a beautiful new gown given to me, and by whom do you think?

"I don't know; Ned Riley, maybe."

"Ned Riley indeed!" replied Bridget, with a sneer; "not a bit of it. By a finer man than ever stood in *his* shoes. Who but Mark Brady?"

Peg's heart sank within her.

"That was n't all I dreamed," and she fixed her wild eyes full on Peg, in a way that made hers fall instantly. "I dreamed that I was married to him."

"To Mark?" whispered Peggy.

"*To Mark!*"

Peggy did n't utter another syllable, did n't even look up, but sat motionless and pale, very pale. Bridget could n't understand her seeming apathy; a more acute observer would have contrasted it with the intense emotion which she felt within, — an emotion not a whit lessened as Bridget continued, with marked expression, "I dreamed all that this blessed morning, and morning dreams, you know, *always come true.*"

Peggy, still silent, seemed to be wholly occupied in demolishing, piece by piece, the remnant of a faded flower which she had taken from her bosom, lingering over its destruction as though a portion of her heart went with each fragment, when Bridget suddenly started up, exclaiming, " Here comes Mark, I declare."

A painful spasm shot through Peggy's frame, yet she did not stir from her seat ; the only evidence that she heard Bridget's exclamation was that her lips grew as pale as her cheek.

" But, law ! what am I thinking about ? I must go and tidy my hair."

And away flew Bridget up to her room, whence she crept stealthily down, and snugly ensconced herself behind the door, — naughty girl ! — to listen to what was then said.

Mark, who, since his conversation with Bridget, had seriously contemplated suicide, but was puzzled about the best mode of making away with himself, had come to the conclusion that to enter the army as a common soldier would be the least criminal, although certainly the most lingering process, and it was to lacerate his feelings by a parting interview with his dearly loved Peg, before he consummated the act of enlistment, that he now came.

Arrived at the door, he hesitated a moment, then, giving one big gulp, lifted the latch and entered. There he saw Peggy herself, looking straight into the fire, never once turning aside or raising her eyes, proof positive to Mark, if he wanted it, that she cared nothing for him. He sat down, and for several minutes there was a dead silence. Mark had fully intended to say something frightfully cutting to his sweetheart ; but as he gazed upon her white, sad face, his resentment vanished, and he felt more

THE MORNING DREAM. 295

inclined to implore than to condemn. He wanted to speak, but what to say he had not the remotest idea.

At last Peg broke the silence, by murmuring softly, as though it were but a thought to which she had given involuntary expression, " May you be happy, Mark! may you be happy ! "

" Happy ! " echoed Mark, with a sharp emphasis, that thrilled painfully through Peggy. "Faith, it's well for *you* to be wishing me happiness."

"Indeed, indeed I do, Mark ! — I mean Mr. Brady," meekly replied the poor girl.

" O, that 's right ! " said Mark, bitterly. " Mr. Brady ! It used to be Mark."

" But never can again."

" You 're right, — never ! "

" Never ! " and poor Peggy sighed deeply.

After another embarrassing pause, broken only by a sort of smothered sound, which *might* have been the wind, but was n't, Mark started up, exclaiming, " I see my company is displeasing to you, but I sha'n't trouble you long. That will be done to-morrow which will separate us forever."

" To-morrow ! So soon ? " replied Peggy, with a stifled sob.

" Yes ! the sooner the better. What is it *now* to you ? "

" O, nothing, nothing ! But I thought — that is — I 'm very, very foolish."

Poor Peggy's heart overflowed its bounds ; burying her face in her hands, she burst into tears.

Mark did n't know what to make of it. " She must have liked me a little," thought he, " or why this grief ? Well, it 's all my own fault. Why did n't I tell her of my love, like a man, and not sneak about, afraid of the sound of my own voice ? I 've lost her, lost the only thing that

made life to me worth enduring, and the sooner I relieve
her of my presence the better."

"Miss May! Peggy!" he said, with an effort at calmness, "this is the last time we may meet on earth; won't
you give me your hand at parting?"

Peggy stretched out both hands, exclaiming through
her tears, "Mark, Mark! this is indeed cruel!"

"It is, I know it is!" said Mark, brushing away an
obtrusive tear. "So God bless you, and good angels
watch over you; and if you ever cared for me —"

"If I ever cared for you! O Mark!"

"Why! did you?" inquired Mark.

"You were my only thought, my life, my happiness!"
There was the same curious sound from the chamber-
door, but the innocent wind had again to bear the blame.
Peggy continued, "Mark, would that you had the same
feeling for me!"

"I had, I had!" frantically he replied. "And more,
O, much more than I have words to speak! Why did n't
we know this sooner?"

"Ah! why indeed?" sadly replied Peggy; "but it is
too late."

"*Too late!*" replied Mark, "*too late!*"

"Not a bit of it!" exclaimed Bridget, bursting into the
room, streaming with tears of suppressed laughter. "Don't
look so frightened, good people; I'm not a ghost. Who
lost a new cap? eh, Peg. And more betoken, who is
likely to lose a new gown? I'll have my bets, if I die
for it. So, you've spoke out at last, have you? You're a
pretty pair of lovers. You'd have gone on everlastingly,
sighing and fretting yourselves, if I had n't interfered."

"You?" cried Peggy and Mark, simultaneously.

"Yes, indeed, it made me perfectly crazy to see the two

of you groaning and fussing, without the courage to say what your hearts dictated. There, go and kiss each other, you pair of noodles."

It is hardly necessary to say that Bridget's explanation brought about a pleasant understanding between all parties, and it will be only needful to add that a few weeks afterwards there was a double wedding in the little parish chapel. One of the brides wore a brand-new calico gown of such wonderful variety of color, and moreover a new cap of so elaborate a style of decoration, that she was the admiration, and of necessity the envy, of the entire female population.

Bridget had won both her wagers, thereby establishing, just as infallibly as all such matters can be established, the truth of the old saying, —

The dream of the morning is sure to come true.

THE TEST OF BLOOD.

"Thou shalt do no murder."

"YOU won't dance with me, Kathleen?"

"No, Luke, I will not."

"For what reason?"

"I don't choose it. Besides, I'm engaged to Mark Dermot."

The above very slight conversation in itself was, to the speakers, full of the greatest import. Kathleen Dwyer was the pretty, spoiled village pet, with quite sufficient vanity to know that the preference was deserved. Every young man in the place was anxious to pay court to her, and, sooth to say, she impartially dispensed her smiles to all, reserving, it must be admitted, her more serious thoughts for one alone. That one was Luke Bryant, and, as he really loved her, the flightiness of her conduct and her interminable flirtations gave him very great uneasiness. Often and often would he reason with her, imploring her to dismiss the crowd of purposeless suitors that ever fluttered round, and select one, even though that selection would doom him to misery.

"No, no!" the little madcap would say, with a bright smile, "I cannot give up altogether the delight of having so many male slaves in my train; they are useful, and if you don't like it, you know your remedy."

"But do you think it is right?" he would say; "suppose there may be some, even one, who loves you truly, to lead him on by the false light of your encouraging smile, to perish at last?"

"Pshaw!" she would answer, "men are not made of such perishable stuff."

"Well, well, Kathleen, have a care; if any one of your numerous admirers feels towards you as I do, to lose you would be the loss of everything."

As may be reasonably supposed, these conversations usually ended in a little tiff, when the wild, good-hearted, but giddy-headed girl would select some one from her surrounding beaux to play off against Luke; generally pitching upon the person most likely to touch his feelings to the very quick; herself, the while, I must do her the justice to say, quite as miserable as her victim, if not more so.

Mark Dermot, or, as he was most generally denominated, Black Mark, was one of those persons we sometimes meet with in the world on whom prepossessing appearance and great natural ability are bestowed, only to be put to the basest possible uses. Character he had none, except of the very worst kind; his ostensible pursuit was smuggling, but crimes of the darkest nature were freely whispered about him, and yet, in spite of all this, his dashing, dare-devil nature and indomitable impudence enabled him to show himself in places where, although his evil reputation was well known, he was tolerated, either from supineness, or, more likely, from the fear of his enmity.

It is not to be wondered at, then, that, as Luke stood by and saw this ruffian carry off his soul's beloved, his very heart should quake with apprehension. He was unaware until this moment that she ever knew him, and his feelings, as ever and anon Mark would seem to whisper something in Kathleen's ear, to which she would seem to smile an approval, can only be imagined by those of my readers, if any such there be, who have seen another feeding upon smiles which they would fain monopolize.

Jealousy of the most painful nature took possession of Luke; he had often experienced sensations of annoyance before, but never to this extent. Her reputation was compromised; for he knew Black Mark to be the worst description of man for a woman to come in contact with, caring nothing for the ties of morality, or for the world's opinion, — reckless, bad-hearted, and moreover uncomfortably handsome in the eyes of a lover.

The dance now over, Luke imagined that she would give up her partner and join him; but no, the silly girl seemed proud of her conquest, and to take a sort of mad delight in wounding Luke's feelings to the uttermost. She approached the spot where Luke with folded arms was standing, and, leaning familiarly upon the arm of Mark, said laughingly, "Why don't you dance, Luke? Come, I'll find a partner for you."

Galled to the very quick, Luke answered, with asperity, "Thank you, Miss Dwyer, you have found one for yourself, and" — looking at Black Mark as a jealous lover only can look — "you'll pardon me, but I don't like the sample."

Mark regarded him with a scowl of the deepest malignity, while Kathleen, the real feelings of her heart kept down by coquetry, exclaimed with a laugh, "Don't mind him, Mark, he's only jealous, poor fellow. Come, will you not dance again?"

"Ay, and again, and for ever," impetuously replied Mark. "Come."

And as they went to rejoin the dancers, Kathleen caught the expression of Luke's features, and there saw so much misery depicted that she would have given worlds to have recalled her words. She yearned to implore his forgiveness, but her insatiable appetite for admiration restrained her. "Never mind," thought she, "when the dance is over, I can easily make it up with him," and away she went, thinking no more about it.

At the conclusion of the dance, her better feelings all predominating, she quitted Mark and rushed over to the place where Luke had been standing, but he was gone; with that unfeeling speech rankling in his heart, he had departed. It was now her turn to be miserable; not all the soft speeches that were poured into her ear had power to console her, but her annoyance was at its height when Black Mark, presuming upon the encouragement which she had given him, seated himself beside her, and in ardent language declared himself her passionate lover. Poor, unthinking Kathleen! she had evoked a spirit which she had not power to quell.

It was more than a week after before Luke could bring himself to venture near Kathleen; but finding that each succeeding day only made him still more wretched he determined to know his fate at once, and with a sorely troubled heart he neared her abode, lifted the latch, and entered. The first sight that met his eyes was Mark and Kathleen, sitting near to each other. The deep blush that crimsoned her to the very throat evinced to Luke the interesting nature of their conversation. She could not speak, neither could he; but, giving her one look which sank into her very brain, he left the place. In vain she called after him, he turned but once — a deep curse was on his lips, but his noble heart refused to sanction it. "Farewell, beloved Kathleen," he cried, while bitter tears flowed fast, "may the good God protect you now, for you will need it." And Luke rapidly strode towards the village, inly determining to go to sea on the morrow, and never look upon her or his loved home again.

Meanwhile, Kathleen, apprehensive that he would do

something desperate, implored Mark to follow and bring
him back. With a contemptuous sneer, he answered,
"Do you think I 'm a fool? No, no! Kathleen, you 've
gone too far with me to retract now. The world sees and
knows our intimacy ; the only barrier to our happiness
was your foolish lover, Luke. He has taken the sulks, and
gone away, — our road is now clear. I love you better
than a hundred such milksops as he could, so come, — say
the word !"

"That word," replied Kathleen, firmly, "shall never be
said by me."

"Have a care, girl !" fiercely retorted Mark, "I 'm not a
man to be trifled with ; you have led me to believe that
you liked me, and you *shall* redeem the pledge your eyes
at least have given."

"Never! Mark Dermot, never !" exclaimed Kathleen,
rising from her seat. But with a fierce gesture, and a determined fire in his eye, Mark forced her down again, saying, in a clear, but terribly earnest manner, "Kathleen,
from my youth up, I never allowed the slightest wish of
my soul to be thwarted ; think you that I shall submit to
be led or driven, coaxed near or sent adrift, at the caprice
of any living thing? — No ! if you can't be mine from love,
you shall from fear ; for," ratifying his threat by a fearful
oath, "no obstacle shall exist between me and my desire."

"What mean you, Mark Dermot?" cried the terrified
girl.

"No matter," he replied, "the choice rests with you.
You cannot deny that your manner warranted me in so-
liciting your hand. Remember, love and hate dwell very
near each other, — the same heart contains them both. Be
mine, and every wish of your soul shall be anticipated ;
refuse me, and tremble at the consequences."

"Heaven forgive and help me!" inly prayed Kathleen, as the result of her weak conduct now made itself so awfully apparent. Thinking to enlist some good feeling from Mark's generosity, she frankly acknowledged to him that her affections were entirely bestowed upon the absent Luke.

She knew not the demon heart in which she had trusted; instead of inclining him to mercy her words only inflamed him into tenfold rage.

"Vile woman!" he exclaimed, starting to his feet. "Have you then been making a scoff and jest, a plaything and a tool, of me? Better for you had you raised a fiend than tampered with me thus. How know I that you do not lie, even now, woman-devil? One word for all!— by your eternal hope, who is it that you do love?"

"On my knees, Luke Bryant," fervently said Kathleen.

"Then woe to ye both!" cried Mark, casting her rudely from him, and, with a look of intense hate, rushing from the cottage.

There was a perfect tempest of rage in Mark's breast, as he quitted Kathleen; plans of revenge, deadly and horrible, suggested themselves to him, and he nursed the devilish feeling within his heart until every humanizing thought was swallowed up in the anticipation of a sweeping revenge. On reaching the village, his first care was to find Luke; upon seeing him, Luke started as though a serpent stood in his path.

"Keep away from me, Mark Dermot," he sternly exclaimed. "If you are come to triumph in your success, be careful, for there may be danger in it."

"Luke," replied the other, in a sad tone, "we are rivals no longer. Nay, listen, I bring you good news; there are not many who would have done this; but what care I

now ? The fact is, like a sensible man, I am come to proclaim my own failure. Kathleen has refused me."

"She has?"

"As true as I'm alive; rejected me for you, Luke.
Nay, as good as told me that she merely flirted with me
to fix your chains the tighter. Cunning little devil, —
eh, Luke? Come, you'll shake hands with me now, I
know."

"If I could believe you, Mark," said Luke, the joy
dancing in his eyes.

"I tell you she acknowledged to me that she never
could love any one but you. Now am I not a generous rival, to carry his mistress's love to another? She
requested me to ask you to call this morning, if you
would have conclusive proof of her sincerity, and you
would then find that *she could never use you so again.*
But now 't is getting late, and, as I have delivered my message, I shall leave you to dream of Kathleen and happiness. Good night; be sure and see her in the morning."
So they parted.

Soon afterwards, Luke missed his clasp-knife with which
he had been eating his supper; but, after a slight search,
thought no more of the matter, his soul glowing with
renewed delight at the thought of seeing his loved one on
the morrow, — that their differences would be made up,
and all again be sunshine.

About an hour after, as he was preparing to retire for
the night, it suddenly occurred to him that he would like
to take a walk towards Kathleen's cottage. Perchance he
might see her shadow on the curtain; he might hear her
sweet voice; no matter, to gaze upon the home that contained her would at least be something; so off he started
in that direction, a happy feeling pervading his every

sense. Arrived within sight of her abode, he fancied he heard a stifled groan, but his thoughts, steeped in joy, dwelt not on it. In a moment after, a distinct and fearful scream, as of one in agony, burst on the stillness of the night. It came from the direction of Kathleen's cottage. Inspired with a horrible fear, he ran wildly forward. Another, and another terrible scream followed; there was no longer doubt; it was the voice of his Kathleen. With mad desperation, he reached the place just in time to see the figure of a man, who, in the doubtful light, he could not recognize, rush from the door and disappear in darkness. In breathless horror Luke entered. Great heaven! what a sight met his eyes. His beloved Kathleen lay on the blood-dabbled floor, in the last agony of departing nature, her beating heart pierced with many wounds; she saw and evidently recognized Luke, for, 'mid the desperate throes of ebbing life, she clutched his hand in hers, trying, but in vain, to speak. She could but smile; her eyes glazed, her hand relaxed its grasp, and with her gentle head resting on his breast her spirit passed away.

All this was so sudden and fearfully unexpected to Luke that he scarcely knew 't was reality, until several of the surrounding neighbors, who had been alarmed by the outcry, came hastily in.

"See!" cried one, "'t is as I thought; murder has been done."

"And here is the fatal instrument with which it has been done," said another, as he picked up a gory knife from the floor. It caught the eye of Luke. "That knife is mine," said he, in the measured tone of one stricken down by a terrible calamity.

"Yours?" they all exclaimed at once. "Then you have murdered her?"

20

Luke only smiled, — a ghastly, soul-crushed smile, most awful to look upon at such a time ; his heart was too full for words. Reason, which had been dethroned by this unexpected blow, had scarcely yet returned to its seat, for all unconsciously he still held the lifeless form tightly clasped in his arms, gazing, with a sort of stony expression, upon the face of her who had been to him the world. It was not until they approached to seize him for killing *her*, that he seemed to be thoroughly aware of his position.

"What would you do, friends?" said he, mournfully, as they endeavored to force him away. "Would you deny me the sad comfort of dying in her presence?"

"Have you not murdered her, wretch?" cried one of the bystanders.

"What! murder *her*! God in heaven forbid," he exclaimed.

"Is this not your knife?"

"It is."

"And how came it here — if not used by you — in this unknown manner?"

"It was stolen from me by that arch-demon, Mark Dermot," said Luke, shuddering to the very heart, as he mentioned that name.

"That has got to be proved," cried one of the crowd, who happened to be a friend of Mark's; "we can't take your bare word for it. Let him be secured."

But Luke needed no securing. Listlessly he suffered them to pinion his arms ; and in the same room with the precious casket which once contained his heart's treasure, he passed the rest of the night, in a state of mental torture utterly indescribable.

The morning after this awful occurrence a coroner's

jury was summoned, and the identity of the knife having
been proved, added to his own admission, and the fact
of his having had a quarrel with her the day before being
testified to, every circumstance tended to fix the guilt
upon him ; a verdict was delivered accordingly, and Luke
Bryant stood charged with the murder of one for whom
he would willingly have shed his last drop of blood.

With a degree of effrontery consonant with his general
character, Black Mark made his appearance amongst the
spectators who attended the inquiry, and was loudest in
denunciation against the supposed criminal. It only remained now for the accused, who had been removed during
the inquest, to be brought into the chamber of death, pre-
viously to the warrant being drawn out for his final com-
mittal, to be tried at the ensuing quarter sessions. He was
conducted into the room ; with a listless, apathetic gaze
he looked around him mechanically, for he cared not now
what fate might do to him, when suddenly his eyes rested
on Mark Dermot. The consciousness of everything that
had taken place seemed all to flash through his brain at
once.

"Murder !" he cried. "Can it be that Heaven's lightning slumbers? Friends! behold that fiend, who, not
content with the life's blood of one victim, now comes to
triumph in a double murder!"

"What means the fool?" contemptuously exclaimed
Mark. "Does he suppose that reasoning men will credit
his ravings, or help him to shift his load of crime upon
another's shoulders?"

"As I'm a living man, as there is a just God who
knows the secrets of all hearts, there stands the murderer,
Mark Dermot!" solemnly replied Luke. "It is not for
myself I care, for Heaven knows that I would rather die

than bear about this load of misery; but that he should brave the angels with a shameless brow, he whose hands are crimsoned with her precious blood, — it is too much! too much!"

"Then, Luke Bryant," said the coroner, "you deny having committed this crime?"

"On my knees, before the throne of mercy, I do."

"I trust, then, that you may cause a jury of your countrymen to believe so; but for me, I have only one duty to perform, and the circumstances clearly bear me out in my assumption. I must send you to trial!"

At this juncture, one of the jurymen, who thought he could perceive a meaning in Mark's peculiar, ill-concealed glance of savage delight, begged to be heard. Keeping his eye steadily fixed on Mark's face, he said, with solemnity, "When the judgment of man is in perplexity as to the author of crimes like these, the aid of Heaven may well be solicited, that it might be mercifully pleased to give some indication by which the innocent may be saved from suffering for the guilty. We have an old tradition here, that if the accused lays his right hand upon the breast of the corpse, swearing upon the Holy Evangelists that he had no act or part in the deed, speaking truly, no results will follow; but if he swears falsely, the dead itself will testify against him; for the closed wounds will reopen their bloody mouths, and, to the confusion of the guilty one, the stream of life will flow once more. It seems to me that this is a case in which *The Test of Blood* might be applied, not vainly."

"Willingly, most willingly, will I abide the test!" exclaimed Luke.

"And you?" said the juror, with a penetrating glance at Mark.

"I!" said the latter, with an attempt at recklessness. "What is it to me? Why should I be subject to such mummery? who accuses me?"

"I do!" thundered Luke, "and I now insist upon his going through the trial. Myself will point the way."

So saying, he approached the lifeless body, and, sinking on his knees, laid his right hand reverently on the heart, saying, "My blessed angel! if thy spirit lingers near, thou knowest that this hand would rather let my life-blood forth than offer thee the shadow of an injury!"

They waited an instant, — all was quiet. Meantime, Mark, persuading himself that it was but a form, and yet trembling to the very core, advanced. All eyes were upon him; he paused, cast a glance around, and, grinding his teeth savagely, cried out, "Why do you all fix your gaze on me? I'm not afraid to do this piece of folly." He advanced another step — again he hesitated; heartless — brutal — though he was, the spell of a mighty dread was on his soul. His face grew livid; the blood started from his lips; large round drops rolled down his ashy cheeks. At last, with a tremendous effort, he knelt, and attempted to stretch forth his hand, — it seemed glued to his side. Starting to his feet again, he cried fiercely, "I will not do it, — why should I?"

"You can not! — you dare not!" said Luke. "If you are guiltless, why should you fear?"

"Fear!" screamed the other, "I fear neither man nor devil, — dead nor living," — and suddenly he placed his hand upon the breast of the dead!

"See! see!" cried Luke, wildly, "the blood mounts up, — it overflows!"

"It's a lie!" madly exclaimed Mark.

But it was no lie; the ruddy stream welled upward

through those gaping wounds, and flowed once more down her snowy breast, a murmur of awe and surprise breaking from the assembled group; whilst, shivering to the very heart, the terrors of discovered guilt and despair seized upon Mark.

"Curse ye all!" he roared. "You would juggle my life away; but you shall find I will not part with it so readily." Hastily drawing a pistol, it was instantly wrested from him. Several of the bystanders flung themselves upon him; but the desperate resistance which he made, added to the frightful internal agony which he had just endured, caused him to break a blood-vessel; and in raving delirium the hardened sinner's soul wended to its last account, in the presence of those whom, in his reckless villany, he had expected to destroy.

Wonder succeeded wonder; and the mystery was soon discovered to be no mystery at all, but the natural instrument in the hands of Providence to confound the guilty. As, relapsing into his former listlessness, Luke was intently gazing on the body of his beloved, suddenly his heart gave one tremendous throb.

"Hush!" he exclaimed, with anxious, trembling voice. "For heaven's love, be silent for an instant! I thought I heard a sound like — Ha! there it is again, — a gasp, — a gentle sob, and scarcely audible, but distinct as thunder within my soul. There's warmth about her breast, — her eyelids tremble. The God of mercy be thanked! She lives! she lives!" and Luke sank upon his knees; a flood of tears, the first he had shed, relieved his overcharged feelings.

It was true, — she did live; from loss of blood only had she fainted, and the excessive weakness had thus far prolonged the insensibility; none of the stabs had reached a vital part, and it was the first effort of nature to resume its suspended functions which had caused the blood once more to circulate, just at the instant which so signally established the guilt of the intended murderer.

It only remains for me to say that Mark Dermot's previous bad character prevented any regret being felt for a fate so well deserved. In process of time Luke's devoted love was rewarded. Kathleen recovered from the effects of her wounds, gave him her hand, and, profiting by the terrible lesson which she had received, made an estimable, virtuous, and affectionate wife.

FATALITY.

A CONDENSED NOVEL.

NOT BY SIR E— B— L—.

CHAPTER I.

NIGHT.

"O, the summer night
Has a smile of light,
And she sits on a sapphire throne."
Barry Cornwall.

"Words, words, words." — *Shakespeare.*

THE moon in tranquil brilliancy shed a soft, spiritual light upon the picturesque and happy village of Oakstown, which, like an innocent child steeped in guilt-less slumber, reposed upon its grassy couch ; that small, low, musical reverberation which fills the air in calm summer nights, rising and falling on the ravished sense like the undulations of some fairy minstrelsy, broke sweetly the intensity of silence ; whilst ever and anon the clear, sharp bay of the distant watch-dog came ring-ing on the ear with startling emphasis.

It was midnight ; the last peal from the village clock had from the ivy-covered tower tolled forth the death of yesterday, while mocking echoes caught up the sound, and to the hills repeated it in myriad voices, then died away and left the scene again to silence ; soft, balmy slumber closed the eyes of all, — all, save one pale watcher ; he, for 't was a man, with anxious gaze peered through the doubtful light, listening eagerly and with bated breath to every passing sound. For one whole hour had this poor, pallid listener, without speech or motion, stood within the half-opened window of a mansion. You would have thought him lifeless, or a statue, so little evidence of vitality did he present, and yet a close observer might have seen by the deep corrugations on that brow, by the strong compression of those lips, by the fixed, steadfast gaze with which those eyes were bent in one direction, that something uncommon had brought that midnight watcher to the open casement, when all around was stillness.

But see, his ear has caught a distant sound, his eyes dilate, he scarcely breathes, as his head is cautiously stretched forth to catch its import; a signal is heard, almost imperceptible, but to the patient listener full of certified assurance; 't is returned; a figure is seen slowly nearing the window; he reaches it, the recognition is mutual; in a low and all but voiceless whisper the now smiling watcher murmurs in the stranger's ear, " Is that you, Bill ? "

A nod and squeeze of the hand was the reply.

"Damn your eyes, I thought you were never coming," said our friend within.

" Hallo, Jim, none of that ere," replied the new-comer ; " I had to establish a crack on my own account, and a jolly good swag I got; so no more palaver, — business is business, — let us go to work, and *stash all jaw.*"

" Well, come on then. Have you got the barkers ? "

" To be sure I have ; you don't suppose I 'd try a knobby crib like this without the persuaders. Do you think the gallows old cove will run rusty ?" inquired Bill, the house-breaker, exhibiting an enormous pair of horse-pistols.

" He might," returned Jim, " so 't is best to be careful, — if he stirs, shoot him, it 's your only security."

"O, never fear me," said the other, with a significant grin. "I'm blowed if I stand a chance of being *lagged* or *scragged* if I can help it; here," he continued, cocking his pistols as he spoke, "here's my best friend in an argument; he does n't speak very often, but when he does he generally has it all his own way; so, now for it."

"Hold!" interrupted Jim, "there's one thing I bargain for before I admit you."

"What's that?" growled the robber.

"The valuables are in the pantry, locked up; the key is in the housekeeper's pocket; should she wake and resist — "

"The knife," savagely whispered Bill, "the knife is a silent argufyer."

"Villain! murderer!" exclaimed the former, energetically seizing the ruffian by the arm, "not for your life. Know, man of blood," continued he, dashing the tears from his eyes, and trembling with suppressed agitation as he spoke, "I love that woman; do with the others as you please, but as you are a man, I charge you to spare her life."

There was a pause; at length the housebreaker gave the required assurance.

"Heaven, I thank thee," fervently ejaculated the other, opening the casement. They entered.

O holy and inscrutable NATURE, who dost in every being plant the imperishable germ of affection, laud be to thee! even this guilty butler, who, leagued with highwaymen, betrays his trust and yields his master to the murderous blade, has within his inmost heart, corrupted though it be, one humanizing influence. CIRCUMSTANCE, thou daughter of the sky, twin-born with DESTINY, creation hinges on thy unerring fiat, the WILL must coincide with thee, the ACT be regulated by thy inclination; thou stretchest forth the hand of man, thou put'st his very tongue in motion; VICE attends thy bidding, enveloping the unrighteous with the attributes of ILL; while virtue at thy summons speeds to earth, and in holy vesture clothes the BEAUTIFUL and the GOOD.

CHAPTER II.

MORNING.

"There's no place like home." — *J. H. Payne.*
"He hath a lean and hungry look." — *Shakespeare.*

THE village of Oakstown, bathed in the sunlight of a summer morning, showed lovely as the home of everlasting joy; the merry woodland choir upraised their song of thankfulness; the gladsome sun-ray danced on the wavelets of the tiny stream, and rained a flood of softened warmth, like breath of seraphs, on the fresh-cut grass with which the morning's labor had bestrewn the meadows, scattering its sweetness on the breeze, and making the morning air one sweet and grateful perfume; the happy villagers thronged the various avenues, seeking their respective homes, for food, and rest from the first instalment of the day's pleasant toil; faces embrowned with ruddy health, and all aglow, looked gladly forth upon the liberal free air of — their sole inheritance; poor serfs of custom, hapless slaves of circumstance, did they but know their misery, shut out from scientific knowledge, far from the inspiring converse of the intellectual, and in melancholy ignorance doomed to wear out life in factitious happiness and unreal comfort!

The breakfast-room in Oakleigh Hall presented a beautiful picture of that domestic elegance which characterizes the
family houses of England. Lord Elderberry, the hereditary owner of some score of miles, of which he formed the
noble nucleus, reclined in his velvet chair, surrounded by
all those luxuries which custom has interwoven with the
wants of life until they have become necessary to the high
in station. He was a tall, graceful, aristocratic-looking
man; his age was about fifty, but he was so carefully
made up that a transient observer would hardly suppose
him to be more than thirty. His fair and ample brow,
well chiselled though slightly exaggerated nose, small
hands, and arch-instepped feet, proclaiming at once the inheritor of noble blood; his beautiful child, the sole sur-
viving daughter of his house, bearing also, in her every
turn, the unmistakable evidences of gentle birth, sat near
him; they, with a taciturn governess, and one male friend
of his lordship, made up the party. It was unusually
late, yet breakfast was not yet served; indeed the table
was but partly laid, and each began to wonder what
could possibly have caused the delay. His lordship was
slightly, but not perceptibly annoyed. To the careless
observer no change could be seen, but MacBrose, his
accommodating distant relation and humble servant, with
the experienced eye of a toady, caught the shadow of an
ungracious expression, and exerted his utmost to avert the
coming storm, ere its arrival should oblige him to seek
shelter in retirement.

"Remarkable fair day, this, my lord," insinuated he in
his blandest manner.

"Very," dryly responded the Earl.

"Hem!" said MacBrose, confidentially to himself. "He
is vexed; that tone is sufficient, — the *deil* take their

laziness," — for inasmuch as his annoyance proceeded from the long protraction of the matutinal meal he supposed the cloud upon his lordship's brow was produced by the same cause.

The Earl sighed heavily, so heavily as to cause the Lady Emily, his daughter, to raise her head from her usual morning's occupation, that of tending her favorite exotics, when, perceiving the sadness which had mantled over her father's face, she approached him affectionately, and, kissing him, exclaimed, " Dearest papa, you are looking quite pale."

O, amidst the thorny path of LIFE, its pangs, its privations, the *pointed rocks*, the *perilous obstructions* fate flings before us as we whirl along the troublous tide of DESTINY, how sweet a comforter art thou, FILIAL LOVE !

His lordship smiled, but 't was as a transient sun-ray on a tomb, showing for one bright instant the external semblance of joy, while all within was dark and dismal ; and yet that insubstantial gleam sufficed to calm his daughter's agitation ; and when the Earl kissed her peachy cheek, and with paternal fondness soothed her apprehension, she cheerfully resumed her task, her happy young heart pure and unsophisticated.

CHAPTER III.

THE APPARITION.

"Morte la bête,
Mort le venin."

"Can I believe my eyes ?" — *Anon.*

MORE than an hour had passed, and yet no sign of breakfast ; the intervening time having been spent by Mac-

Brose in mentally delivering over every servant in the house to the hottest place your memory can suggest, casting furtive glances ever and anon towards Lord Elderberry, and wondering from the inmost recesses of his epigastrium what could possibly have caused this unusual apathy. He was *Hungry*, — uncommonly HUNGRY.

At last the Earl broke silence, exclaiming, suddenly, "Mac Brose"; after a slight pause, continuing, "What's your opinion with regard to Apparitions?"

"Why, my lord, I — that is to say — upon my word — *appareetions* — *gude*ness me, the study of demonology is one of *on*questionable *antee*quity from the earliest stages of the world up to the present time. H*e*story is rife w*e*th *e*llustrations. Pol*ee*bius maintains that — "

Lord Elderberry stayed him in his learned exordium by saying with solemnity, "I saw one last night."

MacBrose forgot his very appetite in more absorbing curiosity. The Lady Emily, arrested in the act of trimming a lotus, caught her father's words, and timidly crept forward to listen.

"You know, MacBrose," continued the Earl, his voice rendered nearly inarticulate from agitation, — "you know the details of my early life, — the mysterious loss of my first-born, my only son, the heir to my name, the last of this noble house."

"Alas! unhappy destiny," sighed forth MacBrose, making liberal use of his cambric, and inwardly exulting that distant relationship was lifted by the circumstance a thought nearer to the broad lands of Oakleigh.

The Lady Emily tried to speak, but could not; so, burying her face within her hands, she knelt on the footstool at her father's feet, and nestled herself in his breast. "My child," faltered he, "my own, my only child!" and the

Earl, stern, cold as was his nature, wept. The grief of father and daughter was sharp but silent. Not so that of MacBrose; he sobbed aloud; and what's more, felt the fell acuteness of his sorrow, for he was hungry even to anguish.

After a space, the Earl resumed his natural, calm dignity, and continued : "'Tis now just fifteen years since my boy was lost; had he lived, he would have been of age to-day; after the three years which I employed in ceaseless search, believing him dead, I endeavored, as you know, to school myself, if possible, into Christian-like resignation."

"Sore blow! *sore* blow! good man! *excellent* man!" sobbed MacBrose, seeing that there was a pause, and he was expected to say something.

"Time, at length, the great softener of human suffering, began to blunt the edge of my anguish; and what was at first a maddening thought, that ever stood up stark and plain before me, sank into a settled melancholy. But as this day comes round, the anniversary of his birth, the greatness of my loss obtrudes itself upon my imagination with renewed violence. Overpowered by such feelings, it was very late last night ere I retired to my bed, and, with my thoughts full of my lost one, fell at last, from very weariness of limb, into an uneasy, broken slumber, from which I was awakened by a sudden noise, and on looking up, great heavens! what was my astonishment upon beholding the apparition of my son; not a sweet, smiling boy, as when last I saw him, but with his manly form developed, his mother's angel face changed into masculine severity, just as it has been my pride to picture what he might have grown to had he lived. Slowly he seemed to near my couch, and then I saw that he was meanly clad, and had a haggard, fearful look; a knife was in one hand, and the semblance of a miniature in the other. I knew it at once : 't was similar to one in my possession, — a likeness of his mother, set in brilliants. His attention seemed to be directed alternately towards it and me. Fear had hitherto fettered my tongue, and froze up the very current of my blood. But in the faint hope of receiving a reply, I determined to address the spectre. For that purpose I raised myself gently, and had just ejaculated, ' In the name of heaven,' when a flash of lightning seemed to break from his very hand ; a loud clap of thunder instantaneously followed, and the apparition vanished."

CHAPTER IV.

RETRIBUTION.

"Do I merit pangs like these,
  That have cleft my heart in twain ?
Must I, to the very lees,
  Drain thy bitter chalice, Pain ?" — *Morris.*

" Revenge is now the cud that I do chew."
                          Beaumont and Fletcher.

SCARCELY had Lord Eldérberry finished the relation when a confused murmur was heard approaching the apartment, and several voices exclaiming, " Bring him along," " We 've caught him," " Villain, robber," etc., the hubbub growing louder and louder, until Simkins, the housekeeper, bounced into the breakfast-room.

" What 's the matter, Simkins ? " sternly demanded the Earl.

" Why, don't you know that you have been robbed, my dear lord," she returned ; "but we 've caught 'em, — that villain, James, to go for to have the impertinence to make up to me, too! O the wickedness of the world!"

"Robbed?" replied the Earl.

"Robbed?" anxiously exclaimed MacBrose, for inasmuch as his posterity *might*, in a century or two, have an interest in the property, it behooved him to be personally concerned.

"And by that rascal, James, too?" said the Earl; "ungrateful fellow!"

"Horrible ruffian!" said MacBrose.

"Unfortunate wretch!" said the Lady Emily.

"Where is he?" demanded Lord Elderberry.

"They're a bringing him, my lord," whimpered Simkins, who, to the honor of womankind, be it said, lamented more at the prospect of a poor fellow's being hanged, and so lost to her and to respectability forever, than for the imminent danger of his lordship's valuables.

At this moment, James, the delinquent butler, was dragged in by several of the under servants, who showed their loyalty for the Earl, and their detestation for crime, by looking awfully indignant, and grasping James tightly by the collar.

"Release him," said the Earl, in a justice of the peace tone. They did so, and the butler shook off his capturers, and, folding his arms across his breast, scowled upon the group.

"Well, sir," said the Earl, regarding the prisoner sternly, "this is a pretty reward for all I have done for you."

"You are right, Earl," replied the fellow in a determined voice, "it is."

"What mean you?" demanded his lordship.

"Patience, my lord; you'll soon know," replied the butler, casting upon him a glance of concentrated malignity.

21

"Come, come, fellow," interrupted MacBrose, who was playing clerk, and noting down the proceedings, "consider where you are, sir, — be respectful."

"Peace, fool!" exclaimed the other savagely. "Mean, crawling parasite, keep to your vocation; cringe, and fawn, and flatter, and eat your miserable meal in silence."

"I wish to the Lord I had it to eat," thought MacBrose, for he was one of those humane, milk-blooded folks who reverence themselves too much to take offence at anything.

"Now, sir, explain," demanded the Earl. "How have I injured you?"

"How?" replied the fellow, with a flashing eye. "How? Ha! I'll tell you how; great lord, *you* endowed me with this load of misery, *you* delivered me up to the tender mercy of a cruel fate. Lord — FATHER! *you* gave me life."

The Earl gasped for breath, shuddering from his very soul as the fellow continued, "Look upon this portrait, most noble lord," tearing a humbly executed miniature from his breast, and flinging it to his lordship.

"Great powers! Maria!" muttered the Earl, sinking back into his chair.

"Ha!" exclaimed the delinquent, "you recognize that face; you saw it when, in youth, health, innocence, and beauty, it beamed like a ray of light; but you saw it not when *vice, misery,* and *degradation* had stamped the impress of a fiend on that angelic countenance; you saw her when she lived the minion of your vicious passion, but you did not see her die a hopeless death, raving in delirium. I *did;* and kneeling beside the corpse of her that *was* my mother, I swore to be avenged upon her soul's destroyer, — upon thee. Ay, writhe, writhe! I've more to tell thee yet. Thy son —"

"Lives," almost shrieked the Earl.

"You shall hear," quietly returned the prisoner. "You never even inquired whether there was such a thing in existence as I, so there was no fear of being recognized. I soon obtained a situation in your household; once there, my first design was to seek your library, upbraid you with your infamy, and shoot you where you sat. Several times did I enter for that purpose, and invariably found you fondling your son, — your only *legitimate* son, — the heir to the house and *honors* of Oakland; when the idea flashed across my brain what glorious revenge it would be to make that much-loved boy the instrument of retribution, to nurture him in vice, to steep him in villany, to blot out every attribute of good, *to destroy him utterly in* LIFE *and in* ETERNITY, — a SON's soul for a MOTHER's. I stole him, kept him concealed for a time, clothed him in squalid rags, and then found means to have him conveyed to the abodes of guilt and wretchedness. Ha! ha! ha! day by day, week by week, year by year, while you incessantly deplored his loss, I watched him in his progress through all the grades of infamy; schooled in wickedness, tutored by robbers and murderers, the heir of Oakleigh grew up a *fit* inheritor of his father's HONOR."

"Merciful heaven!" ejaculated the Earl, as the suspicion flashed across his mind. "Was it he? was it my son that—"

"That aimed the murderous weapon at his father's heart? It was! Ha! ha! it was," triumphantly exclaimed the fellow. "I led him on to the commission of this crime. I planned it, pointed out your room, hoping he would have killed — no, not killed you; for I would have had you *know* the hand that gave the death-wound." At this moment the sound of footsteps was heard approaching.

"Now," roared the ruffian, "*noble* father, prepare to meet thy *honorable* son."

Several dependents entered, having in their custody the man whom the reader will recognize as Bill, of the first chapter. He gave a savage look at the butler, muttering between his teeth, "So, you precious varmint, the whole of this here vos a plant, they tell me."

"Listen," replied the butler, "listen, my lord, to the classic eloquence of your son's language. Honorable Bill, the housebreaker! let me present you to your father. Ha, ha! ha!" and the ruffian's face beamed with savage joy.

The Earl groaned, and covered his face with his hands, in speechless agony.

"What's all this nonsense?" said Bill; "*my* father's far enough away; he's bin *transported* this many a year."

"It's a lie," thundered the butler. "There, there, he sits in that velvet chair, overflowing with paternal love. *Go, go, and receive his blessing before you are hanged.*"

"Will anybody tell me what the fellow means?" replied Bill, looking round the group.

"Why, he asserts," said MacBrose, finding no one spoke, "that you are the undoubted son of his lordship here, whom he, from motives of revenge, stole in infancy, and caused to be brought up in iniquity, hoping by such horrible means to involve father and son in one common destruction."

"O, that's it, is it?" said Bill; "then he'd best have not *hollered* so loud, damn him; I'm glad I can pay him off for getting me into this scrape. I ain't no more your son, my lord, than Oliver Crummles."

The Earl started from his chair, while the butler's face grew livid with rage.

"Proceed," said his lordship; "if there be but the thou-sandth particle of a doubt, you shall be saved, rewarded. Go on, go on, in mercy."

"All I got to say," resumed Bill, "is, that everybody knows who *my* father was; but there used to be a poor little natomy of a creature, that was sommat like me, among us. We called him Slender Jimmy. Nobody knowed where he comed from, or anything about him."

"And where is he?" said the Earl, with intense anxiety.

"Why, you see we couldn't make him useful nohow; he had no taste for picking pockets, and all the whoppin' in the world couldn't drive it into him; so we let him alone until he got up to be a youth. We always knew that there was something queer about him, he had such a curious knack of reading books. Why, if you believe me, I stole nigh hand a whole stall of thim, 'cause he liked 'em, and hadn't the heart to prig for hisself. Well, at last he guv us the slip entirely, and I did hear that he listed and threw hisself away in the army."

"It must, it must be he. O, heaven be thanked!" fervently cried the Earl.

Meantime, the butler, frenzied at the destruction of his plans, suddenly drew a pistol from his breast, levelled it full against the Earl's, and, exclaiming, "Damnation! you shall never behold him," pulled the trigger. There was a loud report, followed by a scream of agony. The barrel had burst, causing the ball to deviate, which lodged harmlessly in the wall, shattering the hand and arm of the ruffian butler, while a fragment of steel pierced his forehead and sunk even to his brain. He raised himself with difficulty, and, fixing his glazing eyes upon the Earl, opened his mouth several times as if attempting to speak, but in vain; shaking his clenched fist, and regarding him with a scowl of malevolence, his jaw dropped, and he fell dead.

CHAPTER V.

C O N C L U S I O N.

"A fair commencement, better far continuation,
And the winding up the fairest of the whole."
Knowles.

"Ne quid nimis." — *Latin Proverb.*

BUT little more remains to be told. The Earl inserted a cautiously worded advertisement in the various newspapers, which very soon had the effect of discovering the individual mentioned by Bill; everything conspired to certify his identity. It appeared that, after quitting the vile society in which his boyhood was passed, he gained much distinction, earning for himself the rank of ensign in the regiment into which he had enlisted, so that, had he not already a name, he would have ennobled one by his own exertions. The interview between father and son was most affecting; and as the latter had passed scathless through so vitiating a trial as the companionship of his early years, it need not be said that he was in every way worthy to shed lustre upon the high position to which he found himself entitled.

The housebreaker was brought to trial, but, inasmuch as this particular transaction was shown to be the contriving of the dead butler, and no other was proved against him, his punishment was limited to a short imprisonment, after undergoing which, his lordship granted him a small farm on his estate, provided that he sincerely promised to amend his life. He did so, and, to his honor be it said, most rigidly kept his word. Who shall say that he has a better hope beyond this life than that reformed sinner? Doth not the holy book declare, "THERE IS JOY IN HEAVEN OVER ONE SINNER THAT REPENTETH"?

THE BLARNEY STONE.

" O, did you ne'er hear of the Blarney,
'T is found near the banks of Killarney,
Believe it from me, no girl's heart is free,
Once she hears the sweet sound of the Blarney."

Lover.

" I TELL you, Mike, agra! it 's no manner o' use, for do it I can't, an' that 's the long an' the short of it."

" Listen at him ; why, it is n't bashful that you are, eh, Ned, avic ? "

" Faix, an' I 'm afeard it is."

" *Gog's bleakey !* why, they 'll put you in the musayum along wid the marmaids an' the rattlin' sneaks ; a bashful Irishman ! why, a four-leaved shamrogue 'ud be a mutton-chop to that, man alive."

" So they say ; but I 've the complaint anyway."

" Well, *tear an aigers*, I never heerd the likes ; it makes me mighty unhappy, for if modesty gets a footin' among us it 'll be the ruin of us altogether. · I should n't wonder but some of them retirin' cockneys has inoculated us with the affection, as they thravelled through the country. Well, an' tell us, how d' you feel whin you 're blushin', Ned ? "

" Arrah ! now don't be laughin' at me, Mike ; sure we can't help our wakeness, — it 's only before her that the heart of me melts away intirely."

" Never mind, avic ; shure it 's a good man's case anyway ; an' so purty Nelly has put the *comether* over your sinsibilities ? "

"You may say that, Mike, *aroon*. The niver a bit of sinse have I left, if it's a thing that I iver happened to have any; an' now, Mike, widout jokin', is n't it mighty quare that I can't get the cowardly tongue to wag a word out o' my head when her eye is upon me. Did you iver see Nelly's eye, Mike?"

"Scores o' times."

"Maybe that is n't an eye?"

"Maybe there is n't a pair of thim, since you come to that?"

"The divil such wicked-lookin' innocince iver peeped out of the head of a Christian afore, to my thinkin'."

"It's nothin' but right that you should think so, Ned."

"O, Mike! to me, the laugh that bames out of thim, whin she's happy, is as good to a boy's feelin's as the softest sun-ray that iver made the world smile; but whin she's sad — O, murdher, murdher! Mike — whin them wathery dimonds flutthers about her silky eyelashes, or hangs upon her downy cheek, like jew upon a rose-lafe, who the divil could endure it? Bedad, it's as much as I can do to stand up agin them merry glances; but when her eye takes to the wather, be the powers of war, it bothers the navigation of my heart out an' out."

"Thrue for you, Ned."

"An' thin her mouth! Did you iver observe Nelly's mouth, Mike?"

"At a distance, Ned."

"Now, that's what I call a rale mouth, Mike; it does n't look like some, only a place to ate with, but a soft-talkin', sweet-lovin' mouth, wid the kisses growin' in clusthers about it that nobody dare have the impudence to pluck off, eh, Mike?"

"Howld your tongue, Ned."

"If Nelly's heart is n't the very bed of love, why thin Cupid 's a jackass, that 's all. An' thin her teeth ; did you notice thim teeth ? why, pearls is pavin'-stones to them ; how they do flash about, as her beautiful round red lips open to let out a voice that 's just for all the world like talkin' honey, every word she says slippin' into a fellow's soul, whether he likes it or not. O, Mike, Mike, there 's no use in talkin' : if she is n't an angel, why she ought to be, that 's all."

"You 're mighty far gone, Ned, an' that 's a fact. It 's wonderful what a janius a boy has for talkin' nonsense when the soft emotions is stirrin' up his brains. Did you ever spake to her ? "

"' How the divil could I ? I was too busy listenin' ; an' more betoken, between you an' me, the rale truth of the matter is, I could n't do it. Whether it was bewitched I was, or that my sinses got dhrounded wid drinkin' in her charms, makin' a sort of a mouth of my eye, I don't know, but every time I attempted to say somethin', my tongue, bad luck to it, staggered about as if it was tipsy, an' the divil a word would it say for itself, bad or good."

"Well, now, only to think. Let me give you a word of advice, Ned ; the next time you see her, take it aisy, put a big stone upon your feelin's an' ax about the weather ; you see you want to bowlt out all you have to say at once, an' your throat is too little to let it through."

"*Be the mortial*, an' that 's a good advice, Mike, if I can but folly it. This love is a mighty quare affection, ain't it ? "

"Thremendious. I had it oncet myself."

"How did you ketch it ? "

"I did n't ketch it at all. I took it natural."

"And did you ever get cured, Mike ? Tell us."

"Complately."

" How ? "

" I got married."

" O, let us go to work ! "

——————

From the foregoing characteristic conversation between Mike Riley and his friend Ned Flynn, it would appear evident that the blind boy's shaft,

    " Feathered with pleasure and tipped with pain,"

was fast imbedded in the heart of the latter, or in plainer and not less expressive phrase, he was bothered entirely by Miss Nelly Malone.

During an interval of rest from mowing, the dialogue took place; that over, they resumed their labor; the convalescent " married man" humming a sprightly air, which kept time to the stroke of his scythe, while the poor wounded deer, Ned, came in now and then with an accompaniment of strictly orthodox sighs.

It certainly was a most extensive smite on the part of pretty Nell; and a nobler heart never beat under crimson and gold than the honest, manly one which now throbbed with the first ardor of a pure and unselfish passion. A short time longer, and they rested again. Ned was sad and silent; and the never-forgotten respect which makes suffering sacred in the eyes of an Irish peasant kept Mike mute also. At last, Ned, with a half downcast, wholly sheepish expression, said, the ghost of a smile creeping over his features, " Mike, do you know what ? "

" What ? " said Mike.

" I 've writ a song about Nelly."

" No," rejoined his friend, with that ambiguous emphasis which might as well mean yes. Adding, with dexterous tact, "Is it a song? An' why the mischief should n't you? shure an' have n't you as illigant a heart to fish songs out of as anybody else? Sing us it."

"I 'm afeard that you 'll laugh if I do, Mike."

"Is it me?" replied Mike, so reproachfully that Ned was completely softened. After the making-your-mind-up minute or two, with a fine, clear voice, he sang : —

THE ROSE OF TRALEE.

All ye sportin' young heroes, wid hearts light an' free,
Take care how you come near the town of Tralee ;
For the witch of all witches that iver wove spell
In the town of Tralee at this moment does dwell.
O, then, don't venture near her, be warned by me,
For the divil all out is the Rose of Tralee.

She 's as soft an' as bright as a young summer morn,
Her breath 's like the breeze from the fresh blossomed thorn,
Her cheek has the sea-shell's pale, delicate hue,
And her lips are like rose-leaves just bathed in the dew :
So, then, don't venture near her, be warned by me,
For she 's mighty desthructive, this Rose of Tralee.

O, her eyes of dark blue, they so heavenly are,
Like the night sky of summer, an' each holds a star ;
Were her tongue mute as silence, man's *life* they 'd control,
But eyes an' tongue both are too much for one's soul.
Young men, stay at home, then, and leave her to me,
For I 'd die with delight for the Rose of Tralee.

And now, after this toploftical illustration of the state of Ned 's feelings, and inasmuch as they are about to resume their labor, let us leave them to their mowing, and look after Miss Nelly Malone, for love of whom poor Ned had *tasted* the Pierian spring.

In a neat little chamber, bearing about it the unmistakable evidence of a tidy woman's care, sits the individual
herself, her little fingers busily employed in knitting a very
small stocking, — her own ; no trace of wealth is to be seen
in this humble abode, but of its more than equivalent,
comfort, it is redolent. At the open casement peep in
the blossoms of the honeysuckle and the sweet-pea, filling the air with a perfume more grateful than art could
ever obtain ; sundry *artless* prints, and here and there a
ballad on some heart-breaking subject, probably amongst
them the highwayman's autoballadography, wherein he
heroically observes,

> " I robbed Lord Mansfield, I do declare,
> And Lady Somebody in Grosvenor Square,"

are fastened to the walls, decorated with festoons of cut
paper of most dazzling variety or color ; a fine, plump, contented lark, in an open cage, which he scorns to leave,
returns his mistress's caress with a wild, grateful song,
whilst, tutored into friendliness, a beautiful sleek puss,
whose furry coat glances like satin in the sun-ray, dozes
quietly upon the window-sill, indulging in that low purr
which is the sure indication of a happy cat. It is the
home of innocence and beauty, fitly tenanted.

And what are pretty Nelly's thoughts, I wonder ; a
shade of something, which may be anxiety or doubt, but
scarcely sorrow, softens the brightness of her lovely face.
She speaks, — 't will be no treason to listen. You will
perceive that the cat is her *confidante,* — a discreet one,
it must be confessed.

" It's foolishness, so it is ; is n't it, puss ? "

Puss does n't condescend to notice the remark.

" Now, Minny, is n't it, I ask you, is n't it folly, the
worst of folly, to be thinkin' of one who does n't think of

me? I won't do it any more, that I won't. Heigh-ho! I wonder if he loves me. I somehow fancy he does, and yet again if he did, why could n't he say so? there's one thing certain, and that is, I don't love *him*, that is to say, I *won't* love him; a pretty thing, indeed, to give my heart to one who would n't give me his in return. That *would* be a bad bargain, would n't it, puss?"

Pussy acquiesced, for silence, they say, gives consent.

"But, O," resumed Nelly, "if I thought he *did* love me — there, now, I've dropped a stitch — what *am* I thinkin' of? — I must n't give way to such foolishness. Why, the bird is done singin', and Minny is lookin' angry at me out of her big eyes. Don't be jealous, puss, you shall always have your saucer of milk, whatever happens, and — hark! that's his step, it is! he's comin'! I wonder how I look," and, running to her little glass, Nelly, with very pardonable vanity, thought those features could not well be improved, and — the most curious part of the matter — she was right.

"He's a long time coming," thought she, as, stealing a glance through the white window-curtain, she saw Ned slowly approach the garden gate; gladly would she have flown to meet him, but maidenly modesty restrained her; now he hesitates a moment, takes a full gulp of breath, and nears the house; at every approaching step, Nelly's pulse beat higher; at last, she bethought herself it would be more prudent to be employed; so, hastily taking up her work, which was twisted and ravelled into inextricable confusion, with a seeming calm face she mechanically plied her needles, her heart giving one little shiver as Ned rapped a small, chicken-livered rap at the door. Nelly opened it with a most disingenuous, "Ah, Ned! is that you? who *would* have thought it! Come in, do."

The thermometer of Nelly's feelings was about fever heat, yet she forced the index to remain at freezing point. "Take a chair, won't you?"

And there sat those two beings whose hearts yearned for each other, looking as frigid as a pair of icicles, gazing on the wall, the floor, pussy, or the lark. Ned suddenly discovered something that wanted a deal of attending to in his hat-band; whilst Nelly, at the same time, evinced an extraordinary degree of affection for the cat. To say the truth, they were both very far from comfortable Ned had thoroughly made up his mind to speak this time, if ruin followed, and had even gone so far as to have settled upon his opening speech; but Nelly's cold and indifferent "Take a chair" frightened every word out of his head. It was essentially necessary that he should try to recover himself, and he seemed to think that twisting his hat into every possible form and tugging at the band were the only possible means by which it could be accomplished. Once more all was arranged, and he had just cleared his throat to begin, when the rascally cat turned sharply round and stared him straight in the face, and in all his life he thought he never saw the countenance of a dumb creature express such thorough contempt.

"It well becomes me," thought he, "to be demeanin' myself before the cat," and away flew his thoughts again.

Of course all this was very perplexing to Nelly, who, in the expectation of hearing something interesting, remained patiently silent. There was another considerable pause; at last, remembering his friend Mike's advice, and, moreover, cheered by a most encouraging smile from the rapidly thawing Nell, Ned wound up his feelings for one desperate effort, and bolted out, "Isn't it fine to-day, Miss Malone?"

This broke the silence so suddenly that Nelly started from her chair, the lark fluttered in the cage, and puss made one jump bang into the garden.

Amazed and terrified by the results of his first essay, fast to the roof of his mouth Ned's tongue stuck once more, and, finding it of no earthly use trying to overcome his embarrassment, — that the more he floundered about the deeper he got into the mud, — he gathered himself up, made one dash through the door, and was off like lightning. Nelly sighed as she resumed her knitting, and this time she was sad in earnest.

"Well, what luck ?" said Mike, as, nearly out of breath from running, Ned rejoined him in the meadow. "Have you broke the ice ?"

"Bedad, I have," said Ned, "and more betoken, fell into the wather through the hole."

"Why, would n't she listen to you ?"

"Yes, fast enough, but I did n't give her a chance ; my ould complaint came strong upon me. Ora ! what 's the use in havin' a tongue at all, if it won't wag the words out of a fellow's head. I 'm a purty specimen of an omadhaun ; there she sot, Mike, lookin' out of the corners of her eyes at me, as much as to say spake out like a man, with a soft smile runnin' about all over her face, and playing among her beautiful dimples, like the merry moonbame dancin' on the lake. O, murther ! Mike, what the mischief am I to do ? I can't live without her, an' I have n't the heart to tell her so."

"Well, it is disgraceful," replied Mike, "to see a good-lookin' man disparage his country by flinching from a purty girl ; maybe it might do you good to go an' kiss the BLARNEY STONE."

"That 's it," exclaimed Ned, joyously clapping his hands

together, and cutting an instinctive caper, "that's it. I wonder I niver thought of it before; I'll walk every stitch of the way, though my legs should drop off before I got half there. Do you think it 'ud do me good to kiss it ?"

"Divil a doubt of it, — sure it never was known to fail yet," said Mike, oracularly.

"Why, then, may I niver ate a male's vittles, if there's any vartue in the stone, if I don't have it out of it." And that very night, so eager was Ned to get cured of his bashfulness, off he started for Killarney. It was a long and tedious journey, but the thought of being able to speak to Nelly when he returned sufficed to drive away fatigue; in due time he reached the far-famed castle,

> "On the top of whose wall,
> But take care you don't fall,
> There's a stone that contains all the Blarney ! "

Mike climbed with caution, discovered the identical spot, and, believing implicitly that his troubles were now at an end, knelt, and, with a heart-whole prayer for his absent Nelly, reverently kissed *The Blarney Stone.*

True, devoted love had lent him strength to overcome the difficulties of access; imagination, that powerful director of circumstance, did the rest. It was with humility and diffidence he had approached the object of his pilgrimage, but he descended from it with head erect and countenance elated; he could now tell his burning thoughts in *her* ear; he was a changed man. A very pretty girl, who officiated as guide, and upon whose pouting lips, report says, the efficacy of the charm has been frequently put to the test, met him at the archway of the castle, — for no other reason in the world than merely to try if he were sufficiently imbued with the attractive principle. Ned watched an opportunity, and, much more to his own astonishment than to hers, gave her a hearty kiss, starting back to watch the effect. She frowned not, she did not even blush. Ned was delighted; his object was attained.

"He could kiss who he plazed with his Blarney"; consequently, feeling supremely happy, without losing another moment, he retraced his steps homeward.

Meantime, Nelly missed her silent swain, whose absence tended materially to strengthen the feeling of affection which she entertained for him. Day after day crept on, yet he came not; and each long hour of watching riveted still more closely her heart's fetters. Now, for the first time, she acknowledged to herself how essential he was to her happiness, and, with a fervent prayer that the coming morning might bring him to her side, she closed each day. Her wonder at last at his continued absence quickened into anxiety, and from anxiety into alarm. Jealousy, without which there cannot be a perfect love, spread its dark shadow o'er her soul, and she was wretched. In vain she reasoned with herself; the sun of her existence seemed suddenly to be withdrawn, and all was gloom; even the very bird, appearing to share his mistress's mood, drooped his wings and was silent; so much are externals influenced by the spirit of the hour, that even her cheerful room felt comfortless and solitary. Nelly loved with a woman's love, devotedly, intensely, wholly; to lose him would be to her the loss of all that rendered life worth living; hers was an affection deserving that which was given for it, although as yet she knew it not.

Gazing out one day in the faint hope of seeing her beloved, her heart gave one sudden and tremendous bound. She saw him; he had returned at last. But how changed in demeanor! Can her eyes deceive her? No, her heart tells her it is he, and it could not err.

Instead of the downcast look and hesitating step, joy laughed forth from his face, and his tread was easy, rollicking, and careless; as he came nearer, she thought she heard him sing; he did sing! what could it portend? Had he found one who knew how to break the shell of reserve? 'T was torture to think so, and yet it was the first image that presented itself to her anxious heart. It was now her turn to be tongue-tied, dumb from agitation; she could not utter a syllable, but, trembling to the very core, sat silently awaiting what she feared was to prove the funeral knell of her departed happiness.

With a merry song upon his lips, Ned lightly bounded over the little paling, and in a minute more was in her presence. Speak or move she could not, nor did his first salutation place her more at ease.

"Nelly," said he, "you drove me to it, but it's done, it's done!"

"What's done? what can he mean?" thought Nelly, more agitated than ever.

"It's all over now," he continued, "for I've kissed it. Don't you hear me, Nelly? I say I've kissed it."

"In heaven's name," cried the pale, trembling girl, "what do you mean? kissed who?"

"No *who* at all," said Ned, laughingly, "but *it*, — I've kissed *it*."

"Kissed what?"

"Why, the Blarney Stone, to be sure," screamed out Ned, flinging his hat at pussy, and executing an extremely complicated double-shuffle in the delight of the moment; indeed, conducting himself altogether in a manner which would have jeopardized the sanity of any one but a love-stricken Irishman.

"Shure it was all for you, Nelly, mavourneen, that I did

it; it has loosened the strings of my tongue, and now I can tell you how deeply your image is burnin' widin my very heart of hearts, you bright-eyed, beautiful darling!"

What more he said or did it will be unnecessary for me to relate; suffice it to say that the world-renowned talisman lost none of its efficacy on this particular occasion. One observation of pretty Nell's, I think, is worthy of record. At the close of a most uninteresting conversation, to anybody but themselves, the affectionate girl whispered to him, "*Dear Ned, you need n't have gone so far !*"

The course of true love sometimes *does* run smooth, a great authority to the contrary nevertheless, for in about three weeks' time the chapel bells rang merrily for the wedding of Edward and Nelly. Ay, and what's more, neither of them had ever cause to regret Ned's visit to THE BLARNEY STONE.

NED GERAGHTY.

CHAPTER I.

BRAVE old Ireland is the Land of Fairies, but of all the various descriptions there is n't one to be compared to the LEPRECHAUN, in the regard of cunning and 'cuteness. Now if you don't know what a leprechaun is I 'll tell you. Why, then, — save us and keep us from harm, for they are queer chaps to *gosther* about, — a leprechaun is the fairies' shoemaker; and a mighty conceited little fellow he is, I assure you, and very mischievous, except where he might happen to take a liking.

But perhaps the best way to give you an idea of their appearance and characteristics will be to tell you a bit of a story about one.

Once upon a time, then, many years ago, before the screech of the steam-engine had frightened the "good people" out of their quiet nooks and corners, there lived a rollicking, good-natured, rakish boy, called Ned Geraghty; his father was the only miller in the neighborhood for miles around, and, being a prudent, saving kind of an old hunks, was considered to be amazingly well off, and the name of the town they lived in would knock all the teeth out of the upper jaw of an Englishman to pronounce: it was called Ballinaskerrybaughkilinashaghlin.

Well, the boy, as he grew up to man's estate, used to worry the old miller nearly out of his seven senses, he was such a devil-may-care good-for-nothing. Attend to any-

GERAGHTY

thing that was said to him he would not, whether in the way of learning or of business. He upset ink-bottle upon ink-bottle over his father's account-books, such as they were ; and at the poor apology for a school, which the bigotry of the reverend monopolizers of knowledge permitted to exist in Ball——, the town, he was always famous for studying less and playing more than any boy of his age in the barony.

It is n't to be much wondered at, then, that when, in the course of events, old Geraghty had the wheat of life threshed out of him by the flail of unpitying Time, Master Ned, his careless, reprobate son, was but little fitted to take his position as the head-miller of the country.

But there is a luck that runs after and sticks close to some people, whether they care for it or not, as if, like love, it despiseth the too ardent seeker.

Did you ever take notice that two men may be fishing together at the same spot, with the same sort of tackle and the same sort of bait, and that one will get a basketful before the other gets a bite ? That 's luck, — not that there 's any certainty about it ; for the two anglers might change places to-morrow. Ah ! it 's an uncomfortable, deceiving, self-confidence-destroying, Jack-a-lantern sort of thing is that same luck ; and yet how many people, especially our countrymen, cram their hands into their pockets and fully expect that the cheating devil will filter gold through their fingers.

But, good people, listen to me, take a friend's advice, don't trust her, and of this be assured, although a lump of luck may now and then — and mighty rarely at that — exhibit itself at your very foot, yet to find a good vein of it you must dig laboriously, unceasingly. Indolent humanity, to hide its own laziness, calls those *lucky* men who, if you investigate the matter closely, you'll find have been simply *industrious* ones.

But to return to the particular luck which laid hold of Ned Geraghty. Everybody thought that Ned the rover would soon make ducks and drakes of the old man's money ; that the mill might as well be shut up now, for there was nobody to look after it. Every gossip, male and female, in the town, had his or her peculiar prognostic of evil. Sage old men shook their heads, grave old matrons shrugged their shoulders, while the unanimous opinion of the marriageable part of the feminine community was that nothing could possibly avert the coming fatality except a careful wife.

Now candor compels the historian to say that the mill-hoppers did not go as regularly as before, and moreover, that Ned, being blessed with a good personal exterior, began to take infinite pains in its adornment. Finer white cords and tops could not be sported by any squireen in the parish ; his green coat was made of the best broadcloth ; an intensely bright red India handkerchief was tied openly round his neck ; a real beaver hat covered his impudent head ; and a heavy thong-whip was in his hand, for he had just joined modestly in the Bally &c. &c. hunt.

This was the elegant apparition that astonished the sober and sensible townfolk a very few months after the decease of the miserly old miller, and of course all the evil forebodings of the envious and malicious were in a fair way to be speedily fulfilled, when my bold Ned met with the piece of luck that changed the current of his life, and gave the lie to those neighborly and charitable prognostications.

It was one fine moonlight night that Ned was walking homeward by a short cut across the fields, for his sorry

old piece of horse-flesh had broken down in that day's
hunt, and for many a weary mile he had been footing it
through bog and brier, until with fatigue and mortification
he felt both heart-sick and limb-weary, when all at once
his quick ear caught the sound of the smallest kind of
a voice, so low, and yet so musical, singing a very little
ditty to the accompaniment of tiny taps upon a diminutive
lapstone. Ned's heart gave one great bound, his throat
swelled, and his hair stuck into his head like needles.

"May I never eat another day's vittles, if it ain't a
leprechaun," said he to himself, "and the little villain is
so busy with his singing that he did n't hear me coming ;
if I could only ketch a-howlt of him, my fortune 's made."

With that he stole softly towards the place whence the
sounds proceeded, and, peeping slyly over a short clump
of blackthorn, there, sure enough, he saw a comical little
figure, not more than an inch and a half high, dressed in an
old-fashioned suit of velvet, with a cocked hat on his head,
and a sword by his side, as grand as a prime minister,
hammering at a morsel of fairies' sole-leather, and singing
away like a cricket that had received a musical education.

" Now 's my chance," said Ned, as, quick as thought, he
dropped his hat right over the little vagabond. " Ha ! ha !
you murtherin' schemer, I 've got you tight," he cried, as
he crushed his hat together, completely imprisoning the
leprechaun.

" Let me out, Ned Geraghty ; you see I know who you
are," squalled the little chap.

" The devil a toe," says Ned, and away he scampered
towards home with his prize, highly elated, for he knew
that the leprechauns were the guardians of all hidden
treasure, and he was determined not to suffer him to
escape until he had pointed out where he could discover a
pot of gold.

When Ned reached home, the first thing he did was to get a hammer and some nails, and, having placed his hat upon the table, to fasten it securely by the brim, the little fellow screeching and yelling like mad.

"Now, my boy, I've got you safe and snug," says Ned, as he sat down in his chair to have a parley with his prisoner. "There's no use in kicking up such a hullaballoo, — tell me where I can find a treasure, and I'll let you go."

"I won't, you swaggering blackguard, you stuck-up lump of conceit, you good-for-nothing end of the devil's bad bargain, I won't"; and then the angry little creature let fly a shower of abuse that gave Ned an indifferent opinion of fairy gentility.

"Well, just as you please," says he; "it's there you'll stay till you do," and with that Ned makes himself a fine, stiff tumbler of whiskey-punch, just to show his independence.

"Ned," said the little schemer, when he smelt the odor of the spirits, "but that's potheen."

"It's that same, it is," says Ned.

"Ah! ye rebel! ain't you ashamed of yourself to chate the gauger? Murther alive! how well it smells!" chirps the cunning rascal, snuffing like a kitten with a cold in its head.

"It *tastes* better, *avic*," says Ned, taking a long gulp, and then smacking his lips like a postboy's whip.

"Arrah, don't be greiggin a poor devil that way," says the leprechaun, "and me as dry as a lime-burner's wig."

"Will you tell me what I want to know then?"

"I can't, really I can't," says the fairy, but with a pleasanter tone of voice.

"He's coming round," thought Ned to himself, and as with a view of propitiating him still further, "Here's your health, old chap," says he, "and it's sorry I am to be obliged to appear so conthrary, for may this choke me alive if I wish you any harm in the world."

"I know you don't Ned, allana," says the other, as sweet as possible ; "but there's one thing I'd like you to do for me."

"And what might that be ? "

"Jest give us the least taste in life of that ilegant punch, for the steam of it's gettin' under the crevices, an' I declare to my gracious it's fairly killing me with the drouth."

"Nabocklish," cries Ned, "I'm not such a fool; how am I to get it at you ? "

"Aisy enough ; just stick a pin-hole in the hat, and gi' me one of the hairs o' yer head for a straw."

"Bedad, I don't think that would waste much o' the liquor," says Ned, laughing at the contrivance ; "but if it would do you any good, here goes."

So Ned did as the leprechaun desired, and the little scoundrel began to suck away at the punch like an alderman, and, by the same token, the effect it had on him was curious : at first he talked mighty sensibly, then he talked mighty lively, then he sung all the songs he ever knew, and some he never knew ; then he told a lot of stories as old as Adam, and laughed like the mischief at them himself ; then he made speeches, then he roared, then he cried, and at last, after having indulged in

"Willie brewed a peck o' malt,"

down he fell on the table with a thump as though a small-sized potato had fallen on the floor.

"O, may I never see glory !" roared Ned, in an explosion of laughter, "if the little ruffian ain't as drunk as a piper."

"Ha! Ned, Ned, you unfeelin' reprobate an' bad Christian; have you no compassion at all at all?" squeaked the leprechaun in drunken but most miserable accents.

"Oh! — oh! — oh!" the poor little creature groaned, like a dying tadpole.

"What's the matter," says Ned with real concern. "Is there anything I can do for you?"

"Air! air!" grunted the leprechaun.

"The fellow's dead drunk," thought Ned, "so there'll be no harm in lettin' him have a mouthful of fresh air"; so he ripped up two or three of the nails, when, with a merry little laugh, the cunning vagabond slid through his fingers, and disappeared like a curl of smoke out of a pipe.

"Mushen then, may bad luck to you, for a deludin' disciple; but you've taken the conceit out o' me in beautiful style," cried Ned, as he threw himself into his chair, laughing heartily, however, in spite of his disappointment, at the clever way the little villain had effected his release.

"What a fool I was to be taken in by the dirty mountebank."

"No, you are not," said the voice, just above his head.

Ned started with surprise and looked eagerly round.

"There's no use in searching, my boy; I've got my liberty, and I'm now invisible," said the voice, "but you're lettin' me out was a proof that you had a good heart, Ned, and I'm bound to do you a good turn for it."

"Why, then, yer a jintleman ivery inch of ye, though it's only one an' a bit," cried Ned, jumping up with delight; "what are you goin' to gi' me, — a treasure?"

"No, better than that," said the voice.

"What then?"

"A warning."

CHAPTER II.

"WHAT the mischief is the matter wid me, at all at all ?" said Ned ; "sure, don't I know every foot of the ground bechune this and the next place, wherever it is ? but bad luck attind the bit of *me* knows where I 'm stau'in' now. Howsomever, I can't stand here all night, so here goes for a bowld push, somewhere or another."

With that, my bold Ned struck at random through the fields in one direction, hoping to find some well-known landmark which might satisfy him as to his whereabout, but all in vain : the whole face of the country was changed ; where he expected to meet with trees he encountered a barren waste ; where he expected to find some princely habitation he met with nothing but rocks. He never was so puzzled in his life.

In the midst of his perplexity, he sat down upon a mound of earth, and, scratching his head, began seriously to ponder upon his situation.

"I 'll take my Bible oath I was on my track before I met with that devil of a leprechaun," said he, and then the thought took possession of him that the deceitful fairy had bewitched the road, so that he might wander away, and perhaps lose himself amongst the wild and terrible bogs.

He was just giving way to an extremity of terror, when, on raising his eyes, what was his astonishment to find that the locality which, before he sat down, he could have sworn was nothing but a strange and inhospitable waste, was blooming like a garden ; and what 's more, he dis-covered, upon rubbing his eyes, to make sure that he was not deceived, it was his own garden ; his back rested against the wall of his own house ; nay, the very seat beneath him, instead of an earthy knoll, was the good, substantial form that graced his little door-porch.

"Well," cries Ned, very much relieved at finding himself so suddenly at home, "if that don't beat the bees, I'm a heathen. May I never leave this spot alive if I know how I got here no more nor the man in the moon : here goes for an air o' the fire, anyway, for I'm starved intensely wid the cowld."

Upon that he started to go in, when he found that he had made another mistake ; it was n't the *house* he was close to, but the *mill.*

"Why, what a murtherin' fool I am this night! sure it's the mill I'm forninst and not the house," said he ; "never mind, it's lucky I am to be so near home, anyway ; there it is, just across the paddock." So saying, he proceeded towards the little stile which separated the small field from the road, inly wondering, as he went along, whether it was the leprechaun or the whiskey that had so confused his proceedings.

"It's mighty imprudent that I've been in my drinkin'," thought he ; "for if I had drunk a trifle less, the country would n't be playin' such ingenious capers wid my eyesight, and if I had drunk a trifle more, I might a hunted up a soft stone by way of a pillow, and made my bed in the road."

Arrived at the stile, a phenomenon occurred, which bothered him more and more : he could n't get across it, notwithstanding the most strenuous exertion ; when he went to step over, the rail sprang up to his head, and when, taking advantage of the opening, he tried to duck under, he found it close to the ground.

The moon now popped behind a dense black cloud, and sudden darkness fell upon the place, while at the same moment the slow, rusty old village clock gave two or three premonitory croaks, and then banged out the hour of midnight.

Twelve o'clock at night is to the superstitious the most terror-fraught moment the fearful earth can shudder at, and Ned was strongly imbued with the dread of ghostly things; at every bang of the deep-toned old chronicler, he quivered to the very marrow of his bones; his teeth chattered, and his flesh rose up into little hillocks.

There he was, bound by some infernal power. The contrary stile baffled all his efforts to pass it; the last reverberation of the cracked bell ceased with a fearful jar, like the passing of a sinner's soul in agony, and to it succeeded a silence yet more terrible.

" Maybe its dyin' that I am," thought Ned; and all that was lovely and clinging in God's beautiful world rushed across his mind at the instant. "If it is to be my fate to leave it all, so full of life and hope, and yet so unmindful of the great blessings I have unthankfully enjoyed, Heaven pity me, indeed, for I 'm not fit to go."

At this moment his ear caught a most familiar sound, that of the mill-hopper, so seldom heard lately, rising and falling in regular succession. Surprised still more than ever, he turned and beheld the old mill, brilliantly lighted up; streams of brightness poured out from every window, door, and cranny, while the atmosphere resounded with the peculiar busy hum which proceeds from an industriously employed multitude.

Fear gave place to curiosity, and Ned stealthily crept towards the mill opening and looked in; the interior was all ablaze with lights, while myriads of diminutive figures were employed in the various occupations incidental to the business. Ned looked on with wonder and admiration to see the celerity and precision with which everything was done; great as was the multitude employed, all was order and regularity. Here, thousands of little atomies pushed along sack after sack of corn; there, number-less creatures ground and deposited the flour in marked bags, while Ned recognized his old friend, the leprechaun, poring over a large account-book, every now and then reckoning up a vast amount of bank-bills and dazzling gold pieces.

Ned's mouth fairly watered as he saw the shining metal, and he heard the crisp creasing of the new bank-notes, which took the little accountant ever so long to smooth out, for each one would have made a blanket for him; as soon as the leprechaun had settled his book affairs to his satisfaction, he, after the greatest amount of exertion, assisted by a few hundred of his tiny associates, deposited the money in a tin case, whereon Ned distinctly read his own name.

While he was hesitating what course to adopt, whether to try and capture the leprechaun again, or wait to see what would occur, he felt himself pinched on the ear, and on turning round, he perceived one of the fairy millers standing on his shoulder, grinning impudently in his face.

"How do you do, sir?" says Ned, very respectfully, for he knew the power of the little rascals too well to offend them.

"The same to you, Ned Geraghty, the sporting miller," says the fairy. "Have n't we done your work well?"

"Indeed, an' it's that you have, sir," replied Ned. "Much obleeged to you, I am, all round."

"Won't you go in and take your money?" says the fairy.

"Would it be intirely convenient?" said Ned, quietly, although his heart leaped like a salmon.

" It 's yours, every rap, so in an' lay a-howld of it," said
the other, stretching up at his ear.

" They would n't be agin' me havin' it, inside, would
they ? " inquired Ned.

" The money that you have earned yourself, we can't
keep from you," said the fairy.

" That 's true enough, and sure, if I did n't exactly earn it
myself, it was earned in my mill, and that 's all the same " ;
and so, quieting his scruples by that consoling thought,
Ned put on a bold front, and walked in to take possession
of the tin case in which he had seen such an amount of
treasure deposited. There was not a sound as he entered,
— not a movement as he walked over to the case ; but as
he stooped down and found that he could no more lift that
box from the ground than he could have torn a tough old
oak up by the roots, there arose such a wild, musical, but
derisive laugh from the millions of fairy throats that Ned
sank down upon the coveted treasure, perplexed and
abashed; for one instant he held down his head with
shame, but, summoning up courage, he determined to know
the worst, when, as he raised his eyes, an appalling scene
was disclosed.

The fairies had vanished, and instead of the joyous multitude flitting like motes in a sunbeam he beheld one gigantic head which filled the entire space ; where the windows
had been, a pair of huge eyes winked and glowered upon
him ; the great beam became a vast nose, the joists twisted
themselves into horrible matted hair, while the two hoppers formed the enormous lips of a cavernous mouth. As
he looked spellbound upon those terrible features, the tremendous lips opened, and a voice like the roar of a cataract
when you stop your ears and open them suddenly burst
from the aperture. The sound was deafening, yet Ned
distinguished every syllable.

"Ain't you afraid to venture here?" bellowed the voice.

"For what, your honor?" stammered out Ned, more dead than alive.

"For weeks and weeks not a morsel has entered these stony jaws, and whose fault is it? Yours!" thundered the awful shape; "you have neglected us, let us starve, and rot piecemeal; but we will not suffer alone, — you, you must share in our ruin."

At these words, a pair of long, joist-like arms thrust themselves forth, and, getting behind Ned, swept him into the space between the enormous hoppers, — the ponderous jaws opened wide, — in another instant, he would have been crushed to atoms. But the instinct of self-preservation caused him to spring forward, he knew not where. By a fortunate chance he just happened to leap through the door, alighting with great force on his head; for a long time, how long he could not tell, he lay stunned by the fall; and indeed, while he was in a state of insensibility, one of his neighbors carried him home, for he remembered no more until he found himself in bed, with a bad bruise outside of his head, and worse ache within.

As soon as he could collect his senses, the scenes of the past night arose vividly to his mind. "It is the leprechaun's warning," said he, "and it's true he said it was better far than gold, for now I see the error of my ways, and, more betoken, it's mend that I will, and a blessin' upon my endayvors."

It is but fair to Ned to say that he became a different man, gave up all his fine companions and evil courses, and stuck diligently to his mill, so that in time he lived to see well filled the very tin case that the leprechaun showed him in the warning.

THE FAIRIES' WARNING.

A BROTH of a boy as ever stood in shoe-leather
was Mickey Maguire. At hurling, wrestling, kicking football, or kicking up a shindy generally, there wasn't
his equal in the barony. It would really do your heart
good to see him, with the fun glancing all over his face,
like sunbeams on the Shannon's water, "batin the flure,"
at a fair or a "pathern," with some bright-eyed colleen;
for there was no better foot at the jig in the country
round, and that the girls knew mighty well, for there
wasn't one of them that wouldn't walk a long mile to
dance "Planxty Molly," or "The Ould Foxhunter," with
Sportin' Mickey Maguire.

Now you must know that our friend Mickey was the
proprietor of the only mill, such as it was, in the vicinity;
consequently, at the early part of his life, the hopper was
continually going, and the result was a very comfortable
living for the thriving miller; but, as he increased in
years, instead of growing wise by experience, and hus-
banding his present resources, so that, in the event of
accident, ill-health, or misfortune of any kind, he might
have a trifle laid by to fall back upon, like too many of
his countrymen he lived from hand to mouth, spending
exactly what he had, be that much or little. To be sure,
a little always satisfied him when he had no more; but if
it were ever so large a sum, he invariably found a way
to get rid of it. It may readily be conceived, therefore, that Mickey was quite unprepared for a rainy day;

23

indeed, he never suffered himself to think of anything beyond the passing moment.   If to-day were only provided
for, to-morrow might take care of itself.

By a singular continuance of equally balanced luck,
Mickey Maguire managed for a number of years to scramble on tolerably well.   The mill was his banker, and it
depended upon its yielding much or little as to whether he
had a "high ould time," or merely satisfied the few wants
to which he could circumscribe himself, if necessary.

Notwithstanding the carelessness of his general disposition, Mickey was a diligent worker in working hours.
No one ever saw him lounging about in idleness when
labor was in demand; and, moreover, he was possessed of
a true, honest, and benevolent heart : the latch of his door
was never lifted without a welcome ; rich or poor, it was
all the same to him.   A bite and a sup, given with pride
to his equals, and with joy to the hungry wayfarer, was
ever to be had at his table; a seat by his cheerful chimney-corner, and a smoke of the pipe, and maybe a drop of
mountain dew, was always proffered to the weary traveller.

It was a thousand pities that to his many heaven-sent
virtues he did not add the worldly one of prudence.   But
he did n't, and there's an end of the matter ; nor was he
to blame for it either, although some self-satisfied, money-
scraping mortals, who, fortunately for their sons and suc-
cessors, happen to have that same grovelling virtue to a
vicious extent, elevate their eyes, shrug their shoulders,
and cry shame upon the open hand, and all the time the
would-be philosophers forget that they might as well find
fault with an individual for the shape of his nose or the
color of his hair as for the peculiarities of his temperament.

Well, it so happened that year after year Mickey's
affairs got worse, and, in the thick of his distress, what

does my bold miller do but take unto himself a wife, — as he said himself, "for to double his joy and halve his sorrow, which was two to one in favor of some comfort, according to the rule of three."

How it answered his expectations, it is unnecessary to inquire ; suffice it to say that inasmuch as she brought him nothing in the way of worldly gain saving a pair of bright blue eyes and a stuff gown, his prospects were not materially brightened by the alliance.

At last came the year of the bad harvest ; the crops all failed, and the mill became quiet and desolate ; that put the finishing stroke upon poor Mickey's perplexities, and, for the first time in his life, he began to think that there was such a thing as a future to provide for.

" Musha ! then it 's time for me to come to my senses," said he, one day, as he took up his pipe after a most unsatisfactory meal. " Many 's the fine night I spint as much as ud last us a month now, and, more betoken, it's suppin' sorra I am for that same, sure enough."

" Indeed, an' ye are, an' sarve you right, too," continued his helpmate. " But it 's me that 's to be pitied, — me, that niver had the good of it when it was goin', and now it 's gone, it 's me that 'll have to cry salt tears for the want of it. Ah ! if you had only put by ever so little of the money that you wasted in rollickin' about, an' threatin' thim that gives you the cowld showldher now, you might snap yer fingers at the harvest ; an' more betoken, I would n't be shamin' yer name by wearin' the same gownd at market an' at mass."

"Arra be aisy," said Mickey, " where 's the use in tellin' me what I know mighty well already ? I 've been a fool, as many 's the one has been afore me ; but I 've had my jig, an' now the piper 's to be paid, out of my bones, if not out of my pocket."

Well, to make a long story short, Mickey went down the hill in a hurry, as easy-tempered people generally do when the light of good fortune does n't show them their way. Puzzled, confused, and blinded, in the thick darkness of distress, he made a few ineffectual struggles towards an upward movement, only to plunge deeper into the mire of disappointment; so that, tired at last of endeavoring to breast the current of misfortune, he made no exertion to sustain himself, but allowed it to float him where it chose. And it is not to be wondered at that amidst the noisy, reckless revelry of the village whiskey-shop was his general anchorage, and, indeed, misfortune's most dangerous flood-tide could not have carried him into a worse haven; for when the prospects grew brighter, and plenteous harvests again smiled upon the land, the habits which he had acquired in his despondency rendered labor distasteful, and the old mill, once more in brisk demand, was deserted for the tippling-house.

Meantime, although the grain was brought as plentifully as ever, the business of the mill was scarcely sufficient to pay the weekly score chalked up against himself and his gay companions; for again they gathered round him, laughing outrageously at his maudlin jests, and pounding the tables at his drunken songs. The labor at the mill was neglected, for without the eye of the master work is badly done; his home was home no longer; his wife's once beloved voice grew cold and tame to his ears compared with the wild hurrahs of his alehouse friends.

Matters had nearly arrived at a desperate state when one summer evening Mickey was making triangular surveys of the road as usual, his locomotion having been rendered extremely uncertain by copious libations of whiskey-punch, and happened to strike his foot against something hard. Stopping in the midst of a fragmentary song, he stooped, and found it was a *horseshoe*.

"Hurrah!" shouted Mickey, at the top of his voice, "luck's come at last; an', indeed, not before it's wanted." For be it understood that, amongst the Irish peasantry, the finding of so commonplace a thing as a horseshoe, under such circumstances, is considered to be the precursor of the most illimitable good fortune; and so it was with Mickey Maguire, although not exactly in the way he anticipated.

"Aha!" he shouted, in glee; "won't this fill the ould woman's heart with joy?" for with the certainty of approaching good luck came back all his warmth of feeling for his wife; it was but the pressure of calamity that deadened it for a while. "The blessed heaven be praised for this," cried he, as with the earnestness of a hearted belief he knelt and offered up a prayer of thankfulness for the precious gift which he felt assured would be the instrument of his delivery from distress.

Rising up, thoroughly subdued by the grateful feeling that pervaded every sense, he dashed the tears from his eyes, exclaiming, "I'll be a man again now, wid a blessin'." Then another mood came over him, and he kissed and hugged the horseshoe, capering about and making the echoes ring with his voluble delight.

Many were the castles in the air poor Mickey built before he reached home, and, amongst other notable intentions, I regret to say that almost his first resolve was to give such a jollification to the whole country round, that the whiskey should flow like pump-water, until every soul at the feast was as drunk as a lord.

He had scarcely made that last resolution when he reached his door, at which, according to his own account

of what then occurred; he was just about to knock, when
he felt a slight tug at the tails of his great coat, which
made him hold back for a second.   Thinking, however,
that it was only his fancy, he lifted his hand again to
knock at the door, when a little stronger pull at his coat-
tail convinced him that there was something mysterious
in it.   The most intense fear took possession of him, as
he tremblingly cried, "May the blessed saints above stand
betune me and all harum!   I do believe the good people
is upon me."

He had scarcely said this when a clear, shrill, distinct,
although infinitely small laugh, ascended from the tufts of
grass at his feet, simultaneously with which his heels were
tripped up, and with another tug at his coat down he
tumbled upon a little mound of "fairy clover," his head
striking against a soft stone.

The blow stunned him for an instant; but when he
opened his eyes again, what was his astonishment to see
the whole extent of ground in his neighborhood perfectly
alive with diminutive creatures in human form, with hundreds upon hundreds of tiny voices chirping out,

> "Aha! Mickey Maguire,
> Luck you 'll have to your heart's desire."

"Musha thin, may long life to yees for that same, and
may yees niver want divarshin yerselves," said Mickey,
taking off his hat and making a low bow to the fairies.

At that instant his attention was directed more especially
to three frolicsome elves, who were carrying, kicking, and
pushing along what appeared to him to be three very
small apples, which were at length deposited immediately
before him, when the whole multitude formed a circle
round, and pointed to the diminutive fruit.

"What 's them for, might I ask?" inquired Mickey.

Whereupon a number of the fairies took up one of the apples, and, presenting it to Mickey, they all shouted, —

" Eat this pippin, Mickey asthore,
And see what you have seen before ! "

Without hesitation Mickey swallowed the little apple at a mouthful, when, lo ! in an instant the house and hill vanished, and in its place appeared the old mill, as it was ten years before. The sound of perpetual industry echoed around, and soon he saw the semblance of himself, but without the careworn traces which the ill-spent intervening time had marked upon his features. The ruddy hue of health was on his cheek, and content beamed from his bright eye. A deep regret smote at Mickey's heart as he closed his eyes upon the happy scene.

" Take it away from my sight," he cried, " it 's too late ! too late ! O for the wasted time once back again ! "

The voices of the fairies recalled him, as they sung, —

" The other, Mickey, eat, and see
What now is, but what ne'er should be."

Mickey did what he was told, but with a sad heart and increasing apprehension. No sooner had he swallowed the second apple, than the mill disappeared, the busy hum of contented labor was hushed ; he found himself within the house, and loud sobs of grief fell upon his ear. He looked around and beheld his wife ; she was on her knees, her head buried in her hands, weeping. Presently a drunken uproar was heard, the door was suddenly burst open, and he saw himself when all manhood was obliterated and nothing but the beast remained. He saw himself in that brutal and degraded condition men would blush into their very hearts to behold themselves reduced to, did even one sense alone remain, — the sense of sight.

"Horrible ! horrible ! " groaned Mickey, as he shut out

the fearful apparition with his clenched hands. "O for the unvitiated mind of other days! but it is too late, too late!"

Again the fairy voices shouted, —

> "*Eat, and see now, with the last,*
> *The future purchased by the past.*"

Infinite terror took hold of him, and it was some time before he could summon up courage sufficient to swallow the apple, so conscious was he of the recompense which his hitherto wasted life deserved. At last, with a sullen determination to know the worst, he gulped it down desperately. The house vanished, and he saw nothing but a black, impenetrable cloud. Striving to pierce through the darkness, at last he distinguished a point of light, which spread and spread until it made a large, luminous circle, within which he could distinguish two forms. On looking closer, he saw that it was his wife and himself, but grown very, very old. There were also joyous children, whom he knew not, making up the happy group. The man was reading from the household book, while a warm, glowing sunset illumined the beautiful picture.

He could have gazed forever upon that calm, glorious scene, but that the tears coursed down his cheeks so abundantly as almost to take away his sight. Suddenly, close by that lovely group, another picture started into view in terrible contrast. It presented the aspect of a bleak, desolate, and dismal heath. Through the dull, misty atmosphere he gazed, and in a few minutes discovered two wretched grave-mounds, the absence of all Christian memorial indicating that they had been hastily thrown up, and in unconsecrated ground. The strong man shuddered to the heart's core, as in burning letters his own name appeared on the miserable wooden grave-mark.

In dreadful agony he uttered a wild cry, and fell insensible. When he came to himself he found that he was in his own bed, and his wife beside him, stanching, as well as she could, a severe cut in his head.

Not a word did Mickey say that whole night about his adventure with the "good people." But the next morning, although suffering considerably from his last evening's accident, he made a clean breast of it, and told his wife everything, together with his determination to take warning by the lessons the fairies had given him, — a determination, I am glad to record, that he kept to the uttermost; for from that time forward there was not a soberer or more domestic and industrious man in the whole country round than Mickey Maguire, the miller.

Great was the delight he took, in after years, when seated in the chimney-corner, surrounded by a friendly circle of bouncing little Maguires, and listened to by such of the neighbors as might drop in to tea with the rich miller, to relate the incidents which caused his reformation, and which he believed as implicitly as holy writ, although Mrs. Maguire would now and then try his temper by declaring that it was very strange indeed, for she was at the window all the time, and he was n't down a minute before she had him lying in bed with a wet towel on his forehead.

O'DEARMID'S RIDE.

ONCE upon a time, a mighty long while ago, when Ireland's green fields and pleasant valleys belonged to those who had a natural right to them, — before her Saxon neighbors overspread the beautiful land, despoiling the rightful possessors of the soil, heaping mountain loads of oppression upon the poor inhabitants, and then deriding them because they could not stand as straight as they did formerly, — there happened to live in the town of Clonmakilty a well-to-do, industrious, and kindly-hearted weaver, whose name was Connach O'Dearmid.

There was then no country but Ireland which could produce such splendid fabrics of every description, from the heavily woven cloth of gold down to the exquisite linen whose texture was so fine that yards upon yards of it could be drawn through a wedding ring; and amongst all the looms in the land, none turned out the equal of Connach O'Dearmid's, — and mind you, the weaver then was not the hunger-wasted, gaunt, phantom sort of death-in-life object one may now see occasionally peering from a miserable aperture called a window, in the very centre of Ireland's once proud capital. No indeed! He had his servants and his grooms, and a retinue like a nobleman.

And if the kings and warriors had their bards to chronicle their high achievements, and inspired minstrels to sing them, so had the handicraftsman his, to hymn the still prouder deeds of holy labor.

A fine, high-spirited, happy, and contented people were they then, until the insatiable and cunning English close by, after vainly endeavoring by open warfare to subdue them, secretly introduced the fruitful elements of discord which unhappily divided those who never more can be united. Colonies of a strange and utterly antagonistic blood and breed were planted in their midst; a new religion brought forth and nurtured with ecclesiastical zeal that most fatal of feuds which results from a difference of faith. Is it surprising then, that, robbed of their inheritance and driven into the woods and savage hiding-places, their hearths usurped and their altars desecrated, the poor, persecuted people, without shelter, without food, and most especially without education, should slowly but surely have retrograded when all the rest of the world has advanced, until centuries of oppression have almost depopulated an entire nation?

But to go back to Connach. He happened, fortunately for himself, to live in a time when every man held his own, in quietness and peace; there were no "evictions," no homesteads levelled to enlarge my Lord So-and-So's estate, no damnable middlemen and agents to plunder equally the unfortunate tenant and the absentee landlord, no intriguing double-faced demagogues, no selfish semi-political priests, — all the accursed spawn of Saxon interference, — but contentment, like an atmosphere of perpetual summer, rested upon the land; and amongst the happy islanders none had more cause to be so than Connach, the weaver; a benignant fate having placed him in that most enviable of all positions, — cheerful and well-satisfied mediocrity, — too high for privation to reach, and too low for envy to assail, with just sufficient intellect to comprehend and enjoy everything enjoyable in nature, and thoroughly impressed with that instinctive religion of the heart which causes it to expand in gratitude to the benign Giver of all good; — true, loving, and considerate in his family relations; free, open-handed, liberal, and conscientious in his friendships.

Such were the characteristics of the representative of the O'Dearmids living at this time; and, with but slight modifications of temperament, such have they been through succeeding generations, even up to the present time; for amidst the chances and changes of conquest, colonization, and foreign absorption, the old house, land, name, and occupation has been transmitted from son to son, in regular descent, and in the town of Clonmakilty may be seen at this very day — if the tourist should ever discover it — a tolerably good-sized but curiously patched tenement, bearing an exceedingly old-fashioned signboard, on which is painted "Connach O'Dearmid, Weaver."

The cause of this strange preservation and uninterrupted transmission of name, property, and occupation for such a number of years, is satisfactorily explained in a family tradition which I had the pleasure of hearing from the present representative; and as it appeared to me to be more graphic in his own diction, I shall endeavor to present it to the reader as nearly as I can in his words.

"You know, sir, I suppose, that at the time luck fell upon the name of the O'Dearmids, makin' somewhere about, it might be, a thousand years ago, — but the date does n't matther a *thraween*, — the fellow that owned it was a bowld-hearted, rollickin', ginerous, divil-may-care boy, as iver breathed the breath o' life. Well, sir, the fairies, you know, was plintier thin nor they are now; by raysin, I suppose, that the ground was trod upon by the raal ould stock, an' not by furrin' schamers and yalla-headed inthruders. More's the pity! A'most every family of dacint behavior thin had somethin' or another in the shape of a fairy visither; some had maybe a *Puckaun*, — them's the divil's own hounds at mischief; others might stumble over a *Leprechaun*, and if they looked sharp, for them's the greatest chates out, would get heaps o' money. Thin there was *Phoukas, Fetches, Banshees,* and hundhereds of sich likes; to some families they comes as warnins, to others as luck signs.

" But I'll tell you how we got one, sir, — long life to him ! He's here now, listenin' to every word I say, — [he reverently lifted his hat as he spoke,] — an' if I tell you a word of a lie, he'll make himself known somehow.

" Well, you must know, sir, that me great ancesther that brought us the luck was oncet riding home from havin' ped a visit to his sweetheart, for he was a coortin' at the time. The night was murdherin' dark, an' he was a little apprehinshus of the 'good people' for the fear of threadin' on a 'fairy circle,' or maybe disturbin' a frolic; so he rode mighty slow across the turf, for there was no roads at the time. Well, sir, all of a sudden the moon bruck out from the black clouds like a red-hot ball from a cannon, an' began to run wild, as I heerd me father say, right across the sky. He had scarcely gazed an instant with terror and wonder upon the quare capers the moon was cuttin', when on turning round agin he saw a phantom horseman ridin' close beside him, that imitated every action. When he galloped, it galloped; when he reined up, it did the same. Fear nearly paralyzed him. He tried to say his prayers, but memory had gone. Still, however, he urged his horse rapidly along; and altho' the sight froze his blood, he could n't keep his eyes off the black rider.

"On comin' to a sharp turn in the road, what did he

see but a little ould woman, sittin' upon a stone, right in
the road of the horseman by his side, now grown into a
solid substance.   Despite of his own terror, me ancesther
shouted out to his strange companion, 'Howld hard, you
black fool !   Pull in, won't you ?   Don't you see the ould
creathur in the road ?   You 'll run over her, you blackguard, you will !'

"But not a hand did the other move in restraint.   On
they went, full gallop.

"'For the love of heaven, ould woman, clear the road !'
cried me ancesther, but not a peg would she stir.   Another
instant, and the black horseman crashed right over the poor
ould sowl, and knocked her as flat as a pancake.

"'Ah ! you murdherin' villain, you 've done it ; I knew
you would !' shouted me ancesther, burnin' wid indignation, and reinin' up his horse as soon as ever he could.   So
did the other.

"What wid the cruelty and the impidence of the fella,
my ancesther could n't stand it any longer ; so, turning his
horse round, he let dhrive at him, but unluckily one of the
big black clouds gradually swallied up the moon, an' in
the darkness the black horseman cut across the fields and
vanished out of sight.   As soon as he was gone, my bowld
Connach groped his way back as well as he could to the
place where the ould woman was run over, an' to his great
surprise found her sittin' upon the same stone as quietly as
if nothin' had happened.

"'God save ye, stranger !' said the ould creathur.

"'God save ye kindly !' said Connach, 'an' I hope yer
not hurted much ?'

"'I 'm not hurted at all, Misther Connach O'Dearmid,
the weaver !' says she.

"'What ! you know me then, do you ?" says he.

" 'Betther nor ye do yerself!' says she. 'It's a good fortune that you desarve, Connach, an' it's a good fortune that ye'll get, both you an' yours, to the end o' time ; for you're respectful an' kind to the ould an' the helpless. You're lovin' and dutiful to them that gav' ye life an' its blessins, your're open-handed to the poor an' the needy, an' honest-hearted to the whole world besides.'

" 'Bedad, I'll come to you for a charadther, if ever I'm in the want of it. Bad-cess to me, av you have n't brought coals of fire into my cheeks, in spite of the cowld weather!' says Connack, blushin' like a girl at the ould woman's praisin' him.

" 'I'll do you a greater sarvice nor that,' says she. 'I'll tell ye yer faults.'

" 'Fire away!' says Connach ; 'let us have them.'

" 'Get down from yer horse, an' sit by me upon this stone,' says she.

" 'Wid all my heart,' says he, jumpin' off in a jiffy ; for he was a little sprung, you see, — the curse of Ireland, sthrong drink, was even then in bein'.

" 'Now for thim faults,' said he, wid a laugh, as he sat down beside the ould woman. 'How many have I ?'

" 'One,' says she.

" 'Is that all ?' says he. 'Pooh ! I know betther.'

" 'Stop !' cries the ould woman, 'hear me out. That one, if suffered to remain within yer heart, will soon breed *all the rest.* For it's the fruitful parent of every crime that has a name.'

" Murdher ! how ye frighten me !' says Connach. 'What the divil is it ?"

" ' *The love of strong drink !* ' says the old woman, seri-ously. ' You behaved kindly to me, an' urged only by the feelins of your kindly nature. I have the power to save

you, an' I will, from this hour forward, as long as time exists. It will be the fault of you an' yours, if misfortunes,
other than those nature imposes, should fall upon yer
name; for yer faults an' vicious inclinations shall be
pointed out to you, by *fairy* power.'

" ' Lord save us ! ' says my ancesther, frightened a'most
out of his siven senses, ' are you a fairy ?'

"'I am,' says she, ' behold the proof ! ' Wid that the ould
rags and tatthers melted away, an', instead of a dirty-look-
ing heap of deformity and wretchedness, Connach beheld
a weeny form, scarcely as big as a blade of grass, but as
bright as if it had been made out o' sunbeams, standin'
an' kissin' its love to him, while the tiniest an' most musical
little voice, like the ringin' of fairy bells, tingled upon his
ear, so small, but so distinct : —

> 'Farewell, Connach ! thou hast had thy warning ;
> Profit by it, and be happy ! '

" The fairy then vanished, an' me ancesther slept upon
that identical stone until mornin'; but when he woke up
he did n't forget the fairy's caution ; for not only did he
never touch liquor, but he left it in his dyin' directions,
to be transmitted from father to son, through every generation, that both house and lands should go away from
him who should get the name of drunkard.

" An' to our credit be it spoke, we have n't had one yet,
though some have needed and received the fairy's warnin'
for that, as well as other faults, an' it 's very wonderful the
various ways they took to tell us of them that 's been runnin' through the family histhory since that time, sometimes in a parable, then again in a dhream, now one way
an' now another. Me own grandfather got his warnin' in
a quare way. His prevailin' fault was harshness, an' a
strong inclinin' to cruel conduct. He threated me father

wickedly durin' his youth, an' at last, because he married
unbeknownst to him, turned him right out of doors.

"Well, it was n't long afther that, grandfather was sittin'
mopin' alone, — for in spite of his hard natur', he missed
his child, — when all at oncet, when he was tryin' to nurse
up his angry feelin', who should he see come in the door
but a favorite cat of his, that had just lost her kittens,
tenderly carryin' in her mouth a bouncin' young rat.
Well, grandfather naturally thought the cat was goin' to
make her supper off the rat ; but not a bit of it. What
does my bould puss do but takes the rat into her basket,
an' pets it up an' plays wid it in the most motherly way !

"At first, grandfather laughed till the tears run down
his cheeks, at the fun of the thing, to see the rat taken so
much care of; but when the cat rowled over on her side,
singin' 'purr-roo,' winkin' at grandfather, an' puttin' her
paw as gingerly over the rat as if she was afraid of breakin'
it, he knew immediately that there was some manein' in
the thing. It was thin that it struck him all at once, that,
if it was an unnatural thing to see a cat nourishin' a creathur that did n't belong to her specie at all at all, it was
more unnatural a mortial sight to see a father turnin' his
back upon his own flesh an' blood.

"'It 's the warnin'!' says he.

"Tears that he had never shed afore — for he was a
hard man — fell in showers from his eyes, an' he prayed
for grace to conquer his faults.

"Well, sir, before the night fell, my father an' his purty
young wife was in the ould man's arms, an' greater joy and
happiness seldom echoed through these ould rafters ; for
next to never doing any wrong, the most heart-satisfyin'
thing in creation is to repent the wrong you 've done ! "

24

JASPER LEECH.

THE MAN WHO NEVER HAD ENOUGH.

THE hero of my sketch, Jasper Leech, was, to use the stereotyped expression, born of poor, but honest parents; his infancy exhibited no remarkable diagnostics by which to illustrate or establish any peculiarity of character, saving, perhaps, the simple fact, that, with him, the process of weaning was protracted to a curious extent, any attempt to cut off or diminish the maternal supply being met with obstinate resistance, in spite of all the ingenious artifices usually resorted to on such occasions to induce a distaste; still he sucked and sucked, until the female visitors, one and all, voted it shameful in a great fellow like that.

At school, young Jasper was famous for the steady snail-pace at which he crawled through the rudiments, and also for the extraordinary *penchant* he evinced for anything in his proximity which was, or appeared to be, unattainable at the moment. If one of his schoolmates was in possession of a new toy, Jasper would first envy him, then covet it, cunningly waiting the moment when, the novelty being past, the boy was open to negotiate; then would he chaffer and diplomatize, almost invariably gaining his desired end. Thus he went on steadily accumulating, until what, with a natural appetite for trading, and a calculating eye to the profitable side of a bargain, he managed to shut up the market altogether by exhaustion. The

very spring-time of life, which generally passes by in glee-
some sport, was to him a period of anxiety and care;
for while his mates were rioting in boisterous play, he
would sit apart, his whole brain wrapped in the maze of
speculation, — a *swop* is in progression, and he must have
the advantage.

Thus passed his boyhood; his schooling over, with his
strong common-sense undulled by too much book-lore, he
was duly inducted into the mystery of shoe-craft. He
served out his time with exemplary diligence, working
leisurely by day that he might keep reserve of strength to
spend the night for his own profit, thereby saving a considerable sum from the employment of his over-hours.

Once his own master, he deliberated long what road he
should travel in pursuit of the blind goddess, invisible as
well as blind, — that phantom which men wear out life
and energy in seeking, only when found to confess with
tears of bitterness how misspent was their time.

At last our ambitious friend ventured humbly into trade
on his own account, declaring that, should anything approaching to success crown his efforts, and at the end of
five or six years he could command a thousand dollars,
he would be the most contented, the happiest fellow on
earth.

He was lucky, curiously lucky; it seemed as though,
Midas-like, all he touched turned to gold; money swept in,
so that before he had been three years in business, instead
of the limited one thousand, he was master of *five.* " Now,"
said he to himself, " if I could but make that five *ten*, I
might not only be enabled to enlarge my stock, and thereby increase my returns, but I think I might even venture
to look about for a helpmate with an equal sum "; for Jasper would just as soon have thought of investing the best

part of his capital in the establishment of a lunatic asylum as of marrying a portionless woman.

The sun shone on : in less time than he could possibly have anticipated, ten thousand was at his command. Very good, thought he ; this, with ten or fifteen thousand more, as a premium for encumbering myself with a comforter of the snarling sex, — for the ungallant Jasper had a thoroughly mercantile business-man's opinion of the angelic species, — will be sufficient. I must investigate. .

So he set out on a tour of the watering-places, and such like wife-markets, where Cupid, the most wide-awake of auctioneers, — it's a libel to say he's blind, — knocks the little darlings down to the highest bidder. Of course, Jasper stopped at the first-class hotels, where he scrutinized the *habitués* of the ladies' ordinary with uncommon interest. There's no use in disguising the fact, he sought not a wife, but a fortune. In extenuation, allow me to say, he was not at all singular : there are plenty of those individuals extant, young, tolerably good-looking fellows, *bien gantés* and redolent of whisker, who linger about the ladies' drawing-room, in the faint hope of fascinating something available (prudent maternity avoids this class with pious horror), middle-aged beaux, who dress sedulously, and toady *chaperons*, carry fans, are always *so* attentive and *so* obliging, dine regularly, and affect a Burgundy decanter, which looks easy-circumstanced, but which the poor waiter is tired of carrying backward and forward, ticketed some hundred and something.

Jasper, though indefatigable, as you may well suppose, met with strange adventures during his wife-hunt. Pretty women, after short experience, he avoided utterly, for he found that they were usually too extravagant in their expectations with regard to *personnel*, and as Jasper could not, by any stretch of his imagination, fancy that he ranked in the category of Fredericks and Augustuses, he endeavored to make up the deficiency by a liberal display of wealth-prefiguring ornament, a kind of strong-box index, which he shrewdly suspected might tempt some ambitious innocent to investigate the contents thereof.

Perhaps it would be well at this period, as our hero is got up at no small expense, to give an outline of his appearance. In the first place, he was twenty-eight years old, by his own account; as he could scarcely be expected to know exactly himself, it's not to be wondered at that he and the parish register differed a few years; but that was of little consequence, for he had an accommodating, curious-colored complexion, which, as it made him look at least forty, will, no doubt, return the compliment by making him look no more at sixty. His hair was about as indefinite, being a factitious auburn, a dry, wiry red, something like the end of a fox's brush in hot weather, crisp and tangible, like fine copper-shavings. One could not help fancying that, if he shook his head, each individual hair would jar audibly against the other. The whole arrangement gave one an idea of intense heat, and an involuntary hope that the poor fellow had but a sprinkle of hydrocephalus. He was of undecided height also, varying from five feet four-and-half to five feet four-and-three-quarters, at the option of his bootmaker; but the most remarkable features, if we may use the expression, in his conformation, were his hands, which were gaunt and bony, of a tanned-leathery consistence, and of a streaky, mottled, castile-soap color, covered with a straggling crop of light, sandy hair, and ornamented with several *wedding* rings, — evidences of broken hearts, which some men are fond of displaying as certificates of gallantry. Dressed in

irreproachable black, and capped and jewelled in the most
orthodox style, it may be imagined that Jasper was the
object of no small solicitude to the anxious mothers of
slenderly-portioned daughters ; he certainly had an air *bien
riche*, if not *distingué*, and that's the marketable *materiel*
after all.

Months were unprofitably spent, and Jasper was beginning to think the time irretrievably lost, when an occurrence of some little interest varied the hotel monotony.
The Blodgerses arrived, *en route* to the fashionable rural
resorts.

Now the Blodgerses were extensive people in their way.
They were originated somewhere in Pennsylvania, and affected the tone of the Far South ; travelled with huge
trunks, two lapdogs, a parrot, and a liveried African.   The
head of the family was a pursy, important, chairman-of-an-
election-committee-looking man, with a superabundance of
excessively white shirt-frill, and too much watch-chain ;
the latter appendage he invariably swung round as he
conversed, its momentum indicating the state of his temper during an argument : let him speak upon uninteresting topics, — literature, for instance, or any of the useless
arts, — you notice but a gentle apathetic oscillation, but
let him get upon the tariff, let him hurl denunciations
against his political enemies, or eulogize his particular
presidential candidate, and round it goes with astonishing
velocity.

Blodgers had been a grocer, or something of the kind,
and having, during a life of assiduous saving and scraping,
accumulated a very large sum, now flung himself with
extraordinary *abandon* upon the full stream of gentility ;
and, to say the truth, most uncomfortable he found it ; for
many a time would he acknowledge to his wife that this

flying about from steam-car to steamboat, was far more fatiguing, and far less profitable, than quietly serving out lump-sugar. Then would Mrs. B. indignantly check such compromising thoughts, for she was a person of great pretension, and had a slight acquaintance with Mrs. Judge Pinning, and once visited by accident Mrs. General Jollikins, so felt herself bound to talk of "society." "They don't do this in our set"; or, " It's not the etiquette in *society"; and* such like side-winded hints of her position, formed the staple of her conversations. As for the heiress to the wealthy grocer's store, there was an indescribable something in her air and manner which plainly indicated, "I am worth looking after!" She talked loudly, stared rudely through a magnificent Parisian double glass, and in fact broke through all the recognized rules of good-breeding with that insolent familiarity which but poorly imitates the *nonchalant* ease of the really *distingué.*

No description of deportment could have made so great an impression on Jasper. She looked ingots, she spoke specie, and her *prestige* was altogether redolent of *rouleaux.* He was struck, but the stricken deer took the precaution to investigate realities before he advanced a step toward acquaintanceship. Now, thought he, if she but happen to have some ten or fifteen thousand, she'd be just the wife for me. The result was satisfactory. He discovered that a larger sum was to be her marriage portion, and so laid vigorous siege instanter.

Now Araminta Blodgers, although decidedly not qualified to grace the pages of the book of beauty, had a strange predilection for "nice young men"; so that at first Jasper met with decided, and not over-delicately expressed opposition. But he was not a man to retire from the first repulse; he persevered, and finally so deceived the sympathetic Araminta into the belief of his ardent affection, that, one fine summer evening, she sighed forth an avowal that she and her expectations were at his disposal.

Fresh from this successful attack upon the heiress's susceptibilities, with a feathery heart Jasper snapped his fingers at love, and danced down the corridor of the hotel to the infinite wonderment of the waiters. Either from force of habit, or as a means of tempering the exuberance of his spirits, he plunged into the mysteries of the guest-book, where — alas for Araminta Blodgers and for true love! — the first name he saw was that of Mrs. Skinning-ton, the rich widow from his own immediate neighbor-hood, — she whom he had sedulously church-ogled from the opposite pew every Sunday, astonished at the vastness of his presumption, — she, the *bona fide* and sole possessor of nearly half his native town. Here was the shadow of the shade of opportunity. She was alone. Jasper hesi-tated. Araminta's fortune was ample; but when there was a chance of more, it was n't *enough!* Finally, he determined to wait the first interview with the widow, and be regulated by her manner.

They met at dinner, and she was singularly gracious. The fact is, those eye assaults had told a little; and I'm sorry to say, for the character of the sex, that the widow, in case the siege should be renewed, had predetermined on capitulation.

The result may be anticipated. The endurable Ara-minta was thrown over for the intolerable widow and her superior wealth. They were married in a curiously short time; and, when Jasper found himself master of the widow's hoard, "Now," thought he, with a glowing heart, "a few thousand dollars more, and I shall be content. One hundred thousand is the acme of my desire; let me but achieve that, and I shall then retire and spend the remainder of my days in quiet comfort."

In process of time he did realize the coveted amount; but did he keep his word and retire? No! he had enough of that. Home was to him the worst of all miseries, — a sort of domestic Tartarus; the presiding fury his elderly wife, who, incapable of inspiring a sentiment of affection herself, yet assumed all the caprice of a girl. Jealous to very lunacy, she gave vent to the agonizing sensations of her soul by scribbling heart-rending sonnets for the Fiddle-Faddle Magazine. Thin, withered, romantic, and exacting, you may suppose that to the unfortunately lucky Jasper home was no *dulce domum*.

The consequence was, that he, dreading the *tête-à-tête* domestic, confined his attention to his monetary affairs. Retirement with such an unlovable and moreover intolerably suspicious companion as Mrs. L., or, as she signed herself, Sappho, was out of the question; so he determined to stick to the counting-house. And now a great idea filled his brain, almost to monomania, which was to make his one hundred thousand *two*. Once conceived, every thought and action were merged in that one absorbing idea. Heedless of the domestic tornadoes that ever and anon swept over his devoted head, he slaved, fretted, lied, I think I may venture to say cheated, but honorably, and in the way of business, until, after a few years of health-destroying worry, he beheld himself within sight of the desired haven. But five thousand more, and the sum would be accomplished; one stroke of luck, one piece of indifferent fortune, and he would then be really content.

Worn out by constant exertion, he fell dangerously ill. During his sickness, news arrived which brought him within a few hundred of his maximum. Notwithstanding his bad health, and in opposition to all remonstrance, he called for his books, and, with weak hand and weaker brain, attempted to calculate. After many hours' labor, altogether unaware that he was thus unprofitably expending his last flickering of life, he gave a long, sorrowful sigh, and, gasping forth, "Not enough! not enough!" expired.

Not many days after, a few feet of earth were sufficient for THE MAN WHO NEVER HAD ENOUGH.

A NIGHT WITH THE SPIRITS.

THERE's old Tom now, sitting sunning himself in his pleasant, little cottage-porch! Nearly fourscore and ten years have dispensed their blessings and their curses on the world since he first breathed its air. Yet see how ruddy are his old cheeks, how firm his nerves, how clear his hazel eyes sparkling with healthy life, — his venerable head shakes not an atom, neither is his back bowed. Is he not altogether a marvel of cheery, vigorous age, —

" As a lusty winter, frosty, but kindly ? "

Listen to the simple secret of this wondrous preservation. It is comprised in one word, and that word is TEM-PERANCE, for

" Never in his youth did he apply
Hot and rebellious liquors in his blood."

No; an occasional foaming beaker of "home-brewed" was the only indulgence that his thirstiest moments yearned for, and even that infrequently. Behold the result! — enjoyable to him, in their every fulness, are the individual delights of each changing season; strong and still active in frame, fresh and unclouded in intellect, with a heart keenly alive to the unnumbered gratifications of this beautiful world, and a soul overflowing with gratefulness to the Giver of all good, who has vouchsafed to him so liberal a store of earth's blessings, in calm serenity he awaits the coming of the inevitable, but by him undreaded summons.

Old Tom Stoddart, however, has had his temptations, as all men have, by the way. Did you ever hear how he raised the spirits, a few years ago, and what effect the supernal visitation had upon him?

No? Then I couldn't have a better opportunity of informing you than the present. Let us step into the parlor of the Blue Lion here. This is the identical room where the strange occurrence took place; that sedulously-cleaned deal table, no doubt, the very circle of his singular incantation.

Old Tom was in an unusually despondent mood — for cheerfulness was his prevailing characteristic — upon the particular occasion of which I am about to tell you, and with some reason; he had but just returned from the hurried, and but little cared-for funeral — if it could so be called — of one his sometime companions, early loved and respected, until the madness for strong drink quelled within him all that was likable, and evoked all that was brutal and degrading, as it never fails to do.

Estranged though they had been for years, yet, when the miserable parish coffin was rudely lowered into its place by careless hands, the old friendliness returned, and flowed once more into his heart upon a flood of tears, — tears which were checked only by indignation at beholding the " maimed rites" indecently hummed through over the wretched clay, which had not left behind it the means of purchasing an ostentatious sorrow.

It was to his own comfortable home and the world-angel who had made that spot sacred for a long lifetime, his dear good dame, — she who had shared his joys and griefs, and so enlinked her existence with his, that from very sympathy they came not only to look alike, but to think alike, exemplifying that harmonious blending of two natures

into one, which is the rarest God-gift to humanity, —
it was to this haven of his best thoughts, this most cherished source of his affections, that old Tom Stoddart always
wended his way whenever anything uncommon or important chanced ; but now he was tempted, in an evil moment,
to take an opposite direction. ˙ Nor was this impulse altogether an unworthy one, for it was the disinclination to
carry his gloomy load into the presence of his kind old
wife, that first induced him to deposit it rather at the door
of the Blue Lion, forgetting that she was heaven-sent to
relieve him from such perilous burdens.

Who among us has not deviated from the wiser road,
at one period or another ?

Well, it so happened that old Tom's reflections were of
such a sort that companionship was repulsive to him, and
he accordingly ordered his tankard of ale, and sat himself
down here — perhaps in this chair — alone, resolving to
let his melancholy thoughts have their full scope, without
the intrusive commonplace condolements of his general
acquaintances, whom curiosity only had urged to be
present at the unceremonious burial.

Left entirely to himself, memory soon began to call up
before his imagination the scenes and friendships of the
olden time.

" Poor Sanders ! " said he, the tears again standing in
his eyes.   " Little did I think, when you and I were boys,
and fought in playful battles against each other, — when
we were men, and ploughed against each other, and went
fishing and shooting together, one heart between us, —
that I should see you flung into the ground like a dog !
There 's not many left now " ; — and old Tom took a long
gulp at the ale.   " Bill Summers is gone : died of a broken
heart, too, because his boy, that he doted on, took to evil

courses; but, above all, to the cursed drink." Alas for
human nature! Here Tom emptied the tankard.

"How they spring up afore me!" he went on. "Jolly
Dick Ryder, the Squire's huntsman, that used to sing Tom
Moody; and little Jack Miller, with them stories of his
that everybody knew by heart at last, — it was gin killed
him, tough as he was." Here old Tom rung the bell for
another pot of ale. "Well, Jack outlived his stories, anyway, and a chap may's well die then." The ale came in,
and Tom took a heavy bite at it, and then pursued his
train of thought.

"O that Dick Ryder, what a fellow he was! what
pranks he used to cut! Do you remember the way he
served the soger-chap that offered to marry his sweetheart?
Ha! ha!" and, in spite of his dreariness, Tom laughed
heartily at a joke which he had all to himself.

"But he's gone, dead and gone; so are they all but me.
I'm the only one left of the lot, and I'll have to go soon,
I suppose. Ale is no use when a man's down in the
mouth this way. I wonder if a drop of brandy would n't
do me good; I don't feel exactly well; and, moreover, the
doctors say that a little of it is mighty healthy. I — I've
a great mind to try; and I will, too, — why should n't I?"
so saying, he pulled the bell, and, in obedience to his wish,
the neat little bar-maid placed a bottle of brandy, with
some sugar, a glass, and a pitcher of hot water before him.
Smacking his lips at the appetizing flavor that escaped in
the process, old Tom carefully mixed himself a huge tumbler of "toddy," and began at first, quietly and slowly, to
enjoy the, to him, very unusual treat. Still, however, his
thoughts continued to be clothed in sombre hue, and to
deepen even in their blackness.

At last, with a firm determination, come what might,

to disperse the cloud that encompassed him, he turned eagerly to the intoxicating draught; his spirits soon began to mount upon the subtle fluid; a pleasant languor stole over his frame, and, erelong, a golden mist hung before his delighted eyes. Reflection was at an end, and all gloomy thoughts fled before the powerful influence of the magician.

It was at this stage of semi-forgetfulness that, as he has often told me himself, with an awe-stricken expression, and, as I think, not knowing exactly at what point the limit of actual circumstance was broken into by the imaginary, he heard a knock at the parlor door, — that little door you are now looking at, — and who should walk solemnly in and seat himself at the table but the identical man he had just seen thrust away to moulder amidst his kindred dust. Old Tom rubbed his eyes, and stared wildly at the new-comer. Sure enough, it was he; not, however, in the wasted and deplorable appearance he presented in his latter terrible days of degradation and distress; but in his strong, healthy, youthful form, ere the demon had fastened upon his energies.

It was some time before Tom could muster up courage to address the phantom; but when he saw him, quite at his ease, reach forth and help himself to a huge quantity of the brandy, which he swallowed in its burning integrity from the bottle, — " Why, Sanders lad," said he, "did n't I see thee buried to-day ? "

" Buried, man ! mayhap you did," replied the appearance, with a chuckle. " What o' that ? I 'm here again, strong and hearty."

" That you be, surely," said Tom. " Gi' us your fist. I 'm woundily glad to see thee." With that he grasped the hand of Sanders, and was pleased to find it was real flesh and blood.

"Ah! Sanders lad," said Tom, sympathizingly, "you don't know with what sorrow I looked upon the severance of our old acquaintanceship. You had found another friend — "

"I know what you mean. This fellow," interrupted the other, seizing the bottle again ; "well, we won't talk about that. Here's to the renewal of our past feeling for each other. Won't you drink that, Tom ? "

"Won't I! ay, if it was in pison, Jemmy, which I'm not sure but it is, but here goes anyhow." So Tom emulated the example of the ghost, and refreshed himself with a long draught of the pure spirit. As he laid down the bottle, he heard another knock at the parlor door.

"Who's coming here ? " said he.

"O, it's only that roistering blade, Dick Ryder," said his companion.

"Ryder! what! " cried Tom, in alarm, "Dick Ryder! Bless my soul, he's been dead these ten years. It can't be he."

His speculation was cut short by the abrupt entrance, not only of his old crony, Dick Ryder, but along with him came tumbling in Jack Miller, and half a dozen other jolly dogs, who, in the olden time, used to make the walls of this little room tremble and roar with their outrageous hilarity.

"This is really very odd," thought old Tom ; "I can't make it out ; I don't of a certainty know whether I am alive or dead, and a ghost as well as themselves. All I do know is that hang me if I did n't see them all under ground years and years ago. Yet here they are, just as natural as life."

As it was they were now evidently full of life and jollity, for they surrounded old Tom, shaking hands with

him, as though they had only been as far as the next
county, and were glad to get back.

"You're looking well, old boy," cried Ryder, slapping
him on the back; "but come, you're not going to treat
us stingily, now we're back? Send out for another bottle
or two."

"O, half a dozen, as he's about it," added Jack Miller;
"and remember, I stick to gin, — it's the wholesomest
liquor, — I always found it so."

Old Tom Stoddart, although much confounded, did as
he was requested. He rung the bell; the bar-maid
entered, and without betraying the slightest agitation at
the presence of so many ghostly customers, received her
orders, and, in due time, executed them.

And now the fun mounted, glass upon glass, until it
got to the topmost pitch of excitement. Jack Miller told
all his stories; Dick Ryder sang all his hunting-songs;
and, steeped to the very lips in a glorious atmosphere of
enjoyment, old Tom echoed every story and chorused every
song, all feeling of awe or surprise obliterated by the
intense excitement of the scene.

Never, in the whole course of his existence, had old
Tom Stoddart felt so supremely happy. All external
interests and solicitudes were shut out; the outer world,
including home itself, — that home where she, without
whose tender ministration it could not bear that blessed
name, was even then trembling within her very heart from
apprehension at his unaccustomed absence, — was forgotten
in the madness of the hour.

And every now and then one or other of the mad group
would pledge the old man in a fresh brimmer, while all
shouted, in discordant chorus, "Hurrah, he's one of us!"

Many and many an anecdote and remembrance of the

25

past was brought up, each serving as food for increased mirth, the most puerile and foolish of which seemed, as the afternoon waned, to awaken fresh outbursts of merriment. There was no cessation to the continuous orgie; it was as though they all had conspired to prevent old Tom from having an instant wherein he could separate his thought from the present on-rushing current of revelry.

The shadows of twilight now began to gather slowly over the land, yet still the joyous laugh resounded through the space; early evening approached, and deeper shade, but louder and louder grew the riotous din; night, black and solemn, fell suddenly down like a shroud, and yet it quelled not the fearful tumult, — while, stimulated thereto by the wild companionship and the thought-destroying influence of the fiery liquor, old Tom's voice rose high above the rest, and he heeded not the flight of time or the increasing darkness.

At length it occurred to him that, as there was a candle on the table, he might as well light it; and, after sundry ineffectual efforts to kindle a match, he at last succeeded in doing so; but the laugh died away on his lips, and the blood rebounded from his heart, when he beheld the abhorrent sight which the illumination revealed. Simultaneously with the first flash of light, all symptoms of hilarity ceased, and was succeeded by a silence appalling from its completeness. Not a sound could old Tom hear but the beating of his own heart, which thumped and thumped against his ribs, like the muffled ticking of a large clock. And, O heaven! the joyous companions with whom he had drunk and revelled to such a pitch of insane enjoyment, stark and denuded of their habiliments and their flesh, were nothing but hideous, grinning skeletons, — all but Sanders, whose yet more fearful appearance was that of a recent corpse, already green with approaching decay, sitting bolt upright in the chair before him, and clad in the garb of the grave !

Old Tom, glued to the spot by the most overpowering terror, tried to cry out, but in vain ; not the slightest approach to an audible sound could he, by the most violent exertion, force his paralyzed tongue to utter.

And still those terrible shapes nodded and gibbered at him, occasionally griping the glasses with their bony fingers, and pouring the useless fluid through their open jaws, whence it would splash upon their whitened ribs and sink into the sanded floor beneath. But more awfully horrible yet it was to see that rigid, dead form immediately before his face, the glazed and rayless eyes fixed upon his, and the half-opened mouth settled into a stony, dread-inspiring smile ! Fascinated, as it were, by the frightful spectacle, he had not power to withdraw his gaze from the revolting object, although instantly rendered sober by the horror of the scene, with all his faculties sharpened to their utmost acuteness of perception.

And now, to his increased terror, the shape opposite rose slowly from the chair, and, standing upright, glared more intently on him with its sightless eyes ; the rigid arms slowly moved into a menacing position, and the thing commenced to make a circuit of the table. Our poor, half-demented friend, old Tom, on witnessing this appalling demonstration, with a desperate plunge and a shriek that startled the surrounding neighborhood, dashed himself through that little door, and fell down beyond, where he lay for some time, deprived of consciousness, and to all appearance as dead as any of his recent companions.

The considerate bar-maid, however, with the assistance of a pitcher of cold water, a vigorous shaking, and other sanitary appliances, had the satisfaction of seeing the russet-brown color deepen over old Tom's cheeks once more. With a prodigious sigh, he ejected the moribund tenant who had taken premature possession of his anatomy, and gazed, but with a half-fearful look, upon the bright world again.

"Where are they?" he asked, in a trembling whisper. "Are they still there?" and he shuddered as he inquired.

"Are who there, Mr. Stoddart?" she asked, with a simper that he quailed at.

"Who?" he continued, "why, the—the shapes, the spirits!"

"Why, deary me, what is the man talking about?" said the girl, with a merry laugh. "Where did you meet with such company, Mr. Stoddart?"

"In that parlor, Mary," replied old Tom, gasping for breath.

"Then they must be in there now, for there has n't even a ghost left since you had that swound; I'll see." So saying, she opened the door and peeped boldly·in. "There's nothing there but an empty bottle, Mr. Stoddart, and a tumbler."

"*One* bottle?" inquired Tom, eagerly.

"Only one."

"Thank you, my dear, — here's a sixpence for you; and — I believe I'll go home."

What conclusion old Tom came to, upon giving the affair his private consideration, I cannot say; but certain it is that from that day to this he never could be prevailed upon to touch a drop of brandy, or on any pretence whatever to enter this little parlor.

V.

POEMS.

✠

"Take up the sword again or take not me."

POEMS.

ST. PATRICK.

SOME centuries back — I'm a little in doubt
With regard to the date, but 't was somewhere about
Four hundred and odd — you can easy find out
The year to a day in Giraldis Cambrensis,
        The sage Nubigensis,
Or else in Henricus Antiodorensis,
        The Book of Ardagh,
        Or the Cath Fiothragh,
The Psalter of Cashel or Comshiorgathagh,
The Leabher Gabhala or Reim Reiogra,
Or the famous Uracept, by Cion Fola ;
        In Solinus the specious
        Or Speed the facetious ;
In Stanihurst, Spencer, or Hector Boetius ;
In Campion, whose streamlet of truth rather shallow ran,
Keating, or Leland, or Doctor O'Halloran ;
Camden or Strabo, the historiographer ;
Pomponius Mela, the great lexicographer :
In any of these you have only to look,
And thus, on your own individual hook,
If you can but make out the archaic philology,
Post yourself up in the proper chronology.

And now to the legend : — In Ireland once,
Or Scotland — and if I know which I'm a dunce ;

But that's not so strange, for a learned inquisitor,
Master Cæsarius, declared, while a visitor,
" Scotia quæ et Hibernia discitur " ;
Welsh Nennius and Bede, Macrobius and Stowe,
      Professors, and so,
      Ought surely to know,
Wrote tomes without number, all tending to show
That Ireland was Scotland a long time ago.
Did n't even Orosius, who flourished before 'em,
Expressly assert that " Hibernia Scotorum
Patria est " ? And though I seldom make use of his
Book for authority, it so abusive is,
Touching the doubt I submit it conclusive is.
England herself was first known as Germanica, —
Vide Lloyd's Archæologia Britannica, —
Scotia as Albion ; and if you but glance
At a primitive map, should you e'er get the chance,
It will show you Great Britain a province of France.
So no matter the name, be it Ir or Iernia,
Heber, Milesius, Iero, or Vernia,
Ogygia, Eirn, Innisfail, or Juerne, — a
Few appellations of ancient Hibernia, —
I love the dear land with the softened affection
That springs from the anguish of sad retrospection.
So now, in right earnest my task to commence,
Nevermore to diverge upon any pretence,
Except when it won't interfere with the sense
Or — pshaw ! I won't promise, for my Rosinante
Is wild, and my equine accomplishment scanty.

In the reign of King Niall, who Ireland swayed
And skillfully followed the conquering trade

In other dominions, (Britannia and Gaul
     He held in his thrall,
To his prowess did nine principalities fall,
     And a hostage from all
     He had within call,
For his faith in the word of the princes was small,)
Religion was certainly rather " so-so,"
And civilization undoubtedly slow.
     The pace it will go
In the same time to come will, most probably, throw
Very far in the shade all that we moderns know.
I wonder what people will think of our lore,
     Our many a score
Of adverse credenda, our limited store
Of truth and true charity, false to the core,
In somewhere about fourteen centuries more !

     As I mentioned before,
Religion was somewhat abnormal and mystic ;
     For spells cabalistic
     And rites druidistic
In horrid detail were the popular creed ;
And benevolent bards saw whole hecatombs bleed
That carnivorous gods might abundantly feed, —
     Not always of cattle,
     For after each battle
     No strict devotee
     But would save two or three
Of his captives to help the ignivorous spree.
These Druids were death upon fighting and fifing,
Still harping or harrying, trilling or knifing ;
Would just as soon sing a cantata as storm a
Fortalice — for more information see " Norma."

They hunted up sinners with clerical zeal,
  And with fire or steel
In the orthodox manner made heretics feel
Humanity's woe for eternity's weal.

It's a singular fact that divergence of creed,
  And even, indeed,
   If on that they're agreed,
Some matter of ritual, useless to heed
In the vital account, will so frequently lead
   Sane men by the nose
   Till the argument grows
   From breath evanescent
   To rage calorescent,
And all a man's diaphragm feels incandescent.

I never could fancy your dons disputatious,
  So very sagacious
On doctrinal points, deeming naught efficacious,
  But foul and fallacious,
That don't coincide with their humor. Good gracious !
I'd rather be served with a *fieri facias*,
  And lose all my chattels
  In litigant battles,
Than listen to one, whatsoever the merit he
Owns, who is swayed by polemic asperity.
   And what is it all about?
   What do they brawl about ?
Finding, perhaps, some ridiculous flaw
  In the letter of law,
Or splitting some thin theological straw, —
The thousand and one serried points of disparity
Ranged on each side to annihilate charity.

For my part I have the completest security ;
Patent highway there is none to futurity ;
  Through the whole universe
Roads there are more than can come in this puny verse.
  Lector benevole, please to excuse
  My intractable muse : —
The fault is n't mine, understand : could I choose,
  She would certainly lose   ·
  No time in digression,
  Absurd retrocession,
Or any such anti-climactic transgression,
Forgetting the earlier scenes she began among,
Straying and playing, delaying the *dénouement.*
All for myself I can possibly say
  In the way
  Of excuse
  For this loose
  And diffusive relation,
Fatiguing and vile anacephalization,
This flow of verbose and ventose etymology,
Is — if you 're conversant with female psychology,
Think of the sex : that 's my only apology ;
Women you know very well.   But my office is
Not analytic — condone the apophasis.

  What time the bold King Niall swayed
  Ierne's realm, and warfare made
  With Anglian, Gaul, with Goth and Hun,
  And Ethiopia's swarthy son,
  Victorious came he from each fight,
  With valor's laurelled crown bedight.
  So peerless in the lists of fame
  Was this renownéd monarch's name

The bravest knight to him might yield
And bear no stain upon his shield ; —
'T was then that in the regal train
St. Patrick wore the captive's chain.

What time the sage King Logar ruled
Ierne, and his people schooled
To wisdom, industry, and peace,
And bade war's fearful woes to cease ;
As vital stream that life imparts
Lived he within his lieges' hearts,
And wheresoever virtue came
All honored was this good king's name.
So did his praise men's voices fill,
Foul crime it was to speak him ill ; —
'T was then that with pure faith imbued
St. Patrick bore the Holy Rood.

What time the base and bloody rite
Of Druidism shamed the light,
When sacrificial altars blazed
Throughout the western world, and raised
Their lurid columns to the sky,
While ever rose the piercing cry
From tender youth of beauty rare,
Or virgin innocent and fair,
In fearful anguish, yielding life,
While reeked the archpriest's dreadful knife ; —
'T was then, amid those scenes of ruth,
St. Patrick spread the light of Truth.

Would you dictum have and date
For the various blessings great

That St. Patrick caused to smile
Upon Erin's lovely isle
During sixty years and four
That the sacred staff he bore?
Are they not inscribed upon
The old Polychronicon? —
All the miracles he wrought:
How the populace he taught
Senseless idols to detest,
And the merciful behest
Of the God of peace and love
To obey all else above?
How, despite of cell and cord,
He still preached the blessed Word,
And its excellence maintained?
How he with a sign explained
The mysterious Trinity
By the shamrock's petals three?
How all serpents from the land
He drove away on every hand,
Till no poisonous thing was found
Did they search the country round?

A ray of light
Beams sunny bright
Upon my clouded brain,
Dispelling quick
The vapors thick
That hung on it amain.
I've found it out
Beyond a doubt, —
The serpents that he banned
Were evil men,

Whose doing then
Disturbed Ierne's land ;
  Who kept the isle
  In squalor vile,
And for their selfish end
  The kindly ties
  That mortals prize
All ruthlessly did rend.
  Men's thoughts to steep
  In darkness deep
It was their only aim ;
  They little recked
  The sad effect,
The sorrow and the shame;
  When sword and flame
  With famine camé
And laid the country waste,
  Less woe befell
  So hard to quell
As from those deeds are traced ;
  For war but gave
  Unto the grave
The bold who nobly bled,
  And famine's dart
  Slow reached the heart
Where hope was not all dead.
  I argue, then,
  It was such men
To whom the Saint did come,
  And frowning say,
  " *Exorcite*
  Secere baculum ! "

THE SWORD OF FONTENOY.

Written for the Hawthorne Literary Union, of Faith Mission.

THE aged Count de Macmahon, ·
    Was at the old chateau
The founder of his name had won
    A century ago.

Knowing the summons had been sent
    That all men must obey,
In calm and Christianly content
    He on his death-bed lay.

His brother's sons stood by him then,
    Three images of ruth ;
Two of them were already men,
    The third was still a youth.

In tears they stood there by his side,
    In tears, but mute as stone,
For from the day their father died
    He loved them as his own.

Then spoke the Count, in accents low
    And weak : " Away with grief ;
Much must you learn before I go
    And now my time is brief.

" Your father, it need not be told,
    Was peer amongst his peers.
He died as die the bravest, old
    In honor, not in years.

" A Frenchman, though his name and blood
    Their origin proclaimed, —
The *Irish* name that while he stood
    In life no falsehood shamed.

" A soldier, with the soldier's creed, —
    Aid and relief to bring
His country first, whoever bleed,
    And after her, the king.

" No matter who Lutetia throned,
    The puppet of an hour,
His heart's allegiance always owned
    France as the regnant power.

Before the heights of La Rothion
    He fell in the advance,
A soldier of the Empire, for
    The Empire then was France.

" Long had he been from home away,
    When his brave death occurred,
Leaving two sons.   Ah ! fatal day,
    He never saw the third.

" For when the sad news came, his wife,
    An angel of true love,
Gave for his being life for life,
    And sought her home above.

" Had he but known the truth, this will
    Would never have been made ;
Unfatherly, unjust, yet still
    His wish must be obeyed.

"The injury was undesigned:
  Through ignorance 't was done ; —
Surely fraternal love will find
  Some way the ill to shun."

The will was read.   The eldest son
  Their home was to receive ;
And for his share the youngest one
  The wealth that he might leave.

And that was all.   The two sons stood,
  With eyes bent on the ground,
" They 'll speak ! " the old Count hoped they would,
  But there was not a sound.

And then he turned, as if ashamed,
  And with a kind of fear,
To Patrick, — so the youth was named,
  Such tale who had to hear.

But there he saw so proud a head
  It made his heart rejoice,
And to the landless youth he said,
  In clear and ringing voice : —

" I have a heritage for thee,
  That beggars house and hoard,
If thou art of our blood, bring me
  Yon old, time-rusted sword.

" That glorious weapon look upon
  With veneration, boy ;
Thy grandsire's grandsire bore it
  On the field of Fontenoy !
                26

"When English, Dutch, and Austrian
From dawn till set of sun
Contended against Frenchmen
All unaided, all alone.

"No, not alone !—what was it then
The tide of battle stayed?
A handful of brave Irishmen, —
The famous Green Brigade, —

"Exiled for loving their old land,
Their faith, and landless king,
Stern retribution nerved each hand
To deadly reckoning.

"That battered piece of sturdy steel
In mean and sordid eyes
And hearts that no emotion feel
Would be a sorry prize.

"A thing of profitless renown,
By such 't would only be.
In some neglected corner thrown,
I give it, boy, to thee !

"Take it, and keep its record bright,
That thy grandchildren may
In after time to theirs recite
The story of to-day !

Silent the youth stood for a space,
Oppressed by feeling great;
Then, lifting up his glowing face,
With joy and hope elate,

He said, as on the blade he wept,
"Go, wealth, and home, and land !
This precious treasure I accept,
From thy more precious hand.

" His name and sword are all I have
Ambition to retain :
And Heaven so aid me as I strive
• To guard them both from stain."

The old Count smiled ; in loving grasp
Their hands were joined awhile,
Till death released the feeble clasp,
But spared the parting smile.

Sad only for that loss, the youth
Turns from his father's land ;
His fortune, faith and hope and truth,
And that time-rusted brand.

Honor's bright pathway he selects,
Like hero of romance ;
And now that homeless boy directs
The destiny of France.

---◆---

POLLY O'CONNOR.

I.

I WILL not venture to compare
Those flashing eyes
To sunny skies ;
To threads of gold thy wealth of hair ;

Thy cheek unto the rose's glow;
Thy polished brow,
To lilies glancing in the light,
Or Parian white;
Thy bosom to the virgin snow; —
For these
Are weak and well-worn similes.

II.

Thine eyes are like — like — let me see;
The violet's hue,
Reflected through
A drop of dew;
No, that won't do.
No semblance true
In ample nature can there be
To equal their intensity, —
Their heavenly blue.
'T were just as vain to seek,
Through every flower to match thy glowing cheek.
No gold could shed
Such radiant glory as ensaints thy head.
Besides, I now remember,
That golden tresses are but flattered red,
And thine are living amber, —
As, when 't is ripest, through the waving corn
The sunbeams glance upon a harvest morn.

III.

To the pale lustre of thy brow,
The lily's self perforce must bow;
Thy bosom as the new-fallen snow

Is quite
As white,
And melts as soon with love's warm glow.
But then,
While that receives an early stain,
Thy purer bosom doth still pure remain.

IV.

Since, to my mind,
I cannot find
A simile of any kind,
I argue hence
Thou art the sense
And spirit of all excellence ;
The charm-bestowing fountain whence
Fate doth dispense
Its varied bounties to the fair,
The loveliest of whom but share
A portion of the gifts thou well canst spare.

THE OPERA OF "LA FILLE DU REGIMENT,"

DONE INTO ENGLISH.

THE Twenty-first Regiment marching one day
In an orderly way,
To sack and to slay
An inadequate mass for their limited pay, —
For, though victory may
Be the sunniest ray
That over a Marechal's caput can play,

I 'll venture to say,
Till the world turns gray
The dollarum dibs will hold paramount sway, —
Well, this regiment marching in valiant array,
With colors so gay,
They
Happened to meet with an overthrown chay,
With a baby inside of it, trying to pray ;
So the *enfant trouvée*
They carry away,
And adopt as their daughter, *sans ceremonie.*

Dear reader, you 'll please to remember this case
Of abduction took place
A long time before the first scene of the *pièce ;*
And Sulpice the sergeant, moreover the bass,
Has had many a chase,
In trying to trace
Out her father and mother, or aught of her race,
That they might embrace
A daughter so lovely in figure and face ;
But vain his endeavors ; so now you may see
That pretty Marie
Is contented and happy as happy can be,
With a step as light, and a will as free,
As a sweet little bird in the boughs of a tree,
Or a nice little fish in some beautiful sea,
Or a frolicsome fawn on a meadowy lea,
Or a bee
Full of glee,
Or a little fairee,
Or anything else that occurs unto thee,
That will with those characteristics agree.

And the soldiers adore their young daughter, for she
Makes most undeniable coffee and tea,
And warbles, moreover, magnificently.

Now our little friend Marie, a short time ago,
Contrived to inveigle a bit of a beau, —
    One Tonio, —
A dapper young Tyrolese peasant, although
    He 's rather so-so,
    As pecuniaries go,
And I 'm angry with Marie for stooping so low ;
    But love's rapid flow
    Will frequently throw
Strange parties together, for weal or for woe,
Let the atoms surrounding them like it or no.
Now Toney and Marie, one day you must know
Were *singing* great love to each other, when, lo !
The sergeant observed them, and he was n't slow
In detecting how matters were going. " Oho ! "
Said he, rushing down with his gills in a glow,
" The pearl of the *vingt unième* must n't bestow
Her hand on a *maudit paysan* and a foe."
    But the sergeant stout
    Was soon put to the rout,
Love had carried the poorly defended redoubt
Of the heart of Marie, and no menace or shout
Can send such a conqueror right about ;
    " For," said she, with a pout,
" If my amiable mother don't know that I 'm out,
    What is it to you,
    Whatever I do ?
So please, Mr. Sergeant, I 'll follow my gout."

" *Mille d'yeux,*
Sacré bleu !
Quelle une audacieuse ! "
Said the *grande militaire,* in a deuce of a stew.
In a most unavoidable passion he flew,
For Marie was true,
To her new
Amoureux,
And stuck to her point like a gallon of glue ;
So they compromised things in a minute or two.
By putting him through
An inductory few
Mere matters of form, to a soldier he grew.
And now I expect
In the *tricolor* decked,
His comrades consider that he might affect
A duchess elect,
Or a queen, if her majesty did n't object.
Now the fun 's what I think I may venture to call
Uncommonly tall,
When a slice of good luck nearly ruins them all,
Making Toney the brave sing prodigiously small.
A Marchioness something, bah ! what is her name ?
I really forget, but it 's all the same, —
Suffice it to say she's an elegant dame,
Of the old *régime.*
All powder and hoop, *à la Louis Cinquième,*
Has come to claim
The glory and pride of the *vingt unième ;*
She calls Marie her niece, and she takes her away,
And, as matter of course, there 's old Harry to pay.

You 'll please to remember, some time has passed
    Since line the last.
    Marie having cast
Her merino for satin that can't be surpassed,
And a natural fund of good breeding amassed,
Grows into a lady remarkably fast,
And she lives in a beautiful palace among
A *magnifique* aristocratical throng;
But you plainly perceive there is something wrong,
For instead of the light-hearted *ran-tan-plan,*
A feeling of sorrow pervades her song.
    A nobleman grand
    Has offered his hand,
With the wealthiest dower that ever was read,
But Toney, the peasant, still runs in her head.
    So the Marchioness said,
"To Toney, the peasant, you cannot be wed,
For a very good reason — because he 's dead ;
So oblige me, and marry the Duke instead."
And the dutiful darling, though tears she shed,
    And her little heart bled,
Prepared to encounter the nuptials dread ;
And they leave her alone, and she gazes around
Those beautiful walls, and declares she has found
But little content on nobility's ground,
When her startled ear catches a well-known sound ;
    With a rapturous bound
She flies to the window, and, marching by,
Her beloved old regiment blesses her eye ;
    And her pulse beats high,
    And she fain would cry,
    But her brain is dry,

And the tears won't come, and she does n't know why,
    No more do I —
But oh ! her delight 's inexpressible, when
The company enters the chamber, and then
She embraces the flag, she embraces the men,
David and *Robert*, *Thomasse* and *Etienne*,
She kisses them over and over again :
But where is poor Toney ? — alas ! now her tears
Flow freely and fast — when she suddenly hears
A voice well remembered through changeable years,
And fancy her joy, when, saluted with cheers,
In an officer's dress her old lover appears.

Dear reader, there is n't much more to disclose,
The Duke has his *congé* as you may suppose,
    The Marchioness shows
    Inclination for blows,
And does n't seem willing the matter to close ;
    When Toney just throws
Out a delicate hint that a secret he knows,
A mistake into which she once happened to fall,
She thought she was married, but was n't — that 's all,
A slight error that gave them a mother apiece,
Making Marie her daughter, instead of her niece ;
So she gives her consent, but I really must say,
'T was brought about in a most scandalous way.

THE AGE OF GOLD.

Read at the convention dinner of the Theta Delta Chi Society, at the
Metropolitan Hotel, New York, February 21st, 1873.

" Aurum omnes, victa jam pietate, volunt."

I AM expected — by the bill it seems —
To read "a Poem." I hope no one dreams
Or has the most remote anticipation
That I 've attempted any such creation.
I only promise a few random rhymes, —
Glancing occasionally at the times.

   .   .   .   .   .   .

In this dilemma, what am I to do?
I would call on the MUSE, but, *entre nous,*
We do not visit, — I have oft before
Rung most politely at the Muses' door,
But always found that they were " not at home,"
And back, abashed, of course I had to come, —
A most conclusive proof, to my own mind,
That the acquaintance is by them declined.
And such a simply personal rebuff
To a retiring rhymer 's hint enough,
Especially when they are more compliant
In other quarters : — WILLIAM CULLEN BRYANT
Is hand and glove with them ; quite at his ease is ;
Can call on them or not just as he pleases.
The intimacy is not at all affected,
E'en by the shameful way they 've been neglected.
To many others they 've been most polite ; —
The classic LONGFELLOW has but to write

A single line, to bring them to his side :
Indeed, so lovingly are they allied,
And so complete their intimacy is,
That now they scarcely know their home from his,
And wonder very often where the deuce it's
Placed, — in Macedon or Massachusetts.
Adventurous TAYLOR through the arctic roves,
Yet they, forgetting their Pierian groves,
Shame not to travel with him side by side,
As through untrodden fields his footsteps guide.

   .   .   .   .   .   .

They heed titanic WHITTIER, — honored soul,
That spurns oppression's infamous control,
And in life's terribly unequal fight,
Whate'er the cause, still battles for the right !
A youthful poet of the present hour,
Strikes with sure hand the chords of western power.
A THETA DELT, we glory in his fame,
And twine this votive garland round his name.
The lowliest subjects, by his pen refined,
Like Zeuxis' paintings, show the master mind.
And what a broad humanity the whole
Pervades, — the true religion of the soul !
The sun shone brilliantly upon the day
The world had garnered in that crop of HAY!
Another form appears, — the wise and witty
Dr. O. W. HOLMES, of Boston city, —
Who, by the will of most capricious fate,
Must his true intuition abrogate,
Enforced to turn on the prudential hose
Above the bright flame that within him glows.
Alas that he should make such great concession
To the requirements of his *grave* profession !

'T is seldom, in their day, the olive crown
Is given to those who best deserve renown.
Great names come filtered through the sands of time
    That, in their time, those very sands obscured;
Even he whose genius was the most sublime
    In his own day the world's neglect endured.

Great Nature's arch-magician, to whose spell
The varied passions of the human soul
Must quick obedience yield, — a myriad minds
In one conjoined, a universe of thought
Within the compass of one mortal brain, —
Obscure, untitled, from the laboring mass
The hand of fate raised up this paragon
To overtop the highest ! Kings will pass
And their whole lineage be forgotten dust ;
Empires will rise and fall, new worlds be found,
Where knowledge now declares a void ; and yet,
While there exists one record of his land
Or language, and mankind would think of one
Who has pre-eminently honored both,
Spontaneous to its lips will rise the name
Of WILLIAM SHAKESPEARE !

What shall his crown be ? Not the laurel leaf,
    That, blood-besprinkled, decks the warrior's head,
Who grasps at glory as destruction's chief,
    A living monument to thousands dead,
Bequeathing a vast legacy of grief ;
    Some pest incarnate, fed with human life,
    Born of ambition or the lust of strife !

In regal diadem shall we proclaim
    Him monarch ? That would circumscribe his worth.

A kingly coronet would only shame
  The kinglier thought, whose realm is the whole earth !
Such petty vanities but mock his fame ;
  Profane it not, He is all crowns above,
  Hero of PEACE ! Evangelist of LOVE !

Erewhile we 've heard how throbbed the mighty heart
Of PEGASUS, yoked to a village cart ;
How strained his trembling limbs to drag the load,
While his frame quivered from the piercing goad !
But only for a space : the indignant soul,
Spurning the savage husbandman's control,
With one prodigious effort burst the traces,
And, as is usual in all such cases,
Smashed up the wagon, and contrived to pitch
The dolt who drove into a muddy ditch ;
Then, pawing with disdain the vulgar ground,
Snorting defiance to the crew around,
Clove with strong pinion the congenial air,
By Phœbus mounted, to the hind's despair, —
Who saw no miracle, nor marked the rise
Of the enfranchised courser to the skies,
But cursed the fate that prompted him to buy
A beast with such a tendency to shy.
This truth, however, his experience told, —
In a horse trade one party must be sold.

Our modern PEGASUS is not so nice ;
Though now and then he may possess a spice
Of the old spirit, and be somewhat restive,
He 's kept in wholesome check by the digestive ;
For he no more ethereally feeds
On Heliconian dews, but rather needs

Robuster fare, and is — the fates deliver us ! —
Amazingly inclined to the carnivorous.
His wings are clipped, and now he seldom soars
Beyond the sphere of advertising stores.
His bated breath no more salutes the gales,
But fills with languid puffs trade's flagging sails,
Lauds, without stint or sense, hats, boots, or coats,
Contented if he earn his daily oats.
And there are many in this " Gradgrind " age
Would rather see him harnessed to a stage, —
Fourteen inside, and just as many more
As can squeeze in or hang upon the door, —
Than have him from his slavery arise,
To range at will the unproductive skies.

Ours is a money-ruled, commercial age, —
Its acts the substance of a ledger's page ;
Its deeds by the prospective profits swayed ;
The universal aim — to make a trade.
The world is one great mart — not over nice —
And nothing is but has its market price ;
Fame, power, pleasure, nay, we have been told,
That even freemen's votes are sometimes sold.
'T is said — of course by some enormous blunder —
That place is but a synonyme for plunder ;
That politicians have been sometimes known
To public welfare to prefer their own ;
And only fools, who don't know how to win,
Go out of office poor as they went in.
'T is hinted — but that must be defamation —
That even in the council of the nation
There are some statesmen who — the Press has said it —
Took shares in schemes not greatly to their credit,

And many long thought honorable names
Were sullied by disreputable aims.
In fine, did we believe what they impart, a
New Lycurgus rules another Sparta,
And the most honored in the common weal
Are those who most successfully can steal.

No change there can be while the money power
Tyrannic rules, the idol of the hour.
Each sordid worshipper his fellow mocks,
Nor counts his worth, except it be in stocks,
And to the glittering apex lifts his eyes,
Nor heeds the mud-heap whence its altars rise.

   .   .   .   .   .

                Its reflected page —
The printed transcript of the passing age —
Is with the weird and terrible so rife,
So filled with images of blood and strife,
That men the daily catalogue of vices
Peruse as calmly as the market prices.
Erewhile, in distant climes, the trumpet's blare
Wakes slumbering WAR from forth his hideous lair,
For cause most causeless; haply the desire
To give some princeling a baptism of fire,
Or else some crafty knavery of state
In wholesale carnage to obliterate;
Meanwhile, as thousands upon thousands bleed,
Religion's dignitaries bless the deed,
Chanting Te Deums, too, from time to time,
As though they 'd fain, with impudence sublime,
Make Heaven itself abettor in the crime.
Thus, to my mind, the anthem's form should be —
The real import of such blasphemy : —

THE HYMN OF PRINCES.

I.

Lord ! we have given, in thy name,
The peaceful villages to flame.
Of all the dwellers we 've bereft, —
No trace of hearth, no roof-tree left.
Beneath our war-steeds' iron tread,
The germ of future life is dead.
We have swept o'er it like a blight ;
To Thee the praise, *O God of right !*

II.

We have let loose the demon chained
In bestial hearts, that unrestrained
Infernal revel it may hold,
And feast on villanies untold,
With ravening drunkenness possessed,
And mercy banished from each breast ;
All war's atrocities above,
To Thee the praise, *O God of love !*

III.

Some hours ago, on yonder plain,
There stood six hundred thousand men,
Made in thine image, strong and rife
With hope, and energy, and life,
And none but had some prized one, dear,
Grief-stricken, wild with anxious fear :
A third of them we have made ghosts ;
To Thee the praise, *O Lord of hosts !*
27

IV.

Thy sacred temples we 've not spared,
For they the broad destruction shared ;
The annals of time-honored lore,
Lost to the world, are now no more.
What reck we if the holy fane
And learning's dome are mourned in vain?
Our work those landmarks to efface :
To Thee the praise, *O Lord of grace !*

V.

Secure, behind a wall of steel,
To watch the yielding columns reel,
While round them sulphurous clouds arise,
Foul incense wafting to the skies,
From our home-manufactured hell,
Is royal pastime we like well,
As momently death's ranks increase :
To Thee the praise, *O God of peace !*

VI.

Thus shall it be, while human kind,
Madly perverse or wholly blind,
Will so complacently be led
At our command their blood to shed,
For lust of conquest, or the sly,
Deceptive, diplomatic lie ;
To us the gain, to them the ruth,
To Thee the praise, *O God of truth !*

———

O age insensate, that for petty crime
Outwears with verbose laws the ear of time;

But when, self-gorged, crime swells to monstrous growth,
Law and the grovelling world, besotted both,
Hail it with frantic shouts, until the shame,
Tossed upward on their breath, mounts into FAME!

. . . . . .

Now to conclude my unambitious rhyme,
(I think I hear you say, 't is almost time,)
I 've but a few more words to say, and those
Reserved, like sweetest morsels, for the close.
How beautiful, amid the cares of life,
The transient bitterness of party strife,
The thousand devious, separated ways
Through which men journey in maturer days,
A scene like this, that for a space renews
On life's meridian the refreshing dews
Of its young morn! to see hands grasping hands
With equal ardor, while the clogging sands
That time has heaped up, since the days of yore,
Are swept away, and we are boys once more!
What is the mystic power that can compel
Such joy as this? 'T is FRIENDSHIP's sacred spell,
FRIENDSHIP, that death's keen arrow cannot quell!
For, while the eternal stars night's purple robe
Begem, while swings in space the pendent globe,
FRIENDSHIP must live! Ah! may its impulse high
Still guard and guide the THETA DELTA CHI!

ROSALIE.

I.

My Rosalie,
So dear to me,
I weep for thee
   Left here·alone.
They say 't is bad
To feel so sad,
As if I had
   A heart of stone.
O, if they knew,
As I well do,
How fond and true
   Thou wert to me,
They 'd silent keep
At grief so deep,
And let me weep
   For Rosalie.

The winds are sighing o'er the plain,
The skies are weeping tears of rain;
All nature seems to grieve with me,
For thou art gone, my Rosalie.

II.

My Rosalie
No more I see, —
So full of glee,
   So fresh and gay !
No more I hear
Those accents dear,

That were so near
  Me yesterday.
Thou art not gone,
My darling one,
For pictured on
  Life's memory,
When in reposo
My eyelids close,
Ah! then it shows
  Mo Rosalie!

My Rosalie,
Since thus to thee
My soul can flee
  When day is o'er,
O, it were best
To be so blest
That I should rest
  For evermore!
I humbly wait
The will of fate
From sorrow great
  To set me free:
The end I 'll greet,
However fleet,
Again to meet
  My Rosalie!

MACSWINEY'S FEAST.

A REMINISCENCE.

" Duos qui sequitur lepores, neutrum capit."

THE ARGUMENT.

[The Right Honorable Peter Paul Macswiney, being Lord Mayor
of Dublin, upon the arrival of the new Viceroy, who has the privilege of bestowing knighthood on the then incumbent, resolves,
although an ardent nationalist, to placate his Excellency by ten-
dering him a grand banquet ; but when *Bacchi plenus*, the truth
which is in wine asserts itself, and patriotism triumphs over ambition.]

IT was night, and the Macswiney tossed restless on his
    bed, —
Ambitious thoughts pervading his right honorable head ;
He saw, amid the darkness, flashing on his mental eyes,
The tributary fount of Irish dignity arise ;
He saw the pomp and panoply of chivalrous parade,
And felt upon his shoulder the viceregal accolade.
' Of temporary honor,' murmured he, ' I 've had enow ;
The sable crown municipal is slipping from my brow ;
It may not be, for this alone, the story shall be told,
That I wore the Saxon fetters, though their links are
    beaten gold.'

Now a brilliant inspiration rained this manna on his soul,
That honor's shining bubbles sometimes sparkle in the
    bowl,
And the stony heart of power, touched as by the prophet's
    hand,
Oft yields to vinous impulse what next morning might
    withstand.

'Within the gorgeous mansion-house I 'll haste me to pre-
pare,
And bid the new lieutenant to a banquet rich and rare.
What boots it that with battle-scars I purchase not this
meed,
For, keener than the body's pain, my purse will have to
bleed.
Meanwhile in courtly minever my breast I will enfold,
And hide the Saxon fetters, with their links of beaten gold.

'Full many a belted knight, I ween, that stomached not
the wars,
By freely shedding blood-red wine achieved his golden
spurs.
Have I not been in peril great with harmfulness imbued,
For what the battle s fury to the rage of party feud?
And in the brunt of such a storm who ever saw me flinch,
Or from the people's side fall back one perdurable inch?'
When sudden he bethought him that such souvenirs as
those
Had best be kept at present underneath his castle clothes,
Till he could fling them from him, and in freedom as of old
Disdain the Saxon fetters, with their links of beaten gold.

Came the feast, and the Macswiney sat in superceltic pride;
For in rosy bonds he held the Saxon ruler by his side.
Passed he quick the brimming amphoræ with civic nectar
full;
Spoke he much in downy accents, soft as double-carded
wool;
Though he felt within his midriff that his honeyed words
were naught,
On his silent coadjutors he relied for what he sought.

"Mel in ore, fel in core," was his motto on that night, —
Monkish, mediæval Latin, but 't will do if read aright;
For amid the heat of wassail came the feeling icy cold
That he wore the Saxon fetters, with their links of beaten
      gold.

Came the morning : and the revelry, fast drawing to a close,
Began to show some symptoms of satiety's repose, —
The extemporaneous speeches to the papers sent away
For the special delectation of the city's *dejeuner*.
The tempest of hilarity had softened to a breeze,
And those who had the strongest heads were weak about
      the knees.
Hands were clasped that never touched before, and hearts
      were welling up,
As passed the proud Amphitrion the mollifying cup ;
Wrapped in measureless content was he, and, as the
      moments rolled,
Forgot the Saxon fetters, with their links of beaten gold.

Breathes there no better Irishman, none better work has
      done,
Than he who led the feast ; but there are spots upon the
      sun.
Both heart and head were armor-clad in patriotic zeal,
But, like the Grecian hero, he was shaky in the heel.
Those golden spurs ! those golden spurs ! the racers of his
      brain
So galled, they bolted reason's track and madly broke the
      rein.
Upon that wild idea he, Mazeppa-like, was bound,
And in circuses Tartarean galloped round, and round, and
      round,

Until a wilder thought arose, that could not be con-
    trolled,
All about the Saxon fetters, with their links of beaten
    gold.

Now, well-a-day! and woe is me such tale that have to
    tell!
'T was through seductive womankind the primal Adam
    fell.
A legacy of paradise his children still inherit.
" *Nulla fere causa est, in quæ non femina moverit.*"
What wonder the Macswiney, in the obfuscating haze,
Took rashly for his guiding star the light of other days !
By pitiless Mnemosyne his soul was tempest-tost,
And, thinking of his grandam, he his mental rudder lost, —
Thinking how she would have suffered could she only have
    foretold
That he 'd wear the Saxon fetters, made of old King
    William's gold.

And he, the famous Jacobite, who had so often bled, —
Macswiney, of the Gallowglasses, — what would he have
    said ?
That ancestor whose battle-axe was crimsoned o'er and o'er
From the blade down to the handle in a flood of Saxon
    gore ?
This spirit 't was that fired his eye and caused his teeth to
    crunch ;
Mixed with a little *usquebaugh*, it made a lovely punch.
Forgot he then the party men, the Ghibelline and Guelph, —
Forgot the spurs, but, most of all, forgot he then himself.
It angered him to think that even phantoms might behold
On him the Saxon fetters, with their links of beaten gold.

Up rose he, and like Jupiter Ferretrius appeared,
While quivered every hair upon his patriarchal beard;
Glared he round on the assembly, in a strange and startling
  way ;
Ah! *Tribus Anticyrus, caput insanabile !*
The collar of his servitude from off his neck he tore ;
' This glittering badge of slavery,' cried he, ' I 'll wear no
  more.'
Away 't was flung, and if the act no deep impression made
Upon the viceroy's heart, it only just escaped his head.
Then hurrah for the Macswiney, who in word and action
  bold
Abjured the Saxon fetters, with their links of beaten gold !

———◆———

PEACE AND WAR.

Peace everlastingly with those
Who still the perfect truth disclose,
And, in all places, nobly dare
The mask from speciousness to tear ;
Who not by words, but actions, show
The attributes of heaven below;
Who never with presumption scan
The failings of their fellow-man,
But those who've fallen in evil ways
By gentle admonition raise,
And thus in deed true homage give
To Him who died that we might live ; —
Peace everlastingly with those
Who still the perfect truth disclose.

NEBULÆ. 427

War to the uttermost with all
Who hold the human mind in thrall;
Be they bold villains, who appear
With bolder faces, scorning fear, —
Who, in their mastery of evil,
Were there a chance, would cheat the devil;
Or be they fat "professors," sleek,
Soft, placid-voiced, and seeming meek, —
Their aspirations worldly greed,
And selfishness their only creed, —
Who in deceit so long have trod,
They fain would hope to cheat their God; —
War to the uttermost with all
Who hold the mind of man in thrall!

—◆—

NEBULÆ.

I FEEL a strange upheaval of the chest,
    To me, at least, a singular sensation,
A pent-up something, — truly, at the best,
    A most unpleasant kind of perturbation.
The difficulty is to solve the question,
If inspiration 't is, or indigestion.

At times I fancy that I 'm big with thought,
    And labor hugely in the parturition;
But for the life of me can bring forth naught
    In anyway presentable condition.
I 'd like to know of what it is symbolic,
The true afflatus, or the windy colic.

Just now a flock of small ideas flew
   Across my brain, but I 'm afraid I 've missed 'em.
It puzzles me to know what I shall do,
   In such severe derangement of the system ; —
Take up my pen, all consequences scorning,
Or take a pill and seidlitz in the morning.

' Throw physic to the dogs,' quoth gentle Will,
   And so say I, my rule is dietetic.
'T is fixed, I 'll scribble; so come, friendly quill
   (Steel pen it is, but that 's not so poetic).
Shall I invoke the Muses' aid, or flout them ?
1 'll independent be, and do without them.

Such antique dames I 'm not inclined to woo
   As those old dowagers ; besides, the *fact* is,
Courting nine women would be, *entre nous,*
   Infringing, rather, on the Mormon practice.
To subjugate so many white-souled creatures
Would task your Brigham Youngs or Brooklyn teachers.

They 've jilted, too, so many a poor wight,
   Who, hapless mortals, thought that they had won 'em,
Oft at the first approaches taking flight,
   There 's no dependence to be placed upon 'em.
To tell the honest truth, I 'm not so smitten
As thus incautiously to risk the mitten.

But if the least of all the nine should chance —
   For women now and then have strange caprices, —
To cast on me the slightest friendly glance,
   Or even introduce me to her nieces,
I must confess that I 'd have no objection
To cultivate the family connection.

As such a prize I dare not hope to win,
    For me, alas ! there 's no such sweet communion ;
It 's pretty nearly time I should begin
    To consummate a less unequal union.
I 'm at the age when love is not potential,
But kept in wholesome check by the prudential.

It just occurs to me there is a dame
    The world, and very righteously, accuses
Of kindling in unnumbered hearts a flame
    For each one lighted by the modest Muses.
A flaunting Jezebel, old, bald, and wrinkled,
Though her false tresses are with gold-dust sprinkled.

Her name is Impudence, and, sooth to tell,
    No place so sacred that her footsteps falter ;
Even where genius worships, she as well
    Kneels, side by side, before fame's glorious altar, —
Not to assist devotion, but to mock it,
For while he 's wrapped in thought, she picks his pocket :

With dextrous fingers filching the great thought
    To which he, haply, gave a life's endeavor,
Deeming celebrity thus cheaply bought, —
    For on time's scroll will he not live forever ?
Delusive hope, she claims the new invention,
Like — well, the names I do not choose to mention.

SUMMER FRIENDS.

As the bee is to the rose,
While the honey-treasure flows,
Gently singing songs of love
To each blossom in the grove,
Pausing only in his flight
Where the sweets of life are bright,
All unwilling to depart
Till he reach the very heart,
And, when all the luscious store
Is exhausted, sings no more ;
As the bee is to the rose,
While the honey-treasure flows,
        Are summer friends.

As the shadow to the boat
On a changeful lake afloat, —
When the lake is in repose,
Like a second boat it shows,
But, when tempests gather round,
Can no longer there be found ; —
As the shadow to the boat,
On a changeful lake afloat,
        Are summer friends.

LOVE'S MISSION.

WHITHER dost thou go, gentle wind?
If thou hast naught to do, to thy mind,
O, betake thee to the west,
To the girl that I love best.
Heavy-laden with those sighs,
To the cottage where she lies;
There, without a living sound
Let them softly hover round;
Let them fan her brow so fair,
Let them stroke her silky hair,
Let them play at hide and seek
Through the dimples on her cheek,
Let them linger but to sip
Heaven's dew upon her lip;
Then commingle with the air,
She is calmly breathing there
That within her gentle breast,
For an instant they may rest
In her heart to whisper deep
Thoughts of me while she doth sleep.

PAULINE.

IF you have n't yet been
    To visit Pauline,
Its representation at Wallack's I mean,
    While memory 's green,
Let me tell you the terrors of sweet Laura Keene —

Fresh now in my mind — brought about by the hein-
ous offences of Lester, whose *rôle* is between
A dove and a hawk, if you know what I mean ;
The most elegant scoundrel that ever was seen,
A Chesterfield cut-throat so aristocratical,
Graciously rude and indeed problematical,
      Pale and piratical, —
Just such a "creature" as causes lymphatical
Boarding-school misses to feel quite ecstatical.

ACT THE FIRST.

Seriatim, the plot to unfold,
Which without any doubt is remarkably bold,
      And new, we are told,
(For the matter of that, it will never be old,)
You 'll please to imagine a brilliant and rare
      Pavilion somewhere
In France, looking out on a pleasant parterre.
      Seated quietly there
Are a daughter and mother, affectionate pair
(Mrs. Stephens, *La Fille*, Mrs. Cramer, *La Mère*).
It 's a beautiful scene.   By the way 't is but fair
To let it be known, as his truest well-wisher would,
All the fine pictures are painted by Isherwood.
It must be confessed that with wonderful skill
      The son of a quill
Who fashioned the drama begins it so dosily,
      Quiet and prosily,
Every one thinks he 'll attend to it cosily,
      Placid and pleasantly,
Little expecting the row we 'll have presently.
And now to continue, the pretty Pauline,
      Miss Keene,

. OF
CALIFORNIA

UNIV. OF
CALIFORNIA

I mean,
Bursts out like a sun-ray upon the dull scene,
And for a few moments it's very serene ;
    Till a jockey in green —
Appropriate colors — requests her to tell
A story that sounds like a regular sell,
    About tigers and jungles ;
A Count, too, who most unaccountably blunders
    In killing the " critter,"
    The way that he " fit " her,
    And hit her,
And how that it was n't convenient to quit her
    Except on a litter.
She piles it all up in a deuce of a twitter,
And then she proceeds quite correctly to faint a bit,
Thinking him dead, but the fact is he ain't a bit.
Meanwhile the neighbors, surrounding the place,
Prepare to assist in the " joys of the chase ";
    And in beating around
    The contiguous ground,
'T is evident something alarming they 've found, —
A boar very likely, such monsters abound
In such pieces, — pshaw ! bless me, I mean in such places.
    There's fear in the faces ·
Of pretty Pauline and her cousin and mother,
    For somehow or other
The animal 's rude to the son and the brother,
By Reynolds enacted, who bravely to lick him meant,
Had n't the best, and is in a predicament ;
Up and down fighting they have on the sward,
And the brute is decidedly running him hard,
When in comes De Beauchamp or Mr. Bernard,
    A little mite " scared."

28

Unsteady, and shaky, and queer in the wrist,
From terror, or toddies he'd taken at yest-
erday's banquet, a hundred to one but he'd missed,
When in glides the Count, and right out of his fist
   He snatches the musket,
    And up to his " weskit "
He raises, and fires it, when right through the tusk it
Is safe to suppose Mr. Boar has the bullet in,
Slap through the gullet, in
Rushes " the crowd " with " the cousin and son,"
And De Beauvale, that's Lester, says, " Very good gun."
   The meeting between
   The Count and Pauline,
To duly appreciate has to be seen ;
   She shivers and shakes,
   And quivers and quakes,
While *à la seigneur*, the Count haughtily makes
Love in a manner 't is perfectly certain ain't
Anything else but extremely impertinent ;
   Using his eyes,
   To the lady's surprise,
As if he had meant to anathematize
The whole of the family, says — but he lies,
As the sequel will prove — he's a capital prize
   In the marrying lottery,
   Choose him she ought, or he
Knows what he'll do — then her eyes become watery,
   Seeing he's caught her, he
Grins, like a good-looking vampire in fun,
   Upon every one,
   While the " cousin and son,"
Young Lucian de Nerval, looks nervously on,
For his recent delivery not at all grateful, he

Strokes his imperial and scowls on him hatefully ;
And this being all that is proper to know,
The curtain descends on a brilliant tableau.

You 'll understand here
There 's a lapse of a year,
During which 't would appear
The Count marries Pauline. But I won't interfere
With the thread of the narrative now waxing queer.

ACT THE SECOND

Discloses a small Cabaret,
A broken-down groggery out of the way,
Where pretty Pauline soon arrives with her " shay."
She 's going to pay
A visit to-day,
Quite extempore,
To Horace, her husband, and wants a relay, —
An order, the hostess, I 'm sorry to say,
Is really unable just now to obey,
For there 's not a postilion, though brave as he may,
Will venture his clay,
Through fear of becoming to brigands a prey,
Who lately in murder have made a display.
Pauline, very properly, says that she 'll stay
Where she 's safe, and is thinking to order a quail
For supper when Harriet comes in (Mrs. Hale),
And they quietly rail
At their lords, and assail
Their faults and their weaknesses ; each has her tale, —
Pauline's is enough to make any one pale,

Though it mainly embraced
Count Horace's — her husband's — equestrian taste.
It happened that she
Discovered that he
Directed *one horse* should in readiness be,
Perpetually,
All saddled and bridled, and ready to flee ;
And when Max and Henri
(Messieurs Chandler and Lee)
Once paid him a visit, why then he had *three !*
She can't make it out,
Or know what it 's about,
Although of his honor she has n't a doubt.
But there is n't much time to discuss the thing here,
For, talk of the fiend, the whole trio appear,
Count Horace de Beauvale, and Henri, and Max,
With guns at their backs ;
But 't is easy to see that their courtesy 's lax,
For Horace attacks
The Countess for coming without his permission,
And she 's in a very distressing condition ;
So, thinking 't is better her grief to disperse, he
Talks blandly enough, though he feels *vice versa,*
And quelling a curse, he
Conveys her right off to the " Château de Burcy."

This awkward rencontre it 's evident suits
Not the men in the boots,
But they 're quickly consoled by a brace of cheroots ;
And one of them — Max, I think — rudely salutes
Mrs. Walcott, who calls them a couple of brutes.

And now we 're transported to " Normandy's shore,"
Where the brother of Pauline has come to explore,

Some remarkable ruins he 'd heard of before ;
    And he will not give o'er
His purpose, though thunder will probably roar,
And the threatening heavens a cataract pour.
(This scene is so real, one prudent old fellow
Looked close, to be certain he had an umbrella.)

Anon to intense and remarkably slow
        Music we go
To the room of Pauline, in the lonely château,
Where she 's sitting in spirits remarkably low ;
The little distinction 'twixt *husband* and *beau*
        She 's beginning to know,
And has a suspicion she 's somewhat *de trop.*
        For certainly though
        Toute à fait, comme il faut,
Her brilliant *boudoir* can but scantily show
Available means of amusement, and so,
As in spite of herself she 's beginning to grow
Excited, and nervous, and very *distrait,*
        She rings up friend Rea,
        The Milesian Malay,
Costumed in a strikingly picturesque way,
All turbaned and bracoleted up to the life,
        A kind of a hyf-
alutin "tame tiger" to Horace's wife,
With a double bass voice and an "ell" of a knife.
She endeavors to pump him, to cross him and wind him, and
Can't get a word from the cunning East Indiaman.
        Putting on airs,
        She sends him down stairs,
Reads "Uncle Tom's Cabin" awhile and declares,
It does n't amuse her, and therefore prepares

To find from the bookcase a volume that bears
A pleasanter character. Doing that thing,
She touches somehow a mysterious spring,
When slowly the bookcase commences to swing
   Right round on its axis,
And she upon one of Count Horace's tracks is ;
For, dreadful to see ! there's *a hole in the wall.*
  To be sure it 's but small,
  Though enough to appall —
'T is so chilly — a lady without any shawl.
With the tact of a woman she fathoms it all,
Exclaiming, "Whenever *he* happens to fall
In love," as is likely with every new face,
  This must be the place
  Where he takes his disgrace-
ful companions, good heavens ! if that be the case,
I 'll soon give him "caudle" for conduct so base.
Meanwhile though the tempest is raging without,
Despite of the lightning that flashes about,
She imprudently will at the window look out,
Where she sees what immediately banishes doubt :
Her husband, Count Horace, with Max and Henri,
  And the reprobate three
Are carrying something wrapt up in a cloak ;
By the aid of a vivid electrical stroke,
She perceives *'t is a female,* a very bad joke
To Pauline, who now seizes the light with temerity,
  Then with dexterity
Touches the spring, and to test its sincerity,
Down to the cellar descends with celerity ;
Where she arrives just in time to take part
In a scene that to view merely makes the blood start
  Right away from her heart, —

Possessing the very peculiar traits
Of a salad of horrors dressed à la Française,
Consisting of crimes of so fearful a texture
That murder's the least in the awful admixture.
  True it is the act ends
With a splendid effect that makes ample amends
  For whatever offends
True taste, and imbues with a ray of vitality
This gallimaufry of Gallic morality.

Perhaps 't is as well to inform you that here
There takes place another delay of a year,
  Or near.
So, being apprised of that fact,
I 'll take you at once to

THE THIRD, AND LAST ACT,

Where Count Horace de Beauvale appears once again,
  The sweetest of men,
A delicate plant from the uppermost ten.
  Pauline has departed,
  And he 's broken-hearted,
And now he 's come back to the place where he started,
To rouse up his spirits the best way in life,
  By taking a wife.
Mam'zelle de Nerval he 's been able to win ;
It 's a good speculation we know to begin ;
  For Lucian comes in,
And, curious enough, only twenty-five min-
utes before the betrothal.   As nearest of kin,
He 's to give her away and to settle the pin-
  Money, titles, and tin,
And the style he goes on is to Moses a sin.

He comes it so grand,
He 'll not condescend to take Horace's hand,
Who won't understand
The cut, 'till he 's put all the business through.
Because, *entre nous*,
She 's, as Lucian insinuates, rich as a Jew.
Now the notary comes, and the witnesses too,
And there 's nothing to do,
But the contract to sign and distribute the u-
sual kisses and blisses and compliments due.
Now, heedless of guile,
La belle fiancée writes her name on the file.
Then Horace advances in drawing-room style,
His single eye upon Lucian the while,
In a manner to rile
The sweetest of tempers right up to the bile.
'T was as much as to say, " Now I 'm sure of the pile."
Lucian immediately waxes irascible,
Horace's features are pale and impassible.
" Scoundrel ! " the former cries, " would you then dare
To write your name there,
And doom to despair
Another poor victim ? " That makes Horace stare.
Then Lucian berates him with might and with main,
Declares he 's the bane
Of his household, and if it so happened the twain
Had been married, 't would never get over the stain.
To which Horace replies, " I 'm afraid we 'll have rain."
Though mad with vexation,
Concealed perturbation,
And rage at the incomplete solemnization,
Without hesitation,
Or manifestation of slightest sensation,

From Lucian he placidly asks explanation ;
Who, looking all mystery, goes to the back.
And leads in Pauline, dressed in very deep black.
The people all gaze in dismay, and with reason,
For she was supposed to be dead a whole season.
   But our hero's *sang froid*
   Even this cannot thaw ;
   He looks at the new-comer
   Cool as a cucum'er,
Plainly implying he cares not a straw.
   The ladies go out,
With the notary too, and the rest of the rout.
And Horace says, seemingly not a bit nettled,
To Lucian, " This little account must be settled."
A sudden and singular duel they fight, —
And further description would hardly be right.
But if you are curious to know how they do it,
Just purchase a ticket and see them go through it.

What we privately think of this drama so terrible,
We 'll, with permission, expound in a parable.
A lion once thought he would give a great feast
   To every beast
Within his dominion, some hundred at least ; —
   So sent for his cook,
An excellent one, who 'd read Soyer's great book,
And told him to furnish it on his own hook, —
   To spare no expense
   On any pretence,
But to get up a banquet in such sort of way
As the palate to suit of each ferine *gourmet.*
   The cook then retired,
   And, duly inspired

With love for his art,
Invented a *carte*
Of such complex variety
That every guest in that mingled society
On his favorite dish might regale to satiety.
When the lion was led
By his *chef*, as he said,
To see if he liked how the table was spread,
He gazed with delight
On the beautiful sight
Of silver and gold, that reflected the light
In a manner emphatic,
Through pendules prismatic,
Till his leonine majesty grew quite ecstatic.
Suffice it to say,
The brilliant display —
To look at — was perfect in every way.
Such exquisite napery naught could surpass,
Such cutlery, china, and monogram glass ;
All well-regulated appointments were there,
From centre-piece floral to *boutonnière*,
And the gratified lion — he could n't do less —
His pleasure was graciously pleased to express.
But, lifting a cover, he
Made a discovery,
Startling and strange, for a sight met his eyes
That caused him to roar out in angry surprise,
"What garbage is this?" "Why, my lord," said the cook,
"It 's a thistle ! Some folk, ay, and very genteel,
Would rather have that than aught else for a meal."
He lifted another, — 't was nothing but mud !
It fired his blood.
" Off with it ! " he cried ; " I have seen quite enough
Of this feculent stuff."

But the cook, unaffected by such a rebuff,
　　Replied, " My good lord,
If lions alone were to dine at your board,
To your own individual taste 't would be stored.
Pray wait till the banquet is over, and deign
To form your deductions from what will remain."
The lion consented, and found the *cuisine*,
Although the unwholsomest ever was seen,
The very best fare for the animal host, —
For the filthiest dishes were relished the most ;
Indeed, it was said he himself, on the sly,
　　Had a little put by,
Rather liking the taste ; but that must be a lie.

———◆———

HONEST MEN.

Not a time is this for lethargy ; give party to the winds,
With all other petty questions that the better judgment
　　blinds,
Thinking only of the infamy throughout the country rife,
And that, like a mordant cancer, slowly eats away her
　　life, —
The infection of jail graduates, distillation of the slums,
That from its own impurity pestiferous becomes !
'T is with you the power rests, though it has slumbered
　　hitherto,
To save the patient victim from the whole pernicious crew.
One decisive course is left, the deadly virus to retard, —
Let it be your war-cry now : Put none but honest men on
　　guard !

Cast aside the old indifference, begotten of your scorn,
That shrinks from contact with the scum to degradation
    born ;
Or its rascal-featured progeny, abhorrent to men's eyes,
That the seething mess political makes to the surface rise.
Do your duty while there's time, and by stalwart action
    show
Far and near to every traitor knave, in office high or low,
That his shameless malefactions must henceforward have
    an end,
And the ballot to oblivion all its branded felons send.
In the conflict which is coming, while your blows fall fast
    and hard,
Let your battle-cry be this : Put none but honest men on
    guard !

Surely, surely, there are patriots enough within the land
The base butchers of her credit in their shambles to with-
    stand !
Do not suffer the assassins of her once exalted fame
In their lust of greed to make it but a monument of
    shame !
Up, then, all who hate rapacity ! Assemble in your
    might !
Your mere numbers will dismay and put the vulture horde
    to flight.
If you would not see your country's glory vanish like a
    dream,
And her name among the nations be of fraud a synonyme,
You must see to it yourselves in every city, town, and
    ward —
In all quarters — that there shall be none but honest men
    on guard !

MADRIGAL.

TO THE PRINCESS ROYAL OF PRUSSIA.

Paraphrased from Voltaire. (1743.)

A<small>MID</small> the wild delusion of our dreams
Faint glimpses of the truth sometimes appear,
When from absorbing thought, the fancy teems
With images of one who is most dear.
Ah! how enchanting then the vision seems!
But all too brief! — I had a dream last night,
A dream like that, as transient and as bright!
Methought I was a king, and madly dared
    To love thee, Princess! Bold indeed is sleep:
My soul's desire while sleeping I declared!
The gods soon punished an offence so deep;
For my awakened sense the treason shared:
My crown and kingdom vanished before day,
My love not even gods could take away!

——◆——

SYLVIA.

AN IMITATION.

U<small>PON</small> some sly affair
    Connubially dishonest —
Vide Lemprière —
    Jupiter was *non est,*
And dame Juno thought
    Scandal and *écarté*
Consolation brought, —
    So gave an evening party.

First, Venus came, and son,
  Who labored to deserve a
Birching, for the fun
  He made of sage Minerva ;
But sooth to say, the boy
  Deems it no great treason
Sometimes to enjoy
  A laugh at sober reason.

Next came a mundane guest
  By special invitation,
And, among the rest,
  Created a sensation.
My SYLVIA 't was, and she
  Perfection so resembled,
For her sovereignty
  The queen of beauty trembled.

When they were all supplied
  With nectar and ambrosia,
To taste undeified
  The mildest of symposia,
Betimes the cards were brought,
  And with them the admission
Celestial skill was naught
  'Gainst mortal intuition.

For *my* SYLVIA soon,
  Playing with discretion,
From each goddess won
  All her rich possession.
OLYMPIA lost her youth,
  Her regnant form and feature,
Everything, in truth,
  Except her jealous nature.

MINERVA lost her mind,
  With wit and wisdom glowing ;
Fair PAPHIA resigned
  Her cestus, charm-bestowing.
Young CUPID then she sought,
  The while with anger swelling,
And from his hand she caught
  His arrow, love-compelling.

She seized the golden gage
  And on the table tossed it,
But, blinded by her rage,
  Played carelessly, and lost it.
When, to yield back the toy,
  Dame JUNO interceded,
She gave it to the boy,
  In fact she did not need it.

When on this earthly ball
  My SYLVIA thus alighted,
With the gifts of all
  The goddesses united,
It is not strange that she,
  Without much endeavor,
Quickly won from me
  Heart and soul forever.

THE RIVAL ARCHERS.

Young Cupid one day, with his quiver well stored,
    Sallied forth, upon wickedness bent.
Right and left his insidious love-tokens poured,
And hearts by the hundred were shamefully scored, —
    To the mischievous archer's content.

He chanced to encounter King Death on his way,
    Whose arrows more fatally flew :
In vain all his skill did the love-god display:
His merciless rival made all hearts his prey,
    For his shafts were, as destiny, true.

Boy Cupid, annoyed at the other's success,
    Invoked cousin Mercury's aid,
Who, having for mischief a talent no less,
Changed their quivers so deftly that neither could guess
    Such a strange transposition was made.

That they 're still somewhat mixed may be easily seen ;
    For if wintry age feel love's smart,
Cupid's arrow by Death surely wielded has been ;
But when youth is struck down while its spring-time is
            green,
    Death's quiver has furnished the dart.

STEAM *vs.* TIME.

A REMINISCENCE.

Ho for the Pacific !
    Three thousand miles away, —
Weather beatific
    And our spirits gay.
Two grand steeple-chasers
    Are about to start,
And the mighty racers
    Ready to depart

Little, for good-bying,
    Time can we afford :
Hark ! the man is crying,
    " Passengers aboard ! "
Laggards, hotly hasting,
    Frantically rush ;
Girls, their kisses wasting,
    On each other gush !

'Mid the cheering hearty
    On the road we are, —
A cosy little party
    In a palace car.
Elegant and spacious
    Carriages throughout,
Airy and capacious, —
    Room to walk about.

29

Or, if you repose would,
  Tempting to the view,
Couches framed in rosewood
  Flecked with ormolu.
Here you rest unjaded,
  Stretched out at your ease,
Backbone uninvaded
  By your neighbor's knees.

Every berth a chamber,
  Linen snowy white,
Reading lamps to slumber
  Pleasantly invite.
Carpeted from Brussels,
  While, in ample swell,
All around you rustles
  Gorgeous brocatelle.

Now the iron courser
  Settles to his work;
Steam, the great enforcer,
  Will not let him shirk;
Onward swiftly speeding,
  While the backward scene,
Rapidly receding,
  Closes like a screen.

Thundering over rivers,
  While, as if in dread,
Solid stonework shivers
  Underneath our tread;
Up the stiff grades dashing,
  Flying o'er the plain,
Into mountains flashing,
  Flashing out again!

Ever changing phases —
   Hill, and dale, and stream,
Lovely as the mazes
   Of a poet's dream —
Momently evolving,
   As we fleetly pass,
Like the views dissolving
   In a magic glass ; —

Pass the cities crowded,
   Scintillant with trade ;
Pass the forests shrouded
   In impervious shade,
Thickly interwoven
   Fir and leafy oak,
Save where seared and cloven
   By the lightning's stroke ;

Pass the homesteads nestling
   In their place of birth ;
Pass the clearings wrestling
   With primeval dearth ;
Pass the cornfields yellow,
   Teeming with their grain ;
Pass the regions fallow
   Of the vacant plain ;

Pass the walls titanic,
   Where, stupendous, rise
Pile on pile volcanic
   Upward to the skies, —
Heaven's architecture,
   Barrier and stay
Of our country's structure, —
   The mighty vertebræ ;

Pass the deserts reaching!
  The horizon's line;
Pass the relics bleaching —
  Horse, and mule, and kine —
On the track they fell in,
  Years on years ago, —
Mute historians, telling
  Tales of want and woe;

Pass the petty log towns,
  Future cities planned;
Pass the prairie-dog towns,
  Where devoted stand
Sentinels Pompeiian
  By each earthy door,
Though the empyrean
  Trembles at our roar.

Pass thy stony border,
  Too uxorious Young, —
Rocks in wild disorder
  On each other flung;
And the Echo Cañon,
  Journey worth alone, —
The cataract's companion,
  Niagara in stone!

By, like darting arrows,
  Donner's fateful lake;
Round the steep sierras
  Coiling like a snake;
Cresting lofty summits,
  Where the miners show
Small as clustered emmets,
  Down the vale below.

Ah ! this is existence, —
Flying like the wind ;
Time, left in the distance,
Lingers far behind :
Long compelled to leave us,
That antiquated team,
The four-in-hand of Phœbus,
Can't run ahead of steam.

Hark ! the bell gives warning
That the race is won ;
On the seventh morning
Five hours we beat the sun !

RISTORI.

AN ACROSTIC.

Art has but little share in thy renown ;
Direct from heaven the sacred radiance came
Enkindling intellect's celestial flame.
Lady, born wert thou to the starlit crown
At whose effulgence all the world bows down, —
Imperial genius thus compelling fame,
Despite itself, to glorify thy name,
Enforcing homage thou alone canst claim.

Resist who can thy soul-subduing sway,
In rapt and sympathetic thraldom bound,
Smiling or sorrowing by turns with thee,
Through every phase of passion's varied round,
On waves impulsive tossed, as on a sea,
Responsive to the deep heart love that we
Instinctive yield to nature's sovereignty.

AN OPENING ADDRESS.

Delivered at the Fifth Avenue Theatre, New York, Monday Even-
ing, September 13, 1875.

An opening address !   The phrase is fine,
But then the thing itself's not in my line :
Yet, as it's promised, why, I must go through it, —
Though, on my life, I don't know how to do it.

When by our chief this task to me was set,
Out of the scrape there was no way to get ;
Remonstrance were but waste of words, for he
Is autocratic — as he ought to be.
I thought at first, not being very apt
At this, that I would steal — I mean adapt —
The thought of those who, from its first invention
Down to the latest copyright contention,
The drama's progress watched, its hopes and fears,
Through the long lapse of intervening years,
While the resounding corridors of time
Echoed their footsteps who made it sublime.
Those crownéd victors, in the Olympic games,
Have left to us their still undying names ;
Nor shall their memory e'er pass away
Whose genius glorified a later day,
When, in the very boyhood of our stage,
It showed more power than its after age
Could equal or approach, — for giants then,
Not pygmies, wielded the dramatic pen !

My fancy was to interview all these,
From Rip Van Winkle to Euripides ;

But, on reflection, I 'm afraid the past
And present would unhappily contrast.
The change is not more grievous than grotesque,
From lofty poetry to low burlesque ;
Where poor Thalia, in her antic days,
Her scanty wardrobe's poverty displays,
" Small by degrees and beautifully less,"
Aggrieved at her abbreviated stress,
On her last legs sues vainly for redress.
Yet this is but an episode in art ;
The drama has to play a nobler part
Upon life's stage.   I am not one of those
Who either doubt its friends or fear its foes, —
In the abiding faith that, though obscure
Its light at times may be, it must endure ;
With justice, truth, and rectitude to side,
And strip the sheepskin from each wolfish hide.

It strikes me now that something I should say
About the recent much-disputed play ; *
And so I would, but it is hard to tell
The facts : what with Michaelis and Michel,
The French in France and French here in New York,
And all the legal, enigmatic work
Of affidavits and injunctions many
(I wonder if they 're understood by any),
So warped the case is, that, beyond a doubt,
The rights or wrongs no fellow can make out.

Old York and Lancaster once came to blows,
And the fierce conflict from two roses rose.

* " Our Boys."

One Rose, through agents and sub-agents, now
Arouses a right royal kind of row
By selling to two parties, nothing loath,
And in the sale, of course, including both.
The very smartest salesman you might get, or
Colonel Sellers, could n't sell them better.
Why they don't pass a law such things to stop
And simplify the literary swap,
Leaving no loophole for chicane to use,
But plainly say what 's what and which is who's,
Not fill with gall the managerial cup,
Is — a conundrum, and I give it up.

Meanwhile our chief to all this adverse luck
Opposes his indomitable pluck,
Untiring industry and active brain,
With courage resolute, to yet maintain
The fight against all odds, and will prevail :
His lexicon "knows no such word as 'fail.'"

MY AIN DONALD.

I.

Hey Donald, my ain Donald !
  The sun is sinkin' doon,
The weary songsters, ere they rest,
  Have piped their gloamin' tune.
The dew is fallin' on the leaf,
  The breezes stir the flower,
And nature's heart is beatin' calm, —
  It is the evenin' hour.

You 're all my dreams by night, Donald,
   You 're all my thoughts by day !
But, ah ! they baith are full of care
   Whene'er you are away.
      Hey Donald, my ain Donald !

II.

Hey Donald, my ain Donald !
   You 'll soon be hame wi' me,
And ilka darksome cloud will fade
   Before your sunny e'e.
The mither bird that frae the nest
   Can never dare to flee,
Greets not its mate wi' blither breast
   Than, Donald, I do thee !

     You 're all my dreams, etc.

III.

Hey Donald, my brave Donald !
   I know that, leal and true,
Your thought is never turned frae me,
   As mine ne'er falls frae you.
Thus, hand in hand and heart in heart,
   We 'll share life's joy or gloom,
And, when the night comes, gently sleep
   Beneath the bonnie broom.

     You 're all my dreams, etc.

THE FIDGET'S SEND-OFF.

TO THE CITY OF CHESTER.

I.

In the old days of gallant chivalry,
  When the last bumper to the health was drained
Of some loved voyager, by land or sea,
  And in the cup no drop of wine remained,
A higher mark of honor could not be
    Than to dash down the goblets to the floor,
    That they the same heart-service should do nevermore.

II.

The steam-yacht Fidget, having on her deck
  Some anxious souls eager to wish God-speed
To those most dear, inspired by "Extra Sec," —
  The boat, I mean, for she held much indeed, —
From that old custom did example take :
    Resolving all such homage to surpass,
    She courtesied her farewell, and smashed up every glass.

CONEY ISLAND, *June* 29, 1878.

THE VISION OF COLUMBUS.

TIME onward passes, and my mental gaze,
O'erleaping centuries, falls on the days
Of the far future.   Lo ! I see a land
Where nature seems to frame, with practised hand,
Her last, most wondrous work !   Before me rise

Mountains of solid rock that rift the skies;
Imperial valleys, with rich verdure crowned,
For leagues illimitable smile around,
While through them, subject seas, fair rivers, run
From ice-bound tracts to where the tropic sun
Breeds in the teeming ooze strange, monstrous things.
I see, upswelling from exhaustless springs,
Great lakes appear, upon whose surface wide
The banded navies of the earth may ride;
I see tremendous cataracts emerge
From cloud-aspiring heights, whose slippery verge
Tumultuous oceans momently roll o'er,
Assaulting with unmitigated roar
The stunned and startled ear of trembling day,
That wounded weeps, in glistening tears of spray;
I see, upspringing from the fruitful breast
Of the beneficent and boundless West,
Unnumbered acres of life-giving grain
Wave o'er the gently undulating plain.
Within the limits of the southern zone
I see plantations thickly overgrown
With a small shrub, whose modest flower supplies
A revenue of millions.

    .   .   .   .   .

I see a river, through whose limpid stream,
Pactolus-like, the yellow pebbles gleam,
Flowing through regions where great heaps of gold
Uncared for lie, in affluence untold,
Thick as autumnal leaves. I see within
My vision's scope small villages begin,
Like twilight stars, to peep forth timidly,
Great distances apart; and now I see
Towns swollen to cities burst upon the sight,

Thick as the crowded firmament at night.
I see brave science, with inspired soul,
Subdue the elements to its control;
On iron ways, through rock and mountain riven,
Impelling mighty freights, by vapor driven,
Or with electric nerves so interlace
The varied points of universal space,
Thought answers thought, though leagues on leagues be-
    tween :
Time is outstripped, and naught is that has been.
But now a form majestical appears,
O'ertopping all, and the obedient years
Proclaim him master, lifting him above
The Past, and the To-come, with reverent love;
For when mankind would think of him whose fame
Surmounts the highest, one beloved name
Up from their hearts will come uncalled, alone,
The immortal name of glorious Washington!
For every heart will be a separate throne
Where that remembrance will forever rest
While the bright stars begem heaven's azure breast,
Or the red flashes streak the clouds, made bright
E'en by their own intensity of light.

FALLING LEAVES.

When winter winds are wailing,
    And death rides on the breeze,
With icy breath assailing
    The stark and sapless trees,

It grieves us not to see —
  For 't is their time to die
And with all nature wither —
  The leaves that round us fly.

But when the day is teeming
  With life, and love, and light,
And in our path is beaming
  The sun-ray of delight,
It saddens us to see —
  O, 't is a mournful thing,
They should untimely perish —
  The leaves that fall in spring.

What though young life has parted
  From earth, ere spring has passed,
Or old and weary-hearted
  It yields to winter's blast?
Grieve not, but humbly bend
  Submissive to the call
Nor scorn their simple teaching, —
  The leaves that round us fall.

University Press : John Wilson & Son, Cambridge.

www.ingramcontent.com/pod-product-compliance
Lightning Source LLC
Chambersburg PA
CBHW052340110726
47901CB00005B/1297